WAITING
ON THE
SIDELINES

The Waiting Series Book 1

BY GINGER SCOTT

To my family and friends
(the members of Team Ginger)
who have always known I could do this. And a special shout out to my husband
who convinced me I should finally just "write the damn thing."
I love you.

1. Trying Out

I LIVE IN A TRAILER. A double-wide manufactured home, to be more accurate. But those are just semantics. No matter how pitched the roof, how long the living room or how fancy the lattice-covered deck is that surrounds your manufactured home, because it is positioned atop giant cinder blocks with a river-rocked driveway, it is, unarguably, a trailer in the eyes of every person fortunate enough to live in a home with a foundation poured directly on the ground.

My trailer is the last one on a long dirt road just on the outskirts of town. We live in Coolidge. It's a small town in Arizona about an hour outside the greater Phoenix area. That means it's about an hour away from anything truly relevant.

Our biggest store is the K-Mart, one of the classic ones with giant orange and yellow toy airplanes by the front door with quarter slots and runny-nosed children begging their parents to let them have "just one ride." The chalky white floor tiles are scuffed with dirt and blue Icee so badly that the daily mopping only moves the filth around, thinning it out with the water rather than actually making things clean.

From the time I started kindergarten my family planned an annual trip to the K-Mart for back-to-school shopping. My family isn't poor. We're comfortable. Lower middle class, sure, but we can afford to buy new clothes at the mall in town, which my parents do from time to time. We usually settled for the K-Mart because of the hour-long drive that a trip to the mall entailed. Our family car is a hand-me-down Oldsmobile from some great aunt I'm pretty sure I never met. It has black vinyl seats and a very sketchy air-conditioning system. Coolidge is separated from town by a lengthy stretch of desert, and one busted radiator hose or a faulty click of the air conditioning control meant we were rolling the windows down. Not a disaster in the winter, but in August, a situation like this almost guaranteed that the striped pattern of the vinyl seats would create a bright pink series of indentations on the fatty parts of the back of our legs, like singe marks on a barbecued hotdog. It is for this reason mostly that all back-to-school shopping is done at the K-Mart in Coolidge.

Up until this year, I had always looked forward to this outing. When I was 5 or 6, I would delight at the latest cartoon-character T-shirts that hung on the walls of the children's department. Those, and the brightly colored soccer shorts in the boys section. A bit of a Tomboy, my wardrobe now consists almost entirely of cut-off jean shorts, tracksuit sweat pants, soccer shorts and sports logo T-shirts. My brother's Nike jacket, made of maroon nylon with sporty white racing stripes down each sleeve, gets me through the winter. Fitting for a girl named Nolan. My dad was a huge baseball fan, and when I was born, his favorite pitcher was Nolan Ryan. Nolan's real first name was Lynn, which of course I got for a middle name. Nolan Lynn Lennox. Not very girly, but I can throw a perfect spiral with the football and my curveball ain't so bad either.

Things like clothing, makeup and hair were always an afterthought. Even during my last year of middle school. I chose my outfit each morning based on whether or not I had P.E. that day or if I had planned on playing kickball or soccer with the boys on the field before the morning bell. I rarely wore a dress, and when I did, I most certainly remembered to put shorts on underneath so I could run without fear of flashing my underwear.

"Dress up," as it were, was reserved for 8th grade graduation and the few school dances we had. And even then my long brown hair was almost always in a ponytail. I found that was the easiest thing to do given the 100-degree temperatures outside and my insistence on playing every sport available. I had a permanent wave in my hair from the spot where the rubber band pulled my hair together.

My life's purpose was to be part of the background. Lightly dusted freckles on my face, brown eyes and a bit of a lanky build, I was too tall for my gawky legs and size 9 feet that were always getting tangled up beneath me. I always wore tie shoes, like Vans or Converse, unless I had my running shoes on. I even convinced my mom to let me wear Converse to my 8th grade graduation – they were pink, which I think is what helped me win my argument.

My daily school outfit was thrown together in seconds every morning; often mismatched, but always clean. That was all I cared about.

Then *Monday* happened.

I'm a freshman. And on Monday I went to the Coolidge High School gym to try out for the school's volleyball team. The concept of tryouts is really arbitrary at the freshman level. Everyone makes the freshman teams; they take as many people as they have jerseys. In fact, the year before they had 26 girls try out with only 25 uniforms. The parent booster club rushed to the rescue with a white, long-sleeved T-shirt (from the K-Mart, of course) and an iron-on number 26 from the craft department.

When I showed up to the gym, most of the other girls had already ran their laps and stretched. I could see them through the doorway window. They were sitting in a circle listening to three older women with clipboards talk, no doubt about the importance of teamwork and the winning record the school was coming off of from the season before. I intended on sneaking in behind them, but the humidity outside was so high that the paint on all of the doors was sticky. As I pulled on the gym door, it made a loud popping sound and an equally awful snarl from the hinges. As it slammed to a sticky close, my cheeks began to burn. The women I intended on sneaking in behind were resting their clipboards against their chests and staring at me with that look that I knew read "we're going to make an example out of you." A group of about 35 girls, many who were there trying out for the varsity squad, stared, too. The two closest to me were definitely juniors or seniors. Their fluffed, curly ponytails and perfectly manicured eyebrows were trademark of high school cheerleaders. And I would have quickly assumed them to be so, except that before I could excuse myself for being tardy, the tallest of the two yelled out 'Ten laps on the stairs, freshman!' before I could utter a word.

"I'm sorry I'm late," I said.

"Tardy people get ten laps on the stairs," she said.

"We had trouble with the car, so…" I tried to eek out an excuse only to be cut off by the tall lanky blonde in shorts so short they really seemed unnecessary.

"You can just start on the north side, run up to the weight room, cross over and come down on the south end."

I was a bit puzzled, but I really didn't mind running. And after all, I had missed warm ups. I nodded yes to the girls in the circle and set my gym bag down in the corner. I don't know why I brought a bag really; it's not like I had a towel or shampoo to take a shower. I wasn't quite ready to experience a group shower yet and thought I'd put it off as long as I could. My bag contained an extra pair of socks, just in case I got a blister, and flip flops so I could pull my shoes off in the car and rest my feet on the ride home.

I heard the other girls start to pull things from the gym's storage closet, and as I made my way up the north stairs, the expanse of the gym came into view. Each girl was getting paired off and pulling balls from a large bin to warm up with. I scanned the lines of girls for anyone I knew, but there were only a few girls who I recognized from junior high. In my circle of friends, I was really the only one into sports. Sienna, who I've known since first grade, was good at things like hair and make-up. She even had her own jewelry business. Her mom ran the local beauty shop and Sienna would make feather earrings and beaded bracelets that her mom would let her sell after school to the ladies in the shop. She actually had a pretty steady stream of customers and could count on a good $15 a week. And I could usually count on her to buy my ticket for the movies because of it. Sports usually resulted in an injury for Sienna, so I didn't even ask her to come with me. Sarah, who I've known equally as long, was more into boys. Her focus was on joining the cheerleading squad. That was "a direct line to dating a football player," she said. Sarah actually has some coordination, so I tried to get her to change her mind and join me, but my efforts were fruitless.

My stomach was starting to sink. I was going to have work into a group of two. I'm not what you would call a natural at breaking the ice. The thought of just running down the south steps and out the back door, hopping the fence and making the 7-mile trek home was starting to sound more and more reasonable. I was reaching for the door to give it a test yank to see if it made the same loud creaking sound as the main door that set my entire punishment run in motion when the door flung open and the sounds of cleats scratching linoleum echoed in the hall leading up to it.

Football tryouts. I recognized most of the boys from junior high, but there were a few new ones. There was really only one feeder school for Coolidge, so it was rare for new names to move into the halls of our school system. But there was one name that the entire town was buzzing about.

The anticipation of the arrival of Reed Johnson was enormous. He went to a private school in the city before he moved to Coolidge to live with his dad over the summer. He may be new to our school, but everyone knew him. His father, Buck Johnson, owned three Buick dealerships in Tucson. He owned several acres of land on the east end of town with a giant two-story home with a four-car garage. The front door was flanked by tall white pillars that made the entire place look like the White House. We always called it the Johnson Ranch, mostly because he had grand iron gates over the bricked roadway leading up to his main house. The entire roadway stretched about the length of a football field and was lined with towering trees that would swallow my trailer up whole, but planted near the Johnson home the trees looked almost like scrub brush.

In a rare moment of clarity, I stopped my run and camped out by the drinking fountain pretending to hydrate and re-tie my shoelaces while the line of sweaty boys rushed up the steps to the weight room. The last thing I wanted was attention right now.

For some reason, I couldn't quit staring at Reed, though. I pulled my hair out of my face and tilted my head sideways while I drank, just keeping him in my periphery. He had perfect boy hair; it was brown and somewhere between long and short with a little curl that stuck out of the sides and back of his hat. A dimple punctuated each cheek at the corner of his lips when he smiled and laughed. He was wearing a purple jersey that read Johnson on the back in big golden letters. *Probably his brother's old jersey, I thought.* His brother, Jason Johnson, was the school's all-star quarterback a few years back, leading Coolidge to their first state title in 34 years. He was recruited by the University of Arizona when he graduated, but spent most of his time as back-up quarterback. He lives in Tucson and runs one of the dealerships with his father now.

Reed was already being touted as the school's next great hope. Sure, his name played into it for the most part. But everyone also knew Buck Johnson didn't like to lose, and his sons were always the best. Since both Johnson boys were able to throw, Buck had them in football, basketball and conditioning camps. Their skills were expensive. And both Reed and Jason could have easily played for one of the big Division I schools in the city. But they wouldn't have stood out as much, and maybe would have only started their senior years. By leading the Coolidge Bears, the Johnsons were sure to be a constant feature of local newspapers. Local heroes, leading a team back from the dead. College scouts love that kind of character. And Buck Johnson knew how to close a deal. And the sizeable donations he was willing to make never hurt.

I must have been in a deep trance, staring at the light freckles on his arms and the shaggy torn sweat pants that showed his muscular calves and Nikes with #13 written on the back, when I was jolted awake by the sound of my last name.

"Lennox! You 'bout done with those laps, lady? Get a move on!"

Everyone turned to stare at me sitting in the stairwell. Reed's eyes are green. I know this because I looked right into them. Then I watched them gaze down my body, taking in my worn-out, extra-large Lake Powell T-shirt, knee-length basketball shorts and tube socks pulled well over my calves to show off the red and blue stripes that this morning seemed so very cool. *Not cool. Not cool, I thought.* That's when I saw the sides of his mouth curl into a half smile. His eyes made it back to mine and he turned around.

I was stunned. Did he approve? Was my style cool? Did I just make an impression on the boy who is clearly our future home-coming king?

I gulped down some water from the fountain and jogged back to the middle of the gym to start passing drills. The next two hours passed in a blur. I remember a lot of running between lines on the basketball court and jumping to reach our hands above the net. I know I aced the passing drills where we had to pass a ball perfectly into a series of large net baskets, and I finished my runs faster than most of the other girls trying out. Just a few hours ago, I would have been soaking up the competitive edge I seemed to be gaining with every challenge. But I couldn't get Reed's eyes out of my head. And that half-smile he left me with as he turned around and raced up the stairs. Every water break, I purposely placed myself at the end of the line so I could get a glimpse of the weight room upstairs. I saw him lying on a bench and lifting weights with another boy I knew, Sean. When they were done, they would bang fists and trade spots. I kept waiting for Reed to look down the stairs at me, clearly standing right in view. But he never did.

Practice was over at 5. I was sitting in the corner rolling down my socks and pulling them off to stuff inside my shoes when the head coach came over to me.

"Lennox, right?" she said, flipping through a few papers on her clipboard.

"Yes. Nolan Lennox," I said, my heart racing now. Is my punishment not over? Or worse, is she going to cut me for being late? I hate that car. My dad had to pour water from a gallon into it just to get us moving. I was mortified and angry.

"You did a nice job today, Lennox. You keep that up, and you'll be playing junior varsity this year." With a small nod of approval she turned and walked into the main coaching office.

I didn't see that coming, but my lungs filled with air as the heavy weight of dread completely dissolved. I was almost proud. I sat there stuffing my shoes into my gym bag and putting on my flip flops for an extra long time. I knew my dad was in the parking lot, so I didn't want to keep him waiting long. I had a feeling after the start of our day that the air conditioning probably wasn't working very well.

As I walked out of the gym I saw Reed sitting on a bench pulling off his cleats and talking to a couple of the other guys. The two older girls from our volleyball practice were sitting on the grass in front of them.

I was just out of their view, but I heard the tall girl with the short shorts start. "Was her name seriously Nolan? That's a dude name. Do you think she's a dude?"

I heard the girls giggle. In a way, I expected that. I'm a girl named Nolan. I spent years defending that, and most of the kids in my class were used to it. In fact, people thought my name was sorta cool by now. What I didn't expect was the next sound. I heard a boy's voice pipe in with a "dang, that ain't right."

I stood still and leaned on the wall for a minute to see if I could tell who was talking. It was Reed. He was pulling a pair of sunglasses out of a cloth pouch and putting them on. Then he looked over at one of the guys sitting next to him and continued. "He, I mean she totally dresses like a dude, though. Maybe she had a sex change."

"Booooom!" Sean, his weight-lifting partner, shouted, as they smashed fists and stood up, throwing their bags over their shoulders. The older girls were in fits laughing at my expense.

I pushed down the urge to cry.

I waited for the girls to leave so I could walk unnoticed to the Oldsmobile. Then came the sucker punch. As they walked back into the building just around the corner from me I heard them continue.

"I think I know her, you know?" said the other girl, who I'm still on the fence about. "I think her mom works at our office."

I do know her, I realize. Her family runs an accounting office that serves most of the small cities south of Phoenix. It has several branches, but the main one was in Tucson, and my mom would work there a few times each month answering phones and assisting clients. Tatum Hernandez. A junior. Beautiful. She was always nice to me when I came to work with my mom. I have a brief moment of hope at this thought. Surely, she'll defend me.

"You know it's not her fault she's so poor. It's sad, really. I think she has to wear her brother's old clothes. I mean, looking like that? She'll never have a boyfriend. I would make her my project if she weren't so embarrassing. She lives in a trailer."

Silence. And just before the door closed I heard Tatum give me one final wound. "We should tell people she's a boy. They'd totally believe it, classic prank!" she roared, laughing so hard she could barely get the words out.

Tatum is not a friend.

———

Staring at the racks of soccer shorts and team logo T-shirts, I felt my mom put her hands on my shoulders.

"OK, kiddo. What do you say we go for a bit of variety this year," she says. "Maybe even branch out into some colors?"

What I say next blows her mind.

"Actually, I was thinking of trying on some of the skirts. I think I need to dress more grown up, don't you think?"

My mom, who has begged me to wear dresses and skirts every school year since I can remember, looks at me with equal parts elation and worry. Elation seems to win, however, because before I know it we're fully enveloped by the junior girl's section and I have a pile of ruffled, colorful garments on the floor of a dressing room.

I leave with eight or nine full outfits. Some of them shorts, but not from the boy's section. As we're checking out, I feel a pang in my gut from the guilt of giving in to peer pressure. I'm disappointed in myself. But I still wouldn't change a thing.

2. First Day

I USUALLY ARRIVE EARLY for the first day of school. My dad does deliveries for Marches Grocery in the city and starts his day at 7 a.m. The warehouse is in Coolidge, a good hub for the produce that comes in through Mexico and Southern California. My dad handles the specialty runs, which are basically special orders from the chains in the Phoenix area that are running low on certain items. Every day my dad loads a big truck based on requested inventory and drives into town from store to store, almost like Santa Claus. This, of course, is another reason we make so few trips into the city as a family. A few thousand miles a week and the last thing my father wants to do is follow his own daily tracks up the interstate.

Given my anxiety about starting high school, I'm okay with getting up early. In fact, I tried to talk my brother, Mike, into driving me when he left the house at 6. Mike's eight years older than me, and he just started working at the nearby junior college. He's an assistant in the kinesiology lab, which is a fancy way of saying P.E. Mike also managed to land a job as an offensive coordinator for the college's football team. He played there when he went to the school and was always a favorite among the coaches. My parents were just thrilled he found a way to make a living. I think they were also looking forward to his moving out soon.

When I asked him for a ride, I could tell it hurt my dad's feelings a bit, so I quickly changed my tune. "Actually, it's okay. I don't want to break my good luck tradition with dad," I said. I could tell immediately that I had mended things. My dad reached for a hidden pack of GEM chocolate donuts in the pantry.

"Here, shhhhhh, don't tell your mom," he half-whispered. "You can eat in the car on the way."

At 6:45, we pulled into the parking lot. The janitor was still pulling back the gate and locking it into position. I felt relief knowing I could slip from the Olds unnoticed and start scouting the locations of my various classes before others arrived.

As I walked to the back of the school where the lockers are located, I could hear the band practicing on the baseball field. The director was yelling at another man who looked like some sort of administrator. Something about how they used to march on the football field before his precious Bears started winning games and how he was single-handedly destroying the arts by relegating them to a baseball diamond.

I scanned the crowd and saw Sienna standing just above third base, her feet wet with freshly mowed grass bits. She tilted sideways a bit and gave me a wave, just enough to not draw attention and ire her already angry teacher.

Among Sienna's many artistic talents was music. She played six instruments at last count. She elected to play saxophone for high school band because the teacher said he had just graduated four players. Sienna figured this was her best shot at first chair. Her competitive spirit was just as alive as mine.

I turned to the endless row of lockers and knelt down to pull the folder from my backpack that they gave each of us at orientation the week before. Orientation felt more like the cattle runs I see out on the big ranches than a real first high school experience. We had two hours on a Friday evening to squeeze through rows and rows of cafeteria tables with our parents, signing forms to participate in sports, registering for school lunch programs, taking flyers from every club on campus and reviewing our schedules with counselors who really didn't care how happy we were with our classes but just wanted to make sure we didn't have anything overlapping a lunch hour. But I studied the folder full of papers from orientation extensively, still wanting to be prepared. I checked and rechecked against my brother's old year book to make sure the teachers I had were the ones with the honors program. I also made sure my lunch hour lined up with Sienna's and Sarah's. Pulling it from my backpack, I opened it to the small Post-It note I pasted on the inside with my locker number and combination written down.

I'm 317. The lockers are clustered in groups of 100. There are the ones, twos, threes, fours and fives. Fours and fives are saved for the juniors and seniors, and the others are spread among the underclassmen. My location was pretty good. Right outside the cafeteria; I would have plenty of time to stop there before and after lunch. It's the only section without a sidewalk cover, though. Already the metal of the black combination dial was burning hot. *"Just like the damn Oldsmobile," I thought to myself.*

I tested out the combination to make sure I could handle it. It opened easily, so I pulled out the heavy load of books and kept only a notebook and my algebra book out so I'd be ready for my first two classes.

I still had 30 minutes to myself. The bell doesn't ring until 7:30. A few people started to arrive. As I walked between the middle rows of buildings, I came to the main area called the quad where the buildings form this large square cut-out filled with picnic tables and grass. You can see a few sad garden experiments along the north wall of buildings, the work of the agriculture club. Some things seem to be growing, but for the most part it doesn't look like it's been tended to in months. In the middle of the square is a large bronze statue of soldiers. There's one from each branch of the military, and they're all bowing their heads and holding hands. Most folks in Coolidge either end up teaching at the school, farming, leaving or joining the military, so the dedication of the bronze statue a few years ago was a big occasion for the town. Right next to it is the school's flagpole. Every morning, members of the school's Junior

ROTC program, which is some type of pre-training military program in high school, hold a ceremony, marching in unison and unfolding, connecting and raising the flag. They take it down every day at 3:30. I stopped to watch as they prepared for today's ceremony, their faces so serious yet so very young. I thought how most of them will be graduating next year and will probably be sent to the Middle East for battle.

Ahead of me was the office, full of activity and packed with parents and students who missed orientation. I was glad that I was at least able to avoid that cluster. I was so intently watching the crowds and daydreaming that I didn't realize the grassy area had ended, marked pointedly by the beginning sidewalk. My toe slammed right into the edge and I flung far forward, my hands bracing my body as I slid several feet across the concrete.

I could feel the heat on my cheeks instantaneously. I knew that my hands were burning and I was pretty sure there was blood. I didn't want to look at my hands and knees to see how much, but rather stood up and grabbed my backpack and looked around to see who witnessed my fall. Several older girls were just entering the quad and I saw Tatum lean over and giggle to a friend, but they immediately climbed on top of one of the picnic tables and began talking to one another. I may have been a source of amusement to her, but at least my show was very temporary – she seemed to move on.

Finally, assured nobody else saw, I took inventory of the damage I'd done to my body, satisfied that the damage to my ego was in a range I could handle. My hands were skinned and bright pink, small scratches from my wrists to my palms. My knees fared far worse. The right knee had a flap of skin bunched in a line, like I had peeled a puffy sticker from my kneecap and left it there to dangle. The blood wasn't dripping, but it was there and it was only a matter of time. The left knee was a little better, though not much.

I knew I had to clean things up. Deep down, I blamed the slipper-style shoes I was now wearing and skirt. If I were wearing my normal clothes, I don't think this would have happened. I walked to the nurse's area, right next to the bustling office, and asked if she had any Band-Aids and alcohol pads.

"Oh honey, what happened," said a large woman wearing jeans and a paisley button-up shirt. She had a badge on that said 'Nurse Carol' – but that was the only thing about her that looked like a traditional school nurse.

"I fell, out in the quad. I'm fine, I just need to clean things up some," I said, a little sheepishly.

"I should say so, you're about to drip blood on my new carpet," she pulled my backpack to get me through the lobby of her office and into a small station in the back. There was a sink and a cabinet on one side and a padded table on the other. She told me to take a seat and started to pull out bandages from the cabinet.

"I really don't need all of those," I protested. The last thing I needed was something that would draw even more attention to my blunder. I just wanted to find a way to cover it up with makeup and move on. But I guess that really wasn't an option.

"I tell you what? You just let me do the nursing now, and if things feel better around lunch time, you can rip off my Band-Aids and pretend none of this ever happened, OK?" she said in a way that felt like my mother.

"OK," was about all I could muster.

I winced as she cleaned things out and then put some ointment and bandages over each knee. My hands were cleaned and didn't have any serious damage. In a matter of minutes she had me back up and on my feet, heading out through the crowded office area. I kept my head down, hoping I could just get back to the quad without anyone noticing my giant wounds. And because I was looking down, the first thing I saw were his shoes.

"Wooahhh, I almost took your head off there," Reed spoke, like we never met. His eyes met mine and he put on the most charming smile, a dimple on one side of his cheek. I could smell the gum in his mouth.

"Sorry, I wasn't paying attention. My bad," *My bad? Really … did I just say that?* I was so flustered at having a conversation with him, and I had no idea why. My first encounter with Reed Johnson

14

resulted in a good three-hour crying fest while I soaked in the tub at home. I didn't owe him anything.

"You OK? Your bandage is coming off?" he said as he bent down and, with one finger, popped the over-sized swath of cotton that Nurse Carol had taped to my leg back in place. I was mortified.

"Oh, thanks. Yeah, I sort of had an accident." *Oh god, realizing that sounds like I peed my pants, I corrected,* "I mean, I fell." *It was just getting worse. I needed to shut up, and leave.*

"Well, be careful. You don't want one of those wrapped around your head," he laughed, swirling his finger around his head to mimic a wrapped bandage, but not in a poking-fun-of-me sort of way.

"Good point," I said, smiling back and swinging my way through the door to the school hallway. He smiled back and turned around, his backpack flung over one shoulder in that perfect sort of way.

That was weird. Clearly, he doesn't recognize me. Of course, why would he? He doesn't really know me. I am being neurotic.

———

My feet were getting blisters, and school had barely started. Knowing I had the back-up Converse in my backpack, I made a plan to stop at my locker before third period. Morning homeroom, which was my math class, was great. I knew most everyone in the class and it was algebra, which I had basically already aced in junior high. I also had my best friends, Sienna and Sarah, in there with me. Truly a great way to start every day. Second period was a bit tougher, English. It looked like I would have a lot of reading to complete this year. I was looking forward to my third period—intro to science.

I didn't want to be late, so I jogged to my locker and threw the evil blister shoes in quickly. I walked barefooted for a few steps with my backpack pulled around in front of me so I could yank out my Converses. I bent down to slip my thumb in the heel of the first one to fit it to my foot, and as I was tilted, head through knees, I saw Reed walking toward me, a grin on his face.

Oh no.

"Now I know you're trying to get knocked over and injured," he chuckled. "Maybe we could just blindfold you and let you walk around campus aimlessly."

Trying to laugh him off, I threw my head straight and flung my hair up as I stood up. "Actually, this is injury prevention," I explained. "My feet aren't made for girly shoes it seems, so my classics are coming out of retirement for an appearance." Grabbing the second shoe from my backpack, I tossed it in the air a little, trying to make it flip over in my hand. Unfortunately, I was distracted by this entire encounter, and when I went to catch the shoe, it bounded off my palm and flipped end over end down the walkway, over a ditch, coming to rest in a drainage pile of dirt and leaves. Embarrassed, I hopped with one foot down the small hill to retrieve it. My backpack slid down my shoulder and fell from my wrist.

"Hang on, I got this," Reed said, lifting my backpack up for me.

"Thanks," I said over my shoulder then turning, red-faced, to my shoe now covered in grass and tree debris. I shook it off, threw it back down and pushed my foot inside. I wanted to find a way to disappear, rewind time, come up with some clever thing to say, but I had nothing.

I shyly turned back around, and Reed was right there next to me.

"Here you go," he said, handing me my pack. "Where you headed?"

"Science," I said, deciding one-word answers were probably my best move.

"Hey, me, too. I'll walk with you," he said.

Oh god.

"I'm Reed, by the way," he said, tilting his head to the side as we walked, his eyebrows raised clearly waiting for my response.

"Oh yeah, I know," I said. Silence. I couldn't seem to keep this conversation rolling and the pause between our words was becoming increasingly awkward. Finally, not able to handle it, I had to fill the space.

"My brother played football here and for Southern Arizona, so I'm sort of *in* on the football scouting," I said. *There, take that!* Reed looked at me with a crooked smile, the sort of smirk that either said 'this girl's a freak' or 'cool, she gets football.'

"Yeah, I guess I have a hard time being anonymous," he said, staring me in the eyes like he was willing me to add something. I just shook my head, smiled and raised my shoulders a bit.

"Like you, for example, are sort of anonymous…at least…I don't know your name?" he sort of asked. *Crap, that's right. I didn't reciprocate the introductions. I'm a nimrod.*

"Oh, right. I'm…(I paused for a moment, remembering the last time I heard him discussing my name with someone). I'm Nolan," I said, sort of scrunching my face a little, like I was saying something disappointing. I had no idea why I was making that face, but my body was full of anxiety. My hands and feet felt as if they were going numb, my stomach rolling over. *Oh please oh please don't bring up the conversation you had about my boy name and my boy clothes and my being nothing like a girlfriend ever. Please oh please.*

Reed jumped back a step while we were walking. He had put two and two together. My only hope was that he would pretend as if he'd never seen me before. Fake it, just for pleasantries.

"That's right. I think I ran into you during practice drills the other day," he was short. I think he wasn't sure where to go from there, but I was fine ending it with that. I didn't want to go into the details. Let's just erase that moment from time.

"So why Nolan?" he asked.

"Why what?" I was confused by his question.

"I mean, why did your parents name you Nolan?" he clarified, with a bit of a laugh. *Again, I am an idiot.* Good grief he was charming. I almost let my mind drift to doodling my name with his last name on a notebook and giggling with my girlfriends about him, me and our future babies…but then I couldn't get the sound of his less charming laugh out of my head, the one that was sparked by the conversation about how absolutely unattractive I was.

I was suddenly glad he asked about my name. I actually liked telling this story, and I thought I could stretch it for the rest of our walk across campus to our class. "Well, my parents were pretty sure I was going to be a boy. The doctor said it wasn't 100-percent conclusive, but he was pretty confident…Anyways, my dad's a huge baseball fan, and after much debate with my mom, who preferred the more traditional names, he talked her into naming their second child after Nolan Ryan…you know, the pitcher?" I paused to look at him to make sure he was following me.

"Well, when I was born, needless to say…not a boy!" I had a certain tone that was both sarcastic and pointed, to both emphasize the story and hint to Reed that I heard his conversation. He didn't seem to flinch, but I was proud of my passive aggression regardless.

"And so they just stuck with the name?" he asked.

"Well, there was some debate. My dad started to go back to the list of girl names they kicked around months before. But my mom, well, she sort of started to get pissed off, yelling at my dad about how girls can do the same things boys can, and why isn't their daughter good enough for a hall-of-famer's name, blah blah blah. So when it came time to put it down for permanent record, they went for it. And voila – here I am!"

We were finally at the classroom and Reed stopped to hold the door open for me, his stupid smile in full force now. As I walked through the rows of tables, I headed for the middle back, not turning to see which direction Reed had gone. I threw my backpack over one of the chairs and slid into the seat and was startled when I heard Reed's backpack hit the floor next to me as he slid into the other seat at my table. I turned to face him, a bit puzzled by his action. He was shaking his head now and chuckling a bit to himself. My confusion must have been apparent on my face because he stopped abruptly and looked right into my eyes.

"That is seriously the best name story I've ever heard. It's actually kind of awesome. You're name's special…just…cool, you know what I mean?"

"I guess so," I said, completely taken aback. And before I could get myself into any embarrassing trouble, the teacher began to talk about his expectations for the school year.

———

So much for the first day being a breeze. Our science class was starting off with a major project, and it would count for at least 20 percent of our grade. We were to work with a partner and build a model of a sustainable community along with a four-page paper explaining our design and how it would help our fake community survive. I was busy taking down notes on the project requirements when I heard my name called. I looked up quizzically, afraid I had missed a question from our teacher, when he finished his sentence with "…you'll be working with Reed, ok?"

I don't know if I spoke or just stared wide-eyed. I felt Reed elbow the side of my arm and I looked over at him. He was just smiling and nodding. He almost looked excited to be *my* partner? I was good at these types of projects. Maybe he had heard about how smart I was and was looking for an easy pass. That was probably it. *Great, I'll be doing all of the work. Well, at least I know it will be done well and I'll get a good grade, I thought.*

When the bell rang, I shoved my notebook back in my bag. Chewing on my pen, I threw my pack over my shoulder and was heading for the door when Reed caught me just before I left.

"Hey, we need to swap numbers," he said, pulling his cell phone from his pocket. I began sweating immediately, knowing the awkward encounter about to come up. I didn't have a cell phone. I was probably the only teenager left in Arizona not to have one, but, frankly, I didn't really have a need…until now. And my dad was always ranting about the dangers of teens with cell phones and how they are a distraction.

"What's your number?" Reed asked. Swallowing, I rattled off our home phone number. Then he looked up at me, insinuating that he was ready to share his. "Want me to just call you now so you'll have a record of my number and you can save it?" he asked.

Oh god.

"Actually, I'm getting a new phone, so I don't have one right now," the words flew out of my mouth so quickly I hardly had time to register the lie I had just told, let alone come to grips with the massive persuasive argument I now needed to develop to talk my parents into buying a phone for me.

"Oh, well…" Reed paused, rather unsure of what to say next. "Huh, well…how about this…I'll call you at your house, that's the number you gave, right? And then we can figure out when we want to start working on this thing and then just take it from there?"

"Sounds good," I said, both thankful that he seemed to not balk at my fib and sick at my further weakening from peer pressure.

"OK, well, I'll see you later," he said as he headed to the quad for his next class.

I just smiled as he walked away and then pretended to bend down to fix my shoelace. When I stood back up, he had blended in with the crowd and was surrounded by his friends.

3. Project

IT WAS a Tuesday afternoon and I was heading to Reed's for our first project session. School and volleyball practice flashed by in a blur. I vaguely recalled a quiz in algebra, which I suppose was a good sign for doing well. Rules of grammar in English, and science class was filled with a video on the relationship between plant life and oxygen. I am sure there was more depth to the video, but I spent 40 minutes pretending to intently watch and take notes, all too aware of my lab partner seated right next to me. From the corner of my eye I saw every doodle he made in the margin of his notebook. At one point, I thought he might have noticed my stealthy stare as he scribbled out a three-dimensional 'HI' that seemed to be daring me. But then he started to add wings and swirls and Nike Swooshes, so I was pretty sure it was just stream-of-conscious drawing.

I had made the junior varsity volleyball team, so practice was fairly intense. I welcomed the two-hour distraction, and clearly put every ounce of myself into conditioning and drills. My dad originally wanted to just drop me off at Reed's straight from practice, but I was *thankfully* able to talk him into taking me home to shower and change first. There was no way I was showing up at his house with a sweat-soaked MicNic Burger shirt and fuzzed out ponytail.

I showered and changed in record time, threw on a pair of hip-hugging denim shorts, loose-fitting tank top and my trusty Converses and we were on our way. My dad was actually really excited to be dropping me off at the Johnson house. He said he always wanted to drive up the entire driveway. I remember him threatening to do it just for fun a few times last year, but my mom would always stop him. I didn't think it was a big deal then, but I think I would just about die if he were to do it uninvited now.

As we rounded the tall trees at the corner of the property and made our way through the main gates, I took the entire thing in. I didn't know how big an acre was, but I knew Reed's dad owned several. His house came into view, classic-style, two stories and a balcony at the front just above the main entrance. The garage to the right was open, showing off a gleaming classic Buick—a 1954 Skylark, according to my dad. I could tell he wanted to stop the car to get out and look at it, but thankfully he just let it idle and told me he'd be back by 6:30 to pick me up. I told him to call if we needed to leave earlier; he was surprisingly good about getting me a phone. I didn't have a fancy plan and it was refurbished, but it would work.

I waved my dad off as I stood in front of the door. For some reason I didn't want the Oldsmobile behind me when Reed opened the door to let me in. But my dad wasn't budging until he knew I was safely inside.

I heard a dog barking after I rang the bell and I could roughly make out the form of someone coming to open the door through the frosted glass. My dad started to pull away and in my mind I thought maybe it was fast enough to not draw any attention to the rust marks on the bumper.

Reed's smile was greeting me instantly. "Welcome to Casa del Johnson!" he said, finding himself terribly clever. "Come on in. I made some space for us in the dining room so we can get started."

I followed him into the house, still not saying a word. He was wearing a well-worn grey t-shirt and loose-fitting jeans that were starting to tear at the feet. He slid across the wood floors in his socks, truly comfortable and not at all bothered by my presence. He pulled out a chair for me at the table and headed into the nearby kitchen, pulling a knit beanie from his head and tossing it on the counter. His hair, still a little wet from his after-practice shower I was guessing, curled a bit at the ends, flopping in random directions.

He came back to the dining room with two Cokes and a bowl of chips. "Brain food," he said.

Finally able to get my mouth to work, I thought I should start by giving him my new phone number. "Hey, I got my new phone, if you want to take down the number," I said, trying to be as casual as possible. I was putting entirely too much thought into even the simplest of sentences. When we had to start seriously talking, I knew I was doomed.

"Awesome. Just send me a text with it later tonight," he said.

"Can do," I said, wincing at my squeaky clean, 'you betcha' response. *Pull it together, Nolan.* "So, I thought maybe we could just go through the project requirements and put together a plan that hit all of the requirements so we could sort of have a list of things to cross as we go. Sound good?"

"Works for me," Reed said, flipping open a notebook to write our list on. I was pleasantly surprised that he was taking such an active role in our project. I was sort of used to carrying the team when it came to group projects.

"OK, first we need a model of our village. It has to include dwellings, food and water sources and be able to accommodate multiple families," I read from the class worksheet. "We will also need a four-page paper describing our village and addressing our challenges and solutions to sustainability."

"Got it," Reed said, scribbling the last bit of our list. "Where do you want to start?"

"Well, I guess we should maybe draw a blueprint of our model and then next time we meet we can build it?"

"I have the perfect thing," he hopped up from the table and ran upstairs in an instant. I heard his feet pound upstairs as they crossed above me. A few minutes later, I heard them cross back and he appeared at the bottom of the stairs with a huge foam cardboard piece in his hand. It was an old Buick credit check sign on one side, but he flipped it over on the table and the back was completely white.

"We can use this as our base," he said enthusiastically.

"Perfect," I said, leaning over the table with a pencil in my hand, realizing I hadn't seen his father, Buck, yet. "Hey, where's your dad anyhow?"

"Oh, he's never home this early. It's just us," he smirked, almost sorry for disappointing me, as if I had been hoping to meet his dad.

I just smiled and shrugged turning back to my drawing, just in time to shield his view of my giant swallow. We were completely alone. My best friends dreamt of this situation. Both Sienna and Sarah had pretty steady boyfriends in junior high, and they had done their fair share of sneaking out to be with their boyfriends. But to be in Reed Johnson's home, completely alone, just the two of us? Even if I still had my reservations about his character, my heart was still racing.

I was so deep in my own imagination that I hadn't noticed Reed answer his phone. I was jolted back to reality when he started laughing with whoever was on the other side. "Sorry, it's Sean. I'll just be a minute," he whispered, walking to his living room. I heard parts of the conversation over the next few minutes as he was explaining what he was doing and who was at his house. "No, dude. It's nothing like that – we're lab partners, that's all…She's cool, man. I swear. You two would actually get along."

I wasn't sure if I was happy to hear him defend my coolness or offended by his categorization of me in the lab partner box. He was back in the dining room soon after. He sat back on one of the chairs, tilting it backwards some, chewing on the cap of a pen and watching me work while I pretended to be oblivious to his studying of my hands. I could tell he wanted to say something, but for some reason was quiet. Finally, I had to break the awkward silence.

"Hey, is this what you were envisioning? Sorry, I just sort of started mapping the entire thing out," I said, looking up and settling my gaze right at the pen cap bobbing up and down on his lip as he chewed.

"Oh, no, this is great! Sorry…I was just trying not to stop your flow," he stopped, and it seemed like he wanted to say more. Chewing a bit longer, he finally pulled the pen from his mouth and continued. "Sean and a few friends are going to stop by for a bit. They'll just be hanging out in the living room, watching ESPN. We can keep working, they won't interrupt."

"Sure, sounds good," I said, closing my lips tightly and putting on the best 'I'm fine with it' smile I could. I wasn't fine with it at all. The last time I was in the presence of the two of them they were high-fiving over their description of how unattractive I was. Being trapped with them again was not high on my to do list. I decided to focus my energy on the project. Maybe, just maybe, I could completely finish the drawing and start actually building the model so I could avoid having to socialize with his friends.

Reed was standing at the head of the table, watching me plot out urban farming squares, when the doorbell rang. Without a word, he jogged over and opened it. I heard Sean first, the familiar 'Boom' that I knew was followed by a knuckle bump with Reed. Vomit was creeping up on me and I knew I was frowning. I heard a few more voices as the footsteps came around the corner and saw Reed whispering something in Sean's ear, presumably reminding him that I was here.

"Noles, what's up man!" Sean said, holding a hand up for me to slap. Completely succumbing to the pressure of the situation, I did. As if I had always done that with him, and we had some sort of relationship. Truth be told, I had known Sean since seventh grade, but we never really talked. "Hey," I said, smiling on the outside.

Pretending, that's what I was doing. I was disgusted at myself for it, but here I was doing it anyhow. *Noles? Since when am I Noles?*

"This is Devin and Cole. They're on varsity with me…juniors. They took the little freshman under their wing," Reed said, laughing it off like he was embarrassed. As absurd as it was, Reed was the one taking the upper classmen under his wing. Though he was not quite 15, he came to Coolidge with such confidence. I know a lot of it came from his name and his father and his brother, but there was also a certain amount that was just his. He owned it, and he was a leader the instant he stepped foot on our campus.

"Mind if we hit the fridge?" Devin, the biggest of the bunch, said. He was clearly a lineman or some type of defensive player. He was built like a college player. I heard the clanking of glass in the kitchen as the fridge door shut. Then I heard the distinct sound of bottle caps snapping. Curious, I rounded the table, pretending to need to work on the other side just to catch a view of what I suspected. All four boys were holding Heineken beers, leaning against the counter, one of them sitting on top of the kitchen island. It was clearly a regular activity, they seemed so comfortable and at home. I was far from 15, several months shy to be exact, and had yet to really kiss a boy, let alone drink a beer. My palms were sweating, I was so nervous at the situation. *Work, busy yourself, Noles!* I thought to myself, smirking at my silently said nickname.

I heard the TV turn on and then the regular banter about the NFL and "great catches" ensued. I continued to circle the table, working, but also putting my ears at their best advantage. Just then, I heard my name. It was Sean speaking up, not quite a whisper but clearly low enough so I couldn't hear, or so he thought.

"Dude, what happened? She's sort of cute now, huh? Weird, right?" he said.

I was dizzy.

"Hmm, you think so?" I heard Reed say.

"Uh, yeah. I do," Sean defended. I had been careful to wear my hair down during school, and I had even toyed with a little make up here and there just to feel a little more grown up.

I heard footsteps coming my direction, so I quickly leaned on my elbows, staring intently on the drawing and the line of my ruler. They were all coming to sit in here with us. Each of them taking a chair and leaning around the table. Their conversation continuing while I busied myself drawing, looking up to react every so often, smiling, just so I didn't appear to be rude or aloof. I heard Cole's phone conversation with Tatum. My mind took in snippets of everything. Something about a party in the desert, Reed getting a ride with them. It was as if I was washing the windows on the outside of an exclusive club. I was getting a glimpse inside, but not fully participating.

The time flew by, and I was startled when my phone rang. My home phone number popped up. My dad was coming to pick me up. Pulling together our notes, the list and the colored pencils I had brought, I threw everything in my backpack and zipped it up.

"Hey, Noles, we could totally take you home if you want to tell your pops," said Cole. He was the quieter one of the group, a bit skinny, but tall enough to make his appearance fool you into believing he was an athlete. *Noles, somehow that nickname was sticking.*

"No, that's ok, I have some family things to do. But thanks!" I said, deep down knowing we didn't have any family plans but that I didn't really want this group pulling up to my gravel driveway after leaving the Johnson palace.

Reed walked me to the door when we heard my dad pulling up, carrying my backpack for me in a sort of traditional gentleman's way. "Hey, sorry I wasn't much help today. It looks great though. How about we pick back up on Thursday?"

"That should work. I'll come by after practice again, OK?" I said, still reeling from the last two hours where I was alone with the *it* boy of my next four years, spent the afternoon listening to tales of underage drinking, all the while in the presence of underage drinking, and earning a nickname that, while I didn't really like, I secretly was honored to be given.

My dad asked mostly about the Johnson garage, curious if I got the full tour. I told him we pretty much just worked on the project the entire time, leaving out the part about Reed's friends and their beer. I sat back in the seat, pulling my legs up from the hot edges of the seat. For once, not really embarrassed by my car or the home we were driving to, but rather impressed with the path my high school self seemed to be on.

———

Thursday was pretty much a rerun of our first afternoon together at Reed's house. Once again, Reed's father wasn't home. And once again, his friends came over and sat around the table while I worked on building miniature casitas, gardens and filtration stations out of modeling clay. I was more involved in the conversation now, adding in my opinion about the Cardinals chances this year (I knew a few things, but was mostly quoting bits I had read on USAToday.com and some of the sports blogs my brother always read).

Our Tuesdays and Thursdays were becoming a regular thing, for at least an hour after practice every time. The guys would say hi to me in the halls at school, and Sienna and Sarah were delighted to flirt with a few upper classmen. A few times, they even joined me at Reed's house, sitting around the table and, while I never did, they also drank a few of the Johnson family beers as well. Sarah was a joiner, and she had been to a few high school parties in junior high where she had gotten buzzed on shots with her older sister. Sienna was a bit more cautious, so she nursed her beer, participating, but not really experiencing.

As the project afternoons progressed, I realized I was pretty much handling the entire thing on my own. But while I usually resented it and did it anyway, this seemed different. I didn't feel taken advantage of, and I liked that the project gave me something to distract myself with when Reed and I were alone, before his friends showed up.

We were fast on our way to becoming friends. I was finally ready to admit to myself that I had a bit of a puppy crush on him for sure, but that I wasn't really interested in anything beyond that. I liked how he made me feel—like I was a part of something, socially accepted, almost cool. I fantasized about our high school years, me catching rides with him, waving at him while he was on the field for a game. One day, after I'd finally met his dad, he'd know me, too. I would pop over to visit and he'd welcome me in, ask me to stay for dinner. Yes, Reed and I could become great friends. And that would be enough.

"Oh. My. God. Your house is so huuuuuuuge!" I heard a squeal come from the front door. That's when I was thrown back into reality.

Tatum was here. In this house. With me and my new group of friends. She showed up with Cole and Devin and threw her purse on the table next to our nearly done project, not even casting a look in my direction. Her heavy and clunky keys slid out the top of her purse, knocking over several toothpick structures I had set aside to dry from gluing. Thoughtless and selfish, was all I could think as I pushed her crap from the table to a nearby chair and reassembled the toothpicks.

"Reeeeeeeeed," she giggled, in a little-girl voice that I thought wasn't fooling anyone. The fakeness oozed from her, and it was utterly transparent—far from attractive. But just then, she threw her arms around Reed and nuzzled her nose into the corner of his neck. She was two years older than him, and she could have any guy in our school. But she wanted to lay claim to Reed. And I was furious.

At first, I thought maybe Reed would be as annoyed by her childish voice and overt flirtation as I was, but he seemed to be eating it up, picking her up and twirling her around in the kitchen, touching her legs with his feet on the couch in the living room and admiring "how cute she was" when she stole his hat from his head and put it on her perfectly tussled head of hair.

For the first time in weeks, the guys didn't sit around the table with me. I continued to work, listening to the conversations in the living room. Tatum giggling at their sports conversations, and asking them what they thought of her hair: Should she cut it? Does it look better up? Should she wear more hats? She had a loose over-shirt on and I watched as she strategically removed it in front of Reed, her back to him as he sat on one of the stools at the breakfast bar. She looked over her shoulder, asking him if he could tuck the tag in on the tight tank she was now revealing.

"Yeah, I got it," he said, a bit taken with her. I could tell he was feeding off of her. Who wouldn't. She was 17 going on 26 and was built like a Hooters waitress. I thought of myself trying to pull off that same move...*I would look idiotic, I disappointed.*

For two hours, the giggling continued. At one point, she had jumped up on his lap and had wrapped her arms around his neck. He was stroking up and down her back with his hand, his thumb flicking the straps of her tank top. He had a smirk on his face and she knew she had him. While I was only a room away, I was an entire world apart.

My phone made me jump, and I knocked over the stack of note cards I had been making about our various model pieces. I told my dad I would meet him outside when he came, fearful that I might start crying at any moment. I bent down to gather the note cards and my eyes started to sting. I saw the bottom of Reed's tattered jeans on the other underside of the table. I begged myself to stop the tears and wished with all my might that he would just leave it at a "see ya next time" or "goodbye."

"Was that your dad?" he asked.

"Yeah, he's on his way. I'm just packing up and then I'll be out of your hair," I said, a bit snarky. I hated myself for letting it get the best of me, and then also dreaded the direction I knew this would go, and the fact that I was taking it there.

"What the hell does that mean, Noles? Something wrong?" Reed said, squatting down to help me with my note cards. Just then, I heard Tatum calling from the living room, "Reeeeeeeeeeeeeed, come back here, I'm cold."

He smiled a little, turning his head sideways, almost as if he was imagining just what he could do to warm her up.

I snapped. "You know, if I was going to do this entire thing by myself, I could have just done it at home, saved us both a lot of hassle. It's not like I need your table to hold up the card board," I shot the words at him, though they were merely a mask for what was eating at my insides.

"Noles, I totally didn't mean to leave you with all of this. I just figured you liked doing this part and you were so good at it. We always have fun, and laugh, and I can totally jump in whenever you need me to. You just never seem to want me to…I'm sorry, dude," he rattled that last part off, just as Tatum let out another cackle of a laugh. And that finally broke me.

"Dude? … Dude?" I stood as he did, getting close enough to him so I could say this last part with enough force but just out of earshot of what was in the next room. "I'm not a dude, Reed, like Cole or Devin. At least …" I looked around as I stepped closer to whisper in his ear. "I haven't had a sex change," I gritted through my teeth. Then, picking up his wrist, I formed his hand into a fist and pounded mine against it, looking straight into his eyes the entire time, unflinching. "Booooom!" I said plainly, with as little emotion as possible, pursing my lips. Staring into his eyes for a few more uncomfortable seconds, I saw realization wash over his face. I had heard the entire thing—and I had heard *him*.

I grabbed my bag from the nearby chair, headed straight to the door and left, never turning back. I walked down the driveway as my dad was pulling up, willing myself to hold it all in until I could lock myself in my room. Reed knew exactly what I meant. He got it all, and I knew it. And as proud as I was of myself, I also silently scolded myself for being surprised that he would cuddle with Tatum in his house while I was busying myself with clay and glue … like a child.

I let the tears fall as soon as I pushed my face into my bed, and I cried until finally falling asleep well after midnight.

4. Words

I WOULDN'T CALL it moping, but I walked to my homeroom that morning with a certain sense of hopelessness. I was exhausted from the previous night's cry fest, and dreading my science class with Reed. As Sienna and Sarah bounded into the classroom, full smiles, I sank further into my seat. We had planned on going to the football game tonight, but that was before I made an ass out of myself in front of our cool new group of friends and lambasted the boy who had repeatedly broken my heart in a matter of weeks. I had to try to get out of this, and so as soon as they sat down next to me I put on a coughing act and said I wasn't feeling very well.

"Like hell," Sarah started. "Girl, you better suck it up and start taking some vitamin C, cuz there's no way we're missing that game tonight. Cole invited us to the desert party after, and we are going, because he is way hot, and I want him."

"I don't know," I started, but was quickly cut off.

"You'll feel fine as soon as we start having fun. If not, my sister will totally drop you off at home on our way to the party, ok?" Sarah said. There really is no reasoning with her when her mind's made up.

"OK," I shrugged, slumping down even more in my chair.

Sienna just looked at me with a soft smile. I think she sensed that there was something more to it, but she was also sweet enough to know when I didn't want to talk. She just squeezed my wrist and whispered, "we'll have fun!"

————

My morning classes flew by and I was on my way to science, walking alone. I spent extra time at my locker to avoid the chance that I might have to walk in with Reed. I scanned the quad on my way to the room terrified that I would still run into him. When I entered the classroom, I snapped my focus right to his seat. I wanted to see him first—before he locked eyes on me. For some reason, I thought that might help me prepare myself and square up my irrational emotions. But his seat was still empty.

I walked over, lopped my backpack over the chair and pulled out my notebook and a pencil. Intently counting the second-hand clicks on the clock, I started to fill with concern that Reed wasn't here. He was skipping school, either because of the dressing down I had given him or because he was off making out with a 17-year-old hoochie. Caught up in the drama in my head, I didn't notice when he slipped in at the last second and slid into his seat next to me.

I could feel the blood rushing to my head. In fact, I could hear it passing over my eardrums in waves, making it almost impossible to hear our teacher. I refused to pull my gaze up from my notebook. I didn't want to see if he was frowning. I didn't want to see if he was furious or sad. I just wanted to shrink down to microscopic size and scamper off unnoticed. The only part of Reed I could see was his feet. They were bouncing up and down, propped on his toes. He was clearly just as affected sitting next to me, but I was pretty sure that he was just counting the seconds that he could be free from me. He smacked his notebook on his desktop and pulled a pen out ready to take notes for the class.

I wrote down various bits of our lesson. Cell structures and mitochondria. It seemed pretty simple so I wasn't too alarmed at my own lack of attention. Reed, however, seemed to be writing down everything our teacher said, word for word. His pen was busy and he kept stopping and scribbling every few seconds. He slowed down some near the end of class and started drumming his pen on his leg to match the tempo of his bouncing. I expected that when we heard the bell he would be off with a sprint.

Finally, after 50 torturous minutes, the bell rang. I slid my note-book sideways on my desk into my backpack and zipped it up. I heard Reed ripping off a page from his notebook and standing up to leave. I thought I would just sit still for an extra minute or two to let him get a head start. I was starting to imagine the pattern of doing this for the next eight months of school and was wondering if I could handle the stress of it when I saw Reed slide a folded piece of paper over to me on top of a blue pocket folder.

Confused, I looked up at him, pursing my lips and crooking the corner of my mouth.

"Just take it and read it, OK?" he said shortly. And then he was walking away.

I flipped open the folder and saw my note cards tucked into one pocket with a rubber band around them. They had been high-lighted and numbered. In the other pocket was a typed and stapled paper. The top sheet was titled "A Sustainable Society: By Nolan Lennox and Reed Johnson." I pulled the paper from the folder and realized it was a full four pages, single spaced. I read the first few paragraphs and they were exactly as I would have written them, minus a few word choices.

Reed had finished our project. By himself. Last night.

I didn't quite know what to make of this. I was equal parts offended that he hadn't included me in our work and awed by his gesture. I was fairly confident that the note he had folded and placed on top of the folder he had given me would provide me with clarity. I started to unfold and read it where I sat, but the next class was already filing in. I was going to be late for PE. Also, as much as I wanted to know what he had written to me, I also was afraid. Was he angry? Is that why he had written so manically during our class? Wondering if I had just bided my time, waiting to yell at him and embarrass him in front of his friends. Did he finish the paper just to be rid of me? Or, maybe they were kind words? And at that thought, part of me wanted to savor it and read it just a few words at a time.

Walking slowly through the grass to the gym, I held the note close to my chest under the folder, my arms crossed over it. When I got to my gym locker, I tucked it inside my backpack and changed for PE. As I sat on the bench waiting for our class to begin, I stared at my locker, wanting to unlock the combination immediately, crawl into a bathroom stall and feign menstrual cramps. But I left it where it was.

We did aerobics for PE and practiced various stretches on the mats upstairs. I could hear the weight room on the other side of the gym and knew Reed was there. Most of the football players had weightlifting as their elective. I felt like I was holding onto a burning secret, but I only knew parts of it. My lack of awareness must have been apparent, too, because I was still laying flat on my back when the rest of the class was folding up mats and carrying them to the stack at the end of the room.

"Nolan, are you OK?" Sienna leaned over and asked. "Are you sick?"

"Huh? Oh, uh no. Sorry, just daydreaming I guess. Thanks for snapping me out of it!" I sat up and started folding my mat. My head still imagining the words that were waiting for me and listening for any hint of Reed's voice just across the basketball court.

As I turned around after throwing my mat on top of a stack, I was stopped by Sienna, hands on her hips and a furrowed brow. "What's up? I know you. I know you really well and have for years. You know you can tell me, right?" she said in her nurturing tone. Sienna was always the friend you could confide in and she often gave the best advice. While Sarah was one to back you up in a fight, Sienna was the one with her head on right. At her words, I let out a huge sigh and leaned back against the wall as we lined up to head back to the locker room.

"It's Reed," I said, not sure where else to go with it.

"Nolan, I know that much. I totally know that you like him… more than friends…and I think there's a part of him that really likes you, too. Did something…happen?" she asked, almost with a look of hope in her eyes.

"Oh god, it's sooooo not what you think," I said, stopping her before she went too far. Then, part of what she said sank in and I flinched, squinting my eyes. "You really think he's got a thing for me?"

"I don't think. I know," she said, matter-of-factly. I wasn't sure she was right on this one, but I was flattered that she would even think that about me. I stood silently, trying to take what she had said in and sorting through the source of my stress for a good place to begin. I decided starting with Tatum's flirtation was the genesis. Sienna winced when I recanted the scene from outside the gym after volleyball tryouts and hugged me when I told her what I said, inches away from Reed's face. Finally, I got to the part about the note, and she shook me by my shoulders.

"You seriously have been holding onto his letter for, like, an hour not knowing what it says?" she was dumbfounded.

"Yeah…I was afraid I wouldn't have enough time to read it, and I'm a little worried about what it says."

Sienna's eyes were wide and her mouth was tightly closed, almost like she was holding something in.

"Nolan, you have to go read that. Like…right now!"

She was right. Now was the perfect time. I had lunch after PE, and I could take all the time I needed and hide out if I needed to. Part of me wanted to just ask Sienna to read it for me, just like when I cover my eyes during scary movies and ask her to tell me when the gory scenes are over and catch me up on the major plot points. But this was personal from Reed to me, and I knew it was something I had to do all on my own.

As she slung her bag over her shoulder in the locker room, she looked back at me and said she'd save me a seat at lunch and tell Sarah I had to talk with the coach. Grateful, I smiled.

Finally alone, I straddled the bench, unzipped my bag and pulled out the note. As I unfolded it, I was first amazed at the length and surprisingly nice penmanship. It was clear that he had written quickly and had a lot to say. Holding my breath, I began:

Nolan:

I don't even know where to start, but I guess the best place would be with sorry. I don't deserve your forgiveness, but please believe me that I am being sincere in asking for it. I am embarrassed ashamed of what you heard and want you to know that that's not the guy I am. I don't have any excuses other than sharing with you the only behavior I've ever known. My parents hate each other. My mom fills me with stories about my cheating father and my father talks about how greedy and superficial my mom is, not that she's any different from any other wife he's had or the many women he's had affairs with. My brother was the most popular guy in school and I'm supposed to be just like him. Jason was is an asshole. I've grown up watching him put people down and have others lift him up for it. Deep down, I've always known it was sort of a douche bag way to be, but I guess I got caught up in it. Again, I don't have any excuses, so I am sorry.

Second, let me just say for the record that you are very pretty. I actually remembered your knee-high socks that you were wearing that first day we met, and they were kinda cute. So, while it might not erase those hurtful things we said that day, I hope it's at least a start.

I'm sure you've noticed that our paper is done. I never intended on having you do all the work. Just so you know, I'm not some stupid jock. I'm actually pretty smart and school has always been easy for me. I'm sure you'll still read the paper word for word to make sure it's of 'Nolan quality,' but I can assure you that it's an A. I will bring the model in on Monday so we can turn them in together for our grade.

I guess that's all. I like hanging out with you and really hope I didn't F things up. Still friends?

~Reed

My knees were numb and I wasn't sure how I was going to make it to the cafeteria for lunch, not that I was hungry in the least. Reed's letter was…well, it just was. I wasn't sure what I had hoped for, but this was certainly not what I expected. I folded it carefully into quarters and pulled out my wallet, tucking it behind my school I.D. I lay back on the bench and pulled my knees up to a bend, resting my folded hands on my forehead. I knew I wasn't going to make it to lunch; I just needed to take some time to soak in this moment. Sitting up, I pulled out my phone from the front pocket of my bag. I typed out a quick text to Sienna that I would fill her in later and that all was good in the world again and hit send. She wrote back immediately, :-).

My next text required more thought. I pulled up Reed's name and stared at the empty screen for minutes. Just as the bell for class was ringing, I typed and hit send.

Still friends, :-)

Almost instantly, he wrote back.

Awesome. C U after the game!

Sarah was going to be happy. There was no way I was missing it now.

5. Friday Night

IN THE PAST, I attended Coolidge High football games wearing my brother's old Bears shirt, cut-off shorts and flip flops. But for some reason, I couldn't seem to settle in on how I looked. I was uncomfortable in my own skin. Of the dozen or so combinations of outfits I tried, I kept coming back to the black-and-white tank top that tied around my neck and the hip-hugging denim shorts. Pulling my hair up into a loose ponytail, I let a few strands fall at the nape of my neck, slightly curled from the humidity. I would be comfortable outside in the desert for the evening, but wouldn't need to worry about climbing over washes. I stuck with the Converse shoes, sockless, so I could navigate my way through the dry brush and rocks at the party as well as climb the bleachers for the game.

I heard Sarah's sister honk the horn out front and I ran out to the living room, kissed my mom and dad and grabbed my overnight bag. I was spending the night at Sarah's house, or at least as soon as we got home from the party that's where I'd be. My parents never would have let me wander around the desert in the middle of the night with a bunch of older boys, never mind the fact that there would be alcohol there. I felt a tinge of guilt at my cover up, but the desire to break the rules for once in my life was too strong.

"I'll be home before lunch tomorrow, ok?" I said, holding the door a crack open as I was leaving.

"Have fun honey!" my mom yelled from the kitchen.

As I made my way down the steps of our porch and heard the crunch of the gravel under my feet, I felt the weight of my lie start to lift. I had made it, and I instantly started busying myself with how my night was going to go. I remembered the words Reed had written…*pretty, he thought I was very pretty.* I had read that part of his letter at least 100 times. I had tucked it carefully in my jewelry lock box when I was done, afraid that someone might find it and throw it away. I never wanted to lose that letter.

As we rounded the corner of the main street in town, Sarah's sister Calley turned the radio up full blast. She was on the dance team and listened to a lot of hip hop music, which was not known for its quiet, subtle language. The students that had gathered early for the tailgate party were walking around the parking lot, sitting on the hoods of cars and in the beds of pickup trucks. As we pulled in and found a spot near the exit, heads started to turn in our direction, no doubt thanks to the F bombs blaring from Calley's car. She turned the ignition off, pulled down the mirror on her car's visor and touched up her lipstick. Finally, with a kissing sound, she flipped the mirror back up and kicked open her door.

"Let's go rule this shit, bitches!" she shouted, followed by a "wooooooo!"

Calley had a way of making you feel like the party started when you arrived, as long as you were with her. Twice suspended for fighting, she had a tough reputation. But she was also gorgeous. Calley and Sarah's dad was from Cuba. He had defected to the United States and met their mother when she was working at a diner in Miami. Her father refused to let them marry, so they ran away to Arizona. They've been married for 18 years now, which I guess goes to show that overprotective parents don't always know best. Anyhow, the Perez sisters had the most beautiful bronzed skin, light brown hair that fell down their backs in waves and curvy bodies built for dancing. I think that's why they both excelled so much at performing.

Sienna and I stepped from the car and shadowed our bolder leaders. When we reached the field, Sienna walked to the far entrance where the band was meeting up. She was nervous about her first time marching and playing an instrument at the same time. I didn't want to crush her spirit, but I was pretty sure most of the people in the stands tonight would be standing in the snack bar line during her performance. They were here for football, not the arts. I was starting to pull my wallet from my purse to pay for my game ticket when Calley grabbed my arm and shook her head.

"Sister, we don't pay. Come with me," she said, leading me by the hand along with her sister. We walked over to the snack bar and I watched as Calley leaned in and whispered something into one of the guy's ears. He smiled and she kissed his cheek. In seconds, he rounded the building and was holding the back gate open for us.

The stands were already getting crowded and our team hadn't even left the locker room to take the field for warm ups yet. The Bears had won their first two games, both away. This was their first home game, and the first home game with a Johnson at quarterback in a few years. We were playing East High School from Yuma, which is on the other side of the state about four hours away. Their travel busses lined the alleyway behind the away stands.

We climbed the middle section of the bleachers and found a seat near the press box at the top, making for a perfect backrest. We were just getting settled when we heard the speaker crackle and the announcer welcome the visiting Lions from East. The band started to play then and the cheerleaders were standing two-girls-high in the end zone, holding a banner for the team to run through as they entered the field. Sarah was watching them intently, I think waiting for one of them to fall. She had made the junior varsity cheer team, but was an alternate for varsity should anything go wrong.

Just as the announcer finished "...your hometown Coolidge High Fighting Bears," the team burst through the banner that read 'Go, Fight, Win!' I saw Cole and Devin right away. Reed wasn't far behind. His helmet in one hand as he side-skipped towards his two friends and bumped into them mid-air in some masculine show of pride. The team circled up in the middle of the field and broke out into lines to start their stretching. You could hear the group of almost men counting down each stretch from blocks away.

The stands were full. There wasn't much else going on in Coolidge on a Friday night, and high school sports were about as elite as it got, given the hour-plus drive to any of the college or professional teams in the state. Calley had left us to save our section of the bleachers while she went to the snack bar for some sodas and candy. Left on my own, I don't think that I would have been able to guard our section from the aunts, uncles and cousins that were quickly filling every spare inch of bleacher. Sarah, thankfully, had no problem shooing away unwanted neighbors, though she did let a few junior and senior boys sit close enough to her that their knees touched her shoulder blades (part of her plan, I was sure).

Calley was climbing back up to our seats with her arms full of drinks and snacks, which I'm sure she managed to convince the freshman boys working the concession area to give her for free. I was reaching to grab two of the sodas to help her free her hands when I noticed Tatum was tailing behind her. Catching my breath a little, my hands stuttered just as Calley was letting the cups go, and I reacted by squeezing the two Styrofoam cups together, spilling about half of the contents of each (Dr. Pepper, I was pretty sure) on my lap.

I was not surprised when Tatum started laughing uncontrollably at my clumsiness. "Oh my god! You dumped, like, that entire thing on your shorts!" *She's really good at the obvious, I thought.*

Smiling with my lips closed tightly, I shrugged my shoulders and stood up. The soda that hadn't soaked into my shorts was now slowly dripping down the fronts and insides of my legs. I was now aware of the stickiness. Just as I bent down to hand the still salvage-able sodas to Sarah, I heard Tatum giggle to Calley and whisper "pathetic!"

I immediately felt ashamed. I am not sure why. I slid along the front of Calley and Tatum. "I'll be right back," I said, looking Calley square in the eyes, half saying "sorry." She gave me a sympathetic look in return, knowing that I probably heard what Tatum had said in her ear.

"Don't worry, we'll hold your seat," she yelled as I made my way down the bleachers. In some ways, I felt as if she was trying to reassure me that I was still cool in her eyes and that she wasn't agreeing with whatever beef it was Tatum seemed to have with me.

As I made my way to the restrooms, I looked at the field as the captains were walking out to toss the coin. Since the captains were all seniors, Reed was standing on the sidelines, jumping up and down, psyching himself up for the game. I started to walk quickly hoping no one would realize the dark wet denim that was starting to chafe my legs. The football restrooms were tiny, and there was a line wrapping around the fence. Knowing I would have to wait for several minutes, I just kept walking. I knew I could get in to the gym through a side entrance and make my way to the women's locker room.

The lights were off when I found my locker. Twisting the combination, I unlocked the door and felt through the piles of T-shirts and socks for my practice shorts. I had only worn them once this week, and while they were plain and cotton, at least they were gray and wouldn't clash with my shirt. Once dressed, I felt my way around the corner to the sinks where I was truly in the pitch black. I managed to find the paper towels and rip a few feet off to wet and wash the stickiness from my thighs.

I was rounding the corner back out to the field and saw Tatum standing in line at the concession stand. She was talking to another group of girls and pointing to our area. As I got closer I heard her tell them that she was with her friend and a bunch of freshmen, so they'd make room. *Great, more of them.* I kept my head down as I passed a few people behind her so she wouldn't notice me. I made my way back up to our seats with only a few minutes left in the first quarter.

"What'd I miss?" I asked Sarah, pointing to the 7 points our team had put on the board.

"Nolan, Reed is uhhhh-maaaazing!" she said, more excited than I had ever seen her at a sporting event.

"Oh yeah? How so?"

"OK, so the other team had the ball first, and they were really close to scoring and then one of the guys on our team, defense, right?" she asked. Sarah's knowledge of sports was amusing. "Anyway, our guy caught the other quarterback's pass in the middle of the air and then started to run it back to our side. He was tackled somewhere in the middle. Then Reed came out and threw the ball three times. Three times! That was it, and we scored!" Sarah gushed.

"Wow! I guess there's something to that Johnson hype, huh?" I said, my inner-self still giggling a bit at my friend's very colorful game commentary.

We sat silent for a few minutes while the clock counted down. Just as the whistles were blowing to signify the end of the quarter, Sarah turned to me with a bit of a sly smile on her face.

"Whaaaaat are you up to with that look?" I asked.

"Nothing," she said, plainly. "I just…I just get why you're so into him, that's all." And at that, Tatum snapped her head in our direction and stared at me. I turned my head to look down at my shoes and bend down to pretend to fix a shoelace. Tilting my head up a bit at Sarah, I reminded her that we were just good friends.

"Yeah, right. You're friends. But you totally want more," she said, leaning into me. I could feel Tatum's stare burning into my cheeks, but I refused to turn and acknowledge it. I just gave Sarah a half-hearted smile to satiate her and end the conversation. I knew Tatum was claiming Reed as hers, at least romantically. And I, of all people, was not a threat to her.

———

We ended up beating Yuma East 49-14, and Reed ended up making plenty more amazing plays. Twice, he ran the ball in for a touchdown himself. I heard one of the older men sitting near us comment on his size and how he was bigger than his brother was when he was a freshman. It was fascinating to hear what these complete strangers knew about him, almost as though they were scouting him well in advance for their future fantasy football drafts.

There was a lot of excitement leaving the game, as a line of cars poured from the parking lot, with honking and hollers from open windows and convertibles. Almost everyone seemed to be headed to the desert party, as we followed pickups and Jeeps to a mile post off the highway to turn down a dirt road. The air was thick with the dust being kicked up and the car shook and bounced along the uneven path. We finally turned off into a hidden camping-type area that was marked by a red sweatshirt tied to a cactus.

We parked next to a tree and got out to stretch our legs. We followed a few of Calley's friends who had pulled in just ahead of us as they walked a few yards towards a wash. You could hear the thumping of music from someone's car stereo and, as my eyes adjusted, I started to focus on the 50 or 60 people gathered around some old picnic benches and large rocks. A few of the pick up trucks were backed up to the seating area and were filled with coolers of various alcoholic beverages. The informal rule seemed to be that if you were drinking alcohol, you needed to bring something to share, as I flipped open one of the coolers and found a mishmash of wine coolers, vodka, tequila and assortments of other liquor clearly swiped from parents and, more likely, the town's various gas stations and convenience stores.

I was starting to panic, as every cooler contained only alcohol, when I finally flipped open a small one with two or three water bottles inside. "Found it!" I said, grabbing one and holding it over my head triumphantly. I grabbed one for Sienna, shut the lid and slid the cooler to the back of the truck, hiding it in case we might want more later in the evening. *Not that water was of an interest to anyone else that was there.*

The party was pretty dull for the first 30 minutes while people just formed small groups and stood around talking. Sienna and I sat on the table of one of the benches just behind Calley and Sarah, who were talking up two upper classmen that they had been flirting with during the game. Jokingly, Sienna leaned her plastic water bottle sideways for me to 'clink' and say cheers. We laughed at our very unhip, straight-edge humor, and I caught Tatum rolling her eyes as she walked up to Calley.

"The guys should be here any minute," she said, smiling. "I am so going to kiss Reed when he gets here. I'm so proud of him." She was saying this just loud enough for my benefit, I knew. Sienna leaned into me with a nonverbal 'sorry.' I shrugged it off, knowing full well what reality was, but my stomach was sinking and I was starting to dread the hours ahead of us tonight.

When the second wave of vehicles started rounding the dirt road, my classmates all started cheering and holding their various bottles in the air in a salute. Cole jumped out of the back of a pickup truck and came running over to the table of cheerleaders, picking two of them up and squeezing their rears with his hands as they laughed. *Pig, I thought.* More and more of the guys started mingling with the rest of the partiers, climbing the trucks and grabbing beers, shaking them and spraying each other and standing on car rooftops to beat their chests. Taken out of context, the entire scene was absurd. *In fact, even in context it was ridiculous, I thought.*

Just then, I felt someone lean into my other side. I jumped a bit and turned to see Reed. "Hey!" I said, bumping him back. This seemed to be an acceptable form of touching, and the warmth of his arm against mine, even in just that split second, sent chills through me.

"So, what'd you think? How'd I do," he said, unwrapping a burger from some fast food joint and shoveling half of it in his mouth. I must have been staring because he felt the need to explain. "Sorry, I would totally share, but I ate one on the way here and I'm STARVING!"

"It's ok, I'm not hungry," I laughed. "And you're game was great! I mean, you did great. So did the rest of the guys, but you were really good tonight." *I was gushing and needed to stop.*

"Thanks! I felt really comfortable out there. Maybe you're my good luck charm!" he said, bumping into me again and polishing off his burger. I let out a tiny laugh in response, but tucked what he said into that place inside where I was holding the words of his letter and any other sign of flirtation from Reed Johnson.

"Hey, you want something to drink?" he asked.

I held up my water and made a crooked smile.

"Ah, good. You found it. I threw a cooler in Sam's truck because

46

I know you don't really like to drink," he said. *He seriously thought about me. I was part of his planning process.*

"Yeah, thanks. I'm not too sure how I'm going to get home, because I know Calley is going to load up tonight," I said, my face showing signs of my concern.

"Don't worry. We'll be here for a while, and it's actually not that far from my dad's, so worst-case scenario, you guys can walk home with me and crash at my house until the morning," he smiled.

"Thanks," I said, my mind turning to the thought of spending the night at Reed Johnson's house.

Not missing a beat, Tatum came running over and plopped herself right on Reed's lap, snapping me right out of my very pleasant daydream where she didn't exist. She had her back to me completely, but I could hear their entire conversation. "Baby, you were so good tonight!" she fawned. *I didn't sound like that when I complimented him, no way.*

"Thanks! What do I get for being so good," he suggested. I was getting uncomfortable and flipped my feet to the ground to get up.

"Hey, talk to you later, Noles, kay?" Reed shouted as I walked away.

"Yeah, sure," I smiled, realizing he was already busy making out with Tatum.

I found Sienna with her feet dangling from the bed of a pickup. I climbed up and sat next to her, kicking my feet at the same rhythm. She turned the side of her lips up in a small smile. "Kinda sucks, huh?" she said.

"Whatcha mean? The party? It's not bad. I just don't drink and I'm awkward and don't really know what to do," I responded honestly.

"No, I mean that," she said, gesturing to Reed and Tatum, now fully enveloped in one another across the lot.

"Oh," I said, turning my head down and knocking the heels of my shoes together like Dorothy from Oz. Sienna smiled at my subtle joke. "Yeah, that kinda sucks. Kinda...a lot," I admitted.

"I know," she said, tilting her water to me again for another half-hearted 'Cheers.'

The party dragged for Sienna and I, as hours passed and teenagers drank more and more. We started making bets on who was going to get sick or stumble first. I was thrilled when I won a dollar after Tatum tripped over her own feet on her way to the cooler. It didn't console me much when she slung her arms around Reed's neck, though.

Things were starting to wind down and a few of the pickup trucks were leaving a trail of dust against the night sky as they pulled out from our desert lot. *No one was in any shape to drive, I thought.*

Sienna and I stood in the middle of the lot, just behind Calley's car. She was definitely not driving. Sarah wasn't as wasted, but she was only 15 and still not in any condition to drive. And Sienna and I, well, we were rule followers.

Devin, Cole and Sean came stumbling over, a few junior cheerleaders with them. "Hey, ladies," Cole slurred. "We're kickin' it at Reed's, you wanna come?"

Knowing I didn't have a choice, we started walking along the wash with them. Reed was leading the way, carrying Tatum piggyback, her legs wrapped tightly around his waist. My stomach felt as if I had just dropped in an elevator and my head felt light. I thought I was maybe going to pass out, but I had Sienna with me to keep me standing. I felt her throw her arm over my shoulder, I think sensing that I needed to be grounded a bit.

Reed was right, his dad's house was close. We walked for maybe 20 or 30 minutes and made our way to the back of his father's property. Reed flipped open a gate and the dozen or so of us following him came streaming through his back yard. He slid open the back glass door and we all followed inside. Some of the guys just fell flat on the floor and the girls all lay on the couch. Sienna and I found two lounge chairs over by the fireplace and curled our feet up. I was trying to make myself small. Invisible.

Reed was the last to walk through the main room, flipping the light off. He looked over at me with a goofy grin, and with a bit of a slur said "g'night, Noles." Then he grabbed Tatum's hand and led her upstairs.

I felt like a pet and I wanted to run away. But it was three in the morning, and I was too many desert miles away from home. I felt Sienna hand me a blanket, and I grabbed it tightly. She patted my arm knowingly and then snuggled in to fall asleep. I pulled the blanket over my entire body and let my eyes fill up with water. I willed myself not to sob, but I sat there, on the verge, for the next several hours.

I was trying to convince Sarah and Calley to wake up to drive me home when the front door burst open and the sound of suitcases rolling filled the foyer. The hung-over teenagers in the living room all started to stir at the noise. I rounded the corner to see who was at the door and ran right into Buck Johnson.

"Oh, hey there, girly," he said, with a hint of Southern charm. "You must be one of Reed's friends?"

"Uh, oh… yeah, I'm so sorry. I'm Nolan. Reed let a few of us stay over because the football celebration lasted so long last night," I was vague, not sure how much information he knew or cared to know.

"Nolan, I've heard about you. Great name, kid!" he said, giving me a bit of a punch on the shoulder. I understood the charm of the best salesman in the business instantly. "Hell of a game last night, huh? I came in from meetings in Tucson for it and had to get back for a breakfast meeting this morning, but it was worth the drive. My boy's something special," he beamed.

I heard steps coming down the stairs and soon Reed was standing behind me. "Hey pops," he said with a wave. "You just get in?"

"Sure did, you wanna roll these bags upstairs for me?" he said, handing over a big garment bag.

"Yep," Reed said, smiling. He was turning to say something to me when I turned quickly as if I didn't notice. I wasn't ready to make eye contact with him. Thankfully Calley and Sarah were walking up with their purses and Calley had her keys dangling from her finger.

"Hey, Nolan. Cole's going to give us a lift back to my car, you ready?" she asked.

"Sounds good," I said. Then, not fully turning to Reed, I half thanked him for letting us stay over last night.

"Uh yeah, anytime," he said, finally turning his attention to moving his father's bags upstairs.

I didn't talk much during the ride to Calley's car or the ride back to my house. I had never been happier to see the wrap-around porch my dad built in my life. I climbed the steps and plopped down on one of the porch chairs next to my dad.

"Have a good time, kiddo?" he asked.

"Sure did," I lied.

6. Without

I DECIDED that I wouldn't be attending any more desert parties after the football games this year. Even without my unhealthy crush on the quarterback, I didn't really enjoy the drunk mingling in the 90-degree desert. And as the fall stretched on, the parties happened less and less as winter settled in and the football season became more and more serious. I wasn't anti-social, by any means. I just didn't let my imagination get carried away.

Reed and I ended up earning the highest grade in the class on our sustainability project. In fact, our teacher was so impressed by our model and paper he entered it in a district competition being sponsored by one of the big solar companies in Phoenix.

Without the project, there was little reason for me to visit or call Reed. I found myself not able to delete the small string of texts I had saved from our few conversations. Most of them were about meeting times and whether or not I was coming over to work on the project. Then there was that last one, when I told him we were still friends. And we were. I just had to create some distance to keep my emotions sheltered until I could overcome this puppy crush.

My volleyball season finished in November, and I was pretty sure

I would be allowed to play up at varsity the next year. Most of the girls were graduating, leaving only Tatum to lead the team. I dreaded the thought of that, but I was pretty sure I could hold my own on the court with her after some practice.

Homecoming went as expected. Reed was named freshman prince and Sarah was his princess. Tatum was the junior royalty and she and Reed spent most of the homecoming dance glued to one another inappropriately. I went to the dance with Sienna and a few of her friends from band. She had just started dating a new boy at our school, Bradley. They were in band together and both were musical prodigies. They competed at the district music challenge with a duet and were sort of inseparable ever since. Thankfully a few other girls were with us, otherwise I would have very much been the third wheel.

District play-offs flew by and Reed and the Bears breezed through allowing their opponents to score 17 points total. He really was a bit of a phenom with the football. The state championship game was a week or two before the holiday break and was held at the university stadium in Tucson. We ended up losing to Valley Christian Prep, a fairly sizeable private school from Scottsdale. They had money and a team of giants whom had played together since Pop Warner at 8. Reed was pretty bummed, losing by two touchdowns. But the papers were pretty fair, talking about his freshman status leading a young team against one that was mostly seniors. "A Force to be Reckoned With" was the headline over the article profiling him in the big paper.

After some serious thought, I sent him a text over the holidays wishing him a Merry Christmas. Surprisingly, he sent back a picture of his smiling face in front of his tree and fireplace. It was amazingly decorated – they must have hired someone, I thought, knowing two men couldn't pull that look off.

I looked at the self-portrait Reed had sent more than I should over the break. But I tucked it back into my taboo file when school started again and I spotted Tatum and Reed holding hands through the quad.

After a few weeks, being friends with Reed was getting easier. We made each other laugh in science and accepted two green medals that we were given for honorable mention prizes in the district sustainability contest for our project. The class joked that we were the green team and I nicknamed Reed 'the Hulk' in the spirit of it all. Our texts were even more regular and caused me less stress. He would ask me my opinion on the upcoming NFL draft or basketball, impressed when I was able to keep up with the text-versation. I could tell he was trying to stump me, and whenever I wasn't sure about something, I consulted Mike, who I had to call now that he'd moved out, and my dad. Reed and I were friends, yes, but I still wanted to remain cool in his eyes.

Track season was starting and I was looking forward to spending my afternoons running for miles with my headphones on. I had brought my own spikes to school and was lacing them up on the bleachers when I heard Reed and a few other guys walking up.

"Noles!" Sean said, sliding onto the bench next to me and putting his arm over my shoulder. "How's my girl?" he added, suspiciously.

"Uh... fine, I guess?" I said, scrunching my brows trying to figure out what he was up to. "What are you guys doing here?"

"Coach wants us to spend the spring running, and I think I'll be pretty good at shot put," Reed said.

"Oh, yeah. I bet," I supported. He would be good, if he could get the technique down, I thought.

A few more people joined us in the bleachers and finally Coach Baker walked up and sat on the railing facing us all. He wasn't the head track coach, but he was the head football coach, and that trumped Coach Stills, who also happened to be a woman. In this good-old-boy's town, she definitely wasn't in charge. She ran the practice and the drills, though, and Coach Baker let her without interference, given her three national championships from her time at Arizona State.

"OK, folks. Here's how it's going to go," Coach Baker started. Reed chuckled a little next to Sean, and they both ribbed each other. They've heard this speech before, I thought. It dawned on me that Sean's arm was still draped over my shoulder. I was curious by it, not wanting it to draw the attention of the coaches. Though I didn't entirely mind, it seemed strange. Not wanting to be singled out, though, I stood up to stretch my legs and work my feet into my shoes, an excuse but it didn't seem to draw a reaction from Sean.

We started practice with a laps exercise. The runner in front would set the pace and the runner at the back would sprint to the front and set a new pace. After about three laps, we all made a pact to gradually slow the pace down some. We were getting away with it until it started to drag a little too much and Coach Stills decided to join us and reset the pace to her more college-level speed. Grumbling made its way down the line, and that's when I heard a breathy whistle behind me. Sean was running behind me, grinning ear to ear. I wasn't sure I had heard him correctly and was even less sure of the meaning.

"What was that?" I said over my shoulder.

"Just enjoying the view," he smiled.

I snapped forward, immediately flushed.

———

Sean's flirtatious comments and overly friendly touching continued for the next few weeks. I didn't react to them, but I also didn't stop them. Tatum decided to join the track team, too. I rarely came in contact with her, she was long jumping and running wasn't really her focus. I think she just joined the team to spend more time with Reed. Things were approaching normal and I was starting to feel like I was my own person again, not trapped by raw neediness and disappointment.

It was the day of our travel meet in Yuma and I was packing a few things from my gym locker in my bag when I noticed Tatum's bronzed legs slide over on the bench next to me. "He's into you, you know," she said, stopping my heart for a brief moment.

"I'm sorry?" I said, not turning to reveal the shock in my face.

"Sean. He's totally into you," she said. "You should hook up with him. You guys would be so cute"

Why was she being nice to me? And what was she talking about? I've known Sean for years and he most certainly did not have a thing for me. "Hmmm, I don't know. I don't think so. He's so... bold." That was the best I could do.

Tatum giggled, that sound flooding my ears and turning my stomach a bit. "Well, I know he likes you. He asked Reed for your phone number, but Reed said he had to ask you himself...you know, because he didn't want to give away your personal information without telling you first."

"Oh," I was stunned.

"Well, now at least you have some time to think about it," she grinned turning to leave the locker room for the bus.

I sat there for a few extra minutes trying to make sense of this new information. Sean was cute, for sure. He was popular and a lot of girls wanted to be his. He had dated a few girls this year. Why was I of any interest to him? I know I should have been excited, but deep in my mind, I knew this also meant that I was putting even more 'friend' definition between me and Reed.

Not able to stall any longer, I grabbed my bag and made my way out to the bus. I climbed the steps and took a seat up front near the coaches, ignoring Sean a few rows back and the wide open space next to him. I was pretty sure he had been saving that seat for me. Luckily, we were on the road quickly and he didn't have time to get my attention. I pulled my headphones out and settled in with some music for the long bus trip ahead of us. I was suddenly wishing I had more amped music and less contemplative selections on my iPod. I listened to two Arcade Fire albums and The National and was about ready to roll my way out of the moving bus from the musical depression I'd forced upon myself when we pulled over at a rest stop about an hour away from Yuma.

I got out to stretch my legs and found my way to the women's restroom and crossed paths with Tatum, who just grinned at me know-ingly. I smiled back briefly and closed the stall door, letting my forehead rest on it for just a moment. I hurried with my business and didn't even stay to dry my hands, opting instead to pat them on my sweatpants. I was one of the first in the bus and quickly put on my headphones to drown out everyone else, mostly Sean as he gave me a smile on his way back on the bus. He looked almost about to speak when I smiled and turned away to look out the window, revealing my headphones so he wouldn't think I was being rude but just didn't hear him. Tatum and Reed crawled on next, and I only watched them from the corner of my eye as they made their way to the back rows. I played a few of the peppy pop tunes on my iPod for the rest of the trip.

We set up camp under the bleachers and I walked over to the table in the center of the field to check in for my races. I was running the 400 and 800 meters and my race wouldn't be until later in the afternoon. I had about 45 minutes to kill before I had to start warm-ups, so I unrolled the towel I brought and lay down, putting my head on my gym bag for support. I closed my eyes briefly letting the music from my headphones put me into a relaxed state.

Turning my head to the side, I saw Reed sitting with his back against a post, his knees bent up, his sweats baggy and long against his running shoes. His sweatshirt was scrunched up under his head and he was laughing, telling some story to Sean with his hands resting comfortably on his knees. His hat was on backwards and the curls of his brown hair were flipping out on the sides and back. I was letting myself take him in for a little too long when Tatum flopped down on the ground in front of him, snuggling against his chest and making her arms at ease wrapped under his thighs. Reed was her personal lounge chair and I was the awkward obsessive watching their intimate moment with my own depressing sound-track pumping in my ears.

Sean walked in front of me and kicked my crossed feet apart to get my attention. I turned to him with a poor reaction but instantly felt guilty. It wasn't his fault he had startled me, and my mood most certainly wasn't thanks to him.

"Sorry, you scared me. What's up?" I said.

"I know your race is soon, wanna warm up a little and check out the snack bar while we're at it?" he asked, almost nervously.

"Uh, yeah. That sounds good. One second." I wrapped my headphones around my iPod and tucked it inside my sweatshirt in my gym bag. Sean reached out his hand to help me up when I sat up and I took it, staring at it like some foreign object. We walked around the front of the bleachers and nearly halfway around the track without speaking. Sean had his hands stuffed in his pockets and was staring out to the middle of the field without much focus, nervously. I wanted to help fill the void in the air, but I really didn't know what to say after Tatum had dropped the bombshell of information on my lap earlier. Unable to take it any longer, I blurted out some obvious strings of conversation.

"So, you're going to try the mile, huh?" I squinted from the sun a bit looking over at him.

"Yep, oh? Hey, here," he said, handing me his sunglasses.

"Thanks," I took them, grateful that I had something to mask the reaction to our conversation in my eyes and also incredibly puzzled at Sean's behavior.

"I think you'll do well," I continued. "You were always good at distance running. I think you were the only person that beat me in junior high," I said with a small laugh. I was so nervous, which was really stupid and unexpected. I felt so foreign to myself.

"Ha, thanks. I don't think I could handle your race, though. The 400? Man, that one makes me puke … literally!" he said, settling in to our conversation. We walked up to the snack bar and I was looking over the menu of sports drinks and energy snacks. I was still studying when Sean stepped up to the counter and ordered two Gatorades and two apples. He handed over five bucks and turned around to hand me a drink and apple.

"Oh, thanks. You didn't have to do that," I said, truly surprised by his gesture.

"You need your energy, Noles. Least I could do," he said, bumping my side a little.

"Well then, thanks," I said, bumping him back. *What was I doing? I was in a full-on flirt fest with Sean. Never in a million years did I see this coming when I got up to start my day this morning.*

We sat over on a concrete curb by the edge of the home stands and bit into our apples, laughing when we both made obnoxious crunching noises and squirted juice out in front of us. Sean pulled his sweatshirt sleeve down over his hand and blotted up the apple drops that fell on my knee. He didn't make eye contact with me, but was very deliberate and gentle. It was strange to see him act this way. Sean was handsome, for sure. His hair was golden brown and short, always styled perfectly. He was one of the tallest boys in school and had broad shoulders. He was pretty fast, but not a sprinter by any means. He was a receiver for the football team mostly because of his height. I watched him as he pulled his sweat-shirt off to reveal the gray track team shirt underneath. He stood and reached his hand down for me again and pulled me up to stand next to him. His hands were strong and his arms had defined muscles. He wasn't as built as Reed, but he was close. I locked into his brown eyes briefly, but looked away not wanting to get caught.

"Hey, you should start your warm ups. I'm gonna go pick a seat to watch your race, k?" he said, his hand softly resting on my arm.

"Sounds good. Wish me luck," I smiled, turning to jog away. *What was happening?*

I took a few practice starts and did a few sprints and knee-highs across the middle of the field before I sat down and started stretching near the shot put area. I watched Reed take his first throw, bending down, his sweats pushed up to his knees revealing his solid calf muscles and long legs. He twisted as he shuffled forward and released the weighted ball through the air. He turned around with a grin and high-fived some guy on the other team, letting out a 'Woooooo!'

He caught my eyes on him and came over to where I was stretching.

"Did you see that? Twenty eight feet! Not bad, huh?" he boasted.

"That's awesome. See, I knew you'd be good at this," I smiled. He smiled back, dimples creasing his cheeks as he knelt down to sit next to me. My heart raced a bit, something that it hadn't done in months, and I was caught off guard. He looked around for a few minutes while I stretched, almost as if he wanted to say something.

Finally, he blurted it out. "You know Sean likes you, right?" he said, seemingly waiting for my reaction.

"Uhm…Tatum sort of said something. And I am starting to get an idea, yeah," I looked up, almost wanting him to tell me what to do. And deeper down wanting him to tell me that Sean wasn't good enough for me and that he was the only boy I should ever kiss. *Stop being ridiculous.*

"He's a good guy. I just wanted you to know," he said, standing up and walking away. He looked over his shoulder at the last minute and threw in, "hey, good luck!" with a wink.

I won my race. I think I let the distraught confusion in my gut fuel my speed, because I pulled out a personal best time, just under 60 seconds. The sun was setting when we were packing up our camp and getting ready to board the bus. Sean had finished third in his mile race, which was pretty good for a field of 15. He was one of the last to run so he was still getting his gear packed and changing his shirt when most of the team was boarding the bus. I wasn't really watching where I was going when I turned to leave the confines of under the bleachers and nearly ran into a kissing Reed and Tatum. "Oh, sorry. I wasn't looking," I said, embarrassed and stung again at the visual reminder.

I was one of the last to board the bus, when I made a spur of the moment decision so completely out of character for me. Sean was standing a few feet behind me with his bag slung over his shoulder. I looked up into the bus window and saw Tatum snuggled into Reed and turned to face Sean, walking right up to him without missing a beat, kissing him full on the lips, from my tip toes and my hand grabbing the back of his neck. That was it, my first kiss. I had spent it now. Sean looked at me with wide eyes, biting the corner of his lip to suppress a big grin.

"So, wanna sit by me?" I asked, riding out my brief moment of confidence and caution-to-the-wind.

"Oh yeah," he said, taking my hand and pulling me on the bus. We settled in a few rows ahead and across the aisle from Tatum and Reed. I put my feet up across the aisle and leaned my head on

Sean's chest and put my headphones in. He stroked my hair, tucking it behind my ear for the entire four-hour trip home. I pretended to have fallen asleep, but was acutely aware of what I had started and pondered if I was ready for or even wanted it. Finally, relenting that it was too late now, I decided to give it, meaning dating Sean, a try.

7. Understudy

THE SUMMER FLEW BY. Sean and Reed had spent most of the summer at a football camp up north and I dedicated myself to complete couch-potato status. It helped that I spent a weekend or two with my grandparents in the Valley and most other days I was with Sienna and Sarah. Sarah couldn't believe I was dating Sean, but she was in full support of me getting the most of it, trying to push me beyond the comfortable make-out sessions I had kept things to before he left for camp.

I talked to Sean a few times a week while he was at camp, finding myself eager to hear stories about Reed as well. I knew that wasn't the right way to feel, but after trying to talk myself out of it for two weeks I decided it wasn't the worst indulgence to allow myself.

The boys were coming back from camp just in time to start official practice at school and I was getting ready for tryouts myself. Tatum had been friendly over the summer, inviting me to open gym volleyball sessions at the school and working with me to improve my hitting before the school year started so I could make the varsity team. I still felt like there was a certain manipulation to everything

Tatum was doing, so I kept my guard up. But I took advantage of her help anyhow.

It was a text from Reed that first alerted me that the boys were back.

We're at my house – pool party! Bring your suit, and tell the girls.

I knew he meant Sienna and Sarah, so I called them and begged them to come along. I was feeling a little unsteady about being around Sean after so long apart. I was also feeling a little strange about seeing Reed.

Calley picked us up and drove us to Reed's house. I had just cut my hair into long layers, but it wouldn't all fit in a pony tail, so I had small pieces that fell along the side of my face. I wore my gray sporty two-piece swimsuit with a pair of board shorts over the bottoms, still not confident in my curvier body.

As we pulled up, the boys were all gathered around a Jeep in front of the main garage. I was barely out of the car when Sean swooped me up and lifted me with a hug, twirling us around. "I missed my girl," he said, his lips completely taking me by surprise. I forgot how easy he was to kiss and was instantly back in form. Dizzy from the spinning, I tapped him on the shoulder to put me down and smiled.

"Oh, sorry. I was a little excited to see you," he said, sneaking in one more kiss on the side of my neck, his finger moving a curl of hair out of the way. "I love your hair."

He was so affectionate and attentive. I was willing my heart to swoon as I reached down and held his hand. "Hey, come check out Reed's new ride," he said, pulling me over to the Jeep.

"Jeep? Not a Buick?" I laughed. Reed smiled as he hopped out of the driver's seat and walked around to the front where I was standing. "Nah, I wanted a Jeep. My dad got a hell of a deal, though," he laughed.

Reed's 16th birthday was just a few weeks away. I was pretty sure that I would not be getting a Jeep for my birthday, embarrassed at the thought of what I would be pulling up to school in. That is, if I had a car to drive at all. I was more likely to be doomed to rides with Sarah and the bus for the rest of my teen years.

We followed the guys inside where bowls of chips and ice chests filled with sodas filled the kitchen. I saw Buck outside on the grill wearing shorts with his shirt off. His belly falling way beyond his waistband and the white of sunscreen not fully rubbed in on his head and chest. Tatum was sitting on a lounge chair outside by the pool rubbing lotion into her legs. She called for me to come sit next to her when I came through the door. Our relationship was truly strange.

"So, are you going to sleep with Sean?" she asked, not even easing me into it. I spit a little soda through my nose as I choked.

"I'm sorry?" I responded with shock.

"You've been going out for a few months now, I just figured maybe you were going to or already have," she continued putting lotion on as if this conversation was no big deal.

"Hmm," I paused. "Well, we haven't. And I don't know. I'm a little…old fashioned, I guess?"

She smiled with a little giggle, winked at me and stood up to walk over to Reed at the outside bar. I watched her in awe of her confidence and maturity. She put her arm around Buck, laughing at something he said. I would never be able to have that relationship with him, and I was stunned by it. I still hadn't brought Sean over to meet my parents. Mostly because I didn't like people seeing my house, especially when they lived in the big ranch houses and wouldn't have the same appreciation of my dad's hand-built BBQ and porch swing.

I saw Sean across the pool and decided to let myself try to fall a little more in love with him. I walked around the pool and put my arms around his neck, making a pouty face at his root beer, which of course he gave to me immediately. He stared at me as I drank for a few seconds and then all of a sudden, a flash of concern washed over his face. "Oh my gosh, put that down, hurry!" He was so urgent, I dropped the can in the grass afraid there was a bee on the can or something. Without missing a beat, Sean swung his arms under my legs and lifted me up, running full force at the pool and jumping, taking both of us in. I screamed when we hit the water from the chill and grabbed the clip from my hair, dunking my head back to get my hair clear of my eyes.

"You!" I teased, splashing him in the face. He pulled me into his arms and kissed me, then stopped and looked me in the eyes. "You're so god damned beautiful." Then he kissed me again, and a hint of butterflies took over in my chest.

———

The first game of the season was packed more than normal. We were starting the season with a rematch against Valley Christian and the entire town wanted revenge. Sarah had taken over the task of sneaking us in, easily manipulating the freshman boys working the snack bar into opening the gate for us. We found a spot in the stands near the press box and I saw Buck sitting with a few older men just a few rows down. Feeling confident I walked down and tapped him on the shoulder.

"Mr. Johnson? I'm Nolan, we've met a few times. I'm friends with…" he cut me off immediately and grabbed my hand with a shake and brought me in for a hug. "Of course, Nolan. I remember you. How you been? You should come by the house more – my son seems to get better grades when you're around," he laughed. I smiled back and nodded as I headed back to my seat, not truly sure what he meant. Reed's GPA was almost as high as mine, in fact I think I was number two in our class and he was number three or four. Shrugging it all off, I took my seat.

"Those are scouts," Tatum whispered in my ear as she sat down behind me. "They aren't supposed to be here yet, but they're personal friends with Buck, so that's how he gets away with it."

I smiled with wide eyes, a little uncomfortable knowing that much information. I turned my attention back to the field for the rest of the game. Sean made two amazing catches in the end zone to score their first 14 points of the half. I worked to keep my focus on Sean and was excited when I caught his eyes as he took his helmet off and turned to face the crowd as they ran in for half time.

His smile stretched his entire face and then he blew a quick kiss before taking off. I was blushing when I caught a glimpse of Reed's eyes as well. They looked…troubled. I wasn't sure why, but I wanted to fix whatever it was.

————

The Bears ended up winning 21 to 7, and everyone was pumped to celebrate. I had promised Sean I would go to the desert party with him, so I rode with Calley, Sarah and Sienna. We sat on the hood of the car watching the dust fill the air as the various headlights highlighted it through the desert brush. The smell of alcohol started to fill the air in an instant, and I pulled out my own cooler, better prepared than I was last year.

Sienna and I clicked our water bottles together in tradition as the first trucks of players started pulling in. Sean was in the back of Cole's pickup truck and jumped over the side as soon as it stopped, running over to me and picking me up and carrying me through the middle of the lot and into the desert brush. "Sorry, super hyper and couldn't wait to see you," he smiled. "Did you see that game? I was good, right?"

He was talking a mile a minute and his body and hair was still warm and damp from his shower. I could feel his shoulder muscles under my fingers as I slid them to his back and tiptoed up to kiss him. He reached around and lifted me up so I could reach his lips and hair, tangling my hands in the wet strands. He walked me backwards until I was sitting on the hood of a truck. I laughed inside realizing I had become one of those couples that made me feel so uncomfortable the year before.

Things stayed heated for about the first hour as we kissed and Sean ran his hands over my thighs and around the back of my shorts, grabbing my butt and pulling me close to him. I was nervous but also felt a bit of a thrill, so I let myself go for a while until we were both nearly dehydrated from the heat and the make out session.

"I'll be right back," Sean said, kissing me one more time so hard that my head leaned back.

I rubbed my lips as he walked away, they were actually raw. I slid from the hood of the truck and was straightening myself up a bit when Reed slid into me with a bump. "Heya," he said, crooking the side of his mouth into a dimple. "Missed ya, how's it going?"

A little rattled by what he said, I shook my head and blinked my eyes a few times. "Uh, good. Hey, great game! Those were some pretty spot-on passes! Gutsy!" I said, knowing that he was really the orchestrator of the great catches that Sean was riding high on.

"Oh, yeah. Thanks! Well…I knew my dad had some friends in the stands, so I wanted to put on a show," he looked at me, his eyes a little troubled.

"Yeah, I … uh, saw them," I responded, showing I understood what he meant.

"You know, I could get in serious trouble if anyone said anything about my dad meeting with those guys. It's all pretty harmless, right now. But if someone took something the wrong way, or made up something just to embellish the story a little, that would be it," he looked frightened, and I understood the look on his face. For the first time ever, Reed was wearing anxiety. It was a look I knew all too well. I just wasn't accustomed to seeing it in his eyes.

"Hey, hey," I said, pulling his sleeve to get his attention, reaching my arms around him to hug him. "Seriously, this kinda thing goes on everywhere, every game, all the time. I promise. I know, because we had people over for dinner a lot when my brother was graduating. And I know in the city it's waaaay worse. So don't worry, ok?" I tried to reassure him.

"You're right; it's just starting so early. I guess…I just…I want this all too much, you know?" he hugged a little tighter, digging his chin into my shoulder and letting out a deep breath. The wind was knocked out of me at his vulnerability. I let him go just before Sean walked around the front of the truck with a water bottle for me, relieved that no one had seen our exchange. I don't know why I felt that I had to hide it, but I expected it had something to do with the aching in my heart when he squeezed me in his arms.

"Hey, man" Sean said, reaching for knuckles from Reed. "Nice tosses tonight. Seriously, it was like pulling apples from a tree, man. Perfect!"

I was comforted to hear Sean praise Reed so. He was a good guy. My stomach twisted a little at my position, and I pushed it down to ignore it.

"Thanks, man. Hey, I'll see you at films tomorrow, ok?" Reed said, walking back to the center of the party and putting his arm around Tatum, who was eyeing me suspiciously. I decided to play dumb and just smiled back and gave Sean a squeeze to throw her off of my scent. It seemed to work when she held up her beer and smiled at me.

Sean opted for water only so he could drive me home. He walked me to my door and kissed me good night at about 1 a.m. I told my parents that I was going to the tailgating party after the game, but didn't bring up the alcohol. I knew it would worry them, or they wouldn't let me go. And I was always going to be responsible, so I didn't see the need. I watched as he ran down my steps and gravel driveway and pulled away in Cole's truck. He would be taking home a lot of the guys tonight, I suspected.

I washed my face and tiptoed into my room, shutting the door and turning on my lamp for a little light. I sat on the end of my bed pulling off my shoes and pulling my shirt over my head. I pulled on my XL overly worn Dr. Seuss T-shirt and kicked off my shorts and pulled up a pair of cut-off sweats. I clicked off the light and lay on top of my covers, still mulling the night over in my head when the ceiling lit up from my phone. It was a text from Reed.

Hey, you up?

I stared at it for a minute or two before replying. I wasn't sure why I was hesitating, but something about it felt like I was hiding something from Sean.

Yep. Wide awake. What's up?

I held the phone in my hand, willing a response to pop up on my screen.

Just feeling a little…blah. Can you talk?

I took a deep breath.

Sure.

And instantly my phone vibrated with his call. I let out a heavy sigh and settled into my pillow. "Hey, what's going on?" I asked.

"Hey. Thanks for talking. I know it's super late. I just wanted to say thanks, you know, for earlier?"

He didn't seem drunk. I wondered if he had left Tatum at the party early. "Sure. You know, we're friends, and I care about you a lot," I cringed hearing the words come out of my mouth. I felt stupid for saying them, half because of how pompous and insincere they always sound and half because I cared about him more than a lot.

"Thanks," he said, with a deep sigh, almost like he was letting a weight off his shoulders. "I had to take Tatum home early. She was pretty drunk. I only had a beer or two."

"You drove?" I said, curiously. "You know, you can get in trouble for that, too, mister. You still have two weeks."

He laughed a little. "Yeah, I know. My dad was going to be out all night and I figured it was safer if I was in charge of getting people home safely, and my dad doesn't really care. I've been driving since I was 12."

The image of a young Reed pulling cars into one of his dad's dealerships amused me. Realizing the awkward silence, I filled it. "Speaking of…what are you doing for your birthday?"

He let out a little groan. "Uhg. Tatum wants to take me out to dinner in the city and then we might stay at one of the resorts. Her parents have a ton of time shares."

I flinched a little at the thought of him and Tatum alone in a hotel room. I didn't know what to say and didn't have it in me to mask my reaction very well. "oh," I said, a little deflated by it and shaken at how *advanced* they were.

"I don't really like to make a big deal of birthdays," he said.

"You're turning 16. Come on, Reed. It's a big deal. Maybe not for boys, but for us girls? It's a big deal. We play 'sweet 16' when we're little girls. It's a thing," I explained, trying to move on mentally from the thought of he and Tatum playing honeymoon together.

"Well, I'll remember that for your birthday then," he said, laughing a little.

"Damn straight you will," I joked.

"Hey, thanks for talking. I feel a little better. I better go to bed. I've got films in the morning," he said.

"Yeah, I've got practice. I'm varsity now, thanks to your girl-friend, you know?" I said, a bit reluctant to give Tatum credit, though she did deserve a little.

"That's right. Congrats – I hear you're pretty strong at that net. I'll have to come check out a game," he said, my heart stopping at the thought of him watching me. I'm sure I would make a fool of myself. Pulling back to reality, I reminded myself of my boyfriend.

"I'm sure Tatum would love to show off for you. You and Sean should come to one of the Tuesday games when you're out of prac-tice early," I said, trying to bring us back to normal.

"Yeah, we should. And she totally would – Tatum's a star, that's for sure. But if I go, I'm team Nolan," he said, leaving it at that. "Good night, Noles."

"Good night."

Noles. It felt special hearing him say it. I lay there holding my phone to my chest, my head swirling with my conversation that borderlined on personal, but never quite got there. I wanted to call him again, right then. But I knew that was a bad idea. So I closed my eyes and let sleep take me over.

8. Two of Me

_____

TWO WEEKS LATER, Reed made good on his promise. It was our toughest game of the year and Sean and Reed were making their way up the bleachers as we were stretching and getting ready for warm ups. I studied Tatum as she stretched with a little extra sexiness in front of them. I tried to mimic her toe-touch, stretching my arms down to touch the ground, but I didn't have the same grace she did. I just looked uncomfortable, and I was pretty sure my knees were bent, making it more of a squat.

I rolled my eyes at myself and grabbed a ball to warm up with one of the other girls on the team, Jaden. We started passing the ball back and forth and setting each other. I was pretty proud of myself for not making any huge blunders up to this point. I looked over at Tatum who was truly enjoying putting on the show. She was talented without doubt, but she had the ability to turn on an extra little showmanship when she knew she was being watched.

When the game started, I caught a glimpse of Sean and Reed. Both of them gave me a thumbs up and I gave one back, laughing a little at our overly obvious secret signal. I had worked my way into a starting position and was glad that the boys didn't come to only see me ride the bench. The game flew by and we ended up winning in two straight games to take the match. I even managed a block in one of the last points to really impress my audience of two.

After the game, Reed and Sean were waiting in the lobby as Tatum and I left the locker room. "Hey, nice block, hops," Reed teased as I walked up to them. "Seriously, nice game Noles. You're so much stronger this year."

Done with my compliments, Tatum wove her arm through Reed's and led him out the door. I turned to Sean who was beaming at me. "My girl's bad ass," he joked, putting his arm around me as we left the gym.

Sean drove me home and we spent a little time on the front porch before I went inside for the night. My dad wasn't too hip on having boys inside unless they planned on sitting in the living room with him and watching the game. After an hour or so, Sean kissed me goodnight and took off.

As soon as I got to my room I pulled out my phone to see if I had a text from Reed. My heart lifted when I did.

Seriously, nice game. Hops ;-p

I smiled and wrote back a quick 'thanks.'

————

Sean and Reed ended up coming to a two more games, the last one on Reed's birthday. Reed and I had been texting every night after practice for the last two weeks, about the stress of his upcoming games and my stress of fitting in on a team full of seniors. I was excited to see him after the game because I had found the perfect birthday present for him. I didn't tell Sean about it, afraid he would be jealous. He probably wouldn't, but I felt a pang of worry nonetheless.

We won our game easily that night, playing one of our rival schools in a lower division. Their team was mostly underclassmen and they really didn't know how to defend against our constant barrage of attacks.

I hurried through my shower and ran out to find Sean and Reed in the lobby before Tatum could make her way out there. I was nervous about sneaking Reed his gift and didn't want to miss my opportunity. As I met them in the lobby, I gave Sean a quick kiss and then looked at Reed. "Hey, I have one of your history papers that I meant to give you earlier. It has some questions on it and I didn't want you to miss an assignment," I said in my most believable voice possible. Reed looked at me strangely but went along with it. "OK, thanks."

"Sean, I'll be right back. Let me just give this to him before I forget," I said, willing Reed to join me out the door. Thankfully he followed.

We walked to the main corridor by the lockers quickly, almost jogging. When Reed caught up he smirked, "what's this all about? There's no paper."

"I know, I totally don't know why I made that up, sorry," I confessed, still hurrying. Intrigued, Reed followed.

"I have a birthday present for you, but I just didn't want to make a big deal out of it. I know you don't like 'big deals'," I said.

I reached into my locker and pulled out the small box that I stuffed in there before our game and handed it to Reed. I watched carefully as he looked up at me and smiled, his hands working on peeling back the paper. I was instantly irritated at myself for wrapping it. It was taking too long. Finally, he slid the box out and pulled back the lid. A huge smile filled his face as he looked up at me.

"Where the hell did you find this?" he said, pulling the small felt patch shaped like the state of Arizona from the tissue paper.

"OK, don't judge, promise?" I said with a serious tone. I don't know why I was so nervous about this.

"Of course," he said, holding it in his hand and his eyes wide and happy.

"Goodwill," I said, waiting for him to make a comment about shopping at Goodwill, something which Tatum would do. When he didn't I continued. "I go there with my mom sometimes to find good deals and the last time we were there I found this old letterman jacket from Coolidge High School. The jacket was pretty beat up, so they gave it to me for $5. I really just wanted the patch. That was your dad's year, right? Didn't he win state in 1976?"

"Yeah," Reed swallowed. He looked up at me and then back at the patch again, reaching his arm out to pull me in for a hug. "Thanks, Nolan. This was really nice."

"I just thought you'd like it," I said, my heart pounding out of my chest at both being in his arms again and at the thought of Sean and Tatum seeing me there. And just then, he kissed the top of my head.

We froze for a few seconds, though it felt like minutes. A line was crossed, however small, and we both felt it. I knew I had to be the first to break it, but I fought against my heart to do so. "Happy birthday, Reed," I said backing out of his arms and looking down. "Hey, we should hurry. Don't want Tatum freaking out," I kidded, though not entirely.

"Oh, right," he said, his eyes holding mine just a little longer than normal.

We ran back to the parking lot and found Tatum and Sean just walking out of the gym doors. Never one for quiet and simple, Tatum squealed Reed's name and came skipping over. I saw that he had shoved the patch in his pocket long before she saw it, and part of me was pleased that he didn't want her to cheapen it with one of her tasteless remarks.

We all piled into Reed's Jeep, which he still wasn't technically licensed for. They dropped me off first, and Sean smacked my ass as I leapt out of the Jeep, whistling as I ran up my driveway and entered my house.

"That Sean with you?" my dad said, as I came in.

"Yeah, sort of. Well, Reed and Sean," I responded, rubbing my rear, a little embarrassed by the swat and catcall Sean gave me.

"Big game this Friday. Reed feel ready?" my dad asked, one thing on his mind – football.

"I think so," I said quickly and turned to head to my room down the hall. My mom stopped me on her way out of the laundry room.

"Did Reed like the patch?" she whispered. My grin giving away a little too much.

"Good…careful, ok?" she said.

"OK," I said, with a bit of an eye roll.

I shut my door and pulled out my phone to wait for my text from Reed. Hours passed and I was starting to think I wouldn't hear from him. Sean called first just to say good night. I was a little quick to get him off the phone, but thought he bought my studying excuse. I was about to give up and take my shower and call it a night when my phone vibrated.

"Hello?" I said, quietly.

"Hey, sorry. Did I wake you?" Reed said.

"No, I was up. I was just waiting…" I stopped short and decided not to finish.

After a short moment of silence, Reed continued. "Thanks for my present. Seriously, that's maybe the most thoughtful thing anyone ever gave me," he said.

"Well, it's not a Jeep," I laughed, self-effacing humor always my go-to.

"No, it's not," he said, without a hint of sarcasm. "Thank you. It meant a lot."

"You're welcome," I said. "I'm glad you like it. Happy birthday, Reed."

"Good night, Nolan," he said, lingering on the phone just a bit before hanging up.

I was in trouble.

9. Not Really

REED SPENT his birthday weekend with Tatum in the city, and I spent the weekend casting evil spells into the air then shaking my head at my own ridiculous thoughts. Imagine my surprise when I heard from Reed Sunday afternoon and he told me that he and Tatum spent the entire night and next day vomiting from food poisoning. I felt strangely guilty for my apparent witchcraft abilities.

While Reed and I continued to talk and text almost nightly, the conversations always remained platonic. Admittedly, I never attempted to take them anywhere beyond our friendship. But neither did Reed. I found myself pulling out Reed's letter before bed to remind myself of the butterflies he could make me feel. Still buzzing from my almost pseudo-intimate moment with Reed weeks before, I oozed school spirit as I prepped myself for Friday's final regular season football game. I even volunteered to work the grill with Sienna and some of the other members of the band and student council for the Big Bear Tailgate Party.

This year's fest was full of extra promise – the Bears were looking to go undefeated. Oddly enough, the last time the school did that was under the leadership of the older Johnson. Reed was undoubtedly feeling extra pressure from the situation.

Sienna and I arrived to the main parking lot at 4 p.m. We were charged with cleaning the grill and getting enough hot dogs and burgers grilled by the time 40 hungry football players and even more boosters showed up for dinner by 5. We were starting to panic when I saw Sean's truck pull into the parking lot, followed shortly after by Reed's Jeep. The boys walked over with their jerseys slung over their shoulders over their gray practice shirts, long purple shorts and flip flops. There was something so mature in their walk and the way they confidently moved toward us.

"Hey, Noles. Thought you could use some extra hands," Sean said, coming up to me and kissing me on my cheek. I blushed when he did and caught myself sneaking a look at Reed to see if he noticed, hoping he didn't. I don't know why, but I suddenly felt like I should hide my relationship with Sean from him, like it would hurt him to see us together. Or perhaps, more the truth, that it would damage whatever sparks I was imagining between Reed and me.

The boys were an enormous help, taking over the grilling and getting most of the burgers and dogs started and well on their way to being done by the time the first fans were arriving. I plated a dinner up for each of them and covered it in plastic wrap so they could head into the locker room to join the other players before coming out for dinner.

The entire team came out at 5:30 to a roaring crowd. Coach announced each of their names to whistles along with small bits of highlights from the season. Reed, of course, was saved for the end. When he made his way to the front of the crowd and climbed up the makeshift stage the student council had built for the party, the parking lot was filled with the thunderous sound of the entire town of Coolidge pounding fists on picnic tables. I saw the look of fear flash across his face briefly, but he was fast to tuck it away – ever the responsible pillar of pride for this community. I knew he took on this role with sincerity, and he truly felt responsible for delivering for his friends, his neighbors, his father and himself.

I stood on top of a picnic table in the back with Sienna to cheer for him loudly, and his half smile back at me stole my breath. He pulled his hat from his head and ran his fingers through his hair, slightly embarrassed by the lingering standing ovation from the crowd. When he put his hat back on, he kept his eyes low and looked up from beneath with a bit of a devious look to his face. Pausing, he held the mic in his hand while the crowd quieted down and waited for just one word from their anointed one. Biting the tip of his tongue, he finally relented to a full blown grin and gave them what they wanted.

"We own this thing – let's do this, Bears!" he shouted and the crowd responded with more pounding and screaming. I was in awe.

The team headed for the locker room to gear up and get ready to take the field for warm-ups. The rest of the crowd lingered until they opened the gates for seating at 6:45. I handled clean up of the grill on my own so Sienna could head in for band warm ups. Sarah sat at a table with her sister and Tatum nearby. I was a little irritated that she didn't offer to help me, but I also knew she wouldn't be much help anyhow. Sarah and manual labor didn't mix well.

I was wiping down the tables and putting all of the leftover buns and condiments in a box when I noticed someone picking up a rag and wiping down the tables with me.

"You grill a pretty mean burger, young lady," Buck said, a toothpick hanging from the side of his mouth. He was wearing a golden shirt with a purple tie and a deep purple suit jacket. On anyone else this outfit would have seemed gaudy, but it was perfect on Buck. He was a force to be reckoned with, and if the man wanted to wear a purple jacket, by God there wasn't anyone that was going to tell him it was a bad idea.

He pulled his jacket off and draped it over my folding chair, then rolled up his sleeves to help me take apart the grill. I smiled at him and inside wondered at his amazing kindness. I wanted to have a meaningful conversation in the worst way, but I couldn't seem to find the words, so instead, in my nervousness, I began to hum "Brown-eyed Girl" by Van Morrison.

"You know, I sing a mean Karaoke of that song. How do you know it, isn't it a little old for you?" he winked.

"Oh, well, my family says I have an old soul," I said, smiling and ringing out my wash cloth with a little flair.

Buck chuckled and continued to pack everything away with me while I hummed, every now and again humming along. I understood why he was so successful. The man had charisma, yes. But he also had that certain special quality that made you want him to like you, to embrace you and take you in as one of his friends. Even as a teenager I felt honored just having this small, tiny thing in common with him. I was running on a sort of high when I looked back over to Sarah and locked eyes with Tatum, who did not look pleased to see me getting along so well with Buck.

In seconds, Tatum was picking up a towel helping clean off the spots on the grill lid. I noticed that, while Buck welcomed her with a "hey there, sugar," he also wasn't humming and whistling anymore. And I felt a small victory at that.

———

Buck helped wheel the grill back into the storage area and headed to the stands to take his spot amid the many reporters and scouts who had come to see his boy pull off the amazing. And Reed did not disappoint.

The score wasn't proof of his performance, the Bears winning 14-7. But every yard, every point and every small spark that helped recharge the team was thanks to something inspiring Reed did on the field. I was amazed by his ability, but even more so, his ability to lead. He was years older than his age on that field.

When the game was over, Reed stayed out on the field for nearly 45 minutes talking to the local newspaper reporters and two TV stations from Tucson and Phoenix that covered the game. I hung out by the gates with Sarah and Sienna for a bit, my eyes dancing between Reed on the field and Tatum, who was sitting in the snack bar window holding court with the underclassmen (all my classmates) who were listening to her talk about Reed and how amazing their relationship was. I wanted to shove her from her perch and tell her how vapid she was, and how fake her entire relationship was, how she didn't really know Reed at all. But, I knew I needed Tatum to like me, or at least tolerate me. And I knew, at the end of the day, she knew what his lips felt like. While I, well, I might have some nice texts and a letter that was falling apart on the folds tucked away in my bedroom.

Reed was finally leaving the field, walking over with his jersey off and his pads exposed, his helmet dangling from his hand. Our smiles met each other and I wanted to run to him and tell him how proud I was. Throw my arms around him. Have him swing me around in circles while I kissed him. I was getting carried away, but my fantasy was delicious. I was just about to walk over to meet him at the track when my legs were swept out from under me and I was slung over someone's shoulder and carried toward the field.

Part of what I liked about being Sean's girlfriend was how much he loved showing his affection, for everyone to see. But for some reason, I only wanted him to stop at this moment. I felt like he had stopped my heart from leaping, if just for a moment, and I resented him for stealing this from me.

I slapped at his back and begged him to put me down and then I found myself on the ground, in the end zone. He started tickling me. I couldn't help but laugh, even though inside I was desperately wanting to rewind. I looked over to where Reed was standing, staring at us and our amateur wrestling match. For a moment, he seemed conflicted, and then he let out the faintest smile and shook his head as he turned and continued over to Tatum, picking her up and twirling her around while she squealed. *Of course she squealed. It was the most awful sound in the world.* He carried her all the way up the ramp to the locker room where he planted her on her feet and told her to wait for him, throwing his jersey to her. She instantly put it on.

I lay there, on the grass, while Sean looked at me. "I played that game for you, you know," Sean said. I barely registered what he said, but knew enough to make eye contact with him, smile and tell him he did it for everyone, also knowing he had nothing to do with that win at all. The boy who did was in the locker room, getting ready to take home another girl, and my heart was breaking.

10. Action, Reaction

COOLIDGE RODE the wave of their newly minted state championship all the way through the holidays. And Reed's popularity and statewide notoriety climbed to new levels. He was only 16, but he was already being heavily recruited. I know his heart belonged to Tucson – the tradition of his father and, while he didn't care for him much, his brother. Despite this, he was being courted by schools from California, Illinois, Texas, Florida and Michigan.

We talked regularly, though never for long, and the focus was always on his college recruitments, football plans for next season and school. Tatum and Sean were merely brought up when we would tell one another to say hi to the other. There was an air of tension, but I couldn't explain it.

School was starting back after the holiday break and the buzz was the upcoming winter dance. Sienna, Sarah and I all volunteered to decorate the gym. We were excited about it but didn't really have much of a choice either as it was Tatum's committee and she was bent on putting us to work.

We had cut hundreds of snowflakes from these sheets of sparkly blue and silver paper that Sienna had picked up from a specialty store in the city. It took us more than three hours to string each one up and tack it to the ceiling. But the final effect was well worth the effort when Tatum switched off the lights and flicked on the glowing disco ball she had ordered to hang from the middle of the gymnasium. The flakes flickered and fluttered above us as the slight breeze from the air system caused them to sway. It seemed as if snow was falling here in the middle of the desert. We were pleased.

We had a little more than an hour to head home and prep ourselves for the dance. I was spending the night at Sarah's and had brought my clothes over to her house to get ready. I had one dress that would work. I had been hanging on to it for two years – my mom and I found it on a clearance rack at the big mall in Tucson when I was graduating from eighth grade and at the time it didn't quite fit me yet, my boobs not quite able to fill the top. It had a flirty and flowing silver and blue skirt that swayed just above my knees and a form-fitting glittery top that hugged my midsection and accentuated my small but mighty bust. Soft quarter sleeves cupped my shoulders to keep everything in place.

I slipped the dress on in Sarah's room while she was finishing up her make up in the bathroom. I was twirling to try to see the zipper on the back when Sarah entered behind me, her hand on her chin and her head turned sideways as if she was studying me for an art class.

"What?" I finally broke.

"Nothing," she said, unconvincingly. "It's just...It's just that something's, I don't know. Just not quite right?"

She started to turn me around slowly, still studying. Finally, she clapped her hands together, her face showing her mind clearly made up.

"Do you trust me?" she asked. I wasn't sure. The truth was, I trusted her with my life, but not necessarily with my outfit.

"Uh, I guess so...what are you going to do?" I waited nervously as she dug in one of her drawers. I gasped a little when I realized she was now holding scissors.

"Close your eyes. I don't want you freaking out on me," she said. I obeyed, holding my breath and scared as hell. *Please don't cut my hair, please don't cut my hair.* I was at first relieved when I felt Sarah pulling on the seams of my sleeves. Then clarity sat in and I realized she was altering my dress, and taking away the only thing holding it up.

"Sarah!" I screamed, pulling away a little. She grabbed my arm with a hard jerk.

"Nolan, for the love of god, just trust me. OK?" she was frustrated.

I relented and waited, still closing my eyes for fear of how this would all turn out. In a few minutes she ordered me to open my eyes. I stood, staring at her, blinking. I was petrified to move for fear that my dress would fall to my ankles. There was no bra underneath as I didn't own one that would hide appropriately under the cut.

"Oh damn, Nolan. You look hot," she said, backing away to admire her work.

Fearful still, I slowly turned to face her mirror. I caught my breath when I realized she was right. What was more, I could actually move without losing the cloth that was hugging my body. My bare shoulders curved from the top of the dress, bronzed from my many hours outside running in preparation for the next track season. My neck looked long and ... kissable.

"We need to put your hair up, like this," she continued, holding most of my hair on the top of my head but letting a few strands fall down my shoulders. I just nodded and let her have her way. Make up, perfume, butterfly clips – whatever she wanted to do. I had never felt more confident than when Sarah was complete with my mini makeover.

I was meeting Sean at the dance. Sarah was working on landing the attention of a senior named Marcus. I was pretty sure she would have success as she slipped on her black strappy heels to match her tight black dress with spaghetti straps at the top. Her hair was straight and fell down her back, her eyes deep and smoky. She may have "jazzed me up," but she looked downright sexy.

———

We walked into the gym and found Sienna standing in a corner by the entrance. My sweet, uncomfortable friend was my solace. I scooted over to her side and put my head on her shoulder. She turned and teased me with a whistle and pawed at me like a cat. I giggled, a little flattered by her compliment.

The dance floor was empty as the mostly freshmen gathered at the dance early sat at the tables picking at cookies and downing paper cups of punch. We picked a table near the dance floor and piled our purses in the middle of the table. Then our fearless leader Sarah led Sienna and me to the middle of the floor, directly under the disco ball that was in full spin. The DJ was playing a hip-hop song that I sort of knew, and Sarah was moving to the music like a girl in the singer's music video. Sienna and I swayed next to her, always the awkward ones.

Giggling and tossing her long hair over one shoulder, Sarah grabbed both of us by the hands. "Girls, we've gotta work on your moves. Here, follow me," she said, showing us some simple moves that helped us look a little less like wallflowers. By the second song, we had it down, and Sienna and I were laughing, our arms over our heads while we moved to the heavy base thumping from the nearby speaker.

I jumped a little when I felt a pair of hands slide over my hips, but relaxed when I smelled Sean's familiar cologne as his chin grazed over my bare shoulders and his lips found my neck.

"You, are downright hot," he said, turning me to face him and pulling me in with both hands on my face.

I blushed when I pulled away to look him in the eyes, his smirk slightly sinister. Truth be told, I was enjoying the attention my new look was getting.

"You like?" I said, twirling a little and showing of my bare back and legs. I could get used to this confidence thing.

"Oh, I like…" Sean said, pulling me closer just as a slow song was starting. I nestled my face into his shoulder and neck and took in a deep breath. There was something comforting in his smell, like my grandfather's wood shop up north. His hair was still a little wet from his shower. He was wearing a black V-neck sweater that accentuated his muscles and showed off his wide upper body. His worn jeans bunched at his feet, his brown leather shoes barely showing. I closed my eyes for a few seconds while we rocked back and forth, willing myself to fall in love. But when I opened my eyes and looked at the couple talking to the faculty chaperones at the door, I knew that no matter how hard I tried, I would never be able to talk my heart into leaping from my chest the way it did when I saw Reed.

He didn't see me at first. His hand was gently placed on Tatum's lower back. She had a short, deep blue, silk dress on that swayed on her lower back, showing off her bare shoulder blades – *always finding a way to one-up me, I thought.*

Reed was joking with one of the football coaches that was helping host the dance. He shook coach's hand and turned to enter the gym with Tatum leading the way. Reed dragged behind a bit, looking down and rubbing the back of his neck with his hand, almost as if he was willing himself to endure this dance. Sarah and Calley had stopped Tatum to admire her dress and Reed kept walking, saying something to her over his shoulder as he held her purse and looked for our table that Sarah had pointed out. He turned and started walking towards it when he froze and locked his eyes on me.

My throat closed. I turned my head in a little to face Sean, but kept my eyes locked on Reed, pretty sure he couldn't tell I was staring at him. He walked slowly to the table, his focus shifting back and forth from his destination to me. Deep down, I knew this was what I had hoped was the result of Sarah's great work. And I was pretty sure this was her goal, too.

Sean and I circled around, and whenever Sean's hands rubbed my back or played with my hair, Reed winced a little. His facial expression was caught somewhere between curiosity and sadness. Even as Tatum and the other girls joined him at the table, he continued to steal glances at me.

The song finished and I told Sean I was thirsty, so we walked back to our table. Determined to find those butterflies that I felt months ago, I searched my brain for a way to make Reed react. When Sean left our group for drinks, I let my guard go and reached for Reed's shoulder, using him to balance myself so I could adjust the strap on my shoe. I felt the heat from his stare as I finished and tossed the ringlets of hair Sarah strategically let fall on my shoulders out of my eyes and gave Reed a "hello" smile.

"Hey…" he said, softly, looking down and swallowing.

"Hey, was wondering when you guys would get here," I said, forcing my most confident self to push forward with an air of disinterest.

"Oh, uh…yeah. Tatum's…well, she's slow. She takes forever to get ready," he said, looking back at her on the dance floor then back to me, now with shock and surprise in his eyes. Sitting down, he looked at the floor again and leaned forward to rest his elbows on his knees. Then he stood up, unable to settle. He was nervous, and it was the most pleasant surprise of my life.

"So, uh…whataya say?" he said, tilting his head to the dance floor.

I looked back to Sean, who was deep in conversation with some of the guys from the team. *Strong self, you can do this, Nolan.* "Sure!" I said, taking his hand and leading him out to the dance floor.

Reed stood there stiffly at first while I danced in front of him, holding my arms over my head while my hips swayed and my hair flirted with my chin and shoulders. He started to relax and I even saw a smirk start to form in the side of his mouth as he watched me, looking at me like he did in my dreams.

When the song faded into a slow song, I started to turn back to our table, but Reed stopped me, grabbing the tips of my fingers and willing me towards him. His smile was stronger. He was turning on the Johnson charm.

"Sean won't mind. I bet Tatum will force him to dance, you know, just to show me a lesson," Reed rolled his eyes.

I laughed, though my gut clenched a little at the thought of Tatum teaching me a lesson.

It was a country song, one that my dad listened to all the time. I knew the words and focused on them to keep my legs from buckling under me as Reed pulled my hand in to his chest and put his warm hand flat against my lower back. *This…was intimate.*

As we rocked to the music, I felt him looking down at my face, his superior height something I was ever so grateful for now. I forced my eyes to look to the side at other couples and caught a quick glimpse of Sean and Tatum dancing across the room. *He was right.*

Unable to stand it, I looked up to try to sneak one look at him, but was caught immediately, his smile fast and captivating.

"Noles, you look amazing tonight. Really," he said, squeezing my hand a little as he held it even tighter to his chest.

"Thanks," I blushed, looking back up at him through my lashes, a move I learned from Sarah. "You clean up pretty good yourself, champ." *And…there I am.*

Reed chuckled a little, then stopped our movement for a moment, lifting my chin with his hand to look him in the eyes. "Stop it; you don't know how to take a compliment. I mean it and I want you to hear me. You. Are. Beautiful."

I was done. I knew it the first time I saw him, but tonight solidified every stray emotion rattling in my body. I loved Reed Johnson, and I was pretty sure I always would. He pulled me back in to his chest and we danced in silence for the rest of the song. My eyes locked on the contour of his jaw line and chest, his chin tucked over my head. In my mind he was holding me as if he never wanted to let go.

Reed guided me back to our table and my head was swirling, my mind trying to wrap itself around the words my ears just heard. My eyes were panicked and looking for Sean, and I worried about what I could ever say. And then one look pulled me right out of my fantasy. Tatum was sitting at our table, her long legs folded over one another and her eyes trained on mine like daggers. She was pissed. And I knew I was her target. She stood and came over to Reed, hooking her arm under his and running her nose along his jaw to reclaim what was hers. But while Reed gave her his attention, he still shared it with me for the rest of the evening.

And Tatum was furious.

11. Untruths

"HEY, I was thinking to kick off track season I would have a little sleepover, you know before the big meet? I thought maybe you, me and a few of the other girls could get together. It'd be fun. Let me know, ok?"

I must have played Tatum's voicemail over a hundred times trying to decipher the tone, get to the root of her plan, understand what she was up to. During the weeks after the winter formal, Tatum had been very short with me. She had also been very possessive of Reed's time, making it near impossible for us to ever be alone together. I had grown nervous for a while that she was sabotaging my relationship with Sean after I'd seen her talking with him in his truck one morning, but despite my anxiety that he would dump me or cause a scene accusing me of cheating on him with his best friend, which I had not done, it never happened.

Regardless, I knew I couldn't trust her. But I also knew that I couldn't alienate myself.

I called Tatum back finally and left her a message confirming my Friday night attendance. It was the night before our first big weekend meet. The meet was at home, so we wouldn't have to leave campus early for travel.

I drove the trusty Olds to her house with my dad in the passenger seat. He was giving me some extra hours behind the wheel before I took my driving test. I was 16, but I wasn't quite comfortable behind the wheel.

He slid over in the seat as I got out and grabbed my bag and sleeping bag from the trunk. I knocked on Tatum's door and she answered, revealing five other girls behind her. I didn't know any of them very well – they were all juniors and seniors – but they were all nice to me during volleyball season and last year's track season.

"Hey, Nolan. You can put your stuff in here," said Becky, the perky blonde who ran the hurdles and high-jumped.

"Thanks!" I said, grabbing my bags and tossing them in a spare bedroom.

I took my spot on the floor where all the girls were sitting, watching the giant T.V. Tatum's house was very large. It wasn't posh, like Reed's, but it was nice. Nicer than mine. But it didn't really feel like a home. It was more like a show gallery, everything in its place and nothing with a sense of home. At least at our house we owned the stains on our carpet and knew what had led to every knick in the door, scuff on the floor and dent in the walls. My home was real. Lived in.

"Pizza, swimming and then movies!" Tatum squealed. She could delight over just about anything, I swear. It was utterly obnoxious.

"Noles, what kind of pizza do you want? My mom's ordering. We all wanted veggie," she stood with a pen and pad of paper dangling at the side of her hip. Truth be told I hated veggie pizza. It was a complete waste of comfort food in my opinion, but I knew I had to be careful tonight. And pizza was not worth making waves.

"Sounds good to me," I smiled.

She turned, almost disappointed I didn't take her first bait. I was sure there would be more.

We all ate our slices around the kitchen counter. Tatum's mom had also made flan for dessert, which we all just attacked with forks until there was nothing left. I was stuffed and not really up for a swim with the other girls, but I put my suit on anyhow and kicked

88

my feet in the water as I sat on the other side of the pool, careful eyes always guarding Tatum.

"You and Sean make a super cute couple," I heard a voice squeak from the water below me. Becky pulled herself up from the pool and sat next to me. The water from her suit made a puddle around us and it chilled me a bit, but I was glad to have someone to talk to.

"Oh, thanks. Yeah, he's a super good guy," I said with a heavy amount of guilt plaguing my gut. I hadn't been a very good girl-friend, I thought. In fact, I was pretty sure I had been nothing but cold towards Sean since the winter dance. I knew sometime soon I had to come clean with my feelings and end it with him, but I also dreaded leaving the safety of our relationship.

"I think you two are so much healthier than Tatum and Reed," she said, with a hint of disdain. *Becky doesn't like Tatum. This might just work out after all, I thought.*

"Oh yeah? How so," I said with genuine interest.

"Well...," she paused for a bit, looking around and moving a little closer so no one would hear. "I think their relationship is pretty much nothing but sex."

My insides were twisting tighter than they ever had before. I knew that Tatum and Reed were physical, but for some reason hearing another girl confirm it just made the vision of it that much more intense.

I nodded in return, hiding how hurt their intimacy made me.

"I mean, I get it. They're hot and young. But, man, they have nothing in common. And...," Becky looked around again, "I think Tatum is really dumb and boring."

I couldn't help it and let out a tight snort laugh. Becky reached up and slapped her hand over my face trying not to laugh herself. Quickly covering up for it she added, "Funniest joke ever, right? My brother told me that one." And with a wink, I knew Becky was my ally.

After an hour or so in the pool, we all started to dry off and gather our things to head back inside. I was looking around the patio for my towel and flip flops when I heard the patio door slide to a close. I turned to walk over and join the rest of the girls when the patio light went dark and I heard the distinct sound of the click of the patio lock.

"Hey! Still out here," I shouted, walking quickly to the door and giving it a useless yank. I knocked on the door for a bit, but then quickly heard the sound of the TV kick on full volume. *I knew she wasn't done, I thought.*

I knocked a few more times, but I knew that there was no way I was getting in that house until Tatum wanted me to. She would tell the other girls I was upstairs or that she wasn't sure what I was up to and then distract them with the movie. It was about 50 minutes before I heard the movie pause and saw the reflection of the light flick on in the kitchen as some of the girls started pulling out chips for snacks. I deliberated whether or not to knock again, not wanting to give her the satisfaction. I think had it been a warmer evening, I would have stuck it out, even slept out here if I had to. But given that I had already wrapped my body as tightly as possible with the towel for warmth, I knew my options were limited.

I knocked again, "Hey, can someone unlock please?" *I was pathetic.*

Tatum's eyes met mine as she flung the shades open on the door. Her smirk gave her away and I dug in with an equally intense stare. She wanted me to know that she controlled everything, but I wanted her to know that I didn't give a fuck. And my face didn't leave anything to the imagination.

"Oh my god, Noles. Have you been out there the entire time? I thought you were just getting ready for bed or something or showering. We had no idea!" she squealed. *So fake.*

I walked in right past her and headed into the room with my stuff and grabbed my pajama pants and long-sleeved T-shirt from my bag to head upstairs and change.

"Noles? I'm sorry, you're not mad, are you?" she trailed off, smirking at me as the rest of the girls were behind her and couldn't see her true evil self. If she wanted a game, then I was ready to play.

Smirking back and batting my lashes in the most over-the-top way I could I walked up to her and gave her a hug. "Tates, OMG! Like I could ever be mad at you. I know it was an accident, silly." I held her stare for a second as I let go, just to signal *are we clear here? I hate you, you hate me. Done.*

I turned to head upstairs to change and caught Becky's attention. She was grinning ear-to-ear and gave me one fast wink to let me know she was on my side. *I liked Becky. We would be good friends.*

————

The night was long. I didn't want to fall asleep, knowing that even though Tatum appeared to be sleeping, she could still wreak havoc on me in a second. I stood it as long as I could, but when the clock read 3 a.m. I let my heavy lids take me over. We had to report for our meet at 7, and I knew I wasn't going to be worth much. I was counting on grabbing an extra hour of sleep at the meet before my race.

As I stretched in my sleeping bag and awoke to the rustling sounds of the other girls stirring in their sleeping bags, I scanned the room for Tatum. She was rolled over on her side on the couch, just where I had left her. A wave of relief flushed over me that I had survived the night.

My face felt tight from the lack of sleep and I desperately wanted to brush my teeth. I headed into the spare room and grabbed my uniform and toothbrush to run upstairs for a quick shower and some freshening up.

Tatum's bathroom was large enough to be a master bathroom. She had both a tub and a shower and a large wrap-around mirror. I imagined it was a luxury for someone like Tatum who probably loved to model for herself at all angles. When I flicked the light on in the bathroom, I squinted at first, the harshness a bit much to take on only three hours of sleep.

I dipped my toothbrush under the water and loaded it with toothpaste and began to brush. Looking in the mirror I noticed one of my eyebrows was curled straight up. *I must have really slept on that wrong, I thought, reaching in the water with my hand to flatten out the gnarled brow. I knew something was wrong the instant I touched my face, though.*

Panic hit me hard. I pushed in close, dropping my brush in the running water. There was a line of hairs missing in my eyebrow. Like they had been plucked. But surely I would have woken up for that. I looked ridiculous, and my stomach was swirling between furious and tortured. I kept rubbing water along the brow to try to bunch the hairs that were left together to cover it up. It was no use, though. No matter what I did, it looked like a mangled mess.

After about 15 minutes, I crawled into the shower and thought about my options. Every nerve in my face wanted to cry, but there was no way I would give Tatum that satisfaction. I wasn't sure, but my instincts told me that Tatum probably put a drop of hair remover on my brow and slid the hairs off my face as I slept. When I was done showering, I grabbed my makeup bag and colored in the missing spot. It wasn't perfect. And up close, you could definitely see that something wasn't right. But with my beanie pulled down far on my forehead, and from far away, I was pretty sure I could fool the group of girls downstairs.

I gathered my stuff and headed down. Most of the girls were dressed by this point and had their bags packed, ready for Tatum to drive us in her mom's van to the school. Smiling at me as we filed out the door, she couldn't help but gloat.

"Something wrong, Noles? You have a rough night's sleep?" she asked with her best concerned tone.

"Nope," I said, clipped. "Slept like a baby." And then I added a pat on the shoulder as I walked out the door.

———

When we pulled up to the school, most of the rest of the team had already arrived. I noticed Sean and Reed's truck and Jeep right away. My stomach was thumping with the beat of my heart from equal parts dread and anger. I wanted to run to Sean for comfort, but I also wanted to rip the Band-Aid off and end our relationship. Sean was a great friend, but he never really made my heart leap out of my chest the way Reed did. I also wanted to slap Reed and question how he could ever be with a girl like Tatum.

I wasn't ready to confront them when I rounded the corner of the locker room to drop off my bags and change my shoes.

"Hey, Noles. You guys just get here?" Reed said, Sean coming closer to grab my hand. I jerked it away in a fit of irrational anger. Sean hadn't done anything wrong, but I didn't want to be touched. Not by him.

"Yep," I said, shortly.

"What's up your ass?" Reed said, looking at Sean to shed some light on my mood.

I turned and without even thinking blurted out, "My ass? Your girlfriend's a bitch. That's what's up my ass." I left them there, bewildered by my outburst, and headed into the locker room. My head was thumping with anger and I was talking to myself. I locked my stuff up and sat on the bench to lace up my shoes, my mouth muttering the words I would say to Tatum's face. And then there she was.

I fought my urge and stood up, snapping my head to stare at her as I headed for the door, but she caught my arm before I could make it out.

"Do not...touch me!" I yelled, my face close to hers.

She leaned into the door to block my exit. Crossing her arms, I saw her face wash over with superiority. This was the Tatum I had first encountered my freshman year. She was asserting her authority over me, and I was not going to have any of it.

"So," she said, kicking her foot along the ground and looking down as she thought about her words. "What do you think Reed will think when I tell him about all the times you've slept with Sean?"

I was befuddled. I was a virgin, that much I knew. Sean had been very respectful and patient with me and I don't think the rumor was floating around that we were having sex. "You're absurd," I bit back. "And you're an idiot." I tried to move her from the door but she wasn't budging.

"Yeah," she laughed a little to herself. "Thing is, all I have to do is say it to a few people and then it's out there. There's no putting that back. Reed will never look at you again. Untouchable. He wouldn't want to *share* you with Sean, and he wouldn't look at you with those doting innocent eyes that he sees you with now."

I was speechless. Was she actually threatening to rumor me to death? Could she do that? Would that work?

"Think about it," she continued. "Are you ready to be a whore? I know you're not in love with Sean. And I bet you're going to break up with him soon. I'll start the rumor about the next guy you're going to hook up with, too. Don't think I won't." She chewed the inside of her cheek with a finality of confidence.

At that moment, I knew there was nothing Tatum wouldn't do to ruin me in Reed's eyes. And if I suffered, too, because of it was of no consequence to her either. In fact, that was icing.

———

I spent the entire meet in my own head. I was careful to avoid situations where I was even near Reed, and Sean's events were spread throughout the meet, so I made sure that I was always on the opposite end of the field…conveniently. I was waiting for my 400 meter race, stretching along the far fences near the end zone when Reed jogged by with a group of guys. *Damn. I didn't see him coming.*

He stopped right next to me and bent down for a bit to catch his breath.

"You know, you're supposed to hold your arms over your head. Opens up your lungs," I said. I figured might as well make it awkward and confrontational right out of the gate. I was still fuming over Tatum. But I was also frightened. I was a good girl, and I planned on staying one. I didn't need the nightmare of a ruined reputation. Lost in my own thoughts, I jumped a bit when Reed bumped me on the side, bringing me back to the present.

"I know, but sometimes it just feels good to hang your head," he said with a faint smile.

"I guess," I shrugged, short with him.

I felt his stare while I continued to stretch and check the tightness on my shoes. I could tell he wanted to say something. But he seemed to be fighting with himself. I stepped a few paces away to sit down and do my butterfly stretches. Reed stayed where he was. When I leaned forward, I snuck a peek to see if he was looking elsewhere, any sign that he may be leaving. I was risking a lot being this close to him with Tatum around. Luckily she was over in the pits for the long jump finals. I was relieved when I finally heard his shoes scuff the pavement as he turned to walk the other way, and I collapsed on my hands in front of me, my face firmly planted in the sleeves of my sweatshirt. *This...was going to be hard.*

———

I ran home after the meet. I didn't want to wait for a ride, and frankly all choices were bad ones. I know that Sean could sense something was wrong, but I wasn't ready to have that conversation either. I would have to soon enough. But first I had to think about how to set off my chain of dominoes in such a way as to keep Tatum from spreading vicious rumors about me.

I was sliding through the gravel in my driveway when I heard the engine rumble behind me. I recognized it, amazingly. The slight spot of the lights that were shining behind me clicked off, followed by the crunch of feet landing on the rocks. I froze, letting out a big sigh as I turned. Reed's eyes locked on mine. He looked furious.

"Hey! You think maybe when someone calls and texts you a thousand times you could at least text them back to let them know you're ok?" he shouted, accusingly.

"You called?" I dug out my phone to see 14 missed calls and a handful of texts. "Oh … sorry. I just left in a hurry and I couldn't hear my phone in my bag. I'm good. Just felt like walkin'."

I was lying through my teeth and I could feel anger seeping up to my mouth. Thankfully, so far, my brain was working in overdrive to keep my words in check.

"Oh, I see," he said, still angry in his tone. He pulled his hat off to run his hands through his hair before putting it back on. He kept turning to leave and then walking back a few steps only to return, each time pressing his lips in a firm line, almost like he was shoving his thoughts back inside. Not sure what to do, I picked up my bags and slung them over my shoulder and when his back was to me, said "Goodnight. Thanks for checking on me."

Despite my best effort, my tone was clipped. There was a sense of snarkiness, and I didn't mean it. I was just emotionally spent and sick, and it was now seeping from me in unexpected ways.

"Seriously? That's all you got? 'Thanks for checking on me,'" Reed repeated mockingly. I turned to face him, my eyes starting to sting a little as I fought to keep the tears at bay. I couldn't tell if they were sad tears, angry tears or both. When I locked gazes with him again I just shrugged and gave him a crooked smile, shaking my head. "Yeah. That's all I've got."

Reed walked up to me deliberately and flung my bags from my shoulder, wrapping his arms around me in the warmest hug of my life after that. And suddenly I couldn't stop them any more. I was toast. The tears came full force now and my body jerked with each heavy sob as I tried to stifle them some, let them out slowly. It was no use. It was as if 24 hours of torture were escaping all at once.

"Shhhhhh, it's ok. Whatever it is, it's ok. Please, Nolan. You can tell me. We can tell each other anything. Please," Reed said, rocking me side to side and stroking my hair. I was clinging to the sides of his sweatshirt, almost as if I was holding fistfuls of the fabric to keep myself from drowning. I pulled my face away from his chest to rub my sleeve across my eyes to dry them. Reed lifted my chin to look at me, and suddenly his face had a look of concern.

"Noles, it looks like something might be wrong with your eyebrow, did you get a bite or something? Let me take a look," he said, reaching up to touch it. I pulled away and pressed my palm to my forehead; I didn't want him to see.

"Oh, it's nothing. Something stupid, really. I'm ok," I said, panicking. I could hear Tatum's warning and I was suddenly terrified that Reed would find out it was of her doing.

"Uhm...ok. It just looks like some of the hair is missing. Are you sure?" he was still concerned.

"I'm sure," I said, staring him in the eyes, almost trying to tell him telepathically without saying the words. When it became uncomfortable, I looked down.

"Noles, what's going on? You're not yourself," he pushed.

I didn't know what to say. I stood there silent, looking down and kicking at the pebbles at my feet, sniffling the last of my emotional explosion away. Finally, I turned my head sideways to meet his eyes again. Chewing on my bottom lip, I paused and thought carefully for a moment, choosing my words.

"Do you love her?" was what came out. Not quite how I wanted to go, but I was going to run with it.

Reed's eyebrows shot up. "Huh? What do you mean?" he said.

"Tatum. Do you love her?" I asked again, my lips tight, fighting to show anything. I had to be careful to not give away my hand.

Reed sucked in his top lip and nodded a little as he thought. He looked up at the sky with a big sigh and then finally looked right at me. "I, uh…I. Hmmmm? Let's put it this way…I haven't said the words to her."

"That's not what I asked." I was getting braver now. "Do you love her, Reed?"

"No," it came out so quickly it surprised both of us. Deep down, I knew he didn't. He was a teenaged boy and she was eye candy. That's about how far it went.

I was going to press on. "OK, understandable. You are young. This is high school. We're supposed to *date* lots of people. But why her?" I paused. I needed to rephrase that so it didn't sound as incredulous as I meant it to. "I mean…what drew you to Tatum?"

Reed walked up to my porch and I followed him, dropping my bags on a chair and sitting next to him on the steps. He had his hat off again and was looking down, rubbing his hair forward almost to hide his shame.

Finally, he spoke. "I'm gonna be real honest here, Noles. I don't even really know any more. I mean, it was exciting at first. But now, every little thing she does irritates me… Wait…why do you ask? Is this about Sean? I mean, I know he's my best friend, but you can still talk to me about him. I would keep it between us."

"No, it's not about Sean…exactly," I said. *Keep going, Nolan. Keep going.* "It's just… I don't think my spark for Sean is going anywhere either. It's sort of stalled. And I'm sort of alright with that," I stopped to look at him sideways. He had an understanding smirk on his face. "And with you…I was just curious. It just seems like you and Tatum are SOOOOOOO different. I mean, you're so nice and thoughtful, and she's…" I stopped and just shrugged and looked down, a bit defeated.

"Nolan, did Tatum say something to you? Is that why you cried?" he reached over and put his hand on mine along the steps. I stared at it and it felt as if time froze. My heart was racing, both from his touch and the fear of Tatum driving by in this instance to see this. I didn't know how to respond, but I needed to stop. This was too far.

I stood up, pulling my hand from under his. "I'm ok, Reed. Really," I said, turning to pick up my bags and reach for the door. His hand was on it fast and he reached for my chin again to turn me to face him.

"You would tell me, right? If she said something to you…" he swallowed. "If she said something that made you cry, something mean or rude, you would tell me?"

I couldn't lie. I just nodded knowingly and smiled with my lips tight, my eyes welling up a little again. Biting my lower lip to keep things in check I reached an arm over Reed's shoulder and gave him one last hug, and then, as I released, I kissed him softly on the cheek. I know he could tell I was holding it in, but he let me go inside anyway. I think he knew I was holding on to my pride. It was all I had. That, and my utter disappointment in myself for letting Tatum break me.

12. Exposed

TWO WEEKS HAD PASSED since my breakdown in front of Reed. He hadn't texted me or stopped by to visit, and I kept our conversations to short 'hellos' and 'see you at practices' in class. I watched him when he was with Tatum in the halls. He was often staring off in the distance, completely detached from her and whatever she was saying to her faithful groupies.

Becky and I were hanging out more, which was nice. I liked her, and so did Sienna and Sarah. The four of us were sitting in the grass at the front of the school while Becky and I went through our gym bags one last time to make sure we had everything for the last track meet of the year. It was against Globe High School in the mountains to the east, and the bus trip would be long and cold.

Sarah was regaling us with some story about a boy she hooked up with from Phoenix over the weekend and we were all giggling and smiling. For the first time in days I felt like a normal girl, weight lifted from my chest. But the ache was still there. I had yet to break things off with Sean, although I barely spoke to him any more and our phone conversations were few and far between. Other than holding hands between a few classes, all evidence of our romance was extinct. It was just a matter of time. Either way, I needed to have a conversation with him. I owed him that.

Reed and Sean were walking down the hill from the gym to where the bus was. "Hey, come on ladies. We're loading," Reed said, waving his hands. Sean stood next to him, smiling at me, but knowingly.

Becky and I grabbed our stuff and jogged over to meet them. Tatum was already holding a seat for Reed in the back, and he headed back there to sit by her. Sean picked a seat a few rows ahead of her. I didn't want to be that close to them, but I also didn't want to show the cracks in my armor.

"Here, let me toss your bag up on the bars," Sean said, taking my bag from me and putting it up on the railing shelf.

"Wait! Can you grab my headphones? I want to listen to some music," I asked. He stared silently for a moment. We would not be talking. Again. I know what he is thinking.

"Sure, hang on," he said, sliding the zipper just enough to pull my headphones and iPod out. He handed it to me and slid down next to me. I picked a playlist and turned the volume up just enough to drown out everyone else as the bus pulled from the parking lot onto the main drag through town. I pulled my knees up and sunk down a bit to keep my body hidden from the presence I still felt behind me. Tatum hadn't done anything in days. But it didn't matter. I was always on edge.

When Sean reached for my hand, I flinched a little. But he held on anyhow. He played with my fingers as I shut my eyes and feigned sleep. It's not that I was ignoring his touch. But rather, I couldn't feel it. I was angry at myself for how I was treating Sean and the more he tried to hold on to a piece of me, the more I pulled away. Finally, after a few minutes, I turned my body so my back was to the window and my legs were bent up in front of me, so I was facing Sean. He winced a little, looked down and then patted the tops of my shoes. Reaching down to his bag, he pulled his headphones out, put some music on and shut his eyes in pretend as well.

The drive to Globe was nearly two hours. We were starting to climb through the mountains when I noticed the chill coming in through the windows. It was only four in the afternoon and already the winds were freezing. I slid my back up along the window, careful not to alert Sean, and looked along the bars for my bag. There wasn't much room up there, so he had put it a little farther back in the bus. When I located it I dropped my gaze to see who I could ask to pass it along to me and locked eyes with Tatum, smirking.

"Cold," she mouthed.

I just gave her a careful nod, and motioned at my bag above her, not fathoming what she would do next. Her smile was venomous as she stepped into the aisle and slid the zipper on my bag slowly. Reed was involved in a video game and paying no attention to her as she pulled out my sweatshirt and sweat pants. She slid back in to sit along the window and then set them on her lap, out of my sight.

I gave her a pleading look. I was so cold already. She lit up with a fake friendly face and reached up to drop the locks on her window. In an instant, she flung my warm clothing out of the bus, dropping it on the side of the desert highway somewhere outside Globe. In seconds she had the window closed again and she was staring at me with narrowed eyes and a mischievous grin.

I sat there staring at her for minutes, my mouth agape. Before this, everything she did was underhanded. But this was so forward. So obvious. Such an attack. I couldn't cry. I was too shocked. I turned back in my seat and slid back into position and put my music on. I was going to freeze and it was going to be terrible, but I would live through it. With one small action, Tatum had won this round.

———

I grabbed my suddenly lighter bag from the bus and hurried down the aisle to the steps. I climbed out and waited while Sean stood by the side of the bus where they loaded the poles for vaulting. When he had his equipment we both walked to the center of the track and dropped our things to set up camp with everyone else. Tatum and her groupies were already running their warm up lap. Sean tugged at my pinky to get my attention.

"Wanna run? It's good to keep warm," he smiled. He had no idea.

I followed him over to the track and then like clockwork we set our steps in sync as we made our way around for a lap. My heart rate was up, and that was helping. It was two hours from now that worried me, though. We stepped back into the grass and started our stretching. I caught a glimpse of Reed and my eyes followed him as he took his lap around the track. With each bend to stretch I picked him up, following his movement as he rounded one end of the track and made his way toward us. I looked over at Sean and gulped when I saw him staring at me…staring at Reed. He looked at Reed and then back to me, nodding once. Knowing.

Reed came up and sat down to stretch with us.

"Fuckin' cold, no?" he said, pulling his hood up over his head.

"No shit," Sean replied, snuggling into his warm ups, too. He didn't make eye contact with Reed though. "Hey, be right back. I have to hit the bathroom," he said, hopping to his feet and running to the back of the stadium stands.

I finished my stretching with Reed, turning away from him some so Tatum didn't think we were talking or that I'd invited his company. My legs were covered in goose bumps and my teeth were already starting to chatter.

"Noles, you should get your sweats on. It's only going to get worse," he stood up, jumping in place and raising his knees to warm up his legs.

"Yeah…I would, but…" I trailed.

"Did you forget them?" he said with raised eyebrows.

"Sorta," I said. Not a total lie. I did forget to keep them safe, I thought.

In an instant, Reed reached up over his head and pulled his hood up, yanking his sweatshirt over his head. Some of his T-shirt came up exposing his muscular stomach and the waistband of his boxers. I sucked in air and quickly looked down as his sweatshirt dropped on my lap.

"Put it on. I'll be ok with just the pants, I swear," he said.

I was about to protest, but he was already walking away. Surely this would set Tatum off even more. But I was so cold. And his shirt smelled so good. I pushed my arms through the sleeves and pulled it over my head, letting the hood stay up. It was extra large, so I had enough slack in it to tuck my knees inside as I sat. I was feeling warmer already. But I don't think it was because it was a sweatshirt. I think it was because it was Reed's. In inhaled its scent, and hugged the sleeves close to me. It was as close to an embrace as I may ever have with him again.

I was so lost in my own fantasy that Sean startled me when he sat back down next to me.

"It's because of him, isn't it," he said, matter-of-fact.

"What?" I pretended, knowing exactly what he meant and dreading the direction this conversation was about to go.

"Reed. You can't take your eyes off of him," he stopped, then chuckled a little to himself, but in a sad way. "It's funny. Now that I think about it, you really never could, could you?" He tilted his head towards me, waiting for a response.

I sat there dumbfounded. He knew everything, without me having to say a word. I blinked, feeling like I should fight away tears. But nothing was there. I couldn't cry over this because I didn't really have intimate feelings for Sean. I cared for him deeply, but as a friend.

He looked down for a while and then finally broke the silence. "It's ok. I mean…I'm not going to lie, it fuckin' hurts. I REALLLLY liked you, Noles. But I'm not mad. Just, maybe give it some time? I'm just not ready to see you flirting with him yet, is that ok?"

I leapt into his arms and hugged him tighter than I ever had. My eyes were welling up now. Sean was so good to me, and I didn't deserve it. But what stung even worse was the fact that he thought he would have to see me and Reed together when I knew that was impossible.

"You are too good for me, Sean Foster. I mean it," I said, pulling out of our embrace.

"I know," he laughed out, his voice cracking a little as he stood up and turned away from me. "I'm going to head over to the guys for a bit. I just need a break from…from this talk."

"I'm sorry Sean. I didn't want it to go this way," I said, hoping he would forgive me for hurting him. "You really are amazing."

He smiled at me walking backwards, pursing his lips and shaking his head. "Not that amazing," he said, gesturing to Reed. "Clearly not *that* amazing."

Then he was gone.

I sat by myself for the next hour, wrapped in Reed's warmth and thinking on how things ended with Sean. I felt oddly lucky. But I also felt lost. I was nobody's now. At least when I was with Sean I felt like I was a part of something. Sitting in the middle of the field alone, I started to feel my gut sink.

I needed to do my warm ups, so I rolled up the sleeves of Reed's shirt and stood to walk to the track. I looked over to the stands where Sean and Reed were sitting by each other. Both of their heads were down, and I could tell Reed was consoling him. Becky came into my view and I realized she was jogging over to join me. She had a sympathetic smile on her face as she came up to me with open arms. I hugged her, not knowing what else to do.

"I heard, Noles. I'm so sorry," she said, patting me on the back. *Good lord, word travels fast out here.*

"Thanks," I said, moving toward the track. She followed me and started to jog my warm ups with me.

"You know," she started. "I'm not surprised. I mean, I think a lot of us saw this coming. You don't look at Sean like you look at Reed."

Becky was smarter than I thought. I shrugged at her, acknowledging my secret to an outsider for the first time. "It doesn't matter, though. Tatum has him wrapped around her...well...her everything," I laughed.

Becky laughed, too, but then got quiet. "She's steaming mad at you, you know," she said, giving me a sideways glance. *What could I have done now? She's the one who decorated the highway with my fleece warm ups.*

Becky continued, "She asked Reed where his shirt was and he pointed to you, said something about you forgetting them?" Becky made a skeptical face. "Which is odd…because we packed together, so…"

I knew where she was going. She thought I pretended to not have them just to wear Reed's. I didn't want her thinking I was that vapid, but I spoke too quickly.

"Yeah, I did pack them. Then Tatum 'unpacked' them for me on the highway," I said, instantly wishing I could retract it all.

Becky's eyes were wide and we both started to slow our jog to walk the straightaway part of the track. "Are. You. Kidding me!?" she said defensively.

Sheepishly, I looked down and nodded. "It's no big deal. Please don't say anything. I don't want it to become bigger than it needs to be."

Becky closed her lips tight and stared straight ahead. After a few seconds of silence she turned to me and grabbed my shoulder. "She's evil, Nolan. Really. I know what she's been doing to you. I've seen her this way before. She's a bully, and a terrible person. You have to tell Reed. Not because you want to steal him from her, but because he needs to know. So he can get the hell away from her!"

I would never tell Reed, and I think a part of Becky knew that. But I nodded anyway, pretending. The announcer called my race and I left Becky, heading for the starting line area. I breathed in the smell of Reed's shirt a few more times before I took it off and set it down on the track. I was in the third heat, so I had some time to kill. I did a few starts and short sprints to get my legs moving. I headed over to the sidewalk side of the track to sit and check my laces but was stopped before I could sit down by a painful shove.

"You just don't get it, do you? He's not into you. He's my boyfriend and you need to back off, trailer trash!" Tatum was yelling in my face. I was without words, something I was vowing to work on while I searched for the right thing to say to her in response. I shook my head, trying to get my mouth to work and then looked over to the stands across the way to see Becky sitting next to Reed and both of them staring at Tatum and I. Becky was talking animatedly with her hands, as if she was angry. In an instant I knew she was telling Reed about the secret cruel pranks Tatum had played on me. Milliseconds were passing so slowly. I wanted to pause everything, get my bearings and ready myself for this next round. But there was no stopping this.

The stinging sensation on my cheek was warm, almost like a burn. My head was flung to the side and my hair was in my eyes. I didn't see her arm coming at me, but the slap Tatum delivered to my face in the cold weather made a ringing sensation in my ear. *So this is what it feels like to get slapped, I thought.* And then there was spit. In my face.

I turned away in disgust and quickly wiped my face with my arms. A nearby coach from the other team came over and grabbed Tatum by the shoulders, moving her away from me. I heard yelling and Becky's voice was nearby. Suddenly someone was wiping my face with a cloth. It burned. It burned so badly.

I opened my eyes and saw Sean frowning at me. I winced as he touched my cheek. "It's going to bruise, Noles. I hate to tell you. What the hell? Are you ok? She went all ape shit on you!"

After everything, Sean was still there for me. I was grateful and hopeful that we'd still be friends. I couldn't process what had just happened, but I knew my fellow runners were getting ready to move into their lanes.

"I, I … I have to run," I said, handing him the cloth. "I'm OK, really," I said, looking over Sean's shoulder into Reed's stunned eyes. He narrowed them and looked down and when his face came up again he was wearing an expression I'd never seen before. He looked cold. Furious.

I headed to my lane and readied myself for the race, stretching my legs and trying to ignore what was probably a beet red hand print on my face. I turned to see Reed standing in front of Tatum, his hands stretched out to either side of him, his voice raised. He looked livid. She was crying and he was yelling. When he finally tried to walk away, she ran after him and grabbed his arm. He brushed her off and said some words that I couldn't make out, but I could tell they were cruel, even if deserved.

———

I came in third overall. It was maybe my best race. I channeled my anger, sadness, confusion and fury over getting slapped in front of everyone into my running. Becky waited for me at the finish line and didn't leave my side until we were on the bus. She insisted I sit next to her, which was probably the best idea I'd been given all day.

As we settled in, Sean passed down the middle aisle and looked at me with sympathy. He moved on without saying a word. I hoped that in time things between us wouldn't be awkward.

Reed was a few people behind him. I felt my heart speed up as he came closer to our seat. When he got to us, he stopped for a second. He didn't make eye contact, but he threw his sweatshirt on my lap. "Keep it for the ride home. It's going to be cold," he said. He kept going to the back of the bus and took a seat across the aisle from Sean. I turned to see his feet dangle in the walkway as he sat sideways taking up the entire seat.

Tatum was the last to get on with her groupie friends. They all sat near the front and huddled around her to console her. *What lemmings, I thought.*

The drive home seemed to take twice as long. I laughed to myself when we passed the point where I thought my warm-ups were probably strung along the highway. When we pulled into the school, I grabbed my bag in my lap and looked at Becky, shaking my head.

"I'm exhausted," I said.

"Uh, yeah," she laughed. "Hey, why don't you come home with me tonight?"

I smiled. That sounded really nice. But I really just wanted to curl up in my own bed. I may throw myself a pity party. Or maybe not. But I just needed to stop my mind, slow things down. I could only do that in the comfort of my own home. "Thanks, but I'm soooo tired. I just want to go home and drop. I'd love a ride, though?"

She smiled and said no problem.

Becky dropped me off at my house at about 11 p.m. and I pulled the keys from my bag to unlock the door. Everyone was asleep, thank God. I didn't really want to explain the hand on my face tonight.

I stripped my clothes and pulled on my cotton pajama pants and a T-shirt and climbed into bed. I lay there flat on my back staring at the ceiling trying to make sense of the last eight hours. When I rolled to my side I noticed Reed's sweatshirt on the floor. I reached over and pulled it to me, hugging onto it. I closed my eyes and started to feel myself drifting when I heard the buzz of my phone.

I reached over to pull it from my night table and saw a text from Reed.

Why didn't you tell me?

This was tricky. I stared at it for about five minutes before I decided honesty was my new path. Hiding things didn't work out so well for me.

I was ashamed.

I waited for him to respond. He did instantly.

You have nothing to be ashamed of.

I waited again. He followed it up with more after a few minutes.

I'm so sorry, Nolan. I had no idea. Becky told me about your warm ups. About the eyebrow. You could have told me. I would have believed you.

I shrunk under my covers. I was so embarrassed. Becky knew about the eyebrow. And she told Reed.

I am so embarrassed.

Honesty. I was going to be honest. I waited.

Don't be. You're not the one who should be embarrassed. Tatum should be. And so should I, for ever going out with her.

I read his text a few times before responding.

Did you two fight over this?

I waited, knowing what I saw. I wanted details, but I didn't want to be pushy. It took him about 15 minutes to write back again, and I was just about to give up when my phone buzzed.

We're done. We were done a long time ago, but this really nailed it. I failed you, and I'm sorry. Dating Tatum is exactly the kind of thing my brother would do. I'm the one who should be embarrassed, not you. I'm so sorry I wasn't there for you.

I wanted to keep this going. I wanted to confess how I felt about him. But I knew that wasn't right. So I resorted to simple things.

Hey, you were there. You gave me a sweatshirt. That saved my ass! :-)

A few minutes later my phone buzzed again.

Ha! It was seriously cold. Tatum really knows how to be mean. Do you still have the shirt?

Honesty.

I'm sleeping with it.

And now I'm suffocating from a panic attack. That was too honest, too honest. How do I take that back? My phone buzzed.

Good. Sleep tight.

I didn't send anything after that. I wanted to end on a high note. Somehow after my nightmares I came out into my wildest dreams. I knew he was just being nice to make me feel better after my ordeal, but it was enough for tonight. I drifted off and slept the night straight through, not waking up until noon on Saturday. I felt refreshed and my bruise was barely showing. I was pretty sure I'd be able to hide it from my parents and avoid any more uncomfortable conversations for the rest of the weekend.

13. Lucky

THE LAST FEW weeks of school passed without much incident, despite Tatum's best efforts. She posted a few nasty things on Facebook about me and Sean, but she hadn't counted on Sean being such a stand-up guy. He would spam her postings with comment after comment about what a liar she was.

And in spite of my ripping of his heart, Sean and I started to hit a nice friendship groove much quicker than I could have hoped for. I think it helped that Becky had a bit of a crush on him, and he wasn't so opposed to her either.

Our little group was quickly expanding—most Friday and Saturday nights, Sienna, Sarah, Becky, Sean, Reed and I all piled into Sean's truck and headed into town for real shopping malls, movies and restaurants. Reed and I were also back to our old selves. We spent most nights before bed texting. Sometimes he would try to quiz me on stupid sports references, and I would amaze him with my brilliance (albeit, not admitting that I was Googling most of the answers). We'd recommend songs to each other and watch stupid videos on YouTube. Everything felt natural, and safe. Only once did our conversation turn to Tatum. Reed still felt guilty, and he seemed to feel like it was his responsibility to make up for her wrongs against me. I wouldn't let him go there, though. If there was one thing I was determined about, it was that if I was ever going to receive kindness, of any kind, from Reed, it would be because he wanted to give it to me…not because he wanted to make up for his nasty ex-girlfriend. *Ex-girlfriend. That made me smile.*

———

Summer hit and I was determined to get a job. My parents didn't really want me to take one on this young; I had just turned 16 before school let out. But I also wanted some independence. I wanted to be able to put gas in the car, and maybe, just maybe, pick up an old clunker that was a step up from the Oldsmobile. (Not that I wasn't thrilled when my parents had officially given it to me at my 16th birthday party, but still.) I was a pretty straight-laced teenager, and I'd never really given them a reason to doubt my responsibilities, so the last time we sat down at dinner to talk about my employment they relented.

My dad got me an interview with the big aquatics center in Chandler, the first main town north of Coolidge. It was a cashier job, but I had hoped that I could train and test for lifeguard before the summer was over; the lifeguards made $13 an hour.

Not thrilled with the idea of me driving by myself 30-45 minutes through the desert, my dad's original plan was that he would time his deliveries and drop me off and pick me up on his way in and out of town. But that just wasn't realistic. He wouldn't even be able to take me to the interview.

Luckily, my mom was a pretty strong woman and reminded him that Mike had been driving himself at that age, and he went a lot farther than 30 minutes away. Plus, Mike was still just a phone call away if I ever had an emergency while they were at work. My newly minted driver's license was dying to be used when my dad finally gave in. Of course, just to make sure I wouldn't speed and would be well surrounded by mass of automobile, I'd be driving the Olds.

I set out early for my interview on the Monday after school let out. My interview with the pool manager was at 11 a.m., but I gave myself a little more than an hour just to be safe. My dad gave the car a once-over before he left that morning and gave me one final lecture about safety on the road, proper signaling and the appropriate breaking distance. I mused to myself about how worried my dad was about me as I rolled down our rocked driveway and made my way to the highway. *If he was really that worried, you'd think he would have sent me in the pickup he bought off of Sienna's dad last month instead of the Oldsmobile, I thought, coming to terms with the realization that the Oldsmobile would be...is now...mine.*

By the time I was a full 20 miles out of town I started to get excited. This was the farthest I had ever been alone, on my own. It felt...amazing. I turned the radio up and rolled down my window to let the warm sunshine-baked air touch my cheek and arm. The small hills on either side of me were speckled with cactus and desert brush, green from the recent rains. The blacktop had recently been paved on this stretch of the roadway and the jet black looked cool against the dusty brown of the surrounding landscape.

I was already halfway there and still had nearly an hour to make it to my appointment. *I could stop at Starbucks, I thought. I always wanted to do that. It felt like an adult thing to do.*

I was startled a little when the radio cut out a few times. The speakers were making loud popping sounds every time, almost like the radio was shorting out. I shut it off thinking maybe if I turned it on again in a few minutes it would kick in – that's how we usually fixed things on the Olds.

When I killed the tunes, though, I became very aware of the sounds the car was making. Almost sputtering. I tried giving it more gas, but it just sputtered more, jerking and whining, louder and louder. Finally, everything on the car just felt limp. I forced my steering wheel to the side of the road, but it was hard to turn. I was traveling at a crawling speed by the time I got to the dirt area off the road and out of the way of traffic, not that there were many vehicles traveling on this stretch at 10:15 a.m. on a weekday.

Son of a...I hate this fucking car!

I got out on the passenger side; at least one thing my dad told me stuck. I pulled the hand towel from the glove box and headed to the hood to unhook the latch. The hood was always blazing hot, so I wrapped the towel around my hand while I held it. I had no idea what I was looking at, but something smelled burnt even though nothing really looked out of place. I walked back to the driver's seat to try to start the car again and it just clicked and then sat there silent.

I beat my hands on the steering wheel a few times and threw the towel up on the enormous dashboard. I put my head down and looked at my watch. I had 45 minutes. *OK, I just need to get Mike here in time. I can still make it.*

I dialed Mike's number and held my breath as I counted the rings. When it went to his voicemail I hung up and repeated. Each time I called, I got his voicemail. I finally left one begging him to call me as soon as he could and pleading with him to rescue me.

I stared at my watch waiting. I would give it until 10:40 before I called the pool number and pathetically explained my situation. *Always, it's always this stupid car!*

I was entranced by the second hand and didn't notice the giant, black Chevy truck that had pulled in front of me. I looked up only when I heard the crunch of boots on the roadway. My heart jumped and bile hit the back of my throat from panic at first, but when my eyes finally focused I realized who it was. Buck Johnson was walking my way, a toothpick hanging out of the side of his mouth and the world's biggest coffee cup loading down one hand.

"Hey, sugar. I thought that was you! Come help me pop this baby up so we can see what's doin'," he said, the words melting from him with charm.

"Oh my god, I'm so glad you drove by," I fumbled my way out of the car and grabbed the towel. I lifted the hood and watched as Buck stared at it, chewed on his toothpick and then stared some more. He lifted a few things and moved some pieces that I, frankly, didn't know could move.

"Smells pretty bad, don't she," he said, taking the hood from me. "I don't know for certain, but it looks like you've got a blown alternator. Probably a whole host of other things, too. I'm shocked this puppy's still runnin'."

I must have looked like I was about to cry because he immediately went into rescue mode. "Where you headed? I can take you home, but I've got a meeting I have to get to in Tucson shortly."

"I have an interview in Chandler," I said. "It's just a summer job. It's…it's ok. I can reschedule, I hope." I threw the last part in unconsciously.

"Nonsense," he said, pulling his phone from his pocket and holding up a hand telling me to just wait a minute.

I just stared as he paced through the desert brush a bit while his phone rang someone on the other end. "Hey, you bozo. Are you still sleeping?" he laughed. "Shouldn't you be at the gym?... Yeah, well, I need you do to something for me."

He looked up at me and gave me his famous wink and half grin. "You know that girly friend of yours? The one that has great taste in cars? … yeah, Nolan. Well, she's out here on highway 89 stuck in the middle of nowhere."

I waited while he listened to the other part of the conversation. "Well of course I would take her home, rocket scientist, but she's got an interview in Chandler and I can't postpone the Tucson thing… Well alright then. I'll tell her."

He hung up and immediately started dialing. I was trying to figure out what was going on when he started up his next call. "Yeah, buzzard, it's me. I need you to send one of the sleds out here to 89, 'bout 20 miles out. Got a friend with a bum Olds we need to take into the shop…Nah, I'll leave the keys. Thanks!"

He was wiping his hands on the towel and closing up my hood and I just couldn't take the waiting any more.

"So, what was that all about?" I sounded sheepish, and desperate.

"Oh, ha! Sorry," he laughed. "Reed will be here in about 20 minutes. If you can call that appointment of yours and tell them you'll only be a few minutes late that should do it. I'll have my guys pull it in. Don't worry about having to get it, I'll get one of them to bring it back up from Tucson."

"Thank you thank you thank you thank you thank you!" I said, reaching for his hand and shaking it over and over and over. He stopped me and put an arm around me, trying to calm me down with his giant, warm hug.

"Sugar, really, stop your worrying," he said. "You're good to my son. That's enough for me to know you're good people."

I dialed the pool while Buck took my keys and readied the car for his crew. I was able to buy myself another 20 minutes or so and was relieved until I was hit with an instant wave of panic. "Buck, I can't pay for this!" I knew it sounded stupid and ungrateful, but I really couldn't. My dad would kill me if I came home with a bill for thousands of dollars in car repairs.

"Girl, you worry too much. I said don't worry about it," he said, patting me on the back.

"Oh, I don't know. That's really nice, I don't think I can accept that…"

Buck interrupted me. "Nolan, do you know how much money I'm worth?"

I was a bit dumbfounded. I just shook my head no.

"Well, let's just say that I could spend an entire year picking up stranded motorists and fixing their cars for free and it wouldn't even make a dent in my bottom line," he grinned and nodded for me to understand.

"Oh," I said, shrugging.

"OK then, get your stuff ready, Reed should be here any minute," he said, climbing back into his truck. "You don't be a stranger this summer, now, you hear?"

"Yes, sir," I said, saluting him.

———

I waited only a few minutes before I saw Reed's Jeep coming closer in my rear view mirror. I hopped out with my purse and small duffle bag of stuff and put a thumb out to the side, pretending to hitch-hike. He cruised up to the side of the road slowly and rolled his window down to let out a dragged out whistle. I blushed and laughed a little.

"Where you headed, hot stuff," he said, pulling his sunglasses down to the tip of his nose. Even feigning to be a backwoods pervert he was still the cutest boy I'd ever seen.

I opened his passenger door and slid in the seat.

"Thanks for coming to get me; I'm so sorry your dad woke you up," I said, looking him over. His hair was disheveled and twisted in all directions. He had a torn T-shirt on and long basketball shorts and Nike flip flops.

"Nah, no worries. I don't need to sleep my day away. He's right," he said, flipping his sunglasses back on his face. "You wanna wait for the tow to get here for your car?"

"Ohhhh nooo. Trust me, no one is ever going to steal that car. Ever," I said wryly.

Reed nodded and pulled back on to the road. He flipped his stereo channels a few times settling on some rap song I didn't recognize. We finished our climb through the mountains and I could see the cityscape off in the distance. I was struggling to find something to say while we rode most of the way in silence. At least a dozen times I opened my mouth and closed it again, staring back out my window. While Reed and I were gelling, we hadn't really spent much time alone. Truly, we have never been alone for long. And the anxiety of this situation was setting in and my stomach felt like it might soon flip out my throat and land in my lap.

"So, summer job, huh?" he said, looking at me for a second or two. His words startled me I was so lost in my own neurotic head.

"Oh, uh… yeah," I nodded. Silence was starting to settle in again. I had to fill it. *Talk, Nolan. Talk.* "I just want some extra cash, you know? I want to be a little more independent. Buy my own gas, maybe get a phone that isn't some off brand that no one's ever heard of," I joked.

"That's cool," Reed said. I looked over and noticed his forehead pinching together some under his glasses, almost like he was thinking.

"I guess it's hard for you to work during the summer even, huh? I mean, not that you have to… but you totally could, if you wanted. I mean… I'm sorry, I'm rambling," I was doing that thing again where I stop making sense.

Reed just laughed. Finally, he responded. "Actually, a job might be nice. Something flexible. I still have a lot of summer drills and workouts. And coach wants me watching tape a lot this summer. Things are really going to get intense. And I'm just a junior. My senior year is going to be ridiculous." He let out a heavy sigh and then turned to me with a tight-lipped smile.

"You can do it. Just take it a day at a time, right?" I said, patting his thigh once like he was a child. I pulled my hand back in my lap immediately, embarrassed by my bold and hokey gesture. "Just turn on Riggs Road up ahead. We can take that all the way to the aquatics center. I don't think my interview will be long if you don't mind waiting for me."

"No problem at all. I'll come in, too. Check the place out," he said.

Just then my phone rang. I pulled it from my purse and looked to see Mike's name.

"Sorry, it's my brother. I have to take this, and yell at him for never being helpful," I said. Reed just laughed.

"Hey, you sorry excuse for a big brother," I half-joked.

"Nolan, are you OK? I'm so sorry. I didn't even have my phone on. I was with Samantha and it was a late night, so…" he tried to continue but I cut him off.

"Stop. Stop. I don't need to know. I'm OK, no need to alert the authorities," I joked.

"Well, where are you? Do you need me to pick you up somewhere?" he asked.

"I'm good. Buck Johnson drove by and he hauled the car in. He sent Reed out here to give me a ride. He'll just bring me home when I'm done," I said quickly, hoping Mike wouldn't dig too deep or tease. No such luck.

"Ooooooh, I see," he chided. "So you're in the car with Reeeeeeeed," he kept going. I pressed the phone tightly to my ear, hoping like hell Reed couldn't hear any of Mike's end of the conversation. I was turning redder by the minute. I just needed this phone call to end.

"We're almost here, so I gotta go. Don't tell Dad anything, he'll just worry. I'll explain when I get home, ok?" I said.

"Yeah, yeah. Call if you need me, though, OK? I promise I'll pick up this time," he said just before hanging up.

I put my phone back in my purse and snuck a sideways glance at Reed to see if he heard any of that. He was smirking a little, so my gut told me he did. I sank down a little in the seat and hugged my purse.

The pool manager's name was Todd. He looked like a PE teacher, with his short hair and shiny sunglasses. He was nice enough. He directed Reed and me to a back office right off the main entrance where we sat on an old sofa and he propped one leg up, half sitting on his desk with a clip board. Chewing his gum, he pulled his sunglasses off and tucked them in the front of his shirt. "So, cashier, huh?" he looked at me.

"Yes. Though, I'd like to test for your next lifeguarding session, if that'd be possible. I would really like to work my way up to that," I said, wringing my hands. I was a little nervous.

"Well, you're in luck. We're actually testing tomorrow, if you'd like to join us. I just need you to fill out this paperwork. I see you have the right CPR and First Aid certifications, so if you pass the tests, you can start this week. We're short on staff and I need to get staffed up pretty quickly. We're opening a new section this season and we're going to be pretty busy."

"You testing, too?" he added, looking over at Reed. Snapping his eyes up to meet the manager's, Reed then turned to me, looking for approval. I just shrugged and smiled, but inside I was begging him to test with me. The thought of spending an entire summer working alongside a shirtless Reed Johnson was too much to handle.

"Yeah, I'd love to," he said, taking the packet of paperwork.

"OK then. When you're done filling this out, leave it with Penny up front and then we'll see you tomorrow at 6 a.m." he said, shaking our hands as he left.

When the door shut, Reed stared at me with wide eyes and mouthed 'Six A.M.' I just laughed and started filling out my paperwork.

When we were done, we dropped our packets off with Penny at the front desk. Penny was an older woman. She spent most of her day answering the phone, it seemed. She took four phone calls all in the span of our stop at her desk.

"See you two tomorrow," she said with a wink as we turned and headed for the parking lot.

We hopped in the Jeep and pulled back out to the main road. I settled my bag and purse down between my feet and adjusted my seatbelt, which was all twisted. Then, the thought struck me. How was I supposed to get to the testing tomorrow? I didn't have a car. I'm sure Reed wouldn't mind taking me, but I really hated imposing. I chewed on the inside of my cheek for a bit then turned to face him.

"So, since we're going to the same place...do you think maybe I could hitch a ride again in the morning?" I said, hating to ask for favors.

"Uh, yeah. I just sort of thought I'd pick you up. You know, to get here in time we'll need to leave at 5, right?" he said.

"Yeah, I'm good with that," I groaned a little. We both laughed and then Reed pulled off the road into a nearby shopping center. A Starbucks. How desperately I needed that.

"I'm buying, whatcha want?" he said, hopping out and flipping his glasses up on his head.

"Vanilla frap?" I said. He smiled back with a thumbs up and headed inside.

I pulled the visor down to open the backside mirror and check my face. My hair was a little tangled from the Jeep ride so I tried to brush out some of the knots with my fingers. My nose and cheeks had a pink sunburn on them, nothing bad, but I definitely needed to lotion up good tomorrow, especially if I was going to be in a pool most of the morning. Reed came out while I was finishing up my untangling. He stuck his arm through the open door across his seat and handed me my frosty cool drink.

"Mmmmmm, thanks," I said. "I love these. Like a dessert with a little kick."

After he climbed in and planted his coffee in the middle cup holder, he reached back behind me, the tips of his hair brushing my shoulder as he leaned into the back seat. My breath stopped at the slight touch and I snuck a look at him, so close. He popped back up with a hat in his hand and then handed it to me. I looked at him, puzzled.

"For your head?" he smirked.

"Jack ass, I know that. Why are you giving it to me?" I said, smacking his arm with the back of my hand. I was getting more and more comfortable with our slight, friendly physical contact.

"Your hair was tangled. I saw you working on it. Thought maybe you'd like this for the rest of the ride?" he said as I took the hat from his hand.

"Oh, thanks," I smiled. I pulled open the back snaps of a dark gray and maroon ASU hat. I smiled a little as I pulled my hair through the back and snapped it into a ponytail. The front was snug over my head and kept my stray hairs in place.

"What's this, UofA boy with an ASU hat," I teased.

"Hey, I haven't made up my mind yet. But don't tell my dad that," he winked, and we were on the road again.

———

We pulled up to my house at about 3 p.m. I hopped out before Reed turned the motor off, hoping I could just run inside without him stopping to talk to my dad or get a good look at my house. But he was quicker than I thought. His motor was off and he was next to me walking across the gravel in no time. I heard some slight noises coming from the side carport and we headed over in that direction to see my dad digging for some tools in the small shed by the back door.

"Hey pops, I'm home," I said as he jumped back, hitting his head on the shed door a little.

Rubbing it, he set his tools down on the shelf and grabbed the dirty towel he left out here to clean his hands off after a little 'tinkering.' My dad was pretty handy. He really didn't have reasons to always be fixing things, but he seemed to search them out anyhow.

He had some garden lattice propped up by the wall and was digging out some brackets and paint, probably something my mom had put him up to.

"Hey there, honey. You home already?" he said, slowing his voice a little when he realized I wasn't alone. "Oh, hey, Reed. Nice to see you, son. What are you up to?"

"Reed gave me a lift," I said, trying to finish the explanation before my dad went into panic, you-had-a-crash, what-happened-to-the-car mode.

"Are you ok? Did something happen?" he said, squeezing my shoulders and looking into my eyes like he was giving me some sort of concussion test. I grabbed his hands and squeezed them and then kissed his cheek.

"I'm fine, daddy. Car just broke down, that's all," I said, filling him with relief.

"Ohhhh, good. Well, guess we should go pick it up. Where'd you leave it," he said, reaching into his pocket for his keys.

I stopped him. "No, no. It's good. Buck actually stopped to help me. I was just outside of town. He towed the car to the shop and then sent Mr. QB1 here to save me," I said, trying to play it off like it was no big deal because I know my dad was going to feel guilty accepting the help and not saving me on his own.

"Oh," he looked down, then back up at Reed, reaching for his hand to shake it. "Well, thanks, Reed. Awful nice of ya. You'll have to give me your father's number, I want to make sure I thank him and find out how to pick the car up and what I owe him."

"No problem, Mr. Lennox. Really, never any trouble. And you probably should just say thanks to my dad and leave it at that. He… well, he pretty much never accepts money when he helps a friend. He'll be offended, sir," Reed said, smiling.

"Oh, well…" my dad shook his head some more and then nodded, finally accepting it. This was hard for my dad, I knew. "Well, then how about we feed you some supper. That'll sure make me feel a whole lot better. And my wife, Susan, makes an amazing roast. She's had one going in the pot all day."

Reed looked at me for approval, but I was more panic stricken. I didn't really want him to see the inside of my house. Truth be told, Tatum's name calling of Trailer Trash was still with me a little. But, since I wasn't objecting either, Reed just shook my dad's hand again and said, "Thanks, I'd love to stay, sir."

"Please, just call me Rich," my dad said, putting his arm over Reed's shoulder and guiding him inside.

We came inside through the backdoor, and thankfully my mom's roast had filled the house with an amazing smell. It made my house feel even homier, and I was hoping it might just distract Reed from our scratched cabinets, old countertops, worn carpet and scuffed walls.

I dropped my purse and bag on the floor by the kitchen counter and guided Reed to the main living room. Our house was very open with the dining room and living space up front with giant windows that looked out over the handmade porch. The kitchen was set off to the back side and had a cute door with a country-style window on it that led to my dad's 'tinkering' space.

My parents' room was at the end of the hall and then my room was to the right and Mike's old room on the left. Mike always liked having his window face the front because he could sneak out easily, his foot landing right on the porch. My window was over one of the only spaces without decking underneath, so the drop was a good eight feet below since our house was lifted up so high. I did have a huge walk-in closet, though, and my own entrance to the spare bathroom. For a girl, it was pretty perfect.

I gave Reed the fast version of the tour, pointing to the other rooms in the house as we strolled the short hallway. He admired the family photos hung on the walls as we walked.

"Hey, is this you?" he said, pointing to a family portrait that was about 10 years old. I was in a red velvet dress and my hair was in two pigtails on either side of my head. My bangs were short and cut in a perfect straight line, following my eyebrows. My socks were pulled up to my knees and my ankles were crossed showing off my shiny black saddle shoes. I have a vivid memory of the outfit, but not much else.

"That's me. I was pretty stylish at six," I joked, hoping he wouldn't take in too many more embarrassing childhood pictures of me.

"You were cute," he said, moving on down the hall. "It's nice that you have these pictures. I don't really have any of these. My parents divorced when I was in kindergarten and I really bounced back and forth until about fourth grade when my parents decided it was best that I stay with my mom. You know, for 'consistency in my young life,'" Reed said, rolling his eyes.

Sometimes I felt bad that he came from a split home. While he might have the fancy driveway and the rich parents, at least mine were under the same roof. And my parents didn't miss anything in our lives, either. My mom had boxes in the attic filled with silly art awards, pictures, ribbons from field day, clay pots from grade school and more. I got the feeling that Reed didn't have a box anywhere.

"Hey, so this is your room then, right?" he said, a devilish grin as he leaned my door open.

"Uh, yes it is…and we don't need to go in there," I said, grabbing for the handle in an effort to stop him. Too late.

He flipped my light on and walked to the center of my room. I leaned against the wall by the door and my dresser. My room was pretty neat. I wasn't your typical messy teenage girl, but I was still self-conscience about everything being on display for his judgment.

"So this is where you are when we text at night sometimes, huh?" he said looking around. "This is where you pick out music and all the 'magic happens.'" He was smiling like he was getting to see some special secret. Admittedly, I liked how it was making me feel. He turned to open my closet and walked in to flip through my things. He thumbed through the hangers, taking note of the two very different sides of my closet. One half was filled with T-shirts and jeans, the other with cute dresses that I rarely wore.

"You know, I like you better in this side of the closet," he said, pointing to the more *me* side with denim and cotton. I blushed a little at his comment.

He turned the light off and shut the door and I continued to watch him. I was trying to think of something witty to say, but nothing was coming to mind. I walked over to the window and slid the blinds up and cracked open the window to let in some air. "I like to sleep with it open at night. I like the way the crickets sound," I shrugged, turning around to see him looking through the various bowls and boxes on my dresser now. Suddenly I gasped a little and lurched forward as he was lifting the lid to my old jewelry box. I felt like my knees were going to buckle underneath me when I caught myself on the corner of my bed. I just sat down and stared, fear stinging my eyes a little, with a touch of mortifying embarrassment. I watched as Reed pulled out the overly worn paper, the creases tearing a bit on the edges. I caught the smirk forming on the side of his lips when he looked at me from a side glance. "Is this what I think it is?" he asked.

"Oh, uh...yeah, I guess. I don't know. I forgot what I put in that thing," I lied. I knew exactly what it was because I looked at that letter from Reed almost every night for two years. I gulped slowly, hoping if I did it slowly enough he wouldn't hear it.

He unfolded it and read over his own words just a little. He carefully folded it and then put it back in the box, replacing the felt lid once again. I just sat there motionless, watching his hands as he slid them in his pockets and tensed his arms just a little, his back to me. He slowly walked sideways, taking in other things in my room, looking at the pictures of Sarah, Sienna and me on my mirror. He ran his finger through the chains and necklaces that were hanging from the small hooks on my cork board. My aunt and mom had a tradition of giving me charms for my birthday, and I had saved every single one since my fifth birthday.

I was starting to feel a little light-headed, probably from holding my breath for so long, when Reed slowly turned to look at me. I both anticipated and dreaded meeting his gaze. I looked down just before his face was looking at mine, staring at my shoes and fidgeting my feet together. I chewed on the inside of my cheek a little and then slowly looked up at him to find him wearing a warm smile. He came over and sat next to me, not too close, but close enough that I could feel the warmth of his body. Thankfully, our silence was broken by my dad's hollering down the hall.

"Hey, Nolan! Bring your guest out on the porch when you can. I made some fresh lemonade and we can wait for your mother to come home. She's on her way," he said.

"OK, be right there," I said, leaping to my feet. I didn't turn around once, just got to my door and said 'come on' over my shoulder, flipping my room light as I turned the corner and headed back to the main room. I could hear Reed's giant shoes clomping behind me and cringed a little that the floor of my house sounded so hollow. Just one more nuance about living in a manufactured home.

I stuck to my mission and flung the screen door open and held it out behind me waiting for Reed to catch up. When we got out on the porch my dad handed Reed a glass and then gave me one, too. "Taste this, son. Right from my own tree. Pretty good lemons this year, I'd say," he said, toasting to his homemade creation.

I stared at the McDonald's glasses we were holding, freebies we'd scored years ago from some giveaway. Suddenly everything in my house didn't feel good enough. I stomped over to the porch swing and sat down folding my legs up underneath me.

"Thanks, Mr. Lennox...uh, sorry. Rich. It's great," Reed said, taking another swallow and puckering a bit at the sourness.

I couldn't even look at him. And here my dad was, trying to impress him with sour lemonade in our pokey mismatched glasses. I just stared at my lap and sighed. Suddenly, the swing was moving and I realized Reed had sat down next to me. I looked up and gave him a closed lip smile, shrugged and took a swig of my sour juice. My dad had gone back to tinkering in the carport – clearly the lemonade was a rouse to keep Reed out of my bedroom alone with me.

"This is actually pretty good, you know?" Reed said, holding up his glass. "I don't think I've ever had fresh-squeezed anything! My dad picks out ready-made everything. Either that or Rose, who comes in to cook sometimes, leaves ready-to-heat leftovers stacked in the fridge."

I smiled a little and then just took another drink, looking out down the dirt road. My mom couldn't get here quick enough.

"So..." he started, then began swinging his legs back and forth like a child. "You kept my letter." He was grinning and looking out into the distance, clearly ready to tease me. I had a choice, be embarrassed or just own it all.

"Yep," I said, swinging my legs, too, and staring off at the same distance, taking another sip of my lemonade and wanting to crawl under the porch and die.

"That's…" he started, then stopped turning to angle towards me a little. He tapped his forearm against my knee, forcing me to look up. "That's really sweet."

I just let my eyebrows raise and nodded, shrugging a little, clearly admitting how embarrassed I was. "Thanks, I guess," that's all I could say.

Like a gift, my mom's car pulled around from the main road onto our stretch. I stood up and stepped down the stairs just a little, Reed joining me.

My mom pulled into the carport right behind my dad's truck and got out of her car, my dad coming over to grab a few bags from her with some extra groceries. She walked up the path to the porch steps and smiled at Reed before leaning in to kiss my cheek. "Hi, Reed. So nice of you to join us," she said reaching out to shake his hand. "Come on in, guys. Food will be served in just a few minutes."

My mom was such a confident woman. I envied her and looked up to her for that. I hoped that my confidence would grow to be more like hers someday. I held the door for Reed as we walked inside, but he took it from my hand and gestured his hand forward, insisting I go inside first.

"Why thank you, sir," I said, in a sort of British accent.

He laughed a little and then said, "Don't expect me to call you lady, Noles."

————

Dinner was amazingly good. My mom had picked up French bread and toasted it with garlic and butter for a side. Reed seemed to be in heaven as he had thirds. By the time I was walking him out the door at 6:30 he was rubbing his belly and complaining that he needed a nap.

"You should see us on Thanksgiving," I said. "It's quite the feast."

He just smiled and then kicked a driveway stone at my feet. "I bet. I'd like to see that…tell your mom to save me a place. Or leftovers. Or leftovers of anything she makes. Like, uh…ever," he joked, smiling and rubbing his satisfied belly one more time.

I walked him over to his Jeep and then waited while he opened the door and sat sideways on the seat, facing me, biting his bottom lip just a bit. Suddenly, I remembered something and ran back to the house.

"One minute," I said.

"Uh, ok," he said, puzzled by my bizarre behavior. *Since when wasn't I bizarre, I thought.*

I ran back out seconds later, holding his hat that he let me wear for the ride home. "Here, can't let you forget this. It's a far superior school, you know," I joked. ASU and UofA were rivals, and I had my heart set on ASU ever since I went to a Sun Devil football game with my dad and brother when I was in third grade. Of course, that's before I knew about the Reed Johnson path. That might have me rethinking everything. *Yeah, throw your life dreams away for a boy, I laughed inwardly.*

"Hey, thanks. I have to keep it in the Jeep. Can't let my dad see it," he winked and flipped the hat on his head backwards, smooshing down the waves and curls of his hair, letting them poke out the sides and back just a bit.

"So, see you in the morning I guess," I said, trying to break the uncomfortable silence that kept creeping in between us. He was back to biting his bottom lip.

"Yep, I'll be here at 5. You better be ready, I know how you like to sleep in late," he said sarcastically.

"Ha, that's a good one, Mr. Johnson. Say, maybe tomorrow you can take a shower before you crawl out of bed," I winked right back.

Reed just laughed a little and looked down, quietly speaking. "I had to rescue some damsel in distress," he smiled.

"Yeah, you did. Sorry about that. But she's REALLLLLY grateful," I said.

"Anytime," he said, swinging his hand into mine for just the briefest touch. It was like it sent fire through my fingers and veins.

He pulled his door closed and leaned his arm out the window some, starting up his engine. I just waved and turned on my feet to head back inside. I was only a few steps away when he called my name.

"Hey, Nolan?" he spoke. I turned to look him in the eyes.

"Yeah, what's up? Need some leftovers to take home," I said, trying to be clever. *Always trying to be clever.*

He curled his left side of his lip up and shook his head. "Nah, I'm good. Probably for hours," he smiled, then dropped his face into a more serious expression. "No, I just wanted to say sorry again. I know you're sick of hearing it, but I am so very sorry. I shouldn't have been with someone like that. Someone that could do that to someone like you."

I was starting to dread his constant apologies. But despite that, I always continued to wonder how he could have been with someone like Tatum. Been so very intimate with someone like her, for that matter. As part of my new promise to be honest, I mustered up the courage to ask Reed the question that had been burning on my mind for days.

"It's really not your fault, Reed. I promise. Please stop worrying about it," I said, smiling genuinely. "But... you know? I sort of was wondering. A couple weeks ago you mentioned that it was over between you and Tatum a long time ago. When did you know it was over?"

I waited. Reed smirked again, pulling his hat off and running his hands through his hair, putting the hat back on his head and then looking down for a few seconds. He patted his hand on the side of the Jeep a few times while he stared off at the sunset, squinting a little and taking in a deep breath. Finally, he turned to look at me and gave me a faint, but honest smile. "The moment I danced with you," he said. "See you in the morning."

And like that, he drove away.

14. Time

I WAS PRETTY TIRED while I tried to force down the toast and eggs my dad made for me before he left in the morning. It would be being generous guessing that I slept for an hour last night. I replayed Reed's words in my mind over and over, at first a bit dazed, not sure I heard him correctly. When I finally had to admit to myself that perhaps I did hear him right, I couldn't slow the speeding beats of my heart down long enough to let my body fall into sleep.

I started to type Reed a text at least a dozen times throughout the night, completely oblivious to the idea that sending him a text at 1 a.m. was probably not the best idea. Deleting paragraphs on a tiny keyboard was hard as I restarted my words time and again. I was ready to confess everything from the moment I first saw him drinking from that fountain in the gym to the way he made me feel when his warm hands touched my bare shoulders at the dance. I knew I was reacting a bit much, but in my wildest dreams did I ever think the door would open for this chance. The slightest crack. I had to be thoughtful about everything. I was not going to mess this up.

I picked an outfit from the *me* side of the closet this morning. Knowing we would be swimming a lot, I pulled out my black Speedo racing suit, which fortunately made my body look like it belonged to an Olympic swimmer. The snug fit sucked in all the right places and the open back and shoulder straps made my upper body look broad and strong. I pulled a pair of cut-off sweat shorts that were a bit big over the suit and rolled the top down to keep them up. I slid my flip flops on by the kitchen door and sat on the chair by the window where I could easily watch the road for Reed's Jeep when it approached.

I could hear the clock ticking slowly and took in every sound of our house. The whishing sound of my blood rushing over my ears as my heart beat was starting to drown out everything else when I saw the front of his Jeep round the corner and head for my house. I grabbed my backpack stocked with towel, sunscreen, extra clothes, granola bars and water and headed out the door, locking it behind me. I ran down the steps to the front gate so he wouldn't have to pull completely into our driveway.

Be cool, Nolan. Be cool.

"Hey, morning person," Reed said as he rolled down his window. "Ready to swim? I bet we're gonna freeze our asses off!"

"No kidding," I said, throwing my pack in the back of the Jeep and climbing into the passenger side. I buckled up as he was peeling out a bit on our driveway. He looked at me sideways and smiled.

"Hope your parents are gone. I always wanted to try that on your driveway," he said.

"Typical boy," I said, leaning into him. *Oh my god.*

We were on the highway in no time and Reed was cranking his stereo at full blast. The sun was barely up and it felt like we were disturbing the peace, but the truth was we were miles from anything but sage brush and rattlesnakes. He had a classic rock station on and it was playing "Wild Thing" and he started singing along, overacting to the lyrics and being freer than I had ever seen him. I giggled and tried to sing along with the chorus, completely blundering the words, which only made him laugh and sing louder, trying to help me.

When the song ended, he turned the radio down a little and silence set in for a few miles. I could tell we were both itching to talk, but holding back. We kept stealing glances and then smiling before looking away. As a rarity, I actually came up with small talk to keep us going for the rest of the trip.

"What do you think the test will be like?" I asked, honestly wondering as I'd never been through this process before.

"Well, Jason lifeguarded all the time. I remember he had to do some speed swimming, nothing fast, just to show you could get to someone in time. There were also a lot of strength drills, like holding the dummy's head above water, CPR, treading water. Why, you nervous?" he asked.

I was actually a really good swimmer. I wasn't fast, but I was strong, so I was pretty sure I could pull it off. I didn't want to come off cocky though, so I just shrugged a bit and said "Nah, I think I'll be ok. I'm going to be tired, though, that's for sure."

Out of nowhere, Reed reached over and touched the tip of his finger to the tip of my nose, crinkling his face a little into a cute new smile I'd never seen from him before. "You better sunscreen that face of yours up," he said. "You're still a little pink from yesterday."

"Aye aye, captain," I said, saluting him. *What the hell? I did that same thing to his dad. I'm a loser.*

I settled back into my seat and looked at my face in the right-side mirror, watching strands of my hair blow around as they came loose from the braid I worked up to keep my hair out of my way in the water. I studied myself for a while, and then it hit me. For the first time in my life, I looked at myself and I felt like a woman. I looked older. My cheeks were more defined, my lips fuller and my hair was in all the right places. If ever there was a day to feel confident about how I looked, this was it. I reached back behind the seat for my bag and dragged it through the middle of us onto my lap.

"Sunglasses," I explained when Reed looked over, wondering what I was doing. I pulled them out and slid them on my face and leaned back to admire myself once more. Yes, I was hot today. And I was going to use it to my advantage.

———

We got to the facility with 15 minutes to spare. Reed speeds a bit, but he never makes me nervous. There were 10 or 12 other life-guards there with sheets of paper and they started calling out names to gather us into groups for testing. I started in the deep end for treading while Reed's group started at the lanes for timed swimming and rescue drills. I dropped my bag over in a shady corner and tucked my sunglasses inside. Reed jogged over to hand his to me for safe keeping as well.

"Where's your purse?" I joked.

"Must've left it at home," he threw right back at me. We were getting good at this type of back-and-forth with one another. It felt comfortable and just right.

I waited for Reed to turn before I slid my shorts down and kicked them to the side. I slipped out of my flip flops and headed to my group at the deep end. When I reached them, I stood at the edge and stretched my arms a bit, dangling them in front of me and relaxing the muscles in my back. When I pulled my head up, I looked at Reed who was looking right back at me with a bit of a wicked smile. I made out the slightest wink and blushed a little from his attention.

Head in the game, Nolan. You're hot stuff, remember?

We all listened closely to the instructions and were soon jumping into the pool and spreading out to give one another space. We treaded for several minutes before the guards on duty stopped us and then handed us small weights and asked us to do it again. A few of the girls in my group couldn't keep up and had to drop out then and there. I was breathing hard, but I wasn't having any trouble holding my weight up.

Whenever I needed a distraction, I would shift my eyes to glance at the racing lanes where Reed stood dripping wet in dark red board shorts and nothing else. In the two years I'd known him, his body somehow filled out even more. His arms were defined and his chest was chiseled like a college football player. I knew he lifted and ran every day, but I never had so long to really take in what was going on underneath those T-shirts and sweatshirts.

Reed caught me staring at least twice, and each time he winked at me, making me laugh and almost lose my weight.

———

The rest of the testing was a breeze after the treading portion, and I was glad I had that part first. I was the fastest swimmer in my group for the timed sessions. I was getting ready to brag about it to Reed when I looked over the sheets posted on the board and realized I was the second fastest overall. Reed was first.

"I think you need to be tested for performance enhancers," I joked behind him, snapping my towel at him a bit as he turned around.

"Hey, what's this with you being this stud swimmer, huh?" he turned, his breath catching a bit when he looked at my full body in a swimsuit. Where I would normally feel embarrassed and want to wrap my towel around me and cover up, I instead felt empowered. I threw it on the bench and just kept talking.

"Yeah, I swam a lot with Mike when we were younger. He swims at the college for exercise all the time and I sometimes join him, but I haven't gone in a while," I said. I loved swimming. Would totally join the swim team if we had one at Coolidge High. We didn't really have a pool in town, so that idea was out.

"Well, you're a bad-ass," he smiled. "I'm pretty sure we're good for the summer gig."

I sat on the bench and grabbed the towel to dry out my hair some. I pulled the braid out slowly to try to preserve some of the waves left behind. As my head was slung over, I heard one of the lead guards pop the bullhorn on and start talking.

"OK, listen up. If I call your name, stick around cuz we need to have you fill out your hiring paperwork. Not everyone will get hired, so I'm sorry for those of you who won't be joining us this summer. But, thank you all for trying out."

I held my breath for just a moment with a brief flash of fear. *What if I don't make it, or Reed doesn't make it?* But the worrying was for naught as our names were the first two they read off. Reed high-fived me and sat down next to me on the bench, our legs touching. He didn't move and I wouldn't dare move.

———

Once the paperwork was done, I pulled out my shorts and slid them back up over my now dry suit. I fished out Reed's glasses and put mine on, too. We waited at the counter for Penny to work out schedules. I leaned against the counter and Reed stood right next to me, casually slinging his arm around my shoulder, holding his hat over my shoulder in his right hand. I didn't dare look at him, but I saw Penny chuckle a little at the surprised look on my face.

"OK, you two kids, here are the slots we have open. How you wanna work it? You can sign up together or work splits, whatever works best for you, but grab your spots quick if you want them," Penny said, sliding over a large clipboard with two months of squares on the papers.

"Together works for me, you?" Reed said, almost sounding hopeful.

"Sure," I shrugged, playing it off while my insides were doing cartwheels.

We signed our names for mostly Sunday, Tuesday, Wednesday and Thursday afternoons, the 1-5 p.m. shift. We threw a few Fridays in, too. I let Reed pick because he had places he needed to be, and I was already at the only place I wanted to be this summer.

The next day was a mandatory work day for everyone. It was camp day, so groups of kids were going to come in every hour to use the facility. It wouldn't be as crowded as normal and would provide some great training, Todd said.

Penny handed us two shirts each and a pair of trunks to Reed and a one-piece suit to me. I went into the ladies locker room to try it on because you never know how those things are going to fit. The center's colors were dark purple and silver, so all staff members had to wear logo shirts and the right kind of suits. Penny explained that the cost of our uniforms would just come out of our first paycheck.

I stuffed mine into the bag I brought and Reed slung his over his shoulder as we headed out. Always the charmer, Reed winked at Penny and told her he'd be sure to bring her a coffee when we reported for duty tomorrow.

"I take tea in the afternoon, pumpkin," she sassed right back at him.

We both agreed that Penny was awesome. Walking out to the parking lot, our hands slung dangerously close to one another, almost as if we were both reaching for each other but also both unwilling to give into the urge. I stared straight ahead, sucking on my lip and just trying not to pay attention to the electricity firing off of my fingertips. *I had never felt this with Sean, I thought.*

Without warning, Reed scooped me up and slung me over his shoulder to join the T-shirts and swimsuit he had put there and took off running. I lost my breath for a second and then the blood rushed to my head as I hung upside down staring at his back and the heels of his shoes. His hands held tight over my upper legs, and I became acutely aware of every place on my body that was touching him. I started giggling uncontrollably, a bit unlike me.

"Reed, no no no, put me down," I begged, lying through my teeth. "Hey, my bag, my bag. I dropped my bag."

He just turned around on the balls of his feet and took off in the direction we came from, refusing to let me go. "I'll get it, not putting you down, nope. Not going to do it!" he said, laughing a bit himself.

He ran back to my bag, stopped and bent forward, telling me to grab the loop on my bag. "I can't!" I laughed uncontrollably. "I can't reach it."

"I'm going to drop you, then," he threatened, jokingly of course.

I reached down and snagged the end of my bag with my fingertips. "Got it, I got it," I yelled. He didn't wait a second longer and just took off running. I couldn't stop laughing, but I was also in wonder over how strong and fast he was. Not that I was very heavy, but he was running in a full sprint and I was clinging to the sides of his shirt, though it never felt like I slipped at all. He slowed to a jog when we got near the Jeep.

"Throw your bag in the back on the count of three, ready?" he said.

"Ready!" I responded, getting a better grip and swinging my bag back and forth to get it ready.

"One. Two. Three!" he yelled, and I let my bag fly. It hit the back of the seats and slid to the back floor next to some football binders and his secret hat.

"OK, I'm going to turn around, and you need to grab the handle," he said.

"OK," I said. "Or, you could just put me down?"

"No, ma'am. I'm afraid that is not an option," he said in an overly serious voice. This silly side of Reed was new, and I was truly loving it.

"Can you see it?" he asked.

"Yep, got it. Open," I said, pulling the door out wide enough for me to get in.

"OK, keep your head tucked," he said, grabbing a hold of my sides tightly and lowering me from his shoulder and into the Jeep so my feet dangled out the side and I sat facing him. I smoothed out the wild hairs from my head, pulled my shorts down a bit and straightened my suit straps, still giggling a bit and squeezing my eyes shut from the rush of blood from my face. I opened them up to see Reed throwing his shirts and suit in the back and then making a dramatic serious face as he stood right in front of me.

"Crisis averted, ma'am," he said, saluting me just like I had done to him so many times. I just smiled, blushing a little at the sudden close attention. Reed's cheesy smile slowly slid into a more natural one, a warm one. He stood there between my feet, so close I could smell the gum on his breath and the chlorine still wet on his shorts. He tilted his head to the side the slightest bit and reached up slowly to tuck a strand of hair behind my ear. I watched his hand come up to my face and then move back down to his side. I was unable to speak. Barely able to breathe. Reed inhaled deeply then looked down my legs. He reached down and scooped up my dangling limbs and slid me the right way in the seat, reaching across my body for the seat belt, stopping when his eyes were right at mine, his mouth inches from mine.

"My duty isn't over until you're completely safe," he said, his right dimple rising with a smirk. He held my gaze for what was probably two seconds but felt like a lifetime. He blinked to look down at the seatbelt holder and clicked my buckle in place, pulling it so it was tight against my skin. "There, we should be able to get you home now."

He stepped back and then closed the door carefully before walking around the back of the Jeep. I exhaled immediately, letting out all of the anxiety from holding my breath for so long. My heart beat was thumping in my ears. I looked in the side mirror to see Reed walking slowly and rubbing the back of his neck. Seconds later he was opening his door and getting in next to me. Without a word he turned the ignition, buckled his own belt and pulled us out on the main road.

I couldn't help but stare at him. The last 10 minutes of my life were a dream. The best dream I have ever had, but they seemed so surreal. I didn't care if Reed caught me staring, and, frankly, I could tell he felt my eyes on him. He was being overly cautious about driving, paying attention to everything on the road, looking every-where but at me. Wanting to break the tension, I leaned forward and turned on his stereo. I put on the oldies station just to get his attention a little, and I saw his face light up with a smile when Elvis started cranking from his speakers. Unable to help himself, he turned to look at me, raising his eyebrows up and down.

"Wow, you know all the latest hits, huh?" he joked.

"Hey, don't knock it 'til you try it, my friend," I defended. "I grew up listening to this stuff. It's the best!"

I sang along to a bit of "Hound Dog" and tapped my hand on the windowsill with the beat. Then, out of nowhere, I felt Reed's hand slide over my other hand that was resting on my leg. He grabbed it tightly, smiled at me and didn't let go until we pulled onto my street.

Reed had a workout scheduled that afternoon, so I didn't talk to him until we texted each other later that night. Feeling like I had a bit of an open door, I sent him a text first:

Hey, you around?

I left my phone on my desk while I busied myself with nonsense around my room, waiting for it to buzz back. A few minutes passed when I heard his reply.

Just got home. Good timing. What's up?

Hmmm. I didn't really have a question. I was just craving more of him, but I sure as hell wasn't going to say that.

Nothing, just wanted to thank you for all the rides this week. My car's supposed to be done tomorrow, might even be waiting for me when we get home. You mind taking me one more time?

While I was excited to have my own car again, I also wasn't ready to give up my commutes with Reed. He wrote back instantly:

You know it! Not sure I'm ready to let you drive yourself. You do drive like a woman, you know :-p

I knew he was kidding. But I was still going to ride his ass about being a pig anyhow.

Do you need me to kick your ass in the pool just to show you who's boss?

He wrote right back:

Uh, no. I know who the boss is, and I'm pretty sure it's you. I'm totally alright with that, tho.

I blushed at his words and my stomach did flips. I turned the light off in my room and plopped down on my bed, curling up to text him back.

Alright, glad we have that settled. So is that what all of the secret service style protection was about today?

I waited for him to take my bait. I wanted to talk about what today meant, where this was going and what he was thinking. But I also didn't want to come off whiny and typical. Minutes passed and I started to worry that I had scared him off. I was about to type something else to change the subject when his next text came in.

Secret service, no. I must admit that today's stunt was all about me figuring out how to flirt with you. Pathetic, I know. But you're…different. I know I've said it to you before, and you hear me, but I think you just dismiss what I'm saying, so let me be clear, Nolan. You. Are. Beautiful.

Holy shit! I shot up from my bed and started pacing the room reading his words over and over again. I wish I could print this out and tuck it away in my jewelry box. As it is, I'm never deleting it and I will read it, every hour for the rest of the night. I had no idea what to say. I just started typing, hoping the right thing would come out.

You really think that? I have never really seen myself that way. I…I wish you could see the face I'm making right now. You are pretty good at this flirting thing, Reed Johnson. You pretty much just took my breath away.

There. That's about as real as I could get. I was getting ready to plug my phone into its charger and call it a night when Reed sent one final text.

You think that's good. Just wait until you see what I have planned for tomorrow ;-)

Tomorrow would not come soon enough.

Reed picked me up at noon, an hour before our training shift. I wasn't quite ready when he arrived, so I ran to the door and let him in while I ran back to my room to grab a few things and finish my hair off in a braid. I was grabbing the can of spray sunscreen from my bathroom medicine cabinet when I felt the shadow of his presence fill the door frame.

He seemed so nervous, and it was refreshing since I always seemed to be the one acting completely idiotic. He had his hands stuffed in the pockets of his long cargo shorts and kept shifting his weight around, almost like he wasn't quite sure how to stand.

"You ok there, soldier," I said, passing by him and brushing against his chest as I passed. This small touch sent shivers through me, and for once, I could see he was affected to. I was pretty proud of myself.

Reed followed me back to the front of the house and we walked out to the porch. I locked the door and tossed my keys in my bag and turned around to see him semi talking to himself. It didn't look like real words, but I could tell his lips were moving. I just giggled a little and he saw that I caught him and turned for the Jeep, a bit embarrassed.

I took control of the stereo again when we hit the road and this time I turned it to the classic rock station he had been blaring before. It was amazing how he knew every song, often most of the words.

"What are you, some time traveler from the '70s?" I joked.

Reed smiled and just started to sing louder before he explained. "My dad loves this shit, and he played it in the garage every summer. It's all they play in the shops, which is where I spent A LOT of my childhood. When I stayed with my dad, I'd usually have to make visits to the lots with him and the mechanics were a lot like family to me."

I loved to watch him talk about his dad. Even though Buck was busy, it seemed like he always made time for his son. And it was clear he loved him, that they loved each other. It made me wonder why he lived primarily with his mom before he moved out here for high school.

"What's your mother like," I blurted out, not really framing the question how I wanted, but it was too late now.

Reed seemed to think about this for a while, scrunching his brows and taking a deep breath through his nose before he started.

"Well…she would like me to say that she's perfect. And I don't mean that in a mean way. I mean, that's what she wants everyone to think, that she's perfect," he started.

"I know my mom loves me, and she did a lot for me when I lived with her. She gave me anything I wanted, made sure that someone got me to anything I needed to get to. But, she wasn't always dialed in, if that makes sense. She's really into status. She remarried a few years ago. A guy named Sam Snyder. He owns a bunch of pharmacies in the East Valley. Millie Johnson-Snyder – she throws all of the high society parties and runs the charities and sits on the hospital board. Their house is on the side of some mountain and there are people that come in and out and do all the work, it's all sort of…I don't know, just sort of gross, do you know what I mean?"

I didn't know how to respond really. I was so far removed from the world he was describing that I couldn't even imagine having someone to cook, clean and drive for me let alone manage my life. I also didn't want to insult his mother.

"Well, she seems to be a woman who knows what she wants, and she seems to be confident and determined. Those seem like strong qualities," I shrugged and hoped it was the right thing to say.

"Yeah, they are. But living with my dad, it's just more…I don't know, more real. I mean, I know he always has a girlfriend, and sometimes he marries one of them. But, he still takes out his own trash. He has an assistant, Rose. She has been working for him for 20 years now. She comes to the house and helps, but it's never like she's working for him, like a servant. She's more like my aunt, who gives my dad shit for being lazy and not putting his shoes in the right place or ironing his shirts the right way or eating enough vegetables. I think that's why I wanted to come live with him so badly. I craved a bit of normalcy."

Reed paused for a bit, and then he looked over at me and grabbed my hand in his. "I'd give anything to have the kind of home you do."

His eyes were right back on the road again, but he maintained his grip on my hand. I just smiled at him, understanding, and squeezed it back a little. "I am lucky," I said, realizing it for maybe the first time ever.

———

Once we got to the center it was all business. We both headed for our locker rooms and changed and reported to Todd for duty. He broke everyone down into assignment locations and reviewed the rotation. "Every 20 minutes, you'll hear the whistle. That means switch. We don't like anyone to get complacent, so by constantly moving, it gives you a new situation to watch over. It's going to get crowded, folks, so let's keep those heads above water and all breathing, OK?"

Everyone seemed pretty excited to start the season. There were six or seven of us new to the team, many that I recognized from the testing. There were a few girls who looked like college coeds. They were enamored with Reed, which gave me a familiar pang of jealousy. Reed was by far the best-looking guy at the pool. It helped that he was more than six feet tall and built like the letter Y. There were a few other good-looking guys, but they weren't in Reed's class. Only one, who I learned was Tyler, Todd's younger brother, was even close.

Reed and I spent most of the day across the pool from each other. Even though we were trained to keep our eyes on the water at all times, I still stole a glance at Reed here and there. I know he looked at me, too, because once when he was sitting up on the chair by the diving boards he stuck his tongue out at me. I laughed and went back to pacing off the deck and telling kids to "quit running."

We rotated into short breaks every hour and a half or so. I took mine with Tyler, and we sat up at the counter, behind the snack bar.

"Here, it's on me," Tyler said, tossing an orange Gatorade at me.

"Oh, thanks. It's ok, I brought cash," I said, sort of uncomfortable.

"I was kidding," he smiled. "We get free drinks. Part of the gig."

I just nodded. That was pretty cool, I thought. I twisted it open and took a big chug, stopping myself before I let it get out of hand. I was thirsty, but I didn't want a cramp. Tyler slid down to sit next to me and reached out his hand.

"I'm Tyler, and you are?" he asked. His confidence reminded me of Buck. He was the sort of guy that would run for fraternity president in college and then move on to some Fortune 500 company and move up the ranks quickly. I caught a glance at Reed in the distance from behind Tyler and he was not happy.

"Oh, I'm Nolan. Nice to meet you," I said, politely but quickly, careful not to invite too much conversation.

"Nice to meet you, too," he said, looking out at the pool and pulling the towel from around his neck. "You'll love working here. It's good money and the days go by super quickly. It's my third year. It helps that my brother runs the place, I sort of get to skip some of the interview process." He winked. It felt a little cocky, but not overtly. There was something a little too shiny about Tyler, and I couldn't quite put my finger on it.

We sat in silence for most of the rest of the break, then when the whistle blew for the next rotation, he caught my arm before I left the snack bar. "Hey, Nolan. If you want, some of us go out after the late shifts some times. Would be great if you came along," he looked hopeful.

I just nodded and shrugged. I didn't know how to handle this. I was just getting used to the idea that the boy of my dreams might be giving me the time of day. There was no way I was prepared to handle any type of showdown. *Slow down there, tiger. Don't get ahead of yourself, no one is fighting for you,* my subconscious put me back in my place.

"Thanks, maybe sometime. I've got a lot going on," I lied. It seemed to be enough. He just smiled and walked away.

When I looked back over at Reed, he was walking in for his break and staring at Tyler with a hard expression. Almost as if to lay a claim on me, he smacked my butt as I walked by. It was probably the most intimate contact we'd had, but it also felt like I was his running back or left tackle. "Sorry, coach, I'll get a hustle on," I said, making a joke out of it. *Always making a joke.*

The day flew by. Tyler was right about that, time passed quickly here. We all finished our shutdown duties, rolling up misters and pool ropes and hanging everything for the next morning. A few staff members were doing trick dives from the diving boards and cannonballs into the deep end. This was the fun time, I guess.

I didn't even hear Reed coming up behind me, but suddenly I felt my legs get swept up and he started marching towards the water. I hadn't been more than ankle deep all day and had heard the water was still pretty cold for the season.

"Reed Johnson, what are you doing?" I said, trying to sound tough. Upon reflection, probably not my best defensive move. He just smiled and took off in a full-on sprint, leaping from the edge and crashing us both in the water. I was completely submerged, but I came back up, still in his arms. He had me held snugly to his chest. I was having a hard time catching my breath from the shock of the cold. I pushed the dripping wetness from my hair back and reached up to clear my eyes before opening them.

"You ass!" I yelled at him, slapping his chest. And at that, he dunked me one more time. "Quit it!"

"Not until you quit calling me an ass," he smiled.

"Fine, I quit. But you're going to have to deal with me cranking the heater on and forcing you to put the top on the Jeep," I said in my whiniest voice possible. The music cranked up a little louder and suddenly everyone was in the pool. Apparently the staff always spent the end of the day goofing off and blowing off steam. *I was going to like it here, I thought.*

I started to get goosebumps on my arms and chest that were exposed from the water. I think Reed could feel me shivering a bit, because he suddenly held me a little closer. I took full advantage and snuggled in under his chin, my face right at his chest. My eyes were out of his sight, so I could look at him all I wanted without getting caught. I admired his tan biceps and perfect abs. I noticed a thin string bracelet on his right wrist. I touched it a little. "What's this?" I said, chattering a little while I talked.

"Oh, that's from my cousin, Shelley. She's 7, and she lives in California. I guess you could say we're sort of pen pals," he joked, lifting his arm so I could get a better look at the bracelet. She had braided it and put tiny beads throughout, the same as our school colors.

"That's pretty sweet," I said, smiling up at him.

"Yeah, it is," he said softly.

Reed just stared down at me, shifting back and forth from eye to eye because we were so close. The music and screaming from other swimmers in the background started to fade out. It was the same sort of feeling I got when I was about to pass out, but I knew my head felt fine. Reed leaned his head forward, pressing his forehead to mine, closing his eyes for a bit. He just sort of spun us, ever-so slowly in a circle, with our lips breaths apart. My lips were tingling, almost numb, but not from the cold water. I bit my bottom lip to try to stop the twitching and keep myself from shaking. I felt Reed shift, getting an even stronger grip on me, somehow holding me closer, which didn't seem possible.

I was frozen, the tip of my nose touching Reed's, as we swayed slowly in the water to some sappy pop song about standing in the rain. I knew the song, it was one of my favorites. But ask me the words right now, and I'd only be able to spit out gibberish. I bit my lip again, licking it a little from this unbelievable, beautiful suspense. And then Reed's lips were touching mine. Not hard, but so incredibly softly. It was barely a kiss, but it was still the best one I'd ever have. He tilted his head up, just barely, taking my top lip between both of his and leaving them there for a few seconds, sucking me in faintly so I felt the tips of his teeth.

When he pulled back, he leaned his face to look at me, still cradling me in his arms. I opened my eyes slowly and couldn't hide my smile. I wanted to cry, the type of cry from a release when you've waited so long for something. He just reached up and brushed water from my face with his thumb and stared at me until finally breaking our silence. "You have no idea how long I've been waiting to do that," he smiled gently.

"You have no idea…" I paused. "Well, there's just so much you have no idea about, Reed."

He walked us over to the steps and we exited the water, his index finger looped with mine as he pulled me behind him. We both changed and headed out to the Jeep. He didn't even wait a second before holding my hand as we drove away.

———

When Reed pulled up to my house, I was both excited and disappointed to see my good old friend the Oldsmobile sitting in the carport. My dad walked out to greet us and flinched for a second when he may have caught a glimpse of us holding hands.

"Hey, sweetie. Buck's guys dropped this off earlier. Boy, she purrs like a dream now. They really did a number," he said, flipping the hood up and urging me to take a look. *Like I have any idea what I'm looking at.* Reed put his hand on my back as we all looked at the engine and listened to my dad go on and on. I loved the thrill of feeling his touch. But I also didn't want to have this conversation with my father. Not tonight, anyhow.

Reed's phone rang, and he stepped back for a second to talk. I heard him asking what time and saying he could get there in 30 minutes. Finally, he was back at my side.

"Hey, it's coach. He has some meeting lined up, something with a scout. My dad's meeting me there. I'm sorry, I gotta go," he said, honestly looking disappointed.

"It's ok, go! I've got a car to test drive," I winked at him.

"Oh no, just try not to drive like a 'woman,'" he said, air quoting. I kicked dirt at him a bit and gave him a playful shove. When my dad wasn't looking, he leaned down and kissed my cheek before flipping his keys in his hand and heading to his Jeep.

My father saw him leaving and yelled after him. "Reed, son. Please give my thanks to your dad, ok? Really, this was an awful nice gesture."

"You bet, Mr. Len…Rich!" Reed yelled back, pointing his finger in the air when he remembered by dad's request for the first-name basis.

I turned to look over the engine some more with my dad and he put his arm around me. "That's a good kid," he said, sort of insinuating that I had his approval, but without actually having the conversation.

"Yeah, he's one of the good ones," I reaffirmed.

"So, you wanna take this puppy for a spin," my dad smiled at me, closing the hood.

"Thought you'd never ask," I said. "But I'm driving!"

My dad winced, still not too good at being my passenger, but he tossed me the keys and climbed into the car. I got in and turned the key to start it right up. The engine made a sound that had never been heard in our family before, and my dad and I both just looked at each other, our eyebrows raising. Then we both laughed. I backed out to turn around and we drove it all the way to the MicNic burger joint for milkshakes. We got an extra one for my mom and made our way home. A perfect day.

15. A Proper Date

REED CALLED me after his dinner meeting with the scout. He wasn't supposed to say anything about it, but he spilled his guts anyway. I was honored to be so trusted. Reed was attracting attention from more schools than he had expected, though I wasn't really surprised. His impromptu meeting was with the quarterback coach for Stanford. His grades were impressive and, to be honest, I don't think Stanford fancied the idea of having Reed attend another school in their conference.

By the time Reed was a junior or senior in college, he could truly have grown into something spectacular. I wondered at the fact that I got to see him mature, see him in his beginning. I also allowed my mind to fantasize about a college world that included a Reed *and* me in it. I didn't let myself dwell there long because I knew I was being naïve, but a month ago I never would have thought I could say I knew what Reed's lips felt like, and well, now I could.

Reed had insisted that we spend tonight celebrating his great meeting and going on our first real date. He was leaving work early to meet with his coach and throw some passes to some promising new receivers now that Devin and Cole were graduated, so I was going to drive my newly made-over Olds. Suddenly, this car that I had spent a lifetime loathing held a special place in my heart. The kind gesture and its connection to Reed played on my perspective. I think my dad was sort of regretting handing the keys over to me permanently now, too. He did a little joy riding on the desert roads last night and said something about 'really opening her up on the open road.'

Reed said he didn't want to waste his first real date with me on a typical dinner and a movie, so he had instructed me to pack clothes that were casual, comfortable and "very Nolan." He also insisted I throw the Nikes in my bag. "Lots of walking," he said.

I must have tried on 15 different combinations of clothes that just days ago all seemed fine. I finally settled on my hip-slung cut-off shorts, double tank tops and plain white socks with my tennies. I had a clip in my bag that I could use to keep my hair up and makeup was always minimal, though I was eager to look more adult lately.

I scarfed down a peanut butter sandwich with some milk, locked up the house and skipped to my car, tossing my bag in the back seat. The engine roared right up for me, a sound I was sure would make my smile beam for months, and I backed out onto our main road.

Driving alone on the stretch of desert highway was finally how I pictured it would be, before my first solo trip was cut short by my car's former insides. I sang out loud all the way into town, rolling my window up as I pulled into the aquatics center, not wanting to draw the attention of the dozens of barely dressed teenagers that were parking around me. I knew I was a staff member and the same age as many of the girls that hung out at the center during the summer, but somehow I still felt inadequate. So many of them looked like, were built like and talked like Tatum. It was going to take me a while to stop trying to measure up to something that I still couldn't believe Reed no longer wanted.

Reed was sitting on the counter talking to Penny when I walked in.

"Uh, I believe she's two minutes late, Penny. Make sure you take note of that," he winked, snapping his towel at me as I walked by and rolled my eyes at Penny.

Penny was clearly always on the woman's side, as she piped up right away, tapping on her watch. "According to my watch, she still has three minutes, sport," she winked right back at him.

I walked through the women's locker room where I stashed my bag for later and met Reed on the pool deck side. He wasn't so subtle as he came over and planted the softest kiss on my right cheek. "I missed you," he whispered. I melted.

Our intimate moment wouldn't last long as Todd called out stations and we all headed out to them. The hours flew by again, and I seemed to always be taking my breaks with Tyler. I was more comfortable with him now as during our first break he asked me how long Reed and I had been going out. He must have witnessed our kiss in the pool yesterday. I told him we hadn't been dating long, though I really wasn't sure what to call us or how to answer that question. Either way, I thought Reed would be fine with my response. I got the feeling he wasn't too keen on Tyler.

I saw Reed head for the locker room at about 2:30 and then come back out dressed in his varsity practice shirt and long sports shorts. He had his secret ASU hat on and slid along the deck in his flip flops over to the chair I was stationed at before he left.

"Hey, you better hurry or you're going to be late," I chided him.

"Well, good thing for me they can't really run receiving drills without someone to throw to them," he smiled. "So, you wanna just meet me at my place? We can leave your car at my house and I'll drive."

He had a devilish grin, bewitching me. "Sure... that seems the best way to go for this... wait, where are we going again?" I tried to bait him but he was having none of it.

"Ohhhh, you will just have to wait and see," he said. "You keep this up and I'm apt to drive you around blindfolded for an hour first just to punish you."

"Oh god please don't do that, or else I'll be apt to throw up all over your Jeep," I wasn't even kidding.

Not wanting to put on a show or get me in any trouble in front of the patrons, Reed just brushed his hands on my shoulder and tipped on his sunglasses before leaving. I watched him pull away from beyond the fence and in my mind started counting down until I saw him next for our official first couple outing.

While the first part of the day raced, the last hour of my shift seemed to tick by so slowly. At one point, I started counting people that went off the high dive, adding decimals for every bounce they took from the board just to make it interesting.

The center was staying open late tonight for lessons, so I didn't have to wind up the ropes and spray the decks like I normally would. When my hours were up, I raced through the locker room, hopped in a shower and did my best to make myself presentable. *He likes you just like this, I reminded myself as I turned from side to side in the distorted bathroom mirror.*

I punched out for the day and told Penny to have a great night. She stopped me and said she'd walk out with me since her day was done, too.

She grabbed her purse, walked around the counter and we were on our way. Penny was extremely short, but she had a spirit and a certain look that warned people she could pack a mighty punch. She was digging for her keys in her purse as we were in the parking lot when she held out a piece of gum to me.

"Here, take one. Hot date tonight, I hear," she winked.

"How'd you know?" I asked, taking the gum. I was grateful. I was nervous as it was, and the Doritos I had during my break were still hanging around a little in my breath.

"That fella of yours? Well, he sure does like you an awful lot," she said, smiling as we started our walk again. I swooned a bit at her words, but had to ask.

"What do you mean," I was curious.

"He got to work a little early today, so we had some time to chat. He was asking me for my opinion on some things he has planned for your date, said it was an important one," she smiled and elbowed my side a little.

I grinned back. "Yeah, it's our first official date. I sort of spent two years chasing him, you know," I said, sort of wanting some credit, but I wasn't sure what for.

"Well, you done caught him," she said as she opened her door.

"Have a good night tonight; and you tell me all about it tomorrow, ok?"

"You know it!" I said as she shut her door and buckled up.

———

I got to my car and threw my bag of wet clothes in the back. I figured I would just run everything through the drier later tonight to freshen things up.

I pulled out onto the main road and started right back where I left off with the singing. I wondered if my dad would be willing to help me save up for a newer stereo, one that I could program with my favorite songs and hook into my phone.

As I drove through the desert, my panic started to set in just a little more. I sat up tall to catch a glimpse of my face in the rearview mirror, scanning for pimples, stray eyebrow hairs (thankfully my eyebrow had grown back), bent lashes, anything that would make Reed run for the hills. I pulled the gum from my mouth, twisting it in a receipt that was in my cup holder, and smelled my breath about 20 times, worried that the Doritos were still lingering. Then I started to question my outfit, thinking that I should swing by my house first. I had nearly convinced myself to do just that when I realized I only had 10 minutes from the time I told Reed I would be at his house. I didn't want to be late.

My stomach was swirling. I was starting to lose the feeling in my hands, so I started shaking them out one at a time. I couldn't seem to get a full breath, and my eyes were watering at the edges a little from my fear. I was pretty sure I was having a panic attack. I stopped at the light in the center of Coolidge and waited for it to turn green, slightly thankful for this small pause in time. I actually started talking to myself.

"You are freaking out for nothing. This is nothing new. You have been out with Reed dozens of times. You have wanted this for so long. Now you are alone with him, and he wants you to be there. Deep breath, Nolan. Deep breath."

My pep talk seemed to work as my fingers suddenly had feeling once again. As the light turned green, I pulled through the intersection slowly, driving through town to the outskirts and onto the long road that led to Reed's house. I could see the tall trees in the distance, and all I could hear in my ears was the beating of my heart.

I turned down his driveway and took one last deep breath as I pulled through the tree-lined lane. I saw the back of his Jeep parked up ahead by the house. I was a little confused when I saw another car pulled up behind it. My head knew it was familiar, but something inside me was keeping the recognition out of the picture. I felt my head start to shake "no" before the realization fully hit me. I was nearly pulled up behind both vehicles when Reed and Tatum came into view. Reed's back was to me, and he was holding Tatum tightly, stroking her hair.

I punched the brakes, and my car squeaked a little as I stopped. They both turned to look at me, still in an embrace. My face stung, and there was no stopping the tears that were already running down my cheeks, leaving hot red streaks in their wake. My hair had slung forward from my abrupt stop, and Reed's eyes were drilling right into mine. His facial expression was ghostlike, and I barely made out the word 'no' as he shook his head and lunged towards me.

"No, no, no, no, no," I screamed, rolling up my window, tears flowing full on now. Reed was walking quickly towards me with his hands waving, and his face pale white. I made the mistake of stealing a glance at Tatum, who was softly smiling, almost like she was sorry for me.

Reed was coming closer, but I had managed to muster enough common sense to put my car in reverse. I was slowly pulling away when he lunged for the hood, smacking it hard with both hands. "Nolan, stop! You don't understand, you don't understand." He was yelling, his face red and his muscles fully flexed. He was yelling at me, angry. Angry at me?

My emotions were a roller coaster. I flung the gears into park, swung my door open so wide it actually came back to close on my leg as I stepped out. It would leave a terrible bruise I knew, but I couldn't seem to stop to care or check on my leg right now. I was swinging between heartbrokenly crushed and furious.

"What's to understand? I just saw you, holding...her!" I said, gesturing to her like she was some tossed aside piece of beef at a cattle show. "How could you? How could you!"

I was spewing venom now, and I couldn't be stopped. "What does this mean, Reed? Are you *with* her?"

He just stood there. Silent. Without words. He frowned slightly, looking down at his feet and then looking back up to me, shrugging. "Nolan, it's just...it's just that. Oh, it's complicated, ok? You have to believe me that I didn't want to hurt you..."

I cut him off at that, raising my hand to say 'stop.' This was it, I was broken now. And I wasn't sure there would ever be a way to come back from this. I got back into my car, and just before I closed my door, I looked him right in the eyes, seething. "Go to fucking hell!"

I spun the car around and allowed myself one last look at him in the rearview mirror. Tatum was walking up behind him, reaching out to take his hand. And still, he just stood there. Silent.

———

I made it home somehow in one piece, avoiding the urge to crash into everything I saw. I didn't want to hurt myself, but I wanted to exhale this pain boiling inside me. I didn't know anything could ever hurt this badly. I managed to get inside my house before my parents were home, giving me an hour to process alone in the comfort of my room. My phone kept buzzing with texts from Reed.

Nolan, please forgive me.

Nolan, I am so sorry. I didn't mean to hurt you.

Please don't hate me.

I finally shot one back after his fifteenth message:

Leave me alone. I am done.

I shut my phone off and threw it into my backpack, crashing face first on my bed and curling into a ball around my favorite pillow. My tears stopped. I felt numb, and for a moment, I thought maybe I had imagined it all. But just when I would start to convince myself I would close my eyes, and as if I were watching a close up, I would see Reed's hand cupping the back of Tatum's head. Their bodies so close. Her face, not at all like this was a trick, but just looking at me with pity. She was pitying me.

I was going to be sick.

I ran to my bathroom and flung open the lid, dry heaving until I heard my mother's keys on the counter in the kitchen and the sound of her high heels treading down the hall in my direction.

"Honey, are you sick? Are you ok?" she said, opening the door and finding me on the floor. As soon as I saw her, the tears started up again.

"Oh, honey. What's wrong?" she said, pulling me into a hug. The only hug that could ever seem to fix anything. Somehow, though, I knew this time my hurt was not meant to be fixed. No. This one was mine to keep. A reminder. A lesson.

She walked me to my room and laid me on my bed, sitting next to me and stroking my hair. I just looked at her, quivering a little with tiny sobs, trying to make them stop. When I finally was able to hold my breath steady for a few moments, I just uttered the truth. "My heart hurts, mommy. Really bad."

She just leaned over and held me tightly again, stroking my hair and rocking me back and forth. "I know sweetheart. I know."

She didn't lecture me. She didn't warn me, or say anything to prevent me from loving a boy ever again. She never even uttered Reed's name. She understood what it was to be a girl with a broken heart. She knew that even though I was 16, what I felt was very real, as real as it would be if I were 37.

She sat there with me for an hour until I finally felt human. We heard the sounds of my dad's truck pulling into the driveway and my mom kissed my forehead and told me that she'd bring me in a plate later. She pulled my door closed and met my dad in the hallway. I could hear them talking, and was so relieved when she was covering for me, knowing that my dad would react to my heartache as a father would.

"Something she ate at work, maybe? She's pretty tired from

being sick just now. I told her I'd check on her later, let's just sit outside tonight for dinner. Give her some quiet," and then they were in the kitchen and soon after I was asleep.

————

The harsh realities of the next morning were upon me. I had to get ready for my shift at work. My shift with Reed. I needed to take control of the power. I packed my bag and drove in for the morning shift, five hours earlier than I needed to be there for the afternoon. Penny was a little surprised when she saw me walk up.

"Sweetie, showing up awful early, aren't you?" she sassed.

I exhaled and plopped my bag up on the counter, leveling with her.

"Penny, I need your help," I pleaded.

"Sure, whatcha need? Help with the timesheet again?" she asked, getting out a form from her desk.

"No...I think I need to change my schedule. I'll work midnight if I have to, but I just can't work my normal hours. I can't be here... with Reed," I said slowly, softly.

Her eyes shot up as she called me back to her desk, pulling out the master schedule. "Well, I'm not so sure what happened between yesterday and today, but I know that look in your eye. I've been there, so let's see how I can help," she said as I sat down next to her.

We went through the weeks and were able to move me to mornings most days. There were a few days that I would still be on his schedule, but none for the next two weeks or so. When we were done, she patted my knee and grabbed my hand for just a second.

"I know what you're feeling, and I know it probably feels like a bullet went through your gut, but I promise darlin'... it gets better," she smiled. I gave her a hug, partly to hide the tears welling up in my eyes.

I left her desk and headed to the locker room to change and join the morning shift. I checked my phone one more time to see that I only had a few more texts and missed calls from Reed. He seemed to be stopping his pursuit, which both made me sad and relieved.

I joined the morning group, which were mostly college-aged staff members who were trying to get their work out of the way early before summer classes. I noticed that Tyler was also here for the morning shift. He spotted me right away and gave me a little shrug, asking what I was doing here. I just shrugged back and mouthed that I would explain later. Probably a mistake since I wasn't really up for talking about Reed, especially with Tyler.

By the time my break rolled around, Tyler was right there next to me. I grabbed a drink and slid into one of the sling-back chairs stashed in the shade by the snack counter. Tyler sunk in next to me seconds later. "Fancy meeting you here," he said, holding out his sports drink as if to toast the day with me. I clinked my plastic bottle to his and just smiled.

"Bottoms up," I said, taking a drink.

"So, this is a new time for you, isn't it?" he shot right out of the gate.

"Yeah," I said, pulling my knees up and exhaling a little loudly.

"OK, not up to talking about it I guess," he said, nudging me a little.

I sat there soaking in the awkwardness. I knew a lot of time was passing, but I wasn't exactly sure what I wanted to say, if I even wanted to say anything.

"I had a fight with Reed," I just blurted out, surprising myself a little. Immediately I wanted to retract it, but instead I just made it worse. "Well, not really a fight. I just saw something. Maybe I didn't. Either way, it wasn't good. Whatever I saw was bad no matter what it meant, and I just can't…"

I just turned to stare at him, shrugging again. He reached his bottle over again for another toast. I reciprocated. "I get it. We're assholes," he took a drink, paused and looked out over the pool. "You deserve better."

I laughed a small awkward laugh and then we sat there in silence the rest of the time. Finally, comfortable silence. I had two or three more breaks with Tyler before my shift was done. He didn't push me to talk more about Reed, but he was exceptionally respectful and friendly. I got the impression he was trying hard to distract me.

When my shift was over, I rushed through the locker room, not changing completely and leaving my suit on just to speed things up. I wanted to get through the parking lot and on the road before Reed arrived. I was rushing by Penny's desk when I snagged the handle of my bag on the door to the supply room, ripping it open and dumping my contents all around the entrance. I hurried on my hands and knees picking everything up, swearing a little under my breath. Penny rushed around the counter to help me, handing me a plastic bag for my things.

"Here, honey, take this," she said. I looked up, fighting the tears in my eyes. The stress of the situation was getting to me.

"Thanks," I said, shoving my clothes, brush, wallet and anything else in as quickly as I could. I managed to get everything picked up and was heading out the door when I saw the parking lights of Reed's Jeep flashing off as he locked the door. I just stopped in my tracks, clutching my torn bag, the plastic makeshift one and my things. I was a mess, and I knew it. I wanted to disappear, but I knew that this was like a bandage. I was going to have to rip it off to move on.

Reed stutter stepped when he saw me, pausing for a minute, his eyes full of sleeplessness and sadness. His hair was its usual disheveled mess, but adorable all the same. He was slowly approaching me and I found my knees starting to get weak. I slowly started to walk forward, avoiding his gaze, making my way to my car.

"Nolan?" he said, almost as if he was surprised I would try to ignore him. "Where are you going? Did you quit?"

I just stopped and turned to face him, staring blankly. "No. I didn't quit."

I turned around and started again for my car when I felt his hand on my shoulder. "Nolan, stop. We need to talk."

"I don't want to talk, Reed. I'm tired. I want to go home," I said, turning to leave again. This time he reached for my hand, but I recoiled. His touch hurt so much.

"Where are you going?" he was starting to sound angry, almost desperate.

I turned to face him, still holding my rag tag bundle of belongings close to my chest, fighting to maintain my breathing. "I switched to mornings."

And with that, he let me go.

———

Sarah welcomed me inside with her typical greeting. "Come on in, beee yatch," she said, hugging me with one arm.

I needed to fill her in on everything, but I really didn't know where to begin. I texted her during one of my breaks and told her I was in desperate need for a little best friends time. She called Sienna and Becky over and they were all waiting there for me.

I stashed my pile of sorry crap in the corner of Sarah's room and we all headed into the kitchen. Sarah opened the fridge and started digging around for something. "Cookie dough. Always fixes everything," she said, slapping the roll of raw dough down on the counter and then slicing it open with a knife. She dug out four spoons from a drawer and gave one to each of us and we sat there on the stools around her kitchen island digging in. I have to admit, the chunks of chocolate and the salted sugar goo was easing my pain just a little. But not for long.

"OK, so spill it," Sarah said. Always a way with words, this one.

I spent the next hour bringing my friends up to speed. They held their hands over their hearts when I told them about how Reed kissed me, but I warned them not to get too comfortable. "Oh I'm going to break your hearts, girls. Get ready for it."

By the time I was done, Sarah was dropping swear words like a paper boy serves up paper. "What a fucking whore," she yelled, slamming the dishwasher door shut on our dirty spoons.

Becky was already conspiring with her, coming up with ways we could get back at Tatum for once again derailing a future of me and Reed. They were quickly on Facebook, trying to dig up dirt. Sienna, thankfully, my thoughtful friend, sat back with me and just held my hand.

"Nolan, I'm so sorry. I know how much you wanted this," she said. "But…isn't it possible that there's more to the story? I mean, Reed doesn't seem like the kind of guy to be a player, right?"

I nodded, sniffling a little. She was right. And I had that thought, too. But every time I wanted to call him and find out his version, I saw his lips carefully brushing along the side of Tatum's neck as he held her close. I couldn't even remember now if I had imagined that part, but something deep down told me I hadn't.

I heard Sarah howling in the living room and we both joined her and Becky. She pulled up a picture of Tatum making out with some other guy, dated just a few weeks ago. "See! I knew she wasn't just into Reed. I'm going to ruin her!" she gave out like a battle cry.

But I stopped her. I walked up and flipped the computer closed. Shaking my head, I sat down at the desk and just buried my face in my hands for a minute. Deep breath.

"I love you guys for wanting to avenge my broken heart, I truly do," I paused. "But…I honestly have just got to get over this. I have spent half of my teenage years…high school…pining after a stupid boy and letting the same girl walk all over me. I think…."

I rubbed my head and stood up to look at them all, just waiting for me to give them the order. "I think I just need to stop. I need to make a turn, turn right or something like that. Pick a different path. Pick a new damn boy to pine after, know what I mean?"

They all sort of looked at each other for a minute, quiet. Finally Sarah broke the silence, as I knew she would. "Party, bitches!"

———

I had finished out that week and the next week on the morning shifts. It was hard at first to get used to getting up so early, but my body was adjusting. I actually liked getting done with work early. I was able to head to the gym for open volleyball practice and take out some aggression, practice my hitting and get in some exercise. It also helped that I was able to leave the campus before Reed showed up for his evening workouts.

My mom never brought up my meltdown again. Only once did she stop me in the hall, pull me into a hug, and whisper "it gets easier." My dad only asked about Reed once. In a way I thought he knew it was best not to, sensed it was taboo. He wondered why we weren't hanging out, and I explained that I had different shifts, had to fill in on mornings. A lie, but a small one. And I think my dad was really happier not hearing about his baby girl's broken heart.

Tyler worked both afternoons and mornings. Sometimes he would slip up and mention Reed, but he also was pretty respectful. He always took his breaks with me, but never flirted. I got to work early a few times to see him practice diving, his sport of choice. He was pretty amazing at it. The thought of flinging myself headfirst from a platform that high just sounded mental to me. I could tell he liked it when I was there, showing off a little. But still, he always managed to keep things 'friendly.'

It was the Friday before the big party weekend. Sarah had planned a party with her sister, Calley. It was going to be a night-time desert party, Calley's last before heading to college in August. I was actually a little excited about it, too. I needed to do something normal, on my own. *Test my strength, I thought.*

I was telling Tyler about the tradition of our desert parties during our last break when I sort of accidentally invited him. I told him he should join us for one sometime, and he said he was free that night. It was sort of throwing a hiccup in my 'stand-on-your-own' plan, but I made it pretty clear that he could join me and my friends, hang out with *us.*

I was giving Tyler directions in the parking lot when I felt Reed's presence behind me. The smell of him was familiar, his shadow familiar. I heard him clear his throat a little as he was walking up and I turned ever so slightly to see his face. He gave me a slight sideways grin, but it still seemed sad.

"What's up, Tyler? Hey...Nolan," he said, swallowing a little as he stopped right at the entrance.

I just shrugged and smiled, putting my pen in my bag and looking for my keys so I could make my escape.

"You working the afternoon today, Ty?" he said to Tyler. *Ty? Since when were they friends?*

"Nah, I've got some shit to do today, man. But hey, maybe I'll see you later," Tyler said, waving the small piece of paper I just gave him with directions and stuffing it in his pocket. "Talk to you later, Nolan," he said, touching my shoulder a little when he stepped off the curb and put his sun glasses on, heading for his car.

I was starting to leave, too, when Reed spoke. "What was that all about," he seemed almost jealous.

"Oh," I waited. "Just one of Sarah's desert parties, you know. Calley's last one. Thought he might think it was cool. Really nothing other than one more person to hang out." *Damn it, why couldn't I lie to him!*

He just exhaled and shook his head, looking to the side in the distance. I hated him for breaking me, but god did I love him, too. Finally turning his head to me he scrunched his brow a little. "Are we ever going to talk, Noles?" he was genuine.

I just stood there, almost speaking, then stopping myself. I took a deep breath. "I don't know, Reed. I don't know if I have it in me. I know you didn't mean to see me get hurt. But I also know that whatever you have to say…well, it's going to suck. Like, reallllllly suck. And I don't know if I'm conditioned enough to take another blow right now, if that's ok."

That was it. I left it all out there on the field for him. Honesty. That was all I could promise him, and all I'd ever given him. He gave me a crooked smile and went to reach for my cheek, but I stepped back quickly, holding up my keys. "I gotta get to Sarah's. Have a good shift."

I cried all the way to her house. She had her work cut out for her when she pulled me into her bathroom and started to work on my hair and make up. She twisted my hair up in a backwards French braid, letting the long parts on the top and side curl down to frame my face a little. It was the perfect style for a summer party in the desert, nice and cool.

Sienna, Becky and Sean came over before the sun set. I hadn't seen Sean in a few weeks and felt bad at the awkward position I was sure he was in. He and Becky had started dating officially, and they were perfect together. They both had similar styles and finished each other's sentences. I could tell Sean was smitten, too, because he would pick her up and carry her around like a back pack, smiling around the house when he didn't think anyone was looking.

We were all getting ready to pile into the back of Sean's truck when he stopped me outside to talk. "Are you ok?" he said, bending down to look me straight in the eyes. At first I nodded yes, but then I shifted into no. I couldn't lie to this boy either. *Damn it!*

"No, I'm really not, Sean. I'm just so confused," I said.

He took a deep breath, looking up for a bit before settling back on my face. "I'm not going to lie, Nolan. It's not good. Tatum is just so…" I stopped him.

"I know, you don't have to tell me how she is, Sean. I know," I said, putting my hand on his heart. He really was one of the good ones.

"OK, but you have to know…you are all Reed asks about, Nolan. I just don't want you thinking that he did this on purpose…"

I smiled a little, but it was fake. The girls came outside just then, so our conversation ended. We piled into the truck and Sarah unzipped her duffel bag to reveal all the liquor she had stolen from her parents bar. They had parties frequently and were always ordering things in bulk. Sarah would slip a bottle here and there so they never noticed. I wasn't planning on drinking tonight, still a bit too nervous to walk on that wild side. I knew Sienna would be my partner in crime. Goody two shoes 'til the end, her and I.

The truck kicked up dust when Sean pulled a sharp right into the desert. It was about 20 minutes in on a hidden dirt road. But there it was. The picnic tables were already full of people. Bon fires were lit, headlights were on and radios were blasting.

"Way to be late to your own party," I yelled at Sarah over the noise.

"Bullshit," she said. "Party doesn't start until I get here!" Sean stopped the truck and Sarah hollered as she stood up on the edge of the bed of the truck, holding a bottle of vodka in her hand.

"Who's drinking with me tonight?" she asked. It didn't take long for a very built, very tall senior from the football team to help her from the truck and carry her over to a table for some making out and underage delinquency.

I shook my head a little as I slid off the tailgate with Sienna. "Shall I grab you one of our usuals?" I asked. She just nodded and smiled. I headed to the front seat cooler to grab a couple of Diet Cokes.

I was glad my hair was up. And as much as I thought it was a risky idea at first, I was also glad I listened to Sarah and wore one of her bikini tops with my cut-off shorts. It was really hot out.

Sienna and I sat on the tailgate of Sean's truck, swinging our feet back and forth. It was the first time in days that I felt almost normal. I wasn't happy, but I also wasn't sad. I let my mind go, looking behind me from time to time to see how Becky and Sean were getting on sitting on the hood of his truck, kissing and giggling. While I could easily resent their happiness, I couldn't help but smile at it.

Sarah came over to grab my hands and dragged me out to the middle of the camp ground to dance to one of our favorite songs. She had made me learn this simple hip-hop routine that the cheerleaders did during basketball games. It was a great Usher song, with a really strong base. I laughed as I slung my head back and looked up at the stars while we kicked and moved our hips. I was pretty sure I looked ridiculous, but she had promised me I didn't when we practiced in her room earlier.

Sienna had joined us now, which made me laugh even harder. For a girl who was so dang musical, she had absolutely no dancing ability. She kept looking at me and shrugging, asking if she was getting it right, which only made me laugh harder. I was having a good time with my friends, just what my soul needed, and then it ground to a stop.

I could barely make out Reed's frame, leaning against the hood of the black Mustang backed into the brush and low trees. He was staring at me, taking long drinks from his beer. A few empty bottles were lined up by his feet. How long he had been here, I didn't know. My throat was closing up and breathing became difficult. I turned to Sarah with wide eyes as I backtracked on my feet and headed back toward the safety of Sean's pickup bed. I was mumbling to myself, I know, but not really words…just short, panicked phrases speckled with the occasional 'shit!' I passed up the back of the truck and climbed into the cab instead, shutting the door and sinking down into the seat. I must have startled Becky and Sean because they both jumped and turned to look at me.

Sean stood up on his hood and then jumped down on the ground and came over to my window. He rapped his knuckles on it gently, a silent plea for me to let him in. I did and slid over to the driver's side. He closed the door, propped his leg sideways on the seat and turned to look at me.

"I was hoping you wouldn't run into him tonight, Noles, I'm so sorry," he said, reaching his hand to hold my shaking shoulder.

"I saw him," I said, tilting my eyes up to look at him. "He's drunk, isn't he?"

Sean turned and stared out the back window, looking right at the darkness where Reed was sitting. He inhaled deeply, pursing his lips tightly. He turned to me finally. "Yeah…he is."

I nodded, but I really didn't know what the hell to do. I promised Sean I wouldn't sit in his truck and sulk, so he left me alone for a few minutes to gather up my thoughts and courage.

Lights glimmered through the brush ahead of me and I knew it was another car coming to the party. When the dusty blue of the BMW came into view, I realized Tyler had made it after all. I wasn't sure if that was such a good idea now, despite the fact that I invited him here under friendly conditions. My stomach turned a bit as I thought about drunken Reed. *Time to suck it up, Nolan.*

When I left the comfort of Sean's truck, I headed to the center of the campsite where Sarah and Sienna were still gathered with a few other girls. I whispered to Sienna that the friend I had invited was here, and she came over to greet him with me.

Tyler was brushing back his longer blond hair with his hand and tucking it neatly under his plaid Hurley hat, looking around the crowded corners for someone he recognized. *Looking for me, I thought.* I caught the relief that washed over his face when he saw us walking up.

"Hey, you made it," I said as we came closer to him. He was wearing long red board shorts and a form-fitting white T-shirt. I knew what Sienna was signaling to me when she kicked my shin with her leg, trying to be subtle. Tyler could be classified as a 'hottie.' He wore everything just right. His light blue eyes were expressive and his hair was out of the pages of a magazine ad. His skin was super tan from his time at the pool and from diving, which also meant his physique was pretty spectacular, too.

But as gorgeous as he was, he still wasn't the best looking guy at the party. No, that title was held by the drunk heartbreaker lurking in the shadows. The one whose presence terrified me, and whose secret terrified me even more.

"Thanks for inviting me; this is pretty awesome," Tyler said, startling me back to the present. "We don't do anything like this in Chandler. I mean, we party…but it's usually in someone's back yard."

We laughed a bit. I introduced him to Sienna and he shook her hand. Uncomfortable by his good looks, she giggled a little uncontrollably. It was cute to see my put-together, level-headed friend a little flustered.

I brought Tyler over to the pickup truck and offered him a drink, a little excited that he just grabbed a bottle of water. I didn't think I could handle more than Reed being drunk tonight. We all sat on the edge of the truck bed for a bit as I pointed out various people at the party to Tyler and explained to him the inner-workings of the football status circle in Coolidge. Who was in, who was out, why the cheerleaders were all drooling over certain seniors who were looking to sign huge contracts with Division I schools, why we were historically so good at football, how the entire town shuts down on Fridays. Pretty much everything except our amazing quarterback, and thoughtfully, he didn't ask anything about it either.

A good hour had passed with Sienna, Tyler and I making up

conversations for the various people at the party. Sienna and I had a good time watching the various forward girls from our school come over and feign interest in us just so they could talk to Tyler. He was always polite, but was also sure to tell people that *I* had invited him here.

Every so often I stole a glance to the black Mustang. Reed was still there. Still drinking. He was hanging out with a couple of the seniors on the team now, trying to keep up with rap lyrics to some song they were blasting. I didn't recognize it, but every now and then it had the word 'whore' in it. I knew because all three of them would sing it loudly and start laughing.

As the night grew longer, Reed and his drunken crew were getting louder and more obnoxious, but they still stayed in their corner. Sarah had finally dragged the three of us out into the center of the party. She said she wanted to dance more, but I think she wanted to show off some of her curvier moves for Tyler. Amazingly, he wasn't interested. He was instead watching me...which, while it was nice to have positive attention after having my heart smashed, it also made me anxious, like a time bomb was waiting to go off.

Sarah made Sean put on her favorite song again and made us do the dance routine that she had drilled into my mind. Sienna joined in to make me more comfortable and we were soon once again lost in the silly happiness of it. When the song ended, Tyler started clapping, I think to make me feel better about how embarrassed I was that Sarah was making me show him my poor dance skills.

When my back was to him, though, his clapping was soon joined by someone else's. I turned to see Reed clapping, with a bottle tucked in his arm so he could use both of his hands. His eyes were blood red, and his face was puffy. He had his cargo shorts on and a long-sleeved gray T. He was messy and unshaven. I had never seen him like this, and it made me feel sad.

"Wooooooo whooooo, yeah baby!" Reed slurred. Sean was walking up behind him, trying to grab his arms to get him to stop clapping, hushing him. He was embarrassing himself. "No, Sean. That was something. We should celebrate it, woooooooo! Come on everyone, give them a round of applause. Our girls can dance, woooooooo!"

I turned to Sienna, my eyes tearing up a little and I just grabbed her hand. I was so uncomfortable from the attention he was drawing. I wanted him to stop, but he wasn't going to.

"That's right…our girls can dance. Let's celebrate!" he flung his head back gulping a half-bottle of beer at once, then throwing the bottle off into the brush behind him. He spun around on his heels, falling backwards a little and taking a minute to right his balance.

"Reed, come on man. Let me get you home," Sean said, trying to get his friend to stop.

"I'm fine, Sean. Come on, let's celebrate," he said, walking over to one of the seniors he was hanging out with, grabbing his bottle of hard liquor. He raised it over his head. "Let's toast. Let's toast. Have you heard? I'm going to be a daddy! Wooooooooooo, fuckin' A! That's right, wooooooo!"

He took a big drink, wiping his mouth across his sleeve when he was done, holding my gaze the entire time. I was frozen, and couldn't help the single tear I let slide down my cheek. "That's right, Nolan. I knocked Tatum up…" he slowly walked closer to me, and the smell of him was making me sick. He tilted his chin up, turned sideways to take another drink, and kept his eyes on me. "So whatcha gonna do about that, huh? How does that fit into your perfect world?"

His eyes flared a bit. He took two fingers and pushed them into my chest, pushing me off balance a little. This pissed Sarah off, who broke our gaze when she yelled at him: "Stay the fuck away from her, Reed. Knock this shit off. You're drunk, and you're being an asshole!"

Reed just started laughing as he turned around in a slow circle, taking in the crowd of onlookers, who were several dozen now.

"Reed?" I said so quietly I wasn't sure it was out loud. It was enough to jolt him to turn right back into my face, the stink of the alcohol on his breath stinging my eyes.

"Nooooooo-laaaaaan," he said in a mean spirited tone, raising his eyebrows and mocking me, but for what who knew.

Suddenly Tyler was between us, and he was pushing me back. "Hey, man. Don't talk to her like that," he defended.

Reed stared at him blankly for a few uncomfortable seconds, and everyone stood silent, wondering if he was going to cry or throw a punch at Tyler's face. Instead he started laughing, laughing so hard that he had to bend over and hold his knees to catch his breath. He started coughing a little when he grabbed Tyler's shoulder to brace himself.

"This guy…" he started, pointing at Tyler with his thumb and looking at me, but not with clear focus. "You fuckin' this guy now? First Sean, now him. Skipped me, huh?"

I don't know how many milliseconds passed exactly, but I'm sure it was very few. My hand flew to his face so hard I knocked the spit from his lips and sent his head tottering to its side and he stumbled to one knee to get his balance. My face was wet with emotion, but my eyes were full of anger. I just stared at him and watched him try to get up. I didn't dare say a word. I said all I needed to when my palm made contact with his face. I may have loved Reed, but right now I hated him.

We all watched in silence as he struggled to his feet, checking for blood on his lip with the back of his hand. He laughed a sinister sound as he walked backwards to the shadows again, still looking at me. There was nothing in his eyes. I wasn't even sure if he would remember this. But I would.

Sean gathered him up and drove him home. Sarah, Sienna and Becky went along, riding in the back. Tyler offered to drive me home, and despite my uneasiness with ever letting anyone see where I lived, I let him.

"You ok?" he said, putting the car in park in my driveway.

I just shook my head in disbelief, staring out his front window, then I turned to him, still wet-faced and red from crying. "No. So completely not OK."

We both took a deep breath and sat there still. I wanted to try to gather myself together enough before I went inside. Tyler didn't hurry me, and he didn't talk. I was finally ready, but then a terrible thought hit me – I was working Reed's shift on Monday.

"Oooooooh crap," I turned to him. "I'm working the afternoon Monday."

I just stared at him, sort of hoping he would convince me to call in sick. "It's ok, I'll work extra. I'll be there, too. Since I'll be in early, I'll make sure the rotation paper puts you on opposite ends all day."

"Ok," was all I could muster.

He just looked at me with sympathy. I sucked in my lips, took a deep breath and then thanked him for the ride. I got out of the car and dug out my key to get inside. I was halfway up the drive when I heard Tyler's window roll down and he called me back.

"Hey, what's your number," he said. I must have made a weird face because he added quickly "oh, I'm not hitting on you. That would be creepy. I just want to send you mine, just in case. If you need anything, ok?"

I smiled and then gave him my number. My phone buzzed with a text from him right away, so I knew I had his, too.

"I'm sorry tonight sucked, Nolan. But thank you for inviting me. I'm glad I was here...for you," he smiled softly, a little sympathy to it.

"Me, too," I said. And I went inside and somehow found sleep.

16. Getting By

MONDAY'S SHIFT was barely tolerable. Reed showed up late for work, so I didn't have to see him at station assignments. When he did finally show up, he looked even more tired than he had the weeks before. I was sure he had slept through most of the weekend and had probably gotten sick the second Sean got him home.

I didn't ask Sarah, Sienna or Sean about that night. I didn't want to relive it any more than I already was every time I had a moment alone. And I didn't want to hear anything that would make me feel bad for Reed.

He and Tatum were having a baby. The weight of that gave me a near heart attack. And the situation had turned Reed into this horrible, mean monster. I knew he was just attacking everything, trying to tear others down with him, just like his brother had always taught him to do. But the words he said to me couldn't be forgiven. I couldn't imagine what he was going through, knowing his future was over, the future he had wanted so badly for both himself and his father. Regardless, I had no part of that, and he had no right to cast any blame my way.

I spent my breaks with Tyler again, and he was back to distracting me and not mentioning Reed at all. I waited in the locker room until Penny told me the coast was clear. I gathered up my things and headed out to the parking lot. Tyler was still there pulling his diving suit and bag from his trunk when he stopped me.

"So…you made it," he smiled softly.

"Yeah, uh…thanks for taking on the extra work. It helped," I was honest. I don't know what I would have done without Tyler's distraction. "Thanks again."

Before I got to my car, Tyler ran over and tapped on my trunk to get my attention. "Hey, didn't mean to scare you," he smiled. "Was just thinking…you maybe want to hang out for a bit while I dive then grab some dinner? Still not a date, I swear."

Despite what he said, I got the impression it was still a date in his mind. But, honestly, the continued distraction sounded more inviting than the warning bells in my mind that told me not to jump into something so fast.

"OK, yeah…let me just call home and leave a message for my dad. He worries," I smiled. Tyler grinned and gave me a wink before he headed back inside.

I promised my dad I'd be home by 7, guaranteeing I wouldn't be out with Tyler too long. I sat on the bleachers and watched as he and a couple of other guys from his team stretched. The other two were good, but Tyler was just a hint better. His precision was shocking. His first dive was a little more plain, just a simple tuck and straight into the water. But the more he did, the more complex they seemed to get. Twists, rolls, backwards; each time he entered the water with such a small splash that if I wasn't looking I would never know the massive movements that were made before he was submerged.

He was toweling off when he came over to sit by me when he was done. I clapped a little like he had done for my silly dance in the desert. "Very impressive," I said, smiling, blushing a little when I noticed his hard muscles and very small suit.

"Thanks. I've been doing it since I was 8, so I hope I at least have some of those down now," he said, raising one side of his mouth for a half grin. "I'm starving. You have time to eat?"

I looked at my watch. It was 6, but I could probably do something quick. "Maybe a quick bite. Sandwiches or something?" I asked.

"Sounds good. Meet you up front," he said, backing away and heading for the locker room.

Penny was long gone, so I sat up front alone waiting for him. When Tyler came out, he was dressed in loose jeans, flip flops and a V-necked white T-shirt. His long blond curls were wet and wrestled in varied directions on his head. He looked like a model, but he still wasn't for me. I was crazy, and I knew it.

We drove separately to the sub shop just down the road. I ordered a ham and cheese and Tyler paid for everything before I could stop him. We talked about normal things over dinner. His brother was a senior at ASU, majoring in engineering. Tyler was hoping to get a scholarship for diving somewhere in California. His parents were both lawyers. He asked about my family, and I talked about my dad's long days driving deliveries. I mentioned how Mike was a coach at Eastern and how I grew up knowing football because of him. Well, that and everyone in Coolidge was taught football from a young age.

For a moment, I was having fun.

We refilled our drinks and left the restaurant to head to the parking lot. The heat from the nearing sunset was burning my shoulders some. It was amazing how evening held so much heat in Arizona. As promised, Tyler kept our dinner very platonic. He clicked his car button to unlock and held his drink in his other hand and nodded goodbye to me. "See you tomorrow?"

"Yep, see ya then," I said, opening my door. I stopped and yelled over my roof at him. "Thanks for today."

"You got it, Nolan. Anytime," he smiled, got in and drove away.

The rest of my shifts were mornings, and I was able to avoid Reed all week. I managed to work a break for the end of every shift so I was in the locker room whenever Reed arrived. I suspected Tyler had a hand in that since I knew he checked the schedule every morning.

I was able to make a few open practices at the school gym, too. I was working out hard, and I was hitting the ball harder than I ever had before. The coaches were impressed and told me to keep doing whatever I was doing. *Ha, just get called a slut by your first love everyday, Nolan, I mused to myself.*

Days had passed since I had seen my friends. I think they were giving me space, but I was starting to feel a little lonely. I was surprised, then, when Sean was sitting on the bleachers during my open gym session on Friday. I waved a few times and he motioned for me to come by to chat when I could. Between games I grabbed a drink and stopped by to talk.

"What's up? What are you doing here?" I said, breathing a little hard from my last match.

"Just getting in some weights. We have workouts tonight, nothing formal. Not allowed," he smiled.

"Ah, that's right," I looked down knowing that meant everyone else would be here soon, too.

"So, Buck's having a BBQ for July 4th," he looked at me, almost expecting me to say I'd see him there. I just nodded and smiled. "Yeah, I know you won't be there. I just know he thinks highly about you. He'll miss you."

"I like him, too. And if you could promise that his son wouldn't be there, then I'd show up. But we both know how stupid that is," I said with a small laugh.

"I know," he stopped, pausing for a long while. I could tell he had more to say. I kicked at his shoe a little getting him to look up.

"Spill it, cowboy," I tried to make light of it.

"Noles, Tatum's making this whole thing up," he just stared at me, waiting for me to react. All I could do was laugh.

"Sean, you're reaching for anything," I said.

"No, I know it, Nolan. I know it," he had the straightest face. "Look, Devin and Cole saw her out drinking at a club in Tempe the night of the desert party. She was with some of her girlfriends. She's registered for ASU and is going there this fall. All of her plans are still the same. Now don't you think if she was having a baby she'd be making a few changes? And drinking on a fake ID would probably be off the table, right?"

I sat down now, deciding to skip out on the next round of games. I just waved a few of the girls off so they could start without me.

"What are you going to do?" I asked, my heart speeding up a little with my anger for Tatum and what she could do.

"I have to tell him. We're hanging out tonight, I'm staying over to help him set up at his dad's for the BBQ this weekend," he said. "Nolan, he's in a bad place. His drinking is out of control, and he's missing practices. I don't want to see him fuck things up. I love that guy like a brother, you know?"

I grabbed his hand and smiled at him, nudging his shoulder with mine. "I know. You're a good guy, Sean."

He stood up and slung his bag over his shoulder. I followed him out the door to the hallway to the locker room entrances. My mind was tumbling between this new information and the anger that still brewed in me over Reed's words and behavior. No matter what my tangled heart was feeling, I still didn't want to see Reed throw his future away. He was so gifted. And I didn't want to see him disappoint Buck.

"Hey, Sean?" I stopped him before he got inside the door. "Would you let me know how it goes? I just…need to know he's ok. Just let me know?"

He smiled tight-lipped and nodded once, heading inside.

I finished another game, packed my stuff and escaped before the rest of the team showed up, avoiding Reed like I had done all week. My phone was buzzing as I got out of my shower and noticed I had a text from Tyler.

What are your plans for 4th?

I sent back:

I got nothing

I wasn't sure where this was going, and I wasn't sure where I wanted it to go.

Wanna see a baseball game? Todd has suite tickets. We're playing the Dodgers.

How could I resist that?

I'm in.

I loved baseball, and there would be a group of us again. It felt safe.

OK, I'll pick you up around 4. We want to get there early enough for the free T-shirts ;-)

I wrote back:

I love free T-shirts!

And it was refreshing to see the embarrassingly awkward Nolan make an appearance again. I tossed my phone on my bed and went into the living room to join my dad for a little dinner in front of the TV. My mom was working late, so dad made chili. I loved these nights, even though I looked forward to my mom coming home. There was something special about watching reruns of old sitcoms with my dad over his greasy chili.

Mom came home around 10, and I gave her a big kiss and decided to call it a night. I was exhausted from my hours of play at the gym and getting up early was making me go to bed earlier and earlier. I checked my phone one more time before plugging it in to charge and noticed another text alert. It was Sean.

I told him. It did not go well. He made me drive him to her house. He confronted her, called her some shit, threw a few things, broke a few things, and then we came back to Buck's. He's drinking again. A lot. Buck's in Tucson. I'm worried.

I sat there and read his note a few times, wondering what to do. I pushed the phone aside and turned my light off, lying down on my bed. There was nothing I could do, but I couldn't get Sean's worry out of my own mind. I looked at my phone again and noted the time stamp. It said 8:30. Two hours ago.

A few more minutes passed before I decided I needed to know how the night ended.

. . .

Sorry, just got this. Was with my dad. Everything ok?

I waited, and waited. Almost 30 minutes passed before I heard from Sean again.

Yes. He passed out a little bit ago. I got him upstairs. I'm in the spare room. He's wrecked. Buck comes home in the morning. I just hope he can hold it together for the party.

I took a deep breath and shut my eyes tightly. I hated the spiral Reed was on. And I just couldn't seem to make sense out of the version of him I was so intimate with just a few weeks ago. This *new* him was so destructive and hateful.

Let me know if I can do anything. Thank you, Sean.

I put my phone on my desk and decided I had to stop.

I don't remember what I dreamt, but I know I woke up every few hours feeling like I needed to cry but nothing would come out. I tried waiting in the bathroom to be sick, but nothing happened there either. I wandered my tiny house in the dark a few times before making my way back to my bedroom and forcing myself asleep again and again. I woke up for the final time at 6, exhausted.

On autopilot, I put on a pair of running shorts and slid my feet into my tennies. I was never much of a long-distance runner, but something in me felt like my body needed it this morning. I drank a giant glass of water in the kitchen and left my parents a note on the counter. They always slept in late on Saturdays; it was their one day.

I laced my shoes tightly on the porch and jumped down to the gravel. I started a slow pace down my small road and ran along the desert trail along the side of the main road all the way into town. I would guess I made it about four miles by the time I got to the school. I was breathing hard and needed water badly. I snuck through a small space in the fence and made my way to the drinking fountain by the baseball field, taking a good drink.

I crawled back out and walked a few blocks through town getting my breath back. I don't know how I ended up at Tatum's house, but there it was. I saw her car in the driveway and noted that all the lights were off. Before I knew it I was lightly knocking on the front door. When the gravity of what I was doing hit me, it was too late and her face was staring right back at me.

She looked fine. Like nothing had ever happened. There was no evidence of spending all night crying (I was well acquainted with what that looked like). She just sighed and put her hand on her hip, looking at me.

"What?" she seemed annoyed.

"How could you," I shook my head. Looking down, I noted the new pedicure on her toes. She was wearing tiny shorts and a tight shirt. Her hair was perfect as always. It was like nothing had ever happened. She was just moving on to her next day, her next victim. She was truly crazy and thought nothing of the lie she spun.

"Whatever," she said, closing the door in my face.

I stood there for a few minutes, stunned. When I realized she didn't matter and there was nothing I could say that would make her feel, I turned to leave. I walked back home and my parents were making bacon and eggs when I came in.

"Breakfast, honey?" my mom offered. It smelled delicious, and I had worked up an amazing appetite. For once, in weeks, I was hungry. Honestly hungry. I just nodded and smiled, stealing a piece of bacon on my way to the bathroom. "Let me take a quick shower. Keep it hot?" I asked.

"Will do," my dad said.

I let the water pour over my face. Every so often I would shudder, trying to force myself to cry, but nothing happened. I wasn't sad anymore. I was tired. I felt grief, in a way, but I wasn't sad. I just didn't have it in me.

Piling my hair in a towel on my head, I threw on a clean shirt and shorts and joined my parents for the most delicious breakfast I had enjoyed in years.

Tyler picked me up promptly at 4. I let him come to the door to meet my parents. I could tell my dad had questions since he had never heard of a Tyler before. My mom nudged me a little because he was cute, and I smiled at her with my cheeks flushed. My dad shook his hand and asked him a few questions about his car, like he always did. Tyler seemed to pass their test as they let me get in the car with him.

It took almost two hours to get into the city and park for the game. We rushed from a parking lot a few blocks away and managed to get into the ballpark before the free shirts were gone. We both were giddy about it and put them on over what we were wearing right away. They said "Diamondback Red, White and Blue" and were hideous, but they were free. I liked that Tyler had the same silly respect for freebies as I did.

The game was awesome. I had never sat in a suite before, and it came stocked with free food and a private restroom. I licked wing sauce from my fingertips and gulped Diet Cokes the entire time. The game was a close one, but the Diamondbacks pulled out a win in the bottom of the 9th. This sent the crowd into overdrive and everyone stayed for the fireworks display after the game.

I jerked a little from surprise when the stadium lights went out. I realized they needed to make it dark for the show, but I wasn't expecting it to be so sudden. Tyler put his arm around me to let me know he was close. I let him leave it there through the entire display.

As we walked out through the crowds, he grabbed my hand. I let him lead me because I hadn't been to a game in years and he seemed well versed in how to best get to our parking lot. I expected him to let go when we made it through the gates onto the streets, but he held on instead. It felt strange. Part of me liked it, but another part knew I just liked not feeling alone.

We got to his car and he opened the door for me and closed it. He got in and then we spent the next 20 minutes trying to dodge the crowds of people leaving the game and the festivities. He managed to find the highway quickly and we were well into our trip back home.

The ride back through the desert was uncomfortably quiet. I

was thinking about calling Sean, wondering if Reed made it through the party for his dad. But I also knew Tyler was thinking about kissing me goodnight. And I didn't know how to make the two connect.

I slipped my phone onto my lap and sent Sean a quick text. I lied to Tyler and told him I was letting Sarah know something for the morning. He just smiled, buying it hook, line and sinker.

We pulled into my driveway a little before midnight. I felt bad that Tyler had to drive so much out of his way, but I wasn't very comfortable driving alone at night yet, especially so far.

"Thanks for tonight, I had a really nice time," I said, pulling my buckle off and closing up my purse.

"I'm glad you came," he said, stopping and just looking into my eyes. He was considering his next move, and I was cowardly waiting, unsure how I would react. When he slowly started to lean forward, I heard my phone buzz and I startled. Blinking and shaking my head a little I told him I should get inside.

He got out of the car and came to open my side. A little overly gentlemanly for my taste, but I appreciated the gesture. He placed his hand on my back as he walked me to the door. Before I reached the step, I turned to look at him and just gave him a sideways smile.

"I'm sorry, I don't know how to do this yet," I said, hoping he wouldn't be offended. He just smiled back.

"It's OK, I can wait," he said, then he leaned in to kiss my cheek. I watched him walk away and when he got to his car he loudly whispered, "Call you tomorrow."

I waved and then quietly went inside. I carefully shut the door to my room and then slid my shoes off and my double set of shirts, putting on the soft worn T-shirt I preferred for sleep. Comfortable, I pulled my phone from my purse and readied myself for the worst.

Thanks for checking, Nolan. Party went OK. Reed was a bit hungover, so he didn't drink. He didn't really talk much, though. Sarah and Sienna came by, said they'd see you tomorrow.

I wrote back, hoping I caught him before he went to bed.

Thanks. I miss you guys. Maybe we can all go to MicNic's tomorrow?

He was up.

Mmmmm, burgers. Let's do it.

Sean was so easy. Why couldn't I have fallen for him? Another text buzzed me right away.

I think I might love Becky.

I smiled at this. It made me happy to see him so happy with someone who cared equally for him. I wrote back right away.

Good. Now tell her!

He just sent back a smile. I went to bed, glad to know Reed was safe and not hurting himself. But I couldn't shake the worried feeling I had. And I was so conflicted over Tyler. He said he'd wait, but what if I made him wait forever? I guess I owed myself time, too. I pulled my head under my covers and fell asleep instantly, my tossing and turning from the night before nowhere to be found.

17. Up and Down

THE NEXT FEW weeks were fairly tolerable. I caught glances of Reed here and there, and the flirtation from Tyler continued, but on an extremely safe level. The attention was a nice distraction, but I wasn't sure I wanted to make a decision just yet. It was like I was sort of stuck, somewhere between the version of me that was ready to grow up a little more and move on and the part of me that was still that silly girl that obsessed over a high school quarterback, drawing my name with his on corners of my homework.

I started to volunteer for a few early morning shifts working with kids with disabilities. It was a form of water therapy that we did in partnership with the Boys and Girls Club, and it was honestly the most amazing thing I had ever done. I had a little girl, Nancy, who would work only with me. She was maybe 7 or 8. The first day I volunteered was her first day in the pool, and she refused to go in with anyone but me. She said I made her feel safe. Nancy had Downs Syndrome and extreme anxiety. But when she floated on her back through the water, staring at the sky, her face would transform into this serene expression. I called her my mermaid princess, because her hair would float around the water in all different directions, just like the Disney movie.

We had to move the last week of sessions to the evening because several of the area swim teams were competing for regional meets and had booked the lap pools for the morning hours. As much as I wanted to avoid my problems by never having to come face to face with them, I also knew that I couldn't run forever. I was bound to have to sort out how to be in the same place as Reed when school began in the fall, and it didn't seem fair to give up something that was bringing me such joy just to put that confrontation off just a little bit longer.

I hadn't seen Reed in so long that I was a little surprised when he walked through the locker room door to the outside deck for the afternoon shift. I was finishing up my last break with Tyler, who was giving me a pep talk before working a double-shift, one with Reed. He seemed to have come back to the world of the living some. His tired face looked well-rested now, shaven and put together. He was wearing an old Detroit Tigers hat, the trucker style ones with mesh netting on the back. His hair was back to being perfect, curling a bit around the edges of his hat.

He seemed somehow older, somehow more mature. And when he slid up on the counter by the front desk to wait for the rest of the afternoon shifters to show up, he turned his face in my direction. I couldn't read the expression from his eyes because of his sunglasses, but I could make out the undeniable dimple on his cheek from his half-smile. I slowly turned to look back at the crowd of swimmers wading in the water, hoping my sunglasses disguised the emotion on my face just as his did.

"You sure you don't need me to stay? I don't mind," Tyler asked, leaning his knee into mine as we sat side-by-side in the deck chairs.

"No, I have to do this sometime. Might as well be now," I said with a heavy sigh.

"OK, but if it's too much, just let me know, and I'll sign up for a double tomorrow, ok?" he said, standing. I nodded with a small smile to show him how much I appreciated his kindness. Tyler walked behind my chair and then leaned his head down above me a bit. I saw his shadow cast over me, but didn't think anything of it until his lips landed square atop my head and he whispered "be careful."

Looking up right away, I'm not sure if my face wore surprise or worry. "Thanks," I said, just watching him disappear through the snack bar behind me. As I turned to sneak another glance at Reed, I know my face turned to sickness. He was staring at me, his glasses off now. His smile was nowhere to be found. What replaced it was a heavy brow and a look that had my heart racing for fear that he was going to shout obscenities at me from across the pool.

Why did I let myself worry over what Reed saw? I knew it didn't mean anything and he gave up all rights to being upset over me and whomever I decided to be friends with the second he called me a whore during his drunken stupor.

I was deep in thought over this when I realized he was walking straight towards me. I was trapped, leaving now would be obvious and cowardly. I dug my heels in and readied myself for a fight.

"You and Tyler seem to be getting along well," he said, short and cold.

I just stared at him through my glasses, keeping them on in case my eyes gave me away. I wanted to show a strong front. "He's a good friend. He was there for me when someone destroyed my character in front of everyone I know," I said, turning my head to look back out over the water. I could feel him staring at me, but I wasn't going to crack. It was killing me.

"Nolan, I don't remember any of that. Sean told me what I said, and I'm sorry. You know I didn't mean it…I was pretty fucked up… and after what Tatum had told me you have to understand that my head wasn't on right. I'm just finally crawling out of the dark place she put me in," he said, his tone not really regretful but almost defensive. This just made me angrier. I realize what Tatum had done was very much about him, but what he didn't seem to understand was it had ruined me, and I was an innocent casualty of it all. And the worst pain was inflicted by him.

Knowing I would regret not showing him the stuff I was holding onto deep down inside, I sucked in deeply and stood to square myself with him. Pulling my glasses off, I made sure to get close enough to make him uncomfortable. "Reed, I'm only going to do this once, so you better listen. I don't know how you've never taken the briefest of moments to ruminate on how this last month played out for me, but let me get you up to speed.

"That night that I drove to your house, I was dreaming, Reed. Dreaming about how I might actually get to be with this stupid fucking boy who had my head all twisted and my heart wrapped around his finger. This boy that I loved secretly for two years, all the while watching him kiss and sleep with this demented bitch who bullied me in the most horrible ways. Horrible, Reed. She was horrible to me!

"And then my world slid off balance the second I saw you holding her again, your lips grazing her face to comfort her. And while you think you fought for me, Reed, you really didn't. You just let me go. And I cried. For days."

He was expressionless staring at me. He was also speechless. And I was shaking from this truth that I'd held so close to my vest. But getting it out felt so liberating, I had to keep going.

"And let's talk about what I think about drunk Reed, huh? Shall we?" I poked a finger in his chest a little, mimicking his drunken gesture. "Boy, Reed. He's an asshole! Like, a major asshole. I know Sean told you that you said some horrible things to me, but did he really give you the play-by-play?" He stilled, his shoulders tensing a little. He was uncomfortable in his skin, and I knew he didn't know the exact words he had uttered.

"You asked me if I was *fucking* Tyler now. You know, after *fucking* Sean." He sucked in a deep breath, his eyebrows raising a little, taking in his own words. "And then you wondered how I could have skipped over fucking you."

Gathering more strength, I stepped into him even closer. "Really? Now, hearing that, is it so hard to wonder?" I held his gaze for a long time. His eyes revealed his shame. I had shamed him, and for once it felt amazing. Not wanting to hear any more excuses or half-ass apologies, I flipped my glasses back on and walked past him over to the front deck to line up for station assignments.

Todd still managed to keep us fairly far apart for the rest of the afternoon. I looked over to see Reed looking at me from time to time, but gone was his cocky smile and angry, jealous glare. He looked like a puppy caught peeing on the rug, and while I was sure I would feel bad about it eventually, for the time being I was still reveling in the superiority.

He was taking one of his breaks with one of the other girls on staff, and though I tried to ignore it, I still snuck in glances to watch over her fruitless efforts to flirt with Reed. This morning, he might have indulged her and made a show of it in front of me. But now? Today I stripped him a bit of his confidence.

———

The regular swimmers had all gone home and I was waiting on the deck for Nancy to arrive. A few of the other members of the therapy class had shown up so I was sure she'd be here soon. I was up front by Penny when Reed came around the corner to the exit, stopping in my view. I turned away from him, and as I did I saw Nancy and her mom walking up from the parking lot. I decided to meet them outside, and when Nancy saw me coming, she ran up to me and jumped at me giving me a huge hug.

"No-line, No-line, No-line!" she said with the most thrilling enthusiasm heard by my ears. She had a hard time saying my name, and it came out with the cutest accent.

"Hey there, pretty mermaid princess. You ready to swim?" I asked her, kneeling down and letting her twirl in front of me. She just turned to me and nodded yes with a huge grin. I stood up and told her mom I'd meet them by the pool and she thanked me and headed into the locker room.

When I turned back around, Reed was staring at me, the faintest of smiles on his face. I just smiled back softly, mostly out of respect for the joy that Nancy brought me. I walked through the gate to Penny's desk and pulled out the paperwork for Nancy's lessons. We had a checklist to work through each day and when she was done I was going to give her a special diploma.

"What's going on?" Reed asked quietly, almost afraid to speak. He coughed a little to clear his unsure throat.

I just looked him in the eye, my brow furrowed a little. I was confused that he was asking and still suspicious. I wondered if I would ever stop being suspicious again. "Uhhh...I'm volunteering?" That's all I gave him.

He smiled with his familiar face, the one he used to show me when I said something sarcastic. "Yeah, I get that. But what's it for?"

"Hmmmm. Well, it's this cool program Todd told me about the other day. I've been thinking that maybe I want to get into special education in college. I've been working with Nancy. She has extreme anxiety, and our swim lessons make her forget about it for a while," I paused for a minute, looking up at him and then back down at her checklist. "We're sort of good for each other, you know?"

One final brief smile shot from my mouth and then I left for the pool deck where Nancy was waiting for me. We slowly climbed into the water and went through our floating exercises, her giggles filling the air with this perfectly soothing sound. She was a magical little girl, and when I saw her conquer her fears, it made me stronger. I knew that I owed my strength today to her.

When I turned her back around to head back to the other end of the pool, I noticed that Reed had stayed to watch our session. He was sitting on the bleachers with his knees bent up and his arms folded on them, his chin down like he was studying me. He seemed lost a little in his thoughts, and when he wiped his nose along his sleeve a little I thought that perhaps Nancy's giggle had gotten to him just a little, too.

———

Reed stayed to watch a little of my next session, too. We didn't talk at all during the day, but he stayed after to talk to Penny for a bit and then I caught him lingering by the bleachers again. I didn't ask Penny what they had talked about, but I had a feeling it might have been a little about me.

Wednesday morning was the first one on my own completely. No Tyler keeping me company. He had a special practice with his private diving coach. It was strange how much time dragged without Tyler or Reed around to distract me, both in their opposite ways. They both walked into the aquatics center at the same time and seemed to be behaving friendly towards one another. Reed sat on the other end of the counter from me, still respecting my need for distance. Tyler slid over and put his arm around me and I saw Reed's face grimace a little.

The day went along as usual until my first break with Tyler. He brought me an energy drink, which wasn't new, but then he toyed with me a little, holding it over my head and pulling it out of reach whenever I grabbed for it. On the last attempt, he caught my arm with his hand and pulled me close, intimately close. "I'll give it to you on one condition," he smirked.

"Hmmmmm, I don't know. I don't want a cherry energy drink that badly, Tyler. I don't know that this deck is really stacked in your favor," I joked, but I was also trying to hide my own fear over where this was going.

"OK, you drive a hard bargain," he smiled again. His body was so strong and wide, his broad chest almost swallowed me whole. "I'll throw in this bag of Red Vines."

That had me laughing uncontrollably. I gathered my composure and then asked "what are your terms, sir?"

"Dinner," he said, but then held up his hand. "Uh…a date. A dinner date."

I gulped a bit, almost like a cartoon. I didn't want to have to answer this. I was at a fork in my road. The one where I told my friends I would turn right, but I instead wanted to pull out my GPS and recalculate.

"Think about it, today. Don't answer now, but before you leave, OK?" he said, almost sensing my panic. I just nodded and he gave me my treats, not that I could stomach them right now. He sat down and I caught the smirk on his face as he leaned back in his chair and shut his eyes.

I tore at the package of Red Vines a little and then looked up to see Reed watching the entire thing, almost as if it was a show I put on just for him. And that made my heart sink, which worried me all the more.

I was waiting for Nancy at the front desk when Tyler came out and my knees went weak. I knew he was expecting an answer, and I didn't know which one to give. In perfect timing, Reed came around the corner after him, which only made it worse. He looked at the two of us standing near one another and the discomfort he had over the scene was apparent. His eyes were scanning, like he was looking for an out, a distraction.

When one of the other girl guards came out of the locker room he approached her right away, careful not to make eye contact with me at all. I think her name was Morgan. She was one of the girls constantly flirting with Reed. Tyler was talking to me, something about where would I like to go if we in fact go to dinner on Friday night. I was nodding and pretending to think, but all of me was else-where. Eavesdropping.

I heard Morgan giggle a little, and I heard Reed say "I'll drive. Just drop your stuff off at your car."

I watched them leave then I saw him pick her up and wrap her around his back like a backpack, turning around for just a moment to make sure I was watching. I was. And I hated it. That was supposed to be us, and seeing him do that with another girl was forcing me to make my turn.

"So what do you think?" Tyler asked, kicking at my feet a little, startling me.

"OK, let's do it. I already ate my Red Vines anyways," I smiled, even though I was screaming and squirming on the inside.

———

I spent the night with Sienna and was in desperate need for a little therapy session with my good friend who always gave it to me straight. I just couldn't understand why I was so torn in my feelings, I knew I needed to move on. And I was also pretty puzzled by Tyler's interest in me. I was never the *it* girl. I was the girl on the edges. I hung out with the right people and was well-liked, sure, but it's not like I was the girl on the playground in grade school that the boys chased or walked home. I was the one they picked first for their soccer team.

"Nolan, do you seriously not see yourself?" Sienna said, grabbing my hand and taking me over to the mirror on the back of her closet door. "Just stop. Stand here, and I'm going to make you look at yourself. Really look at yourself."

I stood there feeling ridiculous, fidgeting and crisscrossing my legs. I didn't know what I was supposed to see.

"Noles, you aren't 12 any more. You're 16, almost 17. You're taller than most of the girls in our class. Your hair makes Sarah, Becky and I so stupid jealous. Your skin is like a baby—seriously, do you even get pimples? You don't have to wear make up because you already look like one of those ads in the teen magazines for clean skin. You have eyes that can't hide anything, which as your friend makes it really easy for me to know when you need me," she kept going, nudging me a little. Then she sat back on the end of her bed, and let out a sigh, almost exasperated.

"Your body is curved in the right places. Unlike me, you actually need to wear a bra for support. You can wear cute little shorts and show your stomach. Yet you don't show it off and flaunt it like Tatum did. You're just you, with all of this stuff going on underneath," she said, waving her hand up and down at me. "And you're smart. Like, really smart. And you're so strong. You have no idea how strong you are, Nolan. I'm so envious of you. But I'm so grateful for you, too."

I turned slowly with a tight smile, a little uncomfortable from all of the flattery but also so grateful to have Sienna in my life. I walked over and slumped on the bed next to her, lying down beside her and staring at the ceiling. After a while of silence, I just said "Thanks."

"You're welcome," she said, giving my hand a squeeze and then we continued to lay there and think. "What are you going to wear on this date?"

I laughed a little. I had no idea.

By the time I showed up for work early Friday morning, my stomach was in knots. Thursday was full of more flirting between Reed and the girl who I now confirmed was named Morgan. Tyler showed up for only the afternoon session. We took our breaks together like normal, but when the work day was over Tyler grabbed his towel and lassoed it around my back and dragged me towards him. I put my hands on his chest, which was spectacular, to stop myself short of making too much contact with him. I was still worrying about Reed seeing me, it seemed.

"Caught you," he teased with a wry smile.

"It seems you have," I just smiled back.

"I'll be back before you're done with Nancy, ok? Going to head home to grab a change of clothes before dinner. You sure you're ok driving back late tonight by yourself?" he asked.

"I'm sure," I nodded and sent him on his way. Truthfully, I wanted to have the ability to high-tail it out of dodge if I had a panic attack, so I wanted to drive myself to wherever we were going.

While I was standing up front waiting for Nancy and her mom I caught a glimpse of Reed walking through the parking lot with Morgan, his hand smack on her ass as he leaned over and kissed the side of her neck. It made me sick. Then I saw him turn to get a glimpse of me, and he nodded just to confirm that we both saw each other, got where we stood. *Yeah, I got it. Loud and clear.*

My final lesson with Nancy was so touching. She had made me a thank you card and her mom gave me a basket of cookies. I presented her with her diploma. I told her mom I was thinking of going into special education and she encouraged it. The entire thing was so very touching. I hugged them both when they left and smiled as Tyler walked in dressed in a dark pair of jeans and a tight gray T-shirt, his hair neatly combed back, minus the few very sexy strays that were flirting with his face.

"You're early," I teased, as I passed him on my way to my car. "I have to change. Mind waiting just a few? My stuff is in the car."

"I've got nowhere I'd rather be," he said with a devilish smile, sliding on the counter to wait for me. I just smiled back and turned to get my stuff.

I reached through the passenger side back seat to grab my bag and slide it over. When I tilted up I noticed something on my windshield. When I walked to the front to grab it I realized it was a white rose with a small note.

You're amazing.

That was all it said. I smelled it to take in the sweetness and then placed it safely on the passenger seat of my car. I wasn't sure when Tyler had left it there, but it was a nice way to start our date. I skipped inside and changed into a knee-length cotton skirt with a soft T and short-sleeved sweater. It was cool for the warm night but would keep me warm if the restaurant was cold.

I followed Tyler a few miles to the busy shopping mall area. We pulled up in front of a restaurant that looked like one of the fanciest places I'd ever seen. My family usually ate out at pizza joints with the occasional family Mexican food place. This place was a steakhouse, Patrick's Grill & Wine Bar. I was instantly regretting my casual outfit. Fortunately, most of the other diners were dressed similarly.

I ordered a small steak with vegetables and Tyler ate shrimp. I was nervous throughout the entire meal, which I know Tyler caught on to, because at one point he placed his hand on my knee to stop it from bouncing up and down.

"Are you planning when to bolt on me?" he teased.

"Sorry," I smiled. "I guess I'm a little nervous. Haven't really been on a date like this before." I took a big bite and smiled sideways while I chewed. This just made him laugh a little.

"You're a hoot," he said, looking down and picking at his plate some more.

When our meal was over, Tyler insisted we head to a nearby ice cream place for dessert. It was across the street, so we just walked. I was stuffed, but I still managed to find room for a small strawberry ice cream cone. While Tyler was licking his, I had an impulse to tap his elbow just a little, and so I did. He got ice cream on his nose, which put me into hysterics.

"Oh, that's funny, huh?" he said, devilishly. And then my cone was on my cheek before I knew what hit me. I was picking up my napkin, laughing at our small food fight, when he grabbed my hand and stopped me.

"I got it," he smiled softly. "My fault, after all."

And with the tenderest touch he wiped the drip of cream from the side of my cheek and down to my top lip. He put a little water on his napkin and then slowly cleaned the stickiness away, his eyes burning through mine the entire time. Seconds later his mouth was on mine, and I lost myself for a bit in the moment.

It was different from kissing Sean, because I'll admit there was a part of me that was seriously attracted to Tyler. And it was much harder than my kiss with Reed had been. I felt the force of his tongue and the strength in his lips as he sucked on my lower lip just a little. His hands clutched my back and he moved his fingers to the back of my head through my hair. It was intense, and I liked it. But it still somehow paled compared to my one small kiss with Reed.

I kissed Tyler once again when he walked me to my car. In fact, I didn't make it on the road until nearly 11. My head was swimming while I drove home. I didn't turn the radio on, instead opting to let the breeze from the open windows lull my thoughts. I drove carefully, still a little nervous about driving this desert stretch at night. I was pulling from my small road onto the gravel slowly, not wanting to stir up much noise this late, when my headlights brought him into full focus.

Reed was sitting on the back of his Jeep, his feet swinging back and forth a bit. He was eating sunflower seeds and spitting them every so often. I shut off my lights and killed the engine, reaching in for my bag. I decided to come back out later for my note and flower, not wanting to rub it in his face.

"Uh, stalk people much?" I half joked as I walked up my driveway.

He swung his feet to the ground and went to his Jeep door to open it just a little, turning to meet my eyes. "Just wanted to make sure you made it home safe," he said plainly. "I know you haven't driven at night much."

"Oh," I swallowed, still half in shock and strangely wanting to run into his arms and just let him hold me tightly.

"Date go well?" he asked, looking ahead to my house, still emotionless. I knew he was avoiding eye contact, not wanting to be able to read me.

"Yeah…I uh, I had steak," was all I could seem to say. *Stupid, Nolan.*

"Steak's good, I guess," he smiled a little weakly, turning to look me in the eyes again. Moments passed and I was fighting internally to get myself inside when he continued. "So, did he…did he kiss you goodnight," he asked uncomfortably, fighting to meet my gaze.

I didn't want to answer. I just blinked a few times, chewing my bottom lip and finally shrugged, not wanting to lie but also not wanting to make it a big deal.

"Hmmm, ok then," he said climbing into his Jeep and starting up his engine. I just stood there meekly. He turned back to look at me one last time before driving away, and just when I thought he was about to go, he said one last thing. "Did you get your rose?"

I nodded and he smiled faintly then drove away as something entirely new washed over my entire body. The rose was from Reed.

18. Shake Some Sense

/

MY FRIENDS WERE AMAZINGLY DIFFERENT. Becky was over-joyed when I told her that Reed had given me a rose. Sarah was indignant and insisted that he owed me bouquets before I even breathed in his direction again. And Sienna, she was more inter-ested in the two tiny words he had written. *"You're Amazing."*

With the three of them around to work out my heartache and romantic dilemmas, there wasn't much left for me to think about, which was refreshing. School had been in session for a couple weeks and we were setting up for the pep rally and booster barbeque. I managed to luck out with only one class with Reed. Granted, it was literature, so it was usually in a block and longer than most other classes. But thanks to the power of seating charts, I was able to put myself on the other side of the room.

Reed was continuing to flirt with every girl in school. I couldn't seem to make sense of his note to me, the fact that he waited until midnight in front of my house just to see me home safe and then his behavior with these other girls. His partying was still a little out of control. I had skipped the last desert party, but Becky let it slip that he had drank heavily and ended up making out with two of the cheerleaders on the same night. Apparently the two cheerleaders weren't swift enough to realize that he was bouncing between the two of them, each leaving the party thinking Reed was *their* one and only boyfriend.

As amusing as the scene played out in my head, it also broke my heart just a little more. Yes, I was still sort of dating Tyler. I wasn't really sure what to call us, but he had texted me every night since our summer jobs ended and he drove out twice just to take me out for MicNic burgers.

When Buck arrived with his large truck filled with boxes of sports drinks and bags of ice, we all walked over to help him start unloading. I hadn't seen him since he helped me with the car, and I honestly missed the man.

"There's my girl," he said, coming over and giving me a big bear of a hug. Always in a sports coat, Buck was also showing off his red and blue dress shirt. This would look hideous on anyone else, but Buck could pull it off. He was dressed in his University of Arizona colors for tonight's festivities. I had heard that their scouts were joining him for the rally to talk over a few things. I knew this one mattered to him more than most.

Looking him over, I reached up and straightened his matching tie and brushed a little bit of ice chip from his lapel. "There, now you're ready to close that deal," I smiled, winking a bit. *He was rubbing off on me.*

Buck just laughed and patted my back before we all got to work unloading. I wasn't sure when Reed and Sean had joined us, but soon the truckload was moving to the tables much faster. I realized how when I went to grab a load of drinks from the truck and reached up to grab Reed's hand to pull myself up into the truck bed. We both realized it at the same time, stilling for a few seconds and letting the sensation of our connected fingers touch just a little too long.

I looked up at his face, startled, and he was just staring down at our hands when suddenly he moved to put his hands in his pockets and jumped down from the bed of the truck, careful to avoid my eye contact. I just sat back on the edge of the wheel well, pretending to catch my breath a little. Buck walked up then and climbed up into the truck and sat on the wheel opposite of me.

"Well, if you say it's break time then it must be," he chuckled, rubbing his hands on his knees and bending forward a little. "Ooooof, I'm certainly not the young man I used to be."

He just looked up and smiled at me and I reflected his emotion as best I could. His grin disappeared quickly though. "What's eatin' at you, sugar?"

I stood up and started to lift another box, just shrugging. I had a feeling he could read me if I looked at him, so I was careful. "I don't know. Just in a bit of a funk, I guess. Probably just the new school year. Classes are hard," I lied.

"Hmmmm," he just stalled, rubbing his chin a bit. "Aren't you the 'smarty pants' in your class? At least, that's what Reed's always telling me," he was on to me.

I just laughed a little, nervously. "Smarty pants, huh? So that's what he calls me when I'm not around," I diverted.

I jumped down from the end of the truck and propped the box up on my hip to adjust my grip, smiling at Buck, who was standing up again and pulling out a napkin from his pocket to wipe at his sunglasses. "Nah, that's not what he calls you. Just said you're really smart that's all," he said as he stepped down from the truck to join me. "Fact is, he calls you *lots* of other things."

OK, I'll admit, I was intrigued. "Oh yeah? Like what?" I half joked, though deep down I was dying to know.

"Oh you're not going to get me that easily, sugar. You wanna know that, you'll need to ask him yourself," he winked at me. We continued to walk over to the picnic tables and then he stopped for a minute. "But I will tell you that you're important to him…" he paused again.

"Reed… he's been off his game a little lately. I'm not sure what's gotten into him, but he seems to be slipping a little. Not that I'm hard on my boy, but he's just always been so self-driven, know what I mean? I never had to worry about that one. And we've always talked. He tells me everything. But something's in his head, I can just tell. He give you any clues?" he asked.

I shrugged, my mind racing to the drama that unfolded on Reed's lap this summer, absolutely wrecking any chance he and I had. I wasn't sure how much Buck knew, so when I saw Tyler's car pull up in the dirt lot near the barbecue pits, my stomach turned a little. "Excuse me, Mr. Johnson, I see a friend and I have to go meet him," I smiled, as he halted me instantly.

"Girl, when are you going to call me Buck?" he smiled, his cheeks creasing under his eyes. It was the winning Johnson smile.

"Buck," I said back. "Sorry, still hard to get used to that."

Tyler was slowly walking over to the tables when he spotted me, taking his sunglasses off and smiling with those killer dimples and pushing his hand through his perfect damn hair. I noticed a few of the cheerleaders that were there hanging posters and anchoring balloons whisper to one another as he walked by. And I heard them lose their breath just a little when he pulled me into a kiss in front of everyone.

Nothing was ever halfway with Tyler. He kissed me for everyone to see, almost like he was laying claim and showing off. The attention from others made me a little uncomfortable, but I managed to come to terms with it since I really did like kissing him.

As I pulled back, I opened my eyes, blinking a little to regain my balance, a stupid smirk on my face for sure. "Hey," I said, sloppily.

"Hey back," he said, kissing me once more softly on the cheek. "So this is the famous pep rally, huh? Where are all the media cameras and stuff," he asked, looking around a little to take in the scene.

I grabbed his hand and brought him over to the stage area and then we peeked around the corner from the back storage building just a little, where the parking lot had three or four media trucks with their satellite antennas raised high in the air. A few reporters were milling around, talking on phones and swapping stories about the upcoming high school football season.

Tyler just nodded, understanding a little more now. "So, he's that good, huh?" he turned back to me.

I couldn't lie, because yes, he was. "Yep, he's that good."

We were walking back over to the back tables where I was

hoping to blend in and hide with the crowd some before I started grilling hotdogs and cooking for the team when we ran smack into Reed. I wanted to bury myself under the loose dirt right then and there. *This was not happening.*

Tyler was the first to speak. "Wow, man. This is quite a media circus you have out here. All for you, I hear?" he just smiled, reaching out his hand to shake Reed's.

Reed was just staring down at it, chewing on the inside of his mouth a little; it looked like he was fighting with himself internally. He finally let out a small chuckle and took his hand and responded. "Yeah, man. It's crazy attention. But it's not just me. We won state, and it was the first time in a while. It's a good story, small town and all that shit," he said, humble as always. He looked at me sideways, almost to check if he was doing ok. Not smiling, just blank.

Then Tyler made things a million times more awkward.

"Hey, man. I hope you're ok with me and Nolan?" he asked. *Uh, I'm standing right here? Oh god, want to die.*

Reed continued to chew on his cheek, nodding yes just a little before he looked Tyler square in the eyes and gave him the winning Johnson grin. "Yeah, sure. We're good," he patted him on the back as he walked past him. "Sorry, I've got some people I need to see. Gotta go take care of some things. Have to work the circus, you know," he said with his hands stretched out, as he looked from side to side, flashing the signature smile.

Tyler turned back to me and smiled faintly. "Hope that was ok?" he asked. I just smiled. It was *so not* ok, but there was no way I was dragging this conversation out any longer.

———

When coach started talking everyone settled into their seats. The flashes from cameras started snapping as he held the state trophy high over his head and the crowd of people roared. This year's pep rally was at least three times the size they had been in the past, no doubt thanks to the big championship year they were coming off of. My parents even decided to come out. I waved at them while I stood on a bench in the back next to my girlfriends and my...Tyler.

Whether I had any control over it or not, I couldn't keep my eyes from veering to Reed while he sat there in the front row of seats right behind coach. The rest of the team was behind him, Sean and two other captains. Reed was wrestling with his hands, looking down at his feet and leaning over a little. He snapped up to sit straight when coach mentioned his name, and he smiled at his coach faintly, just to show he was listening and appreciated him. But almost instantly, his eyes drifted to mine. And he left them there.

I shifted my gaze a few times, looking over at Sienna and whispering non important things to her just to give myself something to do. But every time I turned back to the stage, there he was, locked onto me. The look on his face wasn't one I was used to seeing from him. It was longing. I knew this because I was feeling the same.

When Reed took the mic to address the crowd, he kept his focus on me until he turned to both sides and then around to look at his teammates before finally addressing the screaming town before him. "Thank y'all for coming out here today. Your support, well... it means a lot. To me, to our team," he locked back on me again. "We aren't much without you. I'm not much without you."

I swallowed from the intensity of his stare. I was hoping that Tyler couldn't tell where his gaze was focused. But I knew I wasn't mistaking this.

He continued. "State last year was awesome, am I right boys?" he yelled, and the team responded with a big "Ooooh rahhh!"

"But you know what's more awesome?" he asked, waiting for the crowd's cheering to go a bit wild. So different from the first Reed I saw sitting uncomfortable at the pep rally his freshman year. "I said do you know what's more awesome?"

The entire crowd cheered back. "What?!"

"Repeat champions!" he called, giving the crowd what they wanted. He handed the mic back to his coach and then finished another rally cry with his team. Just as he always does, Reed gave the people what they wanted. Such a burden for a teenager to carry, but he did it almost effortlessly.

Tyler was helping me clean up the grill when Buck came over and put his hand on my back to get my attention. "Darlin? I'm going to head out. I've got a little meeting with some gentleman," he winked.

"I bet you do," I just smiled back. He looked over my shoulder to notice Tyler. He looked back at me briefly, a rush of understanding seeming to hit him.

"Hi, young man. I'm afraid I've been rude. Buck Johnson," he said, reaching out to shake Tyler's hand.

Tyler smiled and shook back right away, taken in by his charms. "Tyler Rawston, sir. Good to meet you. I'm friends with Nolan," he said, leaning into me a little.

Buck just kept his grin in place, reaching in his pockets to get his keys, but careful to keep his eyes on Tyler the entire time. "This girl's a special one now, you hear?" Buck said, his tone somewhere between kidding and dead serious.

"Yes, sir," Tyler said, deciding that respectful was the best way to go.

Buck gave me one last hug before nodding at me a little. *He knows more than I give him credit for,* I thought.

Alone, Tyler reached down for my hand. I kept it low, below the table. Here I was, hiding it from Reed again. My life was a circle, and I was destined to play the same part over and over. "So, can I take you out?" Tyler asked.

"Sure," I smiled. "I just need to finish cleaning up. Mind waiting?"

"Of course not. I'll help," he said, taking a pad to the grill and hurrying things along.

Sean walked up with Becky around his arm. He shook Tyler's hand and then urged me over to the side a bit. "There's a desert party tonight. We're not going, but thought you might want to know. I know our boy will be there," he just grimaced. I knew what that probably meant. I put my hand on his shoulder and just nodded with a tight-lipped smile to show him I was worried about Reed, too.

Becky and Sean left, and Sienna and Sarah weren't too far behind them. Sienna was leaving for a weekend music camp in the morning, so I knew she wouldn't be at the party. And Sarah didn't like to go alone, so I was pretty sure she wouldn't be there either. I would have preferred for someone to have been watching over Reed, but he was also a big boy. And he was distancing himself from me, on purpose. I needed to let that happen.

————

Tyler and I went through the drive-thru at MicNic's for some frosty shakes to take back to my house. I called my parents and asked if we could just hang out in the living room and watch movies for a while, which of course they were thrilled to let us do. Any date that was happening under my father's roof was preferred by him.

My dad had quite the collection of Adam Sandler movies, so we just picked from the home library for the night. Somehow, Tyler had never seen "Happy Gilmore," which was my favorite of the bunch. We watched it and my dad found his way into the living room a few times to watch with us. *Watch over us, I thought.* Tyler was careful around my father. Not confident and respectful like Reed. He was polite, but I always had the feeling that he was wishing we were alone more.

My parents went to sleep at about 11 p.m. with orders that Tyler had to go home by midnight. Tyler questioned me about how hard that time was set in stone, and I told him that the odds were high that my dad had set an alarm just to make sure that we followed his rules. He grimaced a little at that.

Tyler took full advantage of the hour of alone time, however. Within minutes he had me on my back in a full make-out session on the sofa. My heart was racing from his potent kiss. I couldn't lie, they were delicious. But I was also nervous. His hands were firm on my sides, but slowly sliding up my body. For the longest time he was careful to only hold my back and slide up to my face and neck.

When his hand finally slid up the back of my shirt, I felt both a thrill and a rush of nervousness through my veins, my heart double-beating somewhat. I wanted to experience this kind of closeness so badly. Even Sienna had serious kissing sessions with the two or three boyfriends she had. I was always the one hearing the stories, desperate to understand it all on my own. But I had also always fantasized that it would be Reed who was touching me.

Tyler's kissing grew more intense, and he was slowly working from my lips to my neck, his hand sliding from my back to my sides before finally, softly caressing my breast. My breath hitched a bit at the sensation of it. It was more personal than I had imagined it would be, and a little thrilling at the same time.

He kept his hand there, his fingers teasing my skin softly while his kissing slowed, almost as if he was gauging my reaction. I wasn't saying stop. But I wasn't sure I was saying 'go farther' either. He met my eyes for a moment, and I caught a flash of those irresistible dimples as my hand grabbed at the back of his hair. I was in a bit of a trance staring at his lips, unaware of anything around us when he spoke.

"Is that your phone?" he asked.

"Huh? Oh…I don't. Hold on, let me see," I reached into my pocket and brought the screen up to my face. I had two missed calls. Both from Reed. "Hey, I just need to see what this is. Hang on," I said, sitting up and sliding myself from underneath him just a bit, hiding the screen from his view.

I tapped the text screen and saw a string of text messages as I stood up and walked into the kitchen. "Can I get you anything while I'm up? I'll just be a sec. I think it's Sarah," I lied. *Why was I lying? This was so bad.*

"Yeah, a Coke would be great," he smiled, sitting up and straightening his messed hair a bit with his hands. He turned back around to watch the television, thankfully a little distracted.

When I got behind the counter in the kitchen, I scrolled through Reed's texts. There were dozens of them. They started about an hour ago and were stranger as the time stamp went on.

Hey there, pretty girl. Thinking about you.

Nolan? Are you out with Tyler? I thought you were coming to the party. Where are you?

Is he touching you?

Haaaaaaaa, hhaaaawwaaa. I like tequilaaaaa.

Noooooo LAAAAAAAN :-P I'm sorry I M an asshole.

I don't need you. I have a girl. Her name's Tamara. She said she'd do anything I want, so suck it!

I didn't mean that. But if you're with Tyler, fuck you.

The last few made me wince. The rush of making out with Tyler had completely worn off now and I was yanked back to the reality that is my unrequited love for what was quickly becoming a teenaged disaster. Reed was in bad shape, and I knew it. I almost hesitated to listen to the messages, but worried, I did anyhow.

The first one was from Reed, and he was so incoherent that I couldn't really understand him. I thought he might have dialed me from his pocket. He was laughing uncontrollably and I could hear a girl giggling in the background when the message cut off. The next one came about 30 minutes later. This one was from Sarah.

"Nolan. You need to come get Reed. We're at the desert party. I wasn't going to come, but Calley's in town and we thought it'd be fun. He's messsssed up, man. He keeps trying to talk people into fighting. Shit, I think he just asked Calley to hit him. I tried to get him to let us take him home, but he refused. Said the only way he's going home is if Nolan comes to get him herself. I'm so sorry. I know this is the last thing you need, but I'm worried, Noles. Call me as soon as you get this. I took Reed's phone to keep him from making stupid drunk phone calls."

Too late for that, I thought. My head was swirling. I knew I was going to go get him. I had to. Any other choice was one I couldn't live with. But I was also overwhelmed with how to get out of the situation I was in now. Tyler in my house, midnight and my parents not wanting me to be out driving in the desert. I took a deep breath and walked back into the living room to get through my first hoop.

I smiled faintly, showing a little worry in my brow when I sat on the couch next to Tyler. "Hey, so I am so sorry to have to bail on our night like this, but my friend's in trouble and needs some help," I tried vague, hoping I could get out of this without a lie.

"What's going on? Can I help? Let me get my shoes on and I'll take you wherever you need to go," he was being sweet.

I just held my hand on his arm to slow him a bit. I was going to lie. "No, no. It's ok. It's just Sarah. She went to the party and has been drinking too much. She's at her house now, but is really sick. She's alone and she sounds freaked out."

I held my breath hoping he went along with my play, and when he did I was so relieved. *Lying was hard. I needed to do less of this, I thought.*

"Oh, ok," he paused, still seeming to be thinking about trying to come with me. "As long as you are ok. I don't want to make her uncomfortable. Promise you'll call if you need me, though?" he said, standing and holding one of my hands as we walked to the front door.

"I promise," I smiled, and he bent down and kissed me one last time. Still a hard kiss, no less passion than just minutes before. But where my knees went weak earlier, they were only filled with urgency now. I needed to get to Reed.

"Call you tomorrow?" he said, as he hopped down the front steps and into the gravel of my driveway.

"Mmmmm," I smiled and nodded.

As soon as his lights faded around the corner, I shut the front door and paced around the living room a few times, running my hands through my hair and putting it in and out of a ponytail. I didn't know how I was going to get through this next hurdle.

I knew my parents were barely sleeping. I knew that they were waiting for Tyler to leave. If I could just hold out a few minutes in my room, I was pretty sure they would think I had truly gone to bed. I shut out all of the lights, locked the front door (I would go out the back) and made my way to my room where I even went so far as to change into my baggy sweat pants and giant Coolidge football shirt that I had stolen from Mike years ago.

With the lights off, I sat with my knees up to my chest in the far corner of my bed and dialed Reed on my phone. My chest beat rapidly and sped up with each unanswered ring until finally Sarah answered. She was whispering.

"Noles?" she asked.

"Yeah, it's me," I just waited. Not sure how to make my next move.

"Did you listen to my message," she was still whispering.

"Yeah, I got it. I'm trying to wait out my parents and then I'll sneak out the back... why are you whispering?" I was curious. I could hear the party still raging behind her.

"I don't want Reed to hear me. He keeps asking about his phone. He thinks he lost it. Of course, then he forgets about it and five minutes later he asks where his phone is," her frustration coming through in her tone. Sadly, I could imagine how Reed looked. The time he lambasted me in front of everyone drunk was still scorched in my mind, and the way he looked and sounded was hard to erase.

"How bad?" I asked, not sure if I really wanted to know.

"Pretty bad. Like way worse than I have ever been, and you've seen me at my worst, girl," she added. She was right. I was the pro at curing Sarah's hangovers. She's been getting lit up since 8th grade. The product of very loose parenting.

We sat on the phone silent for a long time. When I finally felt like I could make my move, I let out a heavy sigh. "Sarah, I don't know if I can do this," I admitted.

She sighed back. "I know. But Noles?" she was still whispering.

"Yeah?" I responded.

"You have to. You're the only one. And you know it," she said. She was right. I was. And I knew it. Whatever this stupid torture dance was that Reed and I were doing with each other, it was still very much about us. I couldn't understand why he was pulling me close but then pushing me away. It was killing me. And there was

Tyler, who was…unexpected. Part of me felt like I deserved Tyler. But that same part of me was also angry. And I didn't know if that was the right reason to be with him.

I hung up with Sarah and managed to silently escape my room. I made it look like I was in bed, but barely. I didn't really want it to look like I was trying to pull of a hokey sneak-out, which was exactly what I was doing.

I backed out my car slowly, leaving the lights off until I got to the main road. When I made it to the turn off for the desert party, I felt a swift sense of terror. I was scared. Not for me, but for Reed. I had this sick feeling that I was late, but I was also dreading seeing him in this condition.

Parking my car on the other side of some of the brush around the tables to keep it out of sight, I turned the engine off, killed the lights and hit the call button to find Sarah. I ended the call instantly, though, when I saw him standing on the roof of the black Mustang. His shirt was off, tucked into the back of his jeans and hanging behind him. The tops of his plaid boxers were peeking out from the waist of his jeans, his stupid perfect abs on display for the girls who were fawning over them. His hat was on backwards and he was singing something at the top of his lungs, his words not really making sense.

He stilled when he saw me. Thank god Sarah spotted me first. She rushed over to me and shoved his phone in my pocket, leaning my ear to her. "He just started asking for you again, so good timing, chica," she winked, trying to bring levity.

"Great," I smirked, rolling my eyes a little. I sucked in a deep breath as Reed was climbing from the top of the car and winding his way to me on his unsteady legs. His swagger was faulty when he was like this. When he finally stopped to stand a few feet in front of me, he bent down to take a bow and then looked back up with a smile.

"You came," he had a huge grin, but immediately it turned to a frown. "He's not here, is he? Are you mad at me?"

His thoughts were everywhere. How the hell was I going to get him home? Pursing my lips, I nodded once and decided I was going to have to be tough to get through this. "Reed, it's time to go home," I said politely but firmly.

Unfortunately, he started pouting. "Oh, come on. Don't you want to stay and party with me and my friends?" he asked, waving his hands in all directions at the rest of the drunk teenagers littered through the campsite.

"No, Reed. It's time. Now, come with me," I was firmer. I held out my hand and he just stared at it, his arms slumped down at his sides. His face was somber. After a few very awkward seconds, he grabbed my outstretched hand loosely and just looked back up at me shrugging.

"OK," he said.

I made eye contact with Sarah and she mouthed, "do you want me to come?" I just shook my head. I knew Reed was harmless in this state. I could knock him over if I wanted to. The only things he could hurt me with were words, and she couldn't protect me from those.

I got him over to my car and slid his long legs into the front passenger seat, grabbing the seat belt and handing it to him. He just smiled with a stupid grin. "Do it for me?" he asked, like a child. I grabbed his hand and put the belt in it and slammed the door.

Swearing to myself as I rounded the front of the car, I threw my side open and slid in forcefully, slamming it shut again. I started the car and peeled out a little as I backed up. I had no idea how I did that.

Reed looked out the window most of the way to his house. His playful demeanor was now quieter, deep in thought. When I pulled up into his driveway, he turned towards me one more time. "Promise you're not mad at me?" he asked like a kid who broke his parents' lamp.

I may have told a lot of lies tonight, but I still couldn't lie to him. "No, Reed. I can't promise that. But we can talk about that tomorrow," I said, getting out of the car and coming over to his side.

Getting him into his house and up his stairs was a feat in and of itself. I think I blanked out on the last few minutes because suddenly we were in his room with the lights off and he was flat on his bed. I pulled his shoes off and jerked the shirt out from under him that had been tucked in his pants. It was one of my favorites. A dark red and blue plaid button down from Abercrombie. Under different circumstances, I would probably find a way to take it home and sleep with it so I could take in his smell while I slept. But tonight it smelled of alcohol. In fact his entire room did.

His breathing was heavy, so I was pretty sure he was passed out. I fluffed a pillow and slid it under his head. It was pretty dark, but I was fairly sure his eyes were shut. I waved my hand in front of his face a few times to make sure. To be perfectly honest, I may have given him the finger once or twice, too, in my own amusement. I went into his bathroom to splash some water on my face, cracking the door just a little so the light didn't disturb him. When I was done, I sat back on the edge of the tub and let out a heavy sigh.

I turned the light off and came back into his room. I checked on him one final time, looking closely at his face. His face looked flushed in the moonlight that was streaming through his window. I put my hand on his head gently and he felt a little warm. I snuck back into the bathroom keeping everything dark to get a wet wash cloth when I heard him speak.

"Nolan?" he asked softly. I couldn't tell if he was dreaming and talking in his sleep or not. I stood still at the sink and waited a few seconds. He didn't say another word so I came back into his room and carefully put the cloth on his head, pressing it a few times before removing it to cool him off. I left it on his night stand in case he needed it later and then carefully made my way to his door, my footsteps quiet.

"Are you still here?" he asked again. I froze and waited. "Nolan?" he was really talking. This wasn't a dream.

"Yeah, I'm here," I sighed and leaned into the frame of his door. His eyes were closed, but his face looked pained. I walked back to him to get a little closer so I could see his face. I picked up the cloth again and put it on his head. He reached his hand up and put it on mine. His eyes still closed.

"I love you," he said simply. "I fucked up. But I love you."

There was no way I was going to be able to drive anytime soon.

I felt like Dorothy flying through the tornado to Oz. Everything was spinning, and I couldn't get a full breath. I sat down on his bed and just stared at him, his breathing heavier now. He was fully asleep moments after dropping that bomb on me.

It was the earliest hours of the morning, and my friends were sprinkled around town, none of them able to talk me through this. I had to do this on my own. *Reed said he loves me, I thought, over and over.* Arguing with myself, I would one minute have myself set on chalking it up to his drunken state. But my heart was fighting against all other reasoning. The scariest part was I so badly wanted it to be true. And I wanted him to say it to me again in the morning.

I must have spent an hour sitting bedside with Reed, listening to the light rhythm of his breathing and watching his chest rise and fall. I found myself checking his forehead a few more times until I felt like his fever was reduced. It was 2 a.m. by the time I was able to get my feet working enough to tackle his stairs. I stopped in his kitchen for a glass of water and was washing it at the sink when I heard the sound of his front door opening. The lights went on and I didn't know what to do. I was sure it was Buck, but I didn't want to scare him.

"Hello?" I said, loud enough for him to hear but not loud enough to frighten him.

"Hey, who's that here?" I heard him say back.

"It's me, Buck. Just Nolan. I gave Reed a ride home. I was just leaving," I said as I rounded the corner, but then stopped suddenly as Buck was bent over, his bags dropped haphazardly on the ground and his tie pulled out from his neck. He was breathing hard and reaching to clutch at the side table where he set his keys and without warning he fell to his knees and then rolled to his back.

"Oh my god, Buck," I screamed, rushing over to him. I pulled his tie out completely and started to unbutton the top of his shirt, his body was covered in sweat and his face was red. He started to grip at his chest and I knew.

"I'm calling 911, now!" I shouted rushing to the phone in the kitchen to make sure they had an address to go by.

The operator answered right away. "Hi, I'm at 77104 E. Outlaw and someone is having a heart attack," I rushed back to Buck's side. He was still clutching at his chest. I continued to pull at his buttons with my free hand.

"Ma'am, stay on the phone with me. Help is on the way," the other end of the phone was calming me. I was operating on adrenaline now.

"He's having trouble breathing. He keeps clutching his chest, please hurry," I trembled.

"OK, ma'am. I need you to check his breathing. Put your ear near his mouth," she said.

"OK, hold on," I set the phone on the floor and put my ear to Buck's lips. I could hear air, but he was gasping from pain. "He's breathing. He's breathing. But he is in a lot of pain."

"Do you have Aspirin at home?" she asked. I didn't know. And the only other person who would was dead to the world upstairs.

"I don't know. I'm checking," I said, taking the phone with me and rummaging through the cabinets in the kitchen. I finally found one with medicine and I crawled up on the counter to get a good look. I tossed a few bottles out of my way and found a yellow bottle with Aspirin. I ripped the top off and got back to Buck.

"I have it, I have it," I said.

"OK, you need to try to get him to chew one. Do you think he can do that?" she asked.

"I don't know. I'm trying, hold on," I put the phone down. I leaned down to rest my hand under Buck's head. I lifted him a little and forced his eyes to meet mine. "Buck, help is coming. I need you to try to be calm. I know it's hard. You need to eat this."

I put the pill at his lips and felt him try to open his mouth, so I pushed it in. He was chewing sporadically. I picked the phone back up and continued to sit on the ground with his head in my lap. "He's chewing. Are they almost here?" I was desperate.

"Someone should be close now. Can you see anyone out the door?" she asked.

I set Buck's head on his coat and went to the door. "Yes, I see them. Thank you so much, oh God, thank you!" I rushed out to meet the fire truck and ambulance at the top of the driveway.

Watching them work on Buck was like a blur. I saw them place him on a board and get him to a stretcher and into the ambulance, hooking him up to monitors and putting an IV in his arm. In a rush, they were gone. I remembered that the ambulance driver yelled "Southeast Mercy."

Hospital. Hospital. I had to get to the hospital. I was flailing to find my keys when it dawned on me that Reed was upstairs. I knew he couldn't get to his feet. I doubted I could fully wake him up, but I had to try.

I rushed up the stairs and flung his door open. He was snoring, completely asleep. I pet his head a little and spoke softly but firmly. "Reed, Reed. It's Nolan. I need you to wake up. Just for a minute," I said.

He grumbled and tried to roll over, but I grabbed his arm and kept him near me. I lifted his arm to mine and forced myself to sit up with all my strength. *I was definitely full of adrenaline, I thought.* "Come on, buddy. Work with me, get to your feet. Just for a minute."

He scrunched his brow, keeping his eyes shut tight. He let me get him to a sitting position before he started making whining sounds again. "Just one more minute, Reed. I promise."

I slowly got us down stairs, though I had no idea what condition Reed's ankles would be in. He fell a bit and I just let his weight slide him down. It was the only way I would get him there. We made it out front to my car and I moved him into the back seat where he laid down upon contact. I pushed his legs up, bending them so I could close the door.

Rushing back to the house, I grabbed my jacket, purse and shut the front door behind me. I had to get my head on. I managed to find my way to Mercy and decided to just let Reed sleep it off in my car while I went in. The nurses' station wasn't staffed, so I looked around a few stray halls finally finding someone at a coffee room. "Hi, uhm. I need to check on someone. He was just brought in," I was shaking now.

The nurse sensed my fear and came out to help me right away.

"Are you family, miss?" I just nodded. I needed to know, so I thought I could pretend to be his daughter if I needed to.

"Buck Johnson, he just came in with a heart attack," I blurted all the words out at once.

"OK, let me check," she patted my hand and went to her computer. I stood there, my foot bouncing up and down with anxiety.

"Yes, he's here. They are working on him right now. I'll make sure someone comes out to update you as soon as they can. Why don't you sit in our family room?" she gestured to a more private waiting area with comfortable chairs. I just nodded and slowly slid my feet to the seats. By the time my rear hit the cushions I was in full-on tears. I just leaned my head in my hands and let it out. I cried for a solid 15 minutes, my face red and the snot stringing from my nose. I got up to grab a tissue or two and came back to my seat to look for my phone.

It was 3 a.m. now and I knew I couldn't leave. I had to call my parents. *They would understand, I thought.*

"Daddy?" I said softly when he answered on the first ring.

"Nolan?" he shot back. I could tell he was instantly worried.

"I'm ok, I'm ok. But I need you, daddy. It's Reed's dad. I'm at the hospital. He had a heart attack. Reed…wasn't around. I had to help. I'm so sorry, but it was an emergency," I gave him the edited version.

"OK, OK. We'll be right there, sweetheart. Are you at Mercy?" I could hear my dad getting ready, the sink water flowing in the background.

"Yeah, I'm in emergency, in the family area," I sniffled a little. "I'm scared, daddy."

"We're on our way," he assured.

———

My parents had arrived within minutes. I hugged them both and my mom just let me cry in her lap until the sun started to come up. My parents took turns walking to the coffee center. The last trip, my dad came back with a muffin for me and I was nibbling on it.

I had explained that Reed was out with friends and I was checking on him because Sarah and I were worried and that was when I found Buck. My story didn't make much sense, but I just didn't want my parents to know the state Reed had been in lately.

I was sitting in the chair with my legs folded in front of me when I saw Reed stumble through the sliding doors. He looked terrible. He had managed to put the sweatshirt on that I had thrown in the back seat, but it was clear that he had no idea what was going on.

His eyes found mine and his eyebrows shot up. I leapt from my seat and ran over to him, grabbing his hands right away. He just stared down at our interlocked fingers and then back up at me, his mouth open. "Reed, listen to me. Your dad had a heart attack last night. They are performing surgery, but we should hear something very soon," I stopped. I didn't want to overwhelm him until I knew he understood what I'd said.

His face was white with shock and his eyes were starting to pool up. He was starting to shake his head no, and that's when I just grabbed him and pulled him into a tight hug. I felt his arms slowly wrap around me and his face push deep into the hair at my neck. His body started to quiver a little and I knew he was crying.

Rubbing his back, I just kept whispering in his ear. "He's going to be ok, Reed. I called 911. They came in time. He's going to be ok."

I heard my dad's voice behind me. "Reed, son. Come sit with us. We should hear something soon."

I held his hand tightly and led him back to our seating area. Instead of the chairs, I put us next to each other on the small sofa and put my arm around him, letting him lean on me while I rubbed his shoulder to distract him. And we waited together, silent, our hands glued together, for the next hour.

19. The Mend

BUCK HAD MADE it through emergency bypass surgery and my parents went home later that morning. I stayed with Reed, waiting for us to be able to go in to see his dad. My parents said they'd come back to check on me in a few hours.

Alone, we sat in the waiting room just listening to each other breathe. I felt the heaviness around us. And I knew all the words Reed wanted to say. Part of me wanted to drag them out of him, but instead I waited.

When the nurse called us back, I held Reed's hand tightly and walked with him down the hall. When we made it to Buck's room, I heard his breath hitch a little. He was still sleeping from the anesthesia, but the nurse assured us he would wake up soon, though it would be slow. And he wouldn't be coherent right away.

Reed slid a chair over next to his dad and then reached to hold his hand. I sat at a chair at the end of the bed and just watched. He reached up and brushed a hair from his dad's forehead, putting it in place. He was so tender, so quiet. He just sat like this for about 30 minutes, watching his father breathe. His eyes tearing every so often and he would wipe them with the sleeves of the sweatshirt.

Exhaustion was starting to hit me, as was the desperate need for a shower. I checked my phone and saw a text from Tyler. I closed it. *I would deal with that later, I thought.* I decided I would go home to freshen up, maybe get a little sleep and come back to check on Reed later in the afternoon. When I stood up, he turned to face me. No words, but just a question on his face. I wanted to stay, but he also needed this time with his dad. And I was so tired.

"I'll be back. I'm just so tired, Reed. I have to get home. I'll come back with Sean later so we can bring your Jeep, ok?" I said, squeezing his shoulder a little as I walked by. He reached up and grabbed my hand to give it a squeeze, then turned back to look at his father.

The hallways of the hospital seemed so different during the day. So full of people. I pushed the elevator button and leaned against the wall to wait for it.

"Nolan!" I heard Reed call my name, jostling me aware. He was jogging towards me and when he reached me, he just grabbed my hand and kissed it, holding it tight to his lips, and then pressed it against his cheek, closing his eyes.

"Thank you," he whispered, opening his eyes to meet mine. "Nolan, thank you so much," he reached for me and pulled me into a tight hug. I was swallowed by his giant frame and his long arms. This was the only place I ever wanted to be, but never because of circumstances like this.

Then he kissed my forehead, holding his lips there just as he had my hand. He pressed his cheek to me and took a deep breath. "You saved his life, Nolan. You saved my dad," he stuttered. I could hear the emotion cracking in his voice.

My elevator opened and I pulled away stepping in, my eyes just held his gaze. "I'll be back. I promise," I said as they closed.

I must have fallen asleep as soon as my head hit the pillow. It was late afternoon when I awoke. I rolled to my side and reached for my phone and checked for texts. I had sent one to Sean before leaving the hospital and he responded, asking me to call him when I wanted to go back. There was also another text from Tyler, asking if I was ok.

Yeah, sorry. A bit of a crazy morning. Reed's dad had a heart attack. It sort of affected us all. Call you later?

I left it simple. He knew Buck was a loved man.

I called Sean next and told him I'd pick him up to take him to Reed's in about 20 minutes. I jumped in the shower and soaked up the warmth. It was like I was washing away a nightmare. I kept picturing Buck gasping for air and laying on the floor.

My parents had just gotten back from a quick visit and told me that Buck was awake now and talking. They said he was looking forward to seeing me and wanted to thank me, which made me a little uncomfortable. I didn't think I did anything different than what anyone else would have done.

After getting Sean, we drove to Reed's and went inside for the keys to his Jeep and a change of clothes. While the smell of alcohol had worn off of him, he still looked disheveled this morning at the hospital and was in need of a fresh shirt. I smiled a little when I opened his boxer drawer and pulled out a pair to put in a backpack I found under his bed. I put in socks and a new pair of jeans and one of my favorite gray T-shirts.

Sean followed me to the hospital. Reed was getting a drink at the coffee station when we walked in, and he smiled as soon as he saw us. He pulled Sean into a tight hug right away. "Thanks so much for coming, buddy," he said, patting his back hard to toughen up the embrace.

He came over to me and put his arm around me and started to walk us back to Buck's room. "He's been asking for you all day," Reed said.

I smiled a little. I was anxious to see Buck in good condition. As soon as we got through the door I heard his voice, gravelly but comforting like butter. "There she is. That's my angel. Come on over here, darlin'," he charmed. I slowly made my way to his bedside and grabbed his hand. He patted the side of the bed. "Sit down. I don't bite."

I kept his hand in mine and just looked him over. A little uncomfortable from the silence, I broke it with my usual humor. "A lot of fuss just to get a room with a view, don't you think Buck," I winked. He laughed and coughed a little. I reached for his water and handed it to him.

When I looked at Reed, he had a look of wonder on his face as he watched me and his father. He just smiled, his dimple creeping up as he slid his mouth sideways just a bit. Remembering the bag I packed, I looked to Sean. "Hey, I left the bag in my car. You mind getting it for him," I said, nodding at Reed, who looked puzzled. "I packed you some fresh clothes. It's been a long night."

He sighed with relief; he seemed grateful. "I'll go with you, man. Fresh air sounds nice. Be right back, OK pops?"

"Off with you two, I've got Nolan. She's better than you both," he joked, laughing softly since his chest was still so tender.

When the boys left the room, Buck pulled my hand to his chest and squeezed it with both hands. I just stared at him, so happy to see him ok. My eyes starting to tear up a little, he just hushed me. "Oh, shhhhh, girlie. I'm ok," he smiled. "Thanks to you, by the way."

"Nolan, sweetheart, I owe you my life," he continued. "Reed is shocked at everything you did. I gave him the play-by-play this morning. You are very brave, you know that?"

I just looked down, sniffling a little. "I guess so. At least, when it counts," I smirked.

"Now, none of that," he said, lifting my chin. "You're brave. All the time. It's in you. And I'm glad that Reed has you...as a friend."

I just held his gaze and smiled. I knew Buck knew more than he said. He was very perceptive. *And very wise, I was starting to think.*

"Now, tell me about this Tyler fellow," he put on his fatherly, serious face.

I just shrugged. "Not much to tell," I scrunched my eyes, guiltily.

"Well, just make sure you're honest with yourself, girl, ok?" he said, patting my hands a little. "Be honest with that heart of yours. It's the important stuff."

We stopped talking when Reed and Sean walked back in again,

but as I got up to stand by the door, Buck gave me a wink. *Yes, wise indeed.*

———

Buck was in the hospital recovering for nearly a week. I had finally called Tyler back after our visit. He was very compassionate and offered to come visit with me or just come to my house to take my mind off things. I told him I would be OK and we made plans to see each other the next weekend. He had a diving meet and I was going to watch.

Reed played the season opening game and was amazing. He dedicated it to his father and the entire team wore patches with Buck's old number in honor of him. *The booster moms were working overtime, I thought.*

I hadn't really talked to Reed much since the last visit I made to the hospital. He seemed to be a little more focused. He had avoided the desert party after the game, and Sean said he wasn't drinking, which was good, I thought.

We made eye contact and exchanged pleasant nods and smiles in our literature class, but he still walked right to his seat on the other side of the room. If I hadn't locked it away so solidly in my memory, I would start to doubt if Reed had ever told me he loved me. But I knew he did. But I also knew he smelled like a pint of Jack Daniels then, too.

I was talking to Sienna at our locker when my eyes shifted to follow Reed as he walked by, his arm around a sophomore I didn't recognize. I don't know why it surprised me so, because it was the way he had been acting the weeks before Buck's heart attack. But my gut felt a stabbing pain when I coupled the vision of him with someone else along with the drunken words he had uttered.

"Nolan, earth to Nolan," Sienna was snapping in my ear.

"Huh? Oh, sorry. I got lost in him again, didn't I?" I shrugged.

"What's new," she rolled her eyes. We started walking to our last class together.

"I just don't get it, you know?" I needed Dr. Sienna therapy, and I needed it now. "Why does he say one thing and do another?"

She stopped and turned me to face her. "Nolan, you're my best friend. But you can be such an idiot," she stunned me a bit.

"OK? Go on," I said, shaking my head.

"At least he gives you words, Nolan. You don't say anything. Or you say things to me, but never to him. What are you doing with Tyler? Reed's just trying to give you permission to be happy. You can't blame him for that," she shrugged and started to walk again.

My friend was so smart. *That's two wise people I know, I thought.*

———

I had almost talked myself into having a real heart-to-heart with Reed when I walked out to the parking lot at the end of the day and saw him making out with the sophomore at his Jeep. He was leaning her up against it, his arms trapping her. I averted my eyes quickly and just made for the gym for volleyball practice. I had missed a few days when I was at the hospital with Buck, but my coach was good about it. I was a captain this year, and really liked that some of the younger girls looked up to me.

The workout and practice was a hard one, but it was welcomed. It was a nice distraction from seeing Reed locking lips with yet another girl. I heard the whistles from the football field when I left the gym, and I paused a bit to watch Reed throwing passes from afar. My feelings aside, he was amazing to watch. So poised, so in control. *So confident, I thought.*

I pulled my phone out to read another text from Tyler, firming up our plans for the weekend. I told him I'd see him at his meet and just wait for him after so we could go out. I had to get my head back on right, and maybe seeing Tyler was just what I needed.

———

As the weeks passed, I saw Tyler more and more. I went to a few of his meets, all of which he won. It was amazing to me the level of athleticism he had, yet only a few people watched him dive from platforms while thousands drove hundreds of miles to watch Reed throw a ball.

Tyler and I spent a few evenings at his house, our make-out sessions getting a little bit more intense. And I was growing more comfortable with my body and sharing it with him. It was early October, and the air was starting to chill at night, so we would sit out on his parents' patio by a large fire pit they had built-in next to the pool. This was the first time he had managed to completely remove my shirt and bra.

When I drove out to meet him, I had planned for this to happen, wanted it even. But driving home after our date, I felt a little empty about it. Almost a bit used. I didn't have anything to compare it to, so I wondered if it was just my nerves making me doubt it. There was also the lingering guilt I felt for Reed. It wasn't that he was giving me any new signs that he was interested, but I constantly replayed his confession that he loved me in my head. Frankly, it was starting to make me feel numb on some level. I think that's why I was being so forward and sexual with Tyler. It was like I was trying to force myself to feel sparks when I was with him.

Homecoming at Coolidge High was coming up soon. I had purchased a special ticket for the dance, which was always held on the Saturday after the game. I got a pass to bring Tyler with me, but Friday night after the game was a special student lock-in at the school, and only students were allowed to attend. I was going to skip it, but Becky, Sarah and Sienna worked on me for days until I finally gave in. We were all on the planning committee for special events, so at least I had a say in the various activities we scheduled for the all-nighter.

Since Tyler wasn't able to come to the lock-in, I didn't ask him to come to the game. I'm sure he would have, but part of me also wanted to spend one night on my own, with the girls. Sienna got to the field early for a special performance by the band. I picked up Sarah and we both met Becky there a little before the game. We walked up to the top of the stands so we could rest our backs on the solid wall along the press box.

Our team was heading back into the locker room; they would come back out for a special entrance, breaking through the stacked pyramids of cheerleaders holding the giant State Champions banner. The entire scene had a certain entertainment value to it, but we all loved it. I had grown up watching it. And now, now that the team was winning behind our hometown quarterback hero, the tradition made us all feel something extra. Pride, I think.

Sarah and I cheered loudly for Sienna as the band took the field, trying to embarrass her. We were satisfied when we were pretty sure she blushed a bit and sat down to watch her performance. The crowd joined in when they played the fight song as the announcer called the State Champion Bears to the field. Reed and Sean were leading the team, holding their helmets high over their heads as they ran through the cheerleaders and rainbow of balloons. The display was supposed to intimidate our opponents, but we always scheduled our homecoming game against a school we were guaranteed to beat, so I didn't think we could intimidate them much more than just forcing them to stand on the same field with our boys, who were all heads and shoulders bigger than they were.

I caught Reed's attention as he turned around and scanned the bleachers. I gave him a bit of a thumbs up and he gave a small one back. My tummy felt warm from this silly victory, but I took it anyhow. Sarah just rolled her eyes at me.

A crowd was gathering down at the corner of the bleachers when I realized that it was because of Buck. He had come to the game. I knew this meant a lot to Reed, and I was really happy to see him out and on his feet. But I also felt like I needed to check on him, ask him to take it easy.

I excused myself from Becky and Sarah and climbed down clumsily to the bottom steps. I waited patiently until the other boosters and teachers had gotten their greetings in. When I finally caught his attention, he smiled brightly and just reached out for a hug.

"That's my girl," he said, giving me a warm squeeze.

"Hey," I said back, so happy to see him. "You look great. How are you feeling?"

"Oh, I'm getting there. Taking it slow, cross my heart," he swiped his finger over his chest twice. "Was just dying to get back out here, though. I hate that I missed so many of their games. This is it for me, you know. This is the stuff."

I just smiled and nodded. This was 'the stuff' for him. And how envious I was of him that he knew exactly what made him happy in life. I guess deep down I did, too.

"Well you be careful, ok? Take it easy? I'm just sitting up there with the girls if you need anything," I patted his shoulder as I went to climb back up the steps.

"OK then. Same goes for you, you know," he winked. And I did know. Through it all, I had grown to really love Buck, and I was so grateful for my relationship with him.

———

As predicted, the game was a complete blowout. Reed even threw a few Hail Mary passes down the field just for practice. I texted Tyler the score and told him I'd give him a call in the morning after the lock-in. It took him a while to respond, but I didn't really mind. This night was for me, and I was taking it.

Sarah and I worked the check-in table for the students coming into the gym for the lock in. We had secured the gym area, locker rooms and attached health and science hallways and classrooms for the night. Each room had a different activity, and the gym was for dancing of course, which is where I knew Sarah would spend most of the night. I had come up with the idea for an Adam Sandler movie room, which is where I was planning to spend at least a few hours.

The crowd was getting fairly large and most of the students had started to dance to the music in the gym when the football players finally started to arrive. Each time a new one came in, there was a round of screaming from the girls in the gym.

I was counting the cash in our box to see how many $5 entries we had taken when Reed walked in with Sean. Becky ran over to Sean right away, wrapping her arms and legs around him and dragging him to the dance floor. Reed just stood there smiling at his helpless friend. I was staring, and when his eyes snapped to mine, I startled and started counting again, though I had no idea what number I was on.

I could feel his presence when he walked closer to me and started saying random numbers. "Forty five, sixty, three hundred, fifteen," he joked.

I elbowed him in the side, blew the stray hairs from my face and put the money back into a pile on the table in front of me. "You ass, now I have to start over."

He just winked as he pulled out his wallet and gave me an extra $5. "Start with that one," he smiled, *the* smile. It was the first time in a long time we had talked, and the first time he gave that smile to me. It was short-lived as he put his arm around one of the senior cheerleaders and walked over to a corner of the gym with her, dropping his practice bag and taking her by the arm to lead her out into the hallway. His hair was wet from showering, and he was wearing his baggy jeans and a long-sleeved gray T-shirt with the short-sleeved plaid button one over it. *My favorite shirt. The shirt he was half wearing when he said he loved me, I thought.*

Sarah coughed a little to bring me back to reality. "Start counting, sister," she was snarky.

"Oh yeah, uh… sorry," I said, starting with my pile again.

———

The doors were locked by 10:30 p.m. Sarah and I talked to a couple of the teacher chaperones and gave them the envelope of the money we'd raised. Not wanting to waste any more time, Sarah pulled me to the dance floor where Sienna was standing awkwardly waiting for us. She had picked all of the music for the night, so of course it was all something we could dance to.

We spent the first hour of the lock-in dancing with a lot of the other girls. Most of the boys at the party were sitting along the walls watching. *Typical, I thought.*

I could only keep up the poor showing of hip-hop that came

from my feet for so long. I leaned over to tell Sarah and Sienna that I was going to check out the movie rooms and they both nodded. Sienna was determined to learn some step that Sarah was trying to teach her. *Hopeless. But I admired her determination.*

The halls were quiet, no one tucked in a corner making out. I was glad of that, mostly someone in particular. I looked into the room that was showing scary movies and saw a lot of seniors sitting in there, some cuddling a little too close. *The chaperones are going to have an issue with that.*

Not really in the mood for blood and gore, I stopped in at the game room. Sean and Reed were in there playing a competitive game of ping pong. I slid into a seat next to Becky and asked her who was winning. She said it was all tied up and they had to play a tie-breaker game. Just then, Sean hit a shot that nicked the corner of the table and sent the ball flying into my lap. I jumped a little with surprise and then held the ball out in my hand to give it to Reed.

He had a sinister grin as he turned to me, his eyes lowering a little. I felt very much like prey that he was focusing on.

"I believe that's my ball, madam," he snickered.

Oh, he was being playful tonight, huh? I can do this. "That's funny. I heard you didn't have any balls," I smiled right back at him, tossing the ball up in my hand and catching it.

Reed bit his bottom lip a little and nodded with a little laugh. I tossed the ball to him and he caught it, winking at me before he turned around. I sat by Becky for a few more points, mostly to see if this strange flirtation that had been lost for so long was going to make another appearance, but when Reed remained focused on the game, I felt disappointed. Not wanting to be caught moping, I told Becky I was going to check out some of the other rooms and left my seat.

I finally found my room, the Sandler one. This felt like home. There were a lot of people spread about the floor with sleeping bags, pillows and popcorn. This room was full of laughter. Yes, that's what I needed.

When I found a spot in the back, I slid down the wall and

stretched my legs out in front of me. It felt good to rest for a while. I pulled my sweatshirt off after a while and rolled it up behind my back for a little more support. It was "The Wedding Singer," another favorite. I had been watching it for about 30 minutes when the door cracked open, shedding light across the room again. Squinting, I tried to tell who had just come in.

Reed stood by the door for a few minutes, surveying the room. I kept a watchful eye on him from my periphery and my heart jumped a little when I noticed him notice me and start in my direction.

"Hey, this seat taken?" he whispered, kneeling down next to me.

"No sir, I came to this show solo. It's all yours if you want it," I said, immediately regretting the syrupy words as they left my mouth. I was trying too hard.

He just smiled and slid down next to me, our shoulders touching ever so slightly. I had seen this movie dozens of times, which was good, because I most certainly wasn't watching it now.

My legs were getting tired, so I pulled them up to crisscross them in front of me, pulling my sweatshirt out from my back to cover them a little since I was chilly. Reed was watching my lap as I spread the shirt over my knees and tucked it under my legs. I caught a glimpse of the smirk on his face, too. After a few minutes he scooted in front of me and laid his head on my lap, propping it up just enough to see the movie. He tilted it up for just a second and flashed me a big, toothy smile. "Mind?" he said.

My insides were saying "never." But when I responded to Reed I kept it less needy, just shrugging and smiling a bit.

Reed lay there for the next hour, and somewhere along the way, my feet fell asleep, both of them. But I didn't dare move. Not even a twitch. You could amputate my legs after this for all I cared, I was not going to be the reason he got up and left.

The movie ended and someone sitting near the door switched half of the lights on, forcing most of us to groan and throw our hands over our faces. "Ooooooh, that's bright," Reed said, sitting up. I just rubbed my forehead and grimaced back.

Someone up front announced that "The Water Boy" was up next, and Reed smiled, looking at me. "I love that one," he said.

"Me, too. You know, these are all mine," I admitted. "Well, actually...my dad's the collector. But it's sort of our thing."

The million-dollar smile was back. "That's awesome," he said, nodding in approval. He was looking around the room a bit and then came back to me. "I'm thirsty. You want something?"

"Water would be great," I said.

"OK, coming right up," he said, jumping up to a standing position and shaking out his legs a little.

He reached into his back pocket as he walked away, pulling a dark gray beanie hat out that he slid over his hair, which was now dry and sticking up in all directions from laying on my lap. The long pieces were poking out from all sides, dark perfect curls. He was adorable, and I knew I was lost to him again. It was more than just his tall, strong body and perfect smile, though. It was seeing him with his dad. The way he thanked me for being there. It was holding him while he cried. And, to be truthful, it was still hearing his groggy voice say he loved me, though that was becoming more and more of a memory now.

The next movie started, and I rolled up my shirt and made it into a pillow, leaning back and finally propping it under my head by the wall. I shook my feet out and rubbed my legs a little. I was feeling a bit of atrophy for sure.

I was stalking the doorway, holding my breath each time it opened. But it was never Reed. I had sat up again and moved my position a few times, and being as familiar with the movie as I was, I knew that it had been quite some time since Reed had left. Curious, I got to my feet and ventured out the door.

The hallways were still dark and quiet, which was good. I stopped briefly to look through the tiny windows at each of the various rooms. The game room door was still propped open, but the only people in there were playing video games. Reed wasn't anywhere to be found.

I made my way back to the gym and opened the doors. There were a lot of people in the middle dancing, about three times as many from the time I left. I managed to find my way to Sarah who was still going full throttle. She was dancing with one of the senior football players, grinding a little. I noticed a lot of people were doing that, probably because they were in the middle of a crowd and out of the view of the chaperones standing several yards away by the snack table.

Sarah gave me a little nod, a gesture to ask if I needed something. I just waved her off though. I didn't need to admit out loud that I was on a desperate, and almost panicked, search for Reed. I found Sienna dancing with a few of her friends from band toward the edge of the circle. Her hair was damp with sweat.

"Sarah really worked you out, huh?" I said, pulling at the ends of her hair a little.

She just blew up to cool off her forehead and nodded. "I'm going to get it one day, Nolan. I swear," she joked.

I just smiled, still turning my head to scan the crowd. I stayed near Sienna until I spotted Reed. He was with the group near the center. He had managed to find the senior cheerleader he came in with. And his dancing was rivaling Sarah's. My whole world seemed to switch to slow motion as I watched the girl turn to put her back to him and push into him closely. His hands grabbed her thighs and he slid them up as she lifted her arms in the air and he continued all the way up until he grabbed her hands in the air and spun her around into him, rocking his hips with hers...closely.

I had seen enough. I couldn't help the little chortle that escaped my throat as I stifled what I knew was going to be a hard cry. I started walking quickly, almost jogging, to the large double doors that led to the locker rooms and hallway. My sweatshirt caught a little as I slammed into them, making more of a scene than I had wanted. I jerked at it and got myself through the doors and started to run to the women's locker room.

The cold metal of the lockers was like fire on my hot face as I leaned into them, turning to slide my back against them as I let the tears come on full force now. I heard the sound of the doors slam again seconds later and I held my breath, hoping I could hide from anyone coming in, until I saw Reed's frame fill the hallway leading to the lockers.

"Oh god," I said through the tears, embarrassed and not wanting him to see me. I turned to walk quickly, heading farther into the locker room, somehow thinking I could either lose him or he would change his mind and leave.

He didn't, though. His hand grabbed my wrist when I tried to pick up speed and he jerked me back into him, trying to wrap me up in his arms. I fought against his chest, beating against it with my pitiful fists. "Reed, just go. Just let me go, I don't want you to see me," I begged, but he stayed.

I fought harder, my hair flying wild around me and my sweatshirt falling from my waist and dragging on the floor. I was forced to stop when my back hit the bank of tall lockers along the back wall.

"Nolan, stop fighting me. Just stop!" he yelled, slamming one of his hands on the locker next to my head. He took a deep breath and moved his other hand to slide my nest of hair from out of my tear-strewn face, flinching a little when he realized how hard I had been crying.

"Oh, Nolan. You're crying," he was tender, his eyes showing his own hurt. My bottom lip was still quivering and I just looked down at both of our feet. He was so close I could taste him. It was almost like I could feel his lips without them even touching mine.

He tucked my hair behind my ears and moved his sleeve down over his palm a little to wipe away my tears from my cheeks, which of course only made me start to cry again. Exasperated, he let his arms slump next to his sides. He stepped back a little and turned from me, groaning with frustration, kicking at the other lockers and then swearing. When he came back to face me, he put both palms flat against the lockers on either side of my head. He took his thumb and lifted my chin to force my gaze to his. My eyes were puffy and hard to open. Everything was blurry.

"God, Nolan. Is this because you saw me with Stephanie?" he asked.

"That's her name?" I spit back, almost a little nastily.

He just looked down, inhaling deeply. "Yeah, Nolan. That's her name," he paused. "It doesn't matter, though. Who cares who it is, Nolan. It doesn't matter." His eyes were drilling into mine, and he was shifting his gaze between my eyes and my mouth. The sensation made my lips twitch.

Still angry and hurt, I kept my nasty tone. "You said you'd be right back," I said. "That was half an hour ago, Reed."

He just continued to stare at me. I was letting the tears drop down my cheeks again. I wanted him to see them, have to atone for them. Finally he turned his face sideways. "Fuck!" he screamed, smacking his palm on the locker again so loudly that I flinched. "Nolan, I couldn't come back," he stopped, breathing hard. "I needed to stop whatever was happening. If I would have come back, I would have kissed you, Nolan. And I can't kiss you."

"Why?" I blurted out before I could stop myself. The tears still pouring out, my lips shivering even more now.

He looked down and then moved closer, pushing his forehead to mine. He slid his hands to my face, tenderly drying my wet cheeks with the pads of his thumbs. I could smell the mint on his breath and feel the heat radiating off of his body. When he licked his lips I fought against my urge to move my mouth to his. We were inches apart and his hands were holding my head in place. His eyes were closed and his breathing was hard, but steady.

"I can't kiss you, Nolan," he whispered. I reached up and grabbed fistfuls of the sides of his shirt, clinging to it. "You're with him, Nolan. It's not right, and I can't kiss you when you're with him. Why are you with him, Nolan? Why the hell are you with him?"

He just shook his head, still pressed against my forehead. I felt despair and longing unlike I had ever felt before. "I couldn't have you. I didn't know what to do," I pleaded.

With a swift movement, Reed backed away from me, turning to face the other wall and smacking it hard with another loud groan. "You need to make a choice, Nolan," he said quietly, not turning to face me. And then I watched him leave, the doors swinging shut behind him.

20. Doing the Dance

I SPENT the rest of the lock-in holed up in the locker room. I didn't see Reed when I left, and that was probably for the best. My head felt so confused, but my heart wasn't. I never really stopped loving Reed Johnson. I was angry at him. There was a whole lot of anger. But there was always love there, too. That's why it hurt so damn bad.

I was dreading the homecoming dance. I was grateful that Sarah was taking care of my hair and make up. My dress was a short flirty black one with sparkles and no sleeves. It fit perfectly, and up until today I was desperately looking forward to wearing it.

Tyler was meeting us at Sarah's house, so I did a few final turns in the mirror before he got there. Sarah had tucked my hair up in a twist, and she spiral curled the small wispy hairs that didn't fit. My makeup made me look like a college coed. Sarah had a gift for this. My brown eyes against the dark, smoky charcoal colors made me look sexy, mature. She had forced me to try a deep red lipstick, which actually looked amazing. She gave me the tube to tuck into my small purse in case I needed to touch it up later.

My stomach was fluttering, both nervous about Tyler seeing me and about me seeing Reed later. I was also nervous about how I was going to sort things out. I knew what my heart felt, but being honest about it and putting myself on the line again was another thing.

The doorbell rang and Sarah's mom let Tyler in. Sarah's date, a senior named Jax, showed up soon after. Sienna was going to meet us there. She was going with a boy she had dated a few times from band, Micah.

Not wanting to put it off much longer, I finally stepped down Sarah's stairs into the living room. Tyler stood up and let his gaze start at my legs and make its way up to my eyes. He looked awestruck, which stole my breath a little. It was flattering to have someone look at me with that kind of wanting.

"Wow, you look..." he just stopped, raising his eyebrows. I blushed a little.

"Really?" I giggled. "Thanks."

He took my hand and kissed it and then pulled out a small corsage that he slipped on my wrist. It was a beautiful black ribbon with white roses. "Thank you, that's so pretty," I smiled.

We walked out to his car where he held the door open for me. I watched him walk around the car to the other side and admired how nice he looked in his suit. He had slim gray pants on with a straight, fitted gray jacket. His white shirt was open a little at the top, hinting at his perfect chest underneath. *He was handsome, I admired.*

When we were almost to the school, he leaned over and kissed my cheek, smiling. "You are gorgeous," he said.

I just blushed again and looked down at my fidgeting hands on my lap. "Thanks, I feel a little weird. This isn't my normal look," I admitted, shyly.

He just smiled, looking out the window and checking his mirrors as we pulled into the old barn house that was decorated for the homecoming dance. It was a tradition, one we'd kept up for 40 years. The homecoming dance was always held at Winter's Barn, which was really only used for special events now. Years ago, it was a working barn and students had to dance among penned animals. This smell was definitely preferred.

Before we got out of the car, Tyler turned to me, scrunching his face a little like he was thinking. "So, there's this party later tonight. It's by my school, with a lot of my friends. No desert," he joked. "Anyhow, I was wondering...do you think you'd be up to going after the dance?"

I was a little off guard. I thought about it, and it entirely depended on the direction my evening went. I decided to leave it open. "Maybe. I'd like to, but maybe ask me after the dance? You know...in case I'm beat."

There, that was good. He just smiled and nodded an ok.

We walked up to the door the same time as Sarah and Jax and we all went inside together. Everything was perfect. The seniors always get to decorate for the dance. They had strung white lights everywhere and lined the entrance with a twisted arch of black and white balloons. There were fiber strings dangling from the ceiling, too, making it look like sparkling stars were hovering above. Each table had a small, simple candle and white table cloths. The white chairs were tied with giant black ribbons. *It was exactly as I'd want my wedding to be, I thought, minus the balloons.*

I took Tyler's arm and we followed Sarah to a table near Sean and Becky, who were adorably matched, her gray dress complementing his gray shirt and silver tie. "Woah, what a fox," Becky joked, flitting up my skirt a little.

"Thanks," I smiled, my eyes squinting as I shielded myself from the burning attention.

Sean walked over and gave me a small kiss on the cheek, whispering in my ear "you look amazing, Noles." I just smiled back at him and touched his cheek. He was a good one.

Before he left, I grabbed his arm and made an urgent face. He knew what it meant. "Yeah, he's here. He brought Stephanie. They're sitting with us," he cowered a little, afraid of how I would take it. I just nodded and said "OK."

I put my purse down and decided to lead Tyler out to the dance floor. It was a nice slow song, so I put my cheek flat against his shoulder and tucked my hand underneath. We rocked back and forth slowly and I felt his fingertips glide up and down my bare back. It was soothing, somewhat. But whereas it may have possibly lit my body with desire a few days ago, it only lulled me into a feeling of sleepiness tonight.

My eyes wandered around the room, searching for Reed. I knew that my heart would both soar and sink the second I found him, but I had to find him anyhow. He was my drug. I saw Stephanie first. She had on a skin-tight pink dress that hitched way up on her thighs and her golden hair was pulled back into a tight ponytail with layers of curls. My eyes caught her wrist as it dangled over Reed's shoulder. She was wearing a delicate white corsage, mostly baby's breath. It was feminine and subtle. *Exactly the type of thing Reed liked, I thought.*

Reed's back was to me, which gave me time on my own to take him in. He was wearing a formal, fitted sweater, mostly black. I could see the hints of the gray and light blue argyle pattern on the front as he was slowly turning. His straight, black pants were tight on his muscles and melted into his black shoes. He looked like a GQ ad, his hair smoothed back, but still curled a bit on the ends. I could only imagine what this dark look did to his bright green eyes.

I tucked my chin in more to Tyler's chest as we turned, hiding my gaze from Reed, hoping he wouldn't see me watching. His eyes were looking out over the crowd, his interest clearly not in his date. This made my insides warm over.

Finally, he spotted me. I lifted my face a small bit to acknowledge that I was looking, too. Our eyes were locked on each other as we both turned slowly, almost as if we were dancing with one another despite being in strangers' arms. Reed never smiled. Not once. But he also never wavered, holding me in his gaze until the song ended. I watched him walk over to the table and sit in a chair next to Sean while Stephanie went to greet some of her friends, his stare continuing to focus on me while I stayed on the dance floor.

Tyler and I remained out there for another song and then he led me back to our table before he left to find a restroom. My back was to Reed as I sat next to Sarah and Jax, listening to Sarah talk loudly about how the DJs at the school dances never play hard enough music. I feigned listening to her, nodding and smiling some as I looked sideways, but I knew Reed was still watching.

I was acutely aware of the angle of my face and chin as I turned my head, aware of how my eyes looked and which way the strands of my hair fell. I pulled the lipstick from my small purse and held up the tiny mirror from my compact, slowly tracing my lips with it and rubbing them together with the glossy red before putting it away. There was a fire in me that was forcing me to act out, draw Reed in, and I couldn't stop myself.

The sound of the chair scratching along the floor as he stood up caused me to turn slightly more, and then his hand was on my bare shoulder. He leaned down next to me, his mouth actually touching my ear a little as he spoke. "So, do I get a dance?" he asked, his voice full of suggestion and confidence. I could have been held at gun point and there was no way I was saying no.

Turning to face him as I stood, I caught myself a little in awe. He was wickedly handsome, and when his eyes dipped to take in my entire body I melted. Purposely fluttering my eyes and looking up at him, I smiled softly and took his hand to lead him out to the dance floor.

He grabbed both of my hands and pulled them around his neck, sliding his own down my arms until finally letting them land at the small of my back. We swayed slowly, intensely staring at one another, both wearing suspiciously faint smiles. I narrowed my eyes a little and turned my head to our table to see Sarah and Sienna whispering (about us, I was sure).

"So, how's your date," Reed asked, pointed and short. Still focusing on my face, my mouth.

"He's fine, thank you very much," I said curtly. "How's…Stephanie?"

He crooked up the side of his mouth, giving me a dimple and a devious smile. "She's fine."

We continued to sway back and forth, the electricity between us growing just a bit more with every turn. When I noticed Tyler come back to the table and sit by Sarah, I started to grow less sure of myself, the guilt of my actions settling in some. And Reed noticed. Bending his lips down to my ear again, he spoke privately to me.

"What are you doing?" he asked, leaning back to look me in the eyes, his face harder now, determined and slightly angry. I could feel my heart pounding in my chest and my fingers were going numb around his neck. I was so scared to give in, afraid that as soon as I did Tatum would show up just to yank my happiness out from under me again. Afraid Reed was in on the joke the entire time. My five minutes of courage was fading, and fast.

Reed halted us for just a moment, forcing me to look him in the eyes. He could see the doubt in my face. He looked over at the table briefly and then back to me, pulling me back in to continue our dance. "Damn it, Nolan. You are such a coward," he spat. His words stung a little, and I pushed back into his chest freeing myself. I walked over to the table and grabbed Tyler's hand and led him to the dance floor, leaving Reed there alone.

"Hi. I was just waiting for you to get back," I smiled at Tyler, pulling him to me and turning so my eyes targeted Reed, who stood there with his hands in his pockets, shaking his head. I know I was being spiteful, but he had no idea how many bad falls I had gone through over him, and I guess somewhere along the way my trust was shaken too much.

I stayed on the dance floor for a few songs in a row, Sarah and Jax joining us for a few of the fast songs. Tyler seemed to be completely unaware of my internal battle, which gave me some relief.

When we finally started dancing to another slow song, I looked back to the table, obsessed with keeping tabs on Reed's location. This was a mistake, though, as he had pulled Stephanie onto his lap where he was brushing her hair from her shoulders and nestling at the nape of her neck. Then, he looked directly at me, pausing for a second, his jaw hardening, and then reaching for her face, he pulled her into a deep, powerful kiss.

He wanted me to see that! I was filled with rage. I tiptoed up to reach Tyler's ear. "Hey, I think I'd like to go to your party. You wanna leave in a few to get there in time?" I gulped.

He just smiled down at me. "Yeah, that sounds good. I think you'll like it," he was oblivious to the fact that I was taking him up on an escape route.

———

We left when the song ended, and I made sure Reed noticed as I walked by with Tyler in hand. The party was at a huge house in a gated community on the outskirts of Chandler, so we didn't have to drive far from the desert stretch of highway. Tyler was right, this party was different. Even though there was a lot of excessive drinking at the desert parties, something about this one made the alcohol all seem more apparent. Every person in the house was holding a cup, and the music was radiating off of the walls. The house was littered with plates and wrappers. *I would hate to clean this up, I thought.*

Tyler lead me into the kitchen where he introduced me to a few of his friends, one of whom I had met from the diving meets I went to with him. Everyone seemed like they came from wealthy families. The cars in the driveway as we walked in signaled some of what I was getting into. The BMWs and Escalades were numerous. The girls all were dressed in tight jeans and cropped shirts with giant heels, fashionable and much more mature than the flirty prom dress I was wearing.

Tyler handed me a cup and filled it with beer from a nozzle that he stretched out from a keg on the counter. *Oh, I didn't think about this.* I've only ever had a beer or two at family weddings and reunions, because my uncle thought it was funny to sneak it to the youngsters. Afraid of being laughed at or teased, I just smiled and took a sip. The beer was cold and tangy, cheap I was sure.

I followed Tyler to the dining room where a few of his other friends were playing a game. "Let's play," he said, pulling his jacket off and putting it on the back of a chair.

I still wasn't sure, but I had gotten myself to this point and I was pretty sure I had the power to stay in control, so I just shrugged and sat down next to him.

"How do you play?" I asked.

"OK, everyone gets a card. That card is *your* card. Then, we start turning the other cards over one at a time, and any time a card comes up with your number, you have to drink," he said.

I scrunched my brow a bit. "Uh, that doesn't seem like much of a game. How do you win?" I asked, my competitive spirit still alive and kicking.

"Ah, good question. When you see your card, you have to grab it from the pile after you drink. Once you have all four, you shout 'FOUR' and everyone else has to chug whatever is left in their cups."

Taking a deep breath I steadied myself. There was no way I was going to be able to play this for more than a round or two. But I could at least try it. "OK, got it."

We started the game and I was dealt an 8. Within a few cards, an 8 popped up and I took a sip, faking a bit so I didn't drink much, and then grabbed my card. My luck continued as two more 8s came through the round quickly, leaving me with four. "FOUR!"I held the cards up, and everyone at the table gulped down their remaining drink.

Tyler patted my leg and then smiled. "Fun, huh?" he asked. Actually, it was. With everyone's cups filled, we played another round. This time it was a close match between Tyler, me and another girl at the table. Tyler finally got his last card and yelled 'FOUR' and everyone drank. I struggled getting through mine, and started to think that I was going to have to quit if I wanted to keep my wits about me.

I started to stand up and Tyler just looked at me with puppy dog eyes. "One more? Just one more?" he begged, poking his lip out to exaggerate the act.

"OK, but last one," I said, tapping his nose. I was definitely feeling that last drink.

This round went down to the last few cards and finally the tall guy with dreadlocks at the head of the table stood and announced his victory. We all drank and I made it most of the way through mine, cheating a little and leaving my cup on a side table and standing up to leave the game.

Tyler kept his word and we walked back into the kitchen. I grabbed a handful of pretzels and nibbled on them, my stomach growling a little with hunger. I noticed a giant fire pit in the back yard and motioned to Tyler that I wanted to see it.

"Oh yeah, Jake's house is pretty sick," he said as he led us onto the back patio where even more people were gathered. The fire pit was pretty amazing. It was a long wall of fire, more accurately, and it was warm to stand by. I just stared at it, noticing the hot of the blue and the bright orange of the rocks it was coming from. My head was turning on me a little and I stumbled a bit backwards as Tyler caught me.

"Whoa, you're buzzing a bit, aren't you?" he chuckled. "Let's get you inside."

I laughed a little at myself, too, and followed him back inside through a side patio door. We walked down a long hall, still full of people. He leaned back into one of the doors that opened into a dark room. He reached for my hand and grinned a bit, asking me to come in. Still spinning in my mind and fighting to completely erase the face Reed had made when he taunted me with Stephanie, I joined him.

We sat next to each other on the edge of a bed, and I let my hands feel the softness of the comforter. "Whose room is this?" I asked, not really sure why I cared.

"It's Jake's," he smiled, leaning in and kissing at my neck. I let my mind wander and get lost in his attention for a while. He reached behind me while he kissed at my neck and slowly leaned me down against the bed. Lying next to me, he propped his body up sideways and leaned over me to kiss me harder on the lips. It was a kiss I had grown used to, so by natural reflux I grabbed his hair and pulled him in a little closer.

His hands started to run up my leg, raising my skirt a little and roaming over my hip to the top of my dress. He moved his hand to the back of my dress to work down my zipper a little and then slowly slid his hand back to my skirt. This was making me nervous. I kept kissing him, but I was no longer lost in it. And when he reached for my underwear, I instinctively reached for his hand and pushed it away.

This made him stop instantly. Looking at me, he squinted his eyes a little. "Not OK?" he asked, almost offended.

I just shook my head no. "I'm not there yet, I'm sorry," I smiled, embarrassed.

Tyler shrugged a little and started kissing me again as he did before. We continued to kiss for several minutes when his hand slowly found its way to the same spot and I scooted my body backwards and blocked him with my hand again. "Tyler, I said no," I was more forceful now. And despite the small bit of alcohol flowing through me, I was now filled with adrenaline, too.

Tyler was still moving towards me, almost acting as if he didn't hear me. I fought against him, pushing with my arms and legs as he tried to work his body over me. He was strong and the weight of him was growing more forceful and agitated. Panic was filling me and though I wanted to scream, I couldn't seem to make a noise. I didn't want anyone coming to my rescue, I wanted out of here on my own. I was mortified.

Without flinching, I brought my knee up swift and hard to his groin, leveling him into the fetal position so I could stand, grab my purse, straighten my dress, and get to the doorway.

I didn't look back, but I heard him swear at me a little as I moved through the hallway. The music in the background was being drowned out by the heart beat pounding and the sound of blood flowing in my ears. I had no idea how I was going to get out of here, but I was going to.

No one noticed as I walked through the front door and then made my way to the street. I started to jog a little and realized my strappy heels were making it hard. I pulled them off and held them in my hand so I could run faster, my feet stinging from the cold of the sidewalk. When I made it to the gates, I jumped and waved, trying to trigger them to open. When they wouldn't, I laid my body flat on the roadway and slid underneath, tearing the front of my dress a little and smudging my face with the oil from the blacktop.

I started running down the main roadway toward the more crowded neighborhoods. I made it a few blocks and then I thought I saw a car leave the gated community so I ducked into a side street and crouched behind someone's landscaping. My hands were shaking so much it was hard to get the phone out of my tiny purse to dial. When Sean answered, I felt some of my panic finally release.

"Sean, please. I need your help," I'm sure I sounded petrified.

"Nolan? What's wrong? Where are you?" I heard the concern in his voice, and I couldn't deny that I wanted him to be worried.

"Tyler. He tried…" I stopped. I didn't know how to finish that, but I did know that things weren't going in a safe direction when I left that house.

"Nolan, did he force you?" Sean sounded enraged.

"No, no! I left. I got away, but I need you to come get me, Sean. Please? I'm so sorry to ruin your night with Becky," I was shaking more now, my voice cracking.

"We'll both come, Noles. Where are you?" he asked; I heard Becky asking what was wrong, too.

"I'm in Chandler, but barely. I have an address. I'm just standing outside someone's house," I felt helpless. "It's the corner of…" I looked up to see the street sign, "147th and Mountain View. Right down the road from Old Trail Estates, that's where I was."

"OK, stay there. If you get worried, call me. I'll call you when I get close. And I'll speed, Nolan!" Sean said.

I sat down on the curb, pulling my knees in and cradling my shoes in my lap. I squeezed my legs from the chill of the cold and rocked myself a little while I waited for Sean to arrive. He must have gone fast, because he made the 50-mile trek in less than 30 minutes. Becky called and was telling me to look for them when I recognized his truck as it turned down the road and I stood at the corner, waving.

When they pulled to the side of the road, Becky flung the door open and slid to the middle to make room for me. "Oh my god, thank you so much, Sean," I shut the door and belted myself in, holding my frozen hands in front of his heater. Becky lifted herself up for a minute and pulled off her jacket, covering me with it a little.

"Nolan, your pretty dress," she said, sadly.

I just looked down at it and shrugged, then started to laugh nervously. They remained silent, I think knowing that perhaps I was having a momentary bit of madness from the trauma. When I was able to calm myself again, the shaking started. Becky slid closer to me and put her arm around me, forcing me to lay my head on her shoulder.

The rest of the ride home was silent. My eyes wouldn't blink as I stared wide-eyed out the front window at the passing desert brush. When the old streetlights from town started to come into view I leaned my head upright. Sean had taken us to his house. I climbed out of the truck and waited for Becky to help steady my still quaking legs as we walked inside. I tossed my shoes in the corner by the door and followed Becky to Sean's bathroom where she turned on the shower.

I choked a little at the reflection of myself in the mirror. There were a few tiny scratches on my face. I wasn't sure if those were from Tyler or my escape through the gates. I was filthy and my dress was destroyed. Becky closed the door and pulled a fresh towel from the cabinet.

"Nolan? Do you want me to stay?" she asked, softly placing her hand on my shoulder. I just nodded yes. I couldn't bear the thought of being alone right now.

Becky helped me from my clothes and steadied me as I stepped into the shower. She pulled the pins from my hair and set them on the counter. She leaned my head back under the water and filled her hand with shampoo before kneading it into my head softly and then rinsing it out. She wet a sponge and pumped a little shower gel onto it to make it soft with soap and tucked her fingers under my chin.

"Let me clean your face, I'll be gentle," she spoke softly, her eyes pained. I started to cry a little when she wiped at my cheeks and chin.

She shut the water off and held out the towel to wrap me in. "Stay here for a minute, Nolan. I'll go get some of Sean's clothes," she whispered.

I sat on the toilet lid as she left, clinging to my towel, trying to understand what had just happened to me. Becky came back in with a white T-shirt and a pair of sweatpants. "I think these will work," she said.

She steadied me as I dressed myself and then opened the bathroom door to let out some of the steam. I stood looking at myself in the mirror, not recognizing myself. What have I become? Becky started to untangle my hair with a brush and I winced a little when she pulled at the hairs near my temple.

"Sorry, tender?" she asked. I just nodded.

She continued to brush when I saw Sean's reflection appear behind us. I managed a faint smile. "Thank you so much, Sean," I said, then turned to meet Becky's eyes in the mirror, too. "Thank you both."

Becky just stopped brushing and hugged me tightly from behind. "We love you, Nolan. Anything," she said with a squeeze.

Sean stood behind us, shifting his feet a little back and forth, agitated. I lowered my brow a little, looking him in his reflection, curiously. "What is it?" I asked, almost afraid of his answer.

"Nolan, I don't want you to worry," he said and then stopped, looking down.

"Worry about what, Sean?" I was a bit louder, the blood rushing to my head as my eyes widened.

"Reed was here when you called," he said, and I inhaled deeply, holding my breath.

"What does that mean, Sean?" I asked, already knowing.

"Noles, he heard me ask you if he forced you and then he took off through my front door. I heard his tires peel out of here," Sean held his lips together tightly.

I turned to face him. "You have to call him, Sean. You have to call him, or you have to go get him," I was urgent.

"He's tougher than you think, Nolan. He'll be ok," Sean said, sounding almost as if he was convincing himself.

I thought of all of those drunk people at the party and my head flooded with visions of everyone jumping onto him, each getting their lick in on him. They all loved Tyler. I was sure they would defend him.

I walked over to Sean's bed and sat down, my feet flat on the ground and I stared into space. "I am so stupid!" I yelled.

Becky was at my side quickly. "Nolan, stop. You didn't know. You couldn't see this coming," she said, putting her arm around me.

"If he gets hurt, Becky?" I just stopped at that.

The plan was already for me to spend the night with Becky, so I reasoned that the fact that we were staying at Sean's wasn't much different. We were sitting downstairs watching really bad late night TV. Sean was out cold on the love seat and Becky and I were huddled together under a warm blanket.

"What was Reed doing here?" I asked Becky, my senses finally starting to line back up.

She just sighed a little and then turned to look at me. "We were cheering him up," she shrugged. "He left Stephanie as soon as you walked out the door, told Sean he would wait for him at his house. We just ended up coming home, too."

What?

I was really being stupid. We were both working so hard to shock the other half into being the first to break. So damned proud and so damned stupid. *We're both cowards, I thought.*

When we heard a soft knock at the door, we all shot to our feet. Sean jumped up from the sofa out of his deep sleep, tripping a bit over his feet as he went to unlock the door. Reed walked in slowly and I stood completely still, clutching to the soft blanket wrapped around me. It took him some time before he realized I was there, but when he did, his eyes filled with something unrecognizable.

I dropped the blanket and walked over to him. His lip was split open a little and puffy and there were a few cuts and scrapes over his eye. I reached my hand up to tilt his chin so I could get a better look and he flinched a little at my touch, looking at me suspiciously.

Becky and Sean just watched as I took Reed by the hand and lead him upstairs to the bathroom. I sat him down on the edge of the bathtub and opened Sean's medicine cabinet. He had some alcohol and cotton balls in there and a little Neosporin. I found a bandage and laid the supplies all out on the counter.

I tilted his face up to me again and opened the alcohol, dousing a cotton ball with the liquid. I pressed it softly to the scrapes above his brow, his face twitching a little from the sting. I worked at each one, putting antibiotic on the deep ones and covering them with the bandage. I leaned into the shower to grab the sponge and soaked it with cool water in the sink before slowly cleaning his swelling lip. The cut wasn't very deep and it had stopped bleeding.

As I worked to finish cleaning him up I noticed his eyes intent on the corner of the bathroom floor. I turned to see what he was looking at and realized my dress was still lying there. It looked pretty torn and bad.

I lifted his chin to force him to look at me again. "Don't think that," I said quietly. "I tore it sliding under the gate…"

He looked at me with suspicion. "I promise," I reaffirmed.

I was closing the bottle of alcohol when he grabbed my hands to stop me and took the bottle from me, setting it on the tub next to him. He stood up, towering over me as I stood there barefoot. He looked at my face intensely, brushing a little hair behind my ear and narrowing his eyes when he saw the bruising on my forehead.

He touched it gently with his thumb, shaking his head slowly. I took a deep breath and started to speak, but he quickly pressed his fingers on my mouth, staring at it as he slowly slid them along my bottom lip. He took the back of his hand and brushed it slowly from the top of my face down to the nape of my neck, looking at me adoringly, his gaze following the path of his hand.

Looking down, he reached for my hands that were fidgeting nervously in front of me now. He pulled them both into his own and brought them to his lips where he pressed a tender kiss to them several times, closing his eyes and then opening them to look at me with a sureness I hadn't seen before.

"I am so sorry, Nolan. So sorry…for this," he said, brushing a thumb over my sore cheek bone. "Sorry, for this," this time brushing one over the scrapes on my forehead.

"But mostly, I'm so sorry for not taking care of your heart when you gave it to me. I've been a fool," he chuckled softly. "At least, that's what my dad says. But he's right, usually is. I've been a fool."

He reached up to my face and held it tenderly in his hands, his thumbs stroking my cheeks. "I broke you. Over and over. And then I blamed you for being broken…" I tried to interrupt, but he stopped me again. "No, let me say this."

"I was never interested in Stephanie. Hell, Nolan. I haven't honestly been interested in anyone since I met you. I don't know when it happened, but somewhere along the way I fell for you. I fell fucking hard. And it made me stupid to see you with Tyler," he clenched his jaw a little at Tyler's name.

"But I was the one that was stupid, Nolan," he looked at me intensely, tilting his face down more to make sure we were connected. "I know you think I don't remember. I know you think I was probably too drunk, but it was the only moment of clarity I've had in months, Nolan. I love you. I meant it then, and I mean it now. I love you, with everything I've got. It's the only thing I've got, and I've been terrified because I thought you were falling for him. But I'd be a *fool* if I didn't tell you now."

He pulled me closer, reaching his fingers into my hair, cradling the back of my head as he pressed a kiss to my forehead and then my cheek, stopping to look me in the eyes again. "I love you," he was forcing me to take it in, believe it. And I did.

I felt a tear start to slide from my eye and I blinked to shed it. I stared into his perfect green eyes and reached up to brush his bruised lip with my thumb. He grabbed my hand and stopped it there, to hold it against his kiss, closing his eyes and opening them to mine as I stared at wounds and then back to his perfect eyes. My chest squeezed and I took a slow, deep breath. "I love you, too," my voice cracked.

I said it. And when the words left my mouth, Reed pulled me in closer and stopped with our lips barely touching. Looking at one another so closely, he shook his head a little, the sides of his mouth turning up into a tiny grin, and whispered against me, "I knew you did."

And then his mouth was on mine, soft but full. I reached around his back to hold myself to him closely and he cradled me with his strong arms, still wearing his black sweater. I reached to pull it up over his back to feel more of his skin and he slid it over his head, tossing it to the floor and came right back to me, kissing me harder now, hungrier.

I ran my hands up his undershirt to feel the warm skin of his back and he held his hands to my face, helping me reach his height. He was walking us backwards until we reached the back of the door where he leaned me against it and continued to taste my lips, pulling on them with his own, stopping only to run kisses down my neck and back again.

We stayed in the bathroom for almost an hour, never taking it further, but desperate for one another's touch. When we went downstairs, Becky and Sean had fallen asleep together watching television on the sofa. Reed pulled a few of the pillows onto the floor and pulled me down to the floor with him where he wrapped his arms around me tightly and didn't let go until morning.

21. Us

I STILL WOKE up every morning feeling as though I had to convince myself I wasn't just remembering a dream. Reed and I were an actual couple. It helped that when I held his hand as we walked to our literature class, people turned their heads to gossip.

A few of the guys from the football team would heckle Reed. "About time you got off your ass, Reed," they would yell, whistling and telling us to get a room. Not that we were overly affectionate at school, but we were always connected. At lunch, Reed would pull me onto his lap and wrap strands of my hair around his finger. He would wait for me outside the gym when his practice wrapped before mine just to follow me home, or drive me home on the days that he was able to show up at my house before I left for school. And when we rode in the car, his hand was always interlocked with mine. It was like we were both afraid that if we let go, the other one would disappear.

Tyler tried to call me a few times and he sent a few apologetic texts, too, which I ignored. The calls finally stopped when he called me once while Reed was at my house. I couldn't hear Tyler's end of the conversation, but Reed was pretty clear about him staying away from me. And I was a bit mushy over his protective aggression in my honor.

It was closing in on Reed's birthday, and I had a grand plan, but not much time to pull it off. I had been collecting clippings from the paper and photos from here and there since our freshman year. But I missed a few weeks this season; the weeks when I was so seething angry at Reed that I almost threw my entire box filled with his accomplishments away.

I had always planned on building him a scrapbook, but in the back of my mind it was sort of just a fantasy. Like when people say they'd like to run a marathon one day. But I knew if I did it right, and asked for a little help from my crafty friend Sienna, it would be something he would cherish.

Tugging the box from my closet, I started to lay out the items when I heard Sienna come through the front door.

"Hey, I'm in here," I yelled.

She came bouncing in, her hair in a buoyant ponytail and a guilty grin on her face.

"Sienna? What did you do," I teased her. She just smiled and bit her lip a little, finally giving in.

"Nolan, don't get mad, but I sort of slept with Micah," she spilled so quickly that I had to blink a few times to process what it all meant. Before thinking, I spoke.

"You mean...you had sex?!" I sounded shocked and a bit admonishing, because I was.

"See, this is why I didn't want to tell you," she started to pick up her things, and I grabbed her hand and forced her back down.

"No, no. I'm sorry for that bad reaction. You just surprised me. I...I didn't realize you and Micah were that serious," I was slowly trying to acclimate myself with this new information about my best friend. "So...what was it like?"

Deep down, I really wanted to know. I had thought about it with Reed briefly, sure, but only in the abstract. But now that we were dating, the worry about it plagued me a little more. It wasn't something I was ready for, and I was surely shocked that Sienna was.

"Well, little miss obsessed with the football player," she joked, pointing out that I had probably missed a lot of the details of her life lately. "We've been seeing each other a lot over the last few months, and we both went to that same weekend music camp and sort of got really close."

"Uh, exactly how close," I teased, but was desperate for details now.

"Not that close," she corrected, but then smiled. "Not then, at least."

"So, when did *it* happen?" I asked.

"Last weekend after the homecoming dance," she was grinning ear-to-ear. "My parents were out of town, so he sort of just stayed the night…with me."

I needled her for a few more details, like how much it hurt, did she like it and what did they use for protection – *I felt like a parent on that one* – but I really was happy to hear how much he seemed to care for my friend. They were a pretty exclusive item now, and I was happy to see her so loved. It also dawned on me, though, that I was the only one in our group of friends who would be able to check the virgin box at the doctor's office, and that left me conflicted.

———

After a few hours of sorting and working with Sienna's box of supplies, we had a good start on Reed's birthday gift. I was pretty sure I would be able to get it done by the weekend. I just needed to pay one visit to Buck to get what I needed.

I knew he would be home on Sunday watching all of the games, so I stopped in while Reed was out running with Sean. Buck had become like a second father to me over the past few months, and when he found out that Reed and I were officially dating, he beamed with pride. *"That boy and his thick head finally figured it out,"* he joked.

Buck was able to get me more than I had hoped for, including several awards, medals from Reed's youth, older newspaper clippings and the hype articles that I had missed this year, including the mention of Reed as one of the nation's top 25 high school quarterbacks in *Sports Illustrated.* I hid everything under the seat of my car to ensure Reed wouldn't notice and came back inside to curl up on the sofa across from Buck and take in some football.

We were both yelling at the screen when I heard the door shut and Reed came walking in. "That's bullshit!" Buck was flaring at the television, and I was just agreeing, standing with my hands on my hips.

He slid his arms through mine and put his chin on my shoulder to greet me from behind and I squeezed his arms around the front of me as if they were safety belts on a daredevil roller coaster. "Mmmmmm, so what's all the bullshit?" he half whispered in my ear.

Buck started explaining the bad call to him, something about two feet being in, but I had honestly stopped paying attention. All I could hear, all I could feel was Reed's breath on my ear.

"Hey, pops, I'm going to take my girl upstairs while I get changed. I'll be a boy scout, though, I swear," Reed crossed his heart. Buck just waved us off, still mad at the referees on TV.

Reed slung me over his shoulder and started for the stairs. I kicked a little and then forced my way out of his grip. He frowned a little, but I stopped him quickly.

"I've just seen you pull that move on too many other girls…I want something that's my own," I sheepishly grinned, a little embarrassed at how jealous and shallow I could be.

Reed pursed his lips a little and then let them slide into a smile as he swung his arms under my legs and carried me up the stairs like it was our wedding night, my arms slung around his neck. "Well then, this will have to be our move," he joked.

Once in his room, he shut the door and I sat back on his bed, my feet dangling a bit over the edge. I smiled and laughed a little to myself because at my house, there was no way that bedroom door would ever be shut. Especially if Reed was pulling off his shirt to take a shower, which, *oh my,* he was doing now.

He tossed his stinky shirt at me and I chided him for being gross and smelly, but when he went into his bathroom I pulled the shirt in close just to remember his scent. When he came out in just a towel,

I blushed a little, taking less-than-obvious peeks at his abdominal muscles and defined chest. Catching me, he narrowed his eyes and bent his smirking face down just enough to startle my vision back up to his eyes.

"Why, are you checking me out Miss Nolan Lennox?" he teased.

"Uh, yeah, I was. Now, could you turn around and walk that way for a bit," I scratched my chin and acted like a gymnastic judge at the Olympics, not willing to let him embarrass me. He just grabbed a sock and flung it at me, laughing.

Once Reed was changed he sent a text to Sean asking him if he and Becky wanted to come over for the afternoon games and pizza with us.

"Cool, Sean said they'd be here in 30 minutes with some pizza," he said, tossing his phone to the side and crawling on the bed and pushing me backwards until I was laying flat and he was positioned right over me.

"I like pizza," I tried to distract. *Always the smooth one, I was.*

Reed just smiled and continued to move closer until he was propped up on his elbows and hovering over my face, moving pieces of my hair out of my face and sliding them behind my ear slowly.

Reed had been taking things very slow with me. We usually never made it beyond some rough kissing and making out, despite my every attempt to let him know that it would be okay if he pushed the boundaries a little with me. I think he was still freaked out about Tyler, even though I wasn't. He didn't want to be compared (like he ever could).

Not able to take his nearness any more, I tilted my chin up and initiated our kiss. He always kept his hands on my face when he could, and as we rolled to our sides he held my cheeks tenderly now. But I wanted him to give me more, and I was going to bust down the doors a little today on my own if I had to.

After several minutes of kissing, I pushed myself up so I was lying on top of Reed, and this forced him to move his arms and slide his hands around my back. Pushing myself up a little, I scooted on my knees and finally sat so I was straddling him, and the power and intensity of it all was urging me forward. I had never felt like this with Tyler, and I knew it was because it was always supposed to be Reed.

Sliding my hands up his stomach, under his soft T-shirt, I smoothed them over his chest, admiring him and wanting him at the same time. Reed reached up and grabbed my wrists, almost as if he was trying to slow me down. I just shook my head a little and smiled sweetly. "Please? I am ok, I would tell you," I said, as he slowly loosened his grip, his eyes still questioning me, but relenting a little more.

I lifted the bottom of his shirt and slowly slid it over his head, wanting to feel more of his warm skin. I leaned forward and placed tiny kisses along his stomach and up his chest until he couldn't take it and pushed his hands demandingly into my hair, pulling my mouth to his for a hungry kiss, more urgent than ever before.

Twisting my legs with his, we both rolled a little more on his bed and when I felt his hands start to push the back of my shirt up and grip at my skin, I reveled a little at my victory. Willing him on, I dug my hands into his back a little. But when he stopped there, I decided I had to give this one more try, and I moved him back under me where he was more helpless. Sitting up, holding his hands to the sides, I stared into his eyes. They were full of want, but he was restraining. *Can't he see I'm not looking for a gentleman right now?*

Biting my lower lip a little and grinning, I reached for the bottom of my T-shirt and started to pull it up when he stopped me. I stared at him for a moment, my eyes trying to convey my comfort with him, and then soon he was helping me.

I sat there before him, almost bare, and waited for his reaction. When his eyes slid from mine and followed his hand as it traced the curve of my neck and shoulders, I shivered. Reed stilled for a moment, but I smiled softly, my eyes begging. He slowly slid the straps of my bra over my shoulders, first running his fingers over the tops of my breasts before reaching behind me to finally unhook my bra.

Whereas with Tyler I felt ashamed and nervous at this point, with Reed I felt adored and appreciated. He kept his eyes on mine mostly, though I did notice when he would look at my bare skin, taking in a deep breath. Finally pulling at my chin to urge me closer, he grabbed the back of my head again and soon we were back to kissing, though this time, the feeling of our warm skin against each other was the main focus, and it was something I was sure I wanted more of.

———

We heard Becky and Sean pull up outside and managed to finesse ourselves into something presentable in a matter of seconds. After a few hours of games and pizza, I kissed Reed goodbye and headed back home. I could have stayed all night, but I still had a lot of work to do on his gift before his party Friday, though with everything Buck had given me, I was sure it was going to come out well now.

I also had a few assignments to finish, though my junior year so far seemed to be academically easy. My grades were still all A's, which was all that truly mattered as far as scholarships were concerned. And scholarships were a very important part of the Lennox college plan if I didn't want to be saddled with loans.

The week at school flew by. I saw Reed after practice often, but we were both pretty busy, so we weren't able to sneak in much alone time. I dreamt of his touch every night, and a few times we fell asleep with one another on the phone, just listening to each other breathe. I loved these nights, talking until we couldn't keep our eyes open. Reed would tell me stories about growing up when his parents were still married, his first football games and his grade school girl-friends. The more I learned about his youth the more I wished I'd known him all my life.

When Friday arrived, I made plans to arrive at his party on my own. I had bought a new sweater dress at the big mall in town with my mom the weekend before and I wanted to have her help me with my hair and makeup so I could surprise him a little.

Pulling on my big boots with the deep red dress, I stepped in front of the mirror and pulled the clip out that was holding the curls my mom had made atop my head. I shook out my hair a little and added a touch of the lipstick Sarah had given me. I was meeting

Reed's mom for the first time tonight, so I wanted to look mature and good enough for her son. Sadly, that meant I also wanted to look expensive.

I pulled into Reed's driveway behind a few other cars. The only one I recognized was Sean's, but I was relieved that he and Becky were already here. I decided to wait to give Reed his gift later when we were alone, so I moved it to the back seat of my car, making sure the paper was tucked nicely in the box and tightening the ribbon a little more.

As I shut the door I noticed a black Cadillac pulling in behind me. I turned and started to walk up the driveway and rang the bell. Within seconds, Buck was there inviting me in.

"Girlie, get on in here," he wrapped me into a big hug, then whispered a little in my ear. "Don't look, but that's my ex-wife behind you. Just take a deep breath, and you'll be fine. She's a… handful." He leaned back to look at me, winked and smiled.

I appreciated having Buck on my side, but I desperately wanted Reed's mom to like me just as much as he did. I slid behind Buck and into the house before his mother made it up to the doorway. I could hear a bit of their cordial greetings behind me when Reed came flying down the stairs and scooped me up, swinging me around in a circle and planting a big kiss on my lips.

I giggled a little until we both turned and stopped to see his mother handing Buck a giant white wool coat and brushing the front of her dress with her hands.

"Reed sweetie, come give me a kiss," she held her hands out, smiling at her boy. She seemed so proud of her son. She reached up to touch his cheeks and gave them a soft tap and held his shoulders to look him over before hugging him and kissing his cheek. "Oh how I've missed you, darling. You must come stay with me and Sam sometime soon, OK?"

Her hair was immaculate. It was short and blonde and cut to perfection. Her glasses were dark frames and pointed a little on the edges. She was all business and intimidating as hell. It was interesting to see her standing next to Buck, who was more relaxed and down-to-earth. She was a beautiful woman, but I thought to myself that must have been all the connection was for Buck, because at the surface, they seemed so very different.

Reed led his mother over to where I was standing and I gulped hard, waiting for this introduction.

"Mom, I want you to meet my girlfriend, Nolan," my heart dropped at the word girlfriend, but I held it together and smiled, reaching out my hand. It could have been my imagination, but I felt a slight hesitation from Reed's mom as she shot Reed a quick glance before she turned to shake my hand, giving me a tight, closed-mouthed smile and peering at me a little from the top of her glasses.

"What a pleasant surprise," she said, looking between Reed and I. "I didn't know you had a serious girlfriend, son. We haven't talked enough."

"It's very nice to meet you," I smiled, still shaking her hand. When she looked down at it, I pulled it away slowly, realizing how eager and desperate I was coming off.

"Please, call me Millie, dear," she said, turning to set her purse and gift bags on the table by the door, almost dismissing me.

When Sean walked up to greet her hello I finally exhaled, relief washing over me that this part of my night was finally done. I followed Reed into the kitchen where Becky was waiting along with a few of his teammates. There was quite a spread laid out along with all of Buck's barbecue fixings, a Johnson tradition. We all made a plate of food and headed out to the patio for a little more privacy.

There were a few other family members scattered around, uncles and aunts along with some UofA alumni friends of Buck's. Everyone greeted me warmly, but it may have been that I was just imagining them to take to me more since my cold greeting from Millie a few minutes earlier.

Reed kept me close and at his side the entire night. His warmth was comforting, and despite having kissed him so many times now, I still got a thrill every time his arm wrapped around me or his leg brushed beside mine when we sat near one another.

About an hour into the party, Reed's father called everyone inside for an announcement. We all gathered around the large dining table by the wall-to-wall windows that looked out onto the patio. One of Reed's uncles started handing out champagne glasses to all of us. I took a tiny sniff of mine and was surprised when it was real champagne. Waiting, we all looked up to Buck as he coughed a little to get our attention.

"Thank you all for coming today. Millie and I, well…we might fight like cats and dogs," he laughed, and Millie chided him, elbowing his side a little. "Well, you know we do." He said quietly, but still loud enough we all heard.

She urged him to go on, rolling her eyes. "Anyhow, despite that, we've always had one thing we could agree on. Our sons. Jason has decided to move to New Mexico where he is opening up a new Johnson dealership, starting it all on his own, and we couldn't be more proud."

Everyone cheered and clapped, Reed turned to me and raised his eyebrows a little, secretly mocking his older brother whom I knew he didn't necessarily find to be as perfect as everyone else did. He looked back to his parents when his father said his name.

"Then there's Reed, the man of the hour," he joked, holding his glass up for a bit. "Reed, my boy, you have no idea how proud we are of you. You work hard, and you've had your eyes set on a goal since you and I first started tossing the pigskin around the front yard when you were four."

"I think we can all agree that Reed has grown up to be quite a quarterback," Buck boasted, and everyone nodded in agreement. "But, I just wanted to share in front of you all exactly how good he is."

Buck popped open his briefcase that was sitting on the table and started pulling large envelopes out, setting them on the table one at a time. Reed seemed a little surprised and quite a bit embarrassed by this show, his leg bouncing behind the table. But he also knew his father was just trying to brag out of love, so he held my hand tightly and let him continue.

"Oklahoma. Florida. Texas Tech. Oregon. Cal. Utah. Missouri. And finally, Stanford and University of Arizona. Friends, family… what you see right there is the culmination of Reed's diligence and desire. Son, you have worked so hard. So very hard, and I am honored to have fielded every last phone call and every single meeting that came behind each of these offer envelopes. The choice is, of course, always yours, though you may notice a certain red and blue envelope on top of the stack," Buck laughed a little, nudging the UofA folder a little closer to Reed.

Raising his glass again, Buck urged all of us to join him. "I'd like to give a toast, to my son, whom I love with all my heart, no matter what color jersey he decides to wear," Buck said, and we all joined him with a cheer and a drink in Reed's honor.

Buck then slid a small box over on the table to Reed, who took it and held it in his hand for a while before opening it. I could feel him tense a little beside me from all of the attention, like he knew what was in the box. When he opened it and saw his father's college championship ring he inhaled deeply and looked up at his father with the most loving eyes.

"Dad, I can't take this. It's yours," he explained, trying to close the box and hand it back to Buck. But Buck was having none of it, and just closed Reed's hand around it and squeezed tightly, patting him on the back and kissing the top of his head, one of his few unmanly shows of affection.

"Yes you can, and yes you will," he said.

———

Millie came over after Buck's toast to give Reed a gift more privately. Not comfortable being a part of her moment with her son, I retreated to the kitchen with Sean and Becky and looked on as Reed put on the watch his mom had given him, looking over an engraving on the back. *Reed's birthday was a lot different from mine, which usually consisted of cake and a few new T-shirts.*

Reed joined me in the kitchen and showed me the nice leather watch that his mom had given him. It looked fancy, though I didn't really recognize the brand. I just smiled and told him it was nice. I think he sensed my discomfort as he pulled me in close and kissed the top of my head. I clung to the fabric of his shirt, not wanting to let go.

I finally loosened my grip when his mother walked in and discarded an empty plate and went to wash her hands. She looked like she was getting ready to leave, which internally made me grateful, though I kept up the smiling façade I had going. She didn't like me, and I knew it.

Looking around the house a little, she settled her eyes back to Reed while she dried her hands. "Where's that lovely Tatum, girl, honey? I haven't seen her all night."

I immediately went blank, my knees buckling, and I felt Reed sweep his arm behind me to wrap around my waist and hold me up. "Tatum graduated already, mom. She's at college. We don't really hang out any more," Reed answered quickly, trying to diffuse the situation. Sean and Becky were looking at me to try to gage if I was alright. I was pretty sure I wasn't.

"Oh, well that's too bad. I liked her, she was so pretty," Millie piped back, putting emphasis on the word pretty. "Well, I have to get back before it's too late, honey. I'll call you next week and we can make plans for your summer visits, ok?"

She leaned in to kiss Reed on the cheek again and he helped her pull her coat back on. I just stood behind him, feeling nothing but stupid. Finally, she acknowledged me when we were at the door. "Oh, and it was really nice to meet you…" she couldn't remember my name.

"Nolan," Reed finished, his voice exposing his irritation and embarrassment for his mother.

———

By the time all of the guests had left, it was just Reed and I alone on the sofa in his living room. Buck had gone out to join a few of his alumni friends at the bar. Reed stood and walked to the kitchen, where he started to put food away in the refrigerator. I let out a deep sigh, collapsing backwards on the large ottoman, feeling a little bit like the sucker in a match against the prize fighter.

I heard Reed chuckle a little as he walked in and stood over me, reaching his hand down to lift me up. "Come on, it wasn't that bad," he smiled.

"Oh, I don't know. It was pretty bad," I stood up and hugged him, his hands rubbing my back a little. "Your mom does not like me. I mean, like at all."

Reed squeezed me a little tighter before speaking. "Don't be crazy. Of course she does. She just doesn't know you yet. I told you she was a bit image consumed, and she's always in that mode. Now you see why I love living with my dad," he laughed a little, but his voice also sounded sad that he isn't able to be as close with his mom.

I looked over at the stacks of offer envelopes on his table still, now stacked neatly. I walked over to them and he followed me. I slid them apart and took them all in. "Reed, this is amazing," I smiled at him.

He took in a deep breath and then softly smiled, too, turning to look at me. "It's all kind of overwhelming, too," he said. "I'm still not totally sure what I want to do."

"You'll figure it out," I reassured, though a part of me was also flashing forward to the inevitable time when we would have to be apart. Not wanting to dwell any more on that or the sick feeling left over from my first encounter with Millie, I jerked up with energy and grinned largely at Reed.

"Hey! Want your present?" I was so anxious to give it to him. He just closed his eyes and then reached out his hands. "Well, you're going to have to stand like that for a minute. It's in the car. Hold on."

I raced out the door to my car and grabbed the heavy box from my backseat. I brought it inside, where Reed was still standing with his eyes closed and his hands out. I stopped to admire him for a moment, but he sensed I was there.

"You're teasing me. Not nice, Nolan. I'll remember this," his grin was so damned distracting. When I reached him, I placed the heavy box in his hands and warned him to hold on tight.

"OK, open your eyes," I said, pins and needles everywhere I was so excited to see if he loved it as much as he did in my fantasy.

He turned his head a little and smirked, tightening his eyes as he glanced up at me, shaking the box a little.

"Open it already, would you?" I couldn't take it.

He sat down on the ottoman and put the box in his lap, untying the ribbon that was keeping the lid in place. He slid the top off the box and pulled away the tissue paper, lifting the book out and letting the wrapping fall to the floor.

The leather binding for the cover came out exactly as I had wanted it to, almost looking like an old weathered football. My dad helped me brand #13 on the cover along with 'Johnson.' I watched as Reed's fingers worked at the leather straps to open the book and I almost cried a little when his face reacted to the photo on the first page, biting his lip and smiling innocently. It was one that Buck had given me. Reed was 6 or 7 in the picture, and he was sitting on Buck's shoulders holding his first trophy in the air, waving number one with his finger. Buck had told me it was his favorite memory, so I thought there was a good chance it might be Reed's, too.

I could tell he was feeling the emotion a little when he reached up to wipe his eye just a little and then looked up at me with a grin.

"Well, keep looking. There's more than just one picture in there, you know?" I urged him on.

He flipped through the pages, stopping for several seconds to take each one in. There was a mix of news clippings, awards and photos. I had written captions for some of the pictures based on the information Buck had given me. Finally, when he got near the end of the book, he stopped at the section of photos of him with his friends. Selfishly, I stuck one in of him and me taken during the lock-in. Someone had snuck a photo when he was lying on my lap (I was pretty sure it was Sienna). I made a copy for myself, too.

"This…is my favorite," he said, tapping his finger on the picture of us.

"Oh, shut up, no it's not," I teased, tossing one of the sofa pillows at him. He grabbed it and threw it right back at me, laughing but then turning very serious.

"No, really. This is my favorite. Come here," he patted his lap, so I slid over, taking a seat on his knee. "Look, do you see the face you're making?"

I was embarrassed to look, blushing a little. I know the face I was making because it was sheer bliss. I couldn't believe Reed was laying on me, so close. "Yes, I know," I hid my face, embarrassed.

Reed pulled my chin up and gave me the sweetest, softest kiss. "Don't be embarrassed. I love that face you're making. I was making it, too," he smiled. "You loved me then, and I can't tell you how freakin' happy that makes me."

Still a little embarrassed, I just nestled into his shoulder a little, and he held me close, flipping back through the pages of his book, telling me a little about some of the photos I didn't recognize.

After almost an hour, he pulled the binding straps around the scrapbook and placed it back in the box, closing the lid. He picked it up and grabbed my hand, leading me upstairs with him. I watched as he slid the box under his bed and then came over to me, picking me up under the arms and raising me up above him then letting me slide down tightly into his arms. "Thank you, Nolan. You always give me the most amazing gifts, truly special," I could feel his smile against my face.

"It's cuz I love you," I shrugged, growing more and more confident when those words left my lips.

"Yeah, you always did," he smiled big then kissed me for the next hour.

22. Moments

MY JUNIOR YEAR was shaping up to be a fairytale. I attended every single one of Reed's games that season, even the ones that were out in the far corners of the state. Since Sarah and Sienna were always going for cheer and band, my parents were more apt to allow Becky and me to make the road trips on our own.

My heart stopped each time Reed would lift me up after one of his games, either on his way to the bus or coming out of the locker room. So many times had I watched longingly as he held Tatum. Thoughts of her still poisoned my self-esteem, but I was coming around more and more to the realization that Reed was with me; he was mine and I was his.

The Bears made it all the way to the state title game again, losing by a touchdown in a last-minute drive against Yuma. Reed took the loss pretty hard, always feeling like the entire town's hopes were on his back. I knew Buck really wanted to see a repeat title victory for his son, too. But despite the loss, Reed's performance is what seemed to light up the media spotlight. He had set a new record of more than 4,000 passing yards for the season, and ESPN was coming to town to do a short feature on him for a high school round up segment at the start of the next season.

The calls from colleges were really firing now, and Buck was in his element. The stack of offers was growing, and the pressure was starting to get to Reed a little by the time the holidays rolled around. I talked my parents into letting him stay at our house for a few days between Christmas and New Year's because his dad was going to be out of town so much taking meetings. Reed spent most of those days tinkering in the garage with my dad on his pickup, and I think Reed really liked the time away from talking football. My dad really liked having someone who knew a little about cars around, too.

Reed didn't dare sneak into my room at night, I think partly because my father put the fear of God into him. But Reed also respected my dad and his rules. That's not to say I didn't find my way to the couch during a few late nights, but that was different than sneaking Reed into my bedroom. At least, that's what we rationalized during our all-night make-out sessions in front of the television.

———

The hype from football died down some in the spring, a welcome reprieve for Reed and Buck, who was getting a little tired of the traveling. He was also starting to mix up his colleges, no longer able to rattle off who guaranteed to start Reed and which ones would place him in the back-up position.

It was my first road trip on the bus with Reed for the track season, and I was smitten. He and I, along with Becky and Sean, grabbed the back seats on the bus before we hit the road for a three-hour trek up north to Holbrook High School. Reed teased me while I folded up my legs and finished up my pre-calc homework. "Nerd," he jested.

Once done with my studies, though, I spent most of the way there sharing headphones with Reed and forcing him to listen to my favorite songs on the playlist I had downloaded the night before. I snuggled up in between the window and his arm, burying my face a little in his chest as we listened for more than an hour to my favorite Shins album and The Lumineers. I endured his occasional jokes about my 'chick music' and then let him show me what a real man listens to. I was starting to tolerate his rap and heavy rock more, too; probably because it reminded me of him.

We set up camp in the middle of the field and I stilled a little at the sight of my stuff mixed up with Reed's, like I had always pictured it in my dreams. We ran together and took our water breaks together, and I stretched by his field events just to watch him throw the shot put and disc. He was so much stronger now, and it was like watching a young Olympian when he threw, easily taking first place in both of his events.

He, Becky and Sean spread around the field for my event, yelling for me to run faster and cheering me on as I passed each of them. Reed was at the finish line waiting for me when I was done and wrapped me up in his strong arms with such force that you would have thought he was celebrating my win rather than the fourth place tie that had actually happened.

I couldn't wait to climb back into the bus for our trip home. There was something about laying my head in Reed's lap and folding my legs up on the seat, something about the way his soft and warm sweatshirt felt as I snuggled in close that made my already captured heart melt even more. I think this is the moment I had anticipated most since we had begun dating.

Shrouded in the darkness as we wound through the northern mountain passes making our way back home, I felt at complete ease. A lot of the people around us were either sleeping or watching videos and listening to music, and our small little bus seat felt a million miles away and just ours.

"What's on your mind," Reed asked, stroking my hair behind my ear and looking down at me, his perfect dimples simply perfect.

"Nothing," I bit the inside of my cheek a little and blushed, pushing my face into his chest so he couldn't see my embarrassment.

Reed tickled me a little to force me out of hiding, leaning down to push his forehead to mine while he kissed the tip of my nose. "That doesn't look like nothing," he teased. "Come on, you can tell me. Just say it; you think I'm cute don't you!"

He was joking with me, and it was adorable. "Well, you're alright, I guess," I rolled my eyes, joking back.

He dug in for another tickle. "Hey, you're no looker either, sister. Us uglies have to stick together," he shot back, then broke into a huge smile. I stuck my tongue out at him and with lightning speed he pulled me to him and kissed me hard. *Another perk to the back of the bus, I thought.*

I watched our hands together as Reed held me across his lap and chest, twining his fingers with mine and stroking the top of my thumb and then the inside of my palm. I snuck glances at his face and my heart swelled to see him look just as happy as I felt. Then the words just slipped out of me.

"How many girls have you slept with," fire burning on my cheeks, I had no idea where that came from. My eyes lit up, my eyebrows raised and I cupped my hand over my mouth, muffling my next words a little. "Oh my god, I didn't mean to say that out loud."

Reed just hugged me tight, chuckling a little. "You're adorable, you know that?" he tried to make me feel better. He held me tight for a few seconds and I felt him take a deep breath in. I knew he was trying not to talk about Tatum with me, but I also knew it was inevitable. I knew they had slept together…a lot.

"Four," he was matter-of-fact.

His words stunned me a bit, my body growing rigid and my eyes falling to look strictly at our hands again, not wanting to give anything away. *Four? I was not thinking four! Two, maybe. Honestly, I was really thinking one! Who were the other three?*

"I'm not proud of it," he sighed, sensing my growing insecurity. "And I would take all of them back if I could. You know that, right?"

He lifted my chin to look me in the eyes, his so sincere. Mine revealed how shocked and unsettled I was by his confession. I opened my mouth to speak, but didn't know the words, so I just closed it again.

Reed reached down to brush my hair out of my face and touch my cheek. "I don't want to hurt you, Noles, but I'll tell you anything you want to know. Anything you need to know and deserve to know.

But I'm not asking you to have sex with me, not unless you want to. I'll never be that guy," he was stern.

He was still fighting not to be Tyler. "I know," I smiled at him. "You make me feel safe." I hugged him tightly again.

I felt him relax a little and kiss the top of my head. "OK, well, you know about Tatum. She was my first. And, well, that's because I was an adolescent teenaged boy with hormones busting at the seams and...hell, you know the rest," he paused, looking out the window for a few seconds either to see if I would stop him or to gather the courage to continue. I wanted to know, but at the same time I didn't.

"And...numbers two, three and four?" I questioned, meekly, sort of figuring it out by the timing.

"I said I wasn't proud," Reed said, looking at me again and then looking away. "Morgan was my second... you know? The lifeguard that worked with us this summer?"

I gulped at his words, willing myself to be a big girl about this. *He's with me now, he's with me now.* The words played over and over in my head, reminding me.

"Well, Morgan had a friend named Mandy. We were at a party one night and I sort of found myself with her," he said quietly, scrunching his face a bit in shame. "That's sort of when Morgan told me to kiss her ass."

"Good for Morgan," I shot back, then slapped my hand to my mouth again. *Still talking out loud.* "Sorry," I bowed my eyes and grinned for forgiveness. He just squeezed me tighter.

I was curious who the last one was. He was looking out the window for quite some time, not wanting to admit anything to me. I couldn't take the waiting. "I have to know," I held his arm, willing him to say it.

"Calley," he said, and my mouth tasted like bile. *Sarah's sister? This was a sucker punch!*

My reflexes had me turning a little away from him, fighting to process his honesty against my desire to be angry at the new information. I was so sure he was going to say Stephanie or some other cheerleader, not the friend of his ex-girlfriend and one of my best friends' sisters.

But Reed wasn't letting me drift away from him. He held my gaze, willing me to look at him. He wanted to make it ok, and he wasn't going to let me go without making it so. He moved his hand to my face and forced my gaze to his, revealing the puffy eyes I was fighting against to keep the tears inside.

I raised my sleeve and wiped my eyes a little. "Sorry, I didn't mean to cry, that one just...surprised me," I admitted. "I just thought Calley knew how I felt about you."

I shrugged a little and tried to look away, but Reed pulled my face back to look at his. "Don't do that, don't run away from me," he said, sternly. "And don't blame Calley. She was at the desert party the night you picked me up. She was drunk. I was...drunk."

Yes, that I remember. Reed was at his worst that night. The first night he told me he loved me.

"I was running my mouth off to her in the back of her car, telling her how you were with this dickhead and I fucked everything up and she was consoling me and then we both did a bunch of shots of what-the-fuck-I-don't-know," Reed was revealing how that night unfolded. I guess I never really thought about the part before I got there.

"It sort of happened somewhere after that. And that's when I started texting you because I just wanted to erase it, knew I was fucking everything up...even more than I had already, if that was even possible."

"Calley started crying telling me to never tell anyone and to pretend it didn't happen. Noles, she never wanted to hurt you either. You have to know, she was so drunk. She got sick after that, passed out in her back seat and shit."

He just stopped at that, and held my stare, watching me process. I couldn't tell him it was ok, because it stung like hell. But it was the past, before *us*. I didn't like that it was Calley, but I didn't really like that it was Tatum, or Morgan, or... Amanda? And I think what had me more upset than anything was that I was never going to be able to compete with that.

After several minutes, I snuggled into Reed, looking for relief. I felt his shoulders relax as he brought his warm arms around me and his hands rubbed my arms. "I'm never going to be what they were," I confessed, revealing all of my insecurities. I saw each of those girls as women, whereas I was just some stupid girl. I suddenly had no idea what Reed was doing with me.

I was about to give in to my self doubt when I felt his breath near my ear, his lips light on my skin as he whispered. "Baby, you're so much more," he was soft, gentle. "You have no idea. You're so beautiful, and I love you, and if you ever want to be with me, I'll be the luckiest dude on earth…but not unless you want to share that with me," he kissed my neck and then buried his face in it, breathing me in.

Somehow he was erasing the hurt. I didn't know how he had that power, but he did. It still upset me to think about Calley, but here in the moonlight with Reed, it was easier to accept. And I would learn to.

————

I decided to keep Reed and Calley to myself, knowing that it would cause a rift between Sarah and her sister. And I knew deep down that Calley didn't want to hurt me. It took me a little while to bury the sting, but it hurt less and less each time I was with Reed.

Track season ended, as did my favorite bus trips with him. The end of the school year was almost here. Reed and I joked that we wouldn't be spending this summer working at the aquatics center. The thought of seeing Tyler's face again made my gut recoil, and I know Reed would punch him on sight. I had decided to take a job at the MicNic burger, mostly because I liked the novelty of wearing roller skates, which the wait staff got to do. Plus, I got a little thrill out of bringing my dad home free cheeseburgers from time to time.

My birthday was coming up, and I was nervous about Reed's plans. He was taking me out Friday after school and gave me specific instructions. So specific, they came with a list. He said he was making up for the date that never was, the one he had planned to take me on before Tatum ruined us the first time.

I checked my backpack Thursday night to make sure I had

everything Reed asked for: a full change of clothes, sweatpants and sweatshirt, tooth brush, my favorite songs on my iPod, a flashlight and an orange crayon. *The list was strange, I thought, but I was game. I was dying to know his plans.*

I met Reed at his Jeep when school let out, since he had picked me up that morning. I tossed my school bag in the back and pulled the special pack to the front seat with me. Almost giddy, Reed leapt into the seat next to me and buckled up before nearly peeling out of the student parking lot.

"So, where is this mystery date?" I asked, so curious.

"No, no…all will reveal itself," he was smug and knowing, teasing me and enjoying it.

We were on our desert highway for almost an hour heading south before we linked in with the Interstate and just kept on going. When I realized we were travelling far, I got a little worried. I hadn't prepped a way to spend the late evening hours with Reed, and I wasn't sure what time my parents expected me to be home.

"Reed, maybe I should call my dad? I think he was thinking I'd be home by 9 or something?" I said awkwardly.

Reed just shot me a huge grin, his green eyes lit by his deep dimples. "Not a problem, already got it worked out," he smiled. "See…you're spending the night at Sarah's tonight. She worked this whole thing out with me."

My mouth was open as I stared at him. Was I really spending the night with Sarah? I didn't think that was the case, but I was a bit thrown off my game by not being in control of my own destiny.

We drove for more than an hour south to the outskirts of Tucson before Reed exited on a side road and started to wind through the cactus-dotted desert hills outside the city. His Jeep climbed the mountains quickly and I could tell we were gaining altitude when I looked back to see the sun barely kissing the horizon and the lights of Tucson starting to glimmer a bit on the desert floor.

Twilight was setting in when Reed finally pulled off onto a dirt road and wound through a pine forest grove. It always amazed me that you could climb the desert mountains and find a forest revealed.

He stopped his Jeep and hopped out with gusto, pulling a large pack from his Jeep back and started to set up a tent. *Oh my god, we were camping! I had never been camping, ever!*

I sat there watching him, grinning like a child, until he startled me with his voice. "Are you just going to sit there, or are you going to help me set up camp," he teased, the rods for the tent flinging in every which direction.

"Oh! Yes, sorry. I was just taking it in," I grinned, ear-to-ear. Reed dropped the tent pieces for a minute and lifted me up, looking at my face as his spun me around slowly.

"Happy birthday, Nolan!" he was proud of himself. He did good, and he knew it.

————

We had the tent set in a few minutes and Reed was already working to get a fire going and setting up our site a little. I was just sitting on his sleeping bag that he had laid out for me, holding my backpack and watching him in wonder.

"What's up?" he smiled at me, wanting to know my thoughts.

"I was just thinkin'," I smiled.

"Yeah, I get that," he rolled his eyes. "Whatcha thinking?"

"Well, I get the clothes, and the toothbrush. And the flashlight?" I furrowed my brow a little.

"OH, yeah. Thanks! I'll need that. I don't have one of those," he grinned, grabbing the light from my backpack and pushing it in his back pocket.

"But, why my music?" I asked.

Reed stopped what he was doing and reached for my hand, pulling me into him tightly, kissing my lips lightly. "Duh, so I can dance with you under the stars," he shook his head like I was slow for not getting it, always teasing me.

"OK, OK. But...orange crayon?" I pulled it out of the bottom of my backpack and held it up and Reed just started laughing, so hard he had to hold his knees to catch his breath.

"Damn it," he yelled to the sky. I scrunched my forehead at him, pinching my brow, confused. "Oh, it's nothing really. I just owe Sarah $20."

I was still confused, and he could tell.

"She said you'd pack anything I told you to, and I didn't think you would. You know, because you're so pig headed," he pulled at my hair a bit like a fifth-grade boy. "I threw that on the list as a test, and she won!"

He went back to work, building a spread of sandwiches and fruit slices. "I could just sort of pretend I didn't bring it, you know," I smiled, willing to do what it takes for my boyfriend to win $20.

He just shot me a huge smile and shook his head, taking the crayon from my hands and tucking it in his other back pocket. "No, that's ok. I don't go back on my bets," he touched his thumb to my lip and then sat down next to me, handing me a paper plate with half a sandwich on it.

We ate our picnic spread and cuddled close to stay warm in the cooling air. The temperatures at this height were so much nicer than the desert campgrounds near home. When we were done eating, I pulled on a sweatshirt and followed Reed down a short trail thanks to my flashlight to a small lake. It was small enough to see the other side of the shore in the moonlight, but the stars still reflected beautifully along the surface.

We took turns picking up flat stones and trying to skip them across the water. Naturally, Reed was much better at this than I was. When I finally felt defeated he gave me a lesson, and he celebrated when I finally skipped one with three bounces.

We kicked our shoes off and splashed water at each other at the shoreline, the water freezing cold. When my feet started to go numb, Reed picked me up and let me wrap my legs around him as he held me to his chest and kept me close, kissing me over and over until my cheeks hurt from the constant smile spread on my face.

He carried me and my shoes all the way back to our small campsite where he set me down on the sleeping bag he had spread out. He lay sideways, propping his head up with his elbow, while I sat and stared straight up at the stars. There were millions and I could never take them all in up here.

"So, do you want your present?" he said, sounding more excited to give it to me than I was to receive it. Honestly, I hadn't expected anything else. Just this night was enough for me.

"OK," I said, closing my eyes and holding my hands out like Reed had done for me on his birthday. I felt the folded up paper in my hand and I opened my eyes. Squinting, I stared at the plain, lined paper with notebook shreds along the side and then looked back up to Reed, not sure what to make of it.

"You...wrote me a poem?" I questioned. He started laughing immediately.

"Oh, god no. You don't want me to do that, trust me. It'd be awful!" he laughed. "It's a letter."

I looked back down and started unfolding it. It was two pages and it was well creased and took me a while to pull at the ends and unfold it to flatten it out. Before I could take in the words, Reed blocked the top from my view with his hands.

"Wait, you need to know something first," he started. I stared at him, my eyes wide, unsure of how this night could get any more amazing. "You need to know when I wrote this."

I held my breath, waiting. "OK? So...when did you write this," I asked, my heart suspended.

"That night after the winter dance our sophomore year," he swallowed, his gaze holding mine as if he was trying to prove to me that he was being honest.

My hands were a little shaky now and I bent my head forward to read the words this boy, so much a man, had written to me a year and a half ago.

Dear Nolan:

Dear seems so sappy, sorry. I don't really know how to write things like this. I'll probably just shove this in my desk drawer for nobody to ever find. Damn, I'm already so fucking mushy, I hope they don't find it.

I looked up at Reed, matching his shy smile with my own and I looked back down and continued to read.

I don't know what took me so long to see it, but you are so beautiful. Like, yeah, you're hot! But not in a stupid sounding way – I know, I sound stupid now, huh? Anyhow...sure, I'm going out with Tatum, and yeah she's hot. But, you're different.

I'm not going to lie, I went out with Tatum because all of the guys think she's hot, she's a senior, and she's a lot of fun. Well, not like I can really do things with her, but... OK, I'm not going to sound like a prick in writing, but you know what I mean.

Focus, Reed Johnson .

So, I'm writing this as sort of a confessional. I guess this is like my diary, huh? I've never had one of those, but maybe I should start one. Not that I have a lot to say. But I've got this. I've got what happened tonight. Tonight I danced with a girl that stole my breath away.

My dad's always telling me shit about how 'the heart doesn't lie' and how one day I'll meet a girl that will make me stupid. I always thought he was crazy because there have been a lot of women who have made my dad act stupid. I guess he just likes falling in love.

But you, Nolan, you make me act stupid. I don't know if I'll ever have the courage to tell you any of this. You're not easy (and no, I don't mean that in the perverted way). I mean you come with a lot of feelings, you make me feel. It's weird, but when I touched you tonight it felt like tiny shockwaves hitting my skin. I was afraid to touch you, but I also had to.

I felt my lips twitch, so close to you. That was new, that's never happened before. I almost kissed your neck out of habit then I snapped out of it and realized that you're not mine. But what's strange is it felt like you've always been mine.

I don't know what happened, and I know that you would just rationalize all of this and say something about me being struck by the song and you in that pretty fucking dress, your bare shoulders so perfect and soft. But as beautiful as you were tonight, I think maybe you've been beautiful all along. And I'm just stupid.

Anyhow, like I said. I'll probably just shove this in my desk drawer. But I feel better getting it off my chest. Who knows, maybe some day I'll just kiss you and give it to you anyway. Yours, apparently?

Reed

I've never cried tears of joy, but I was doing that now. I was also fighting to breathe, suffocating a little from this amazing gift. Knowing what I needed, Reed just pulled me into his arms and held me tight against his chest, his mouth at my ear.

"I guess I knew I loved you then, too," I could feel his smile. "I'm sorry it took me so long."

I held onto his arms around my front and kissed them, squeezing him back. Turning in his arms to face him, I folded up the letter and shoved it deep in the pocket of my jeans. "That just kicked the shit out of my scrapbook and the varsity letter," I joked, trying to lighten the mood and bring myself back from the brink of delirium.

Reed just chuckled and smoothed the hair from my face, kissing me softly on the lips. As our lips held on to each other, I knew then that I was ready to give myself to Reed. And it wasn't just because of his letter, though that helped. I didn't want him to think that I thought he was just trying to get into my pants.

I stopped our kiss and held his stare as I sat up and stripped my sweatshirt, followed by my T-shirt and tight undershirt I had worn until I was bare in front of him. He was careful, waiting until I reached to pull his shirt from him, too. I snuggled tightly along his side and kissed my way up his shoulder, neck and face until we were intertwined and kissing hard again.

I kicked at my feet, pulling my shoes off and then working my pants open without Reed noticing. When I started to reach down to slide them down, he stilled, tense, and held my hands. "Nolan, you don't have to do this, that's not what tonight was about," he was serious.

"I know," I just kept my eyes on his, my breathing heavier now and my heart determined.

I stood up and slid my jeans down my body followed by my underwear until I was standing before him completely bare, cold and terrified. Not of what might happen, but that he might reject me.

When he slid his hands up my leg slowly and pulled himself to stand with me, taking the rest of his clothes off, too, I finally started to breathe again. He swung his arms around and picked me up without effort and carried me into our tiny tent, never breaking our kiss when he laid me on the soft comforter laid out on the earth floor.

Reaching for his wallet, he pulled out a condom and tore it to put it on, and my heart started to speed at what was next. Reed could sense my fear, leaning his face to my ear and whispering to me. "I'll be slow. And if you want, tell me to stop," he pulled back to look at me to make sure I understood and was still with him in this.

"I know," I smiled softly, kissing him and grabbing the back of his head, clutching his hair in my fingers as he slowly made his way over me until he was holding my body to his and slowly becoming my first.

I held my breath for what felt like minutes, my body tensing from the sharp pains until my nerves started to give way to passion, and we pulled at and tasted one another until I felt Reed's pulse quicken. My body heat was rising and I was starting to understand why this was so special and why I was so happy it was Reed I was giving it to. When I felt a rush of impulses fire through my core, I bit into Reed's shoulder a little, muffling a tiny cry.

Reed rolled me to his side and held me close, brushing his fingertips over my back and kissing my neck, whispering in my ear. "I love you, Nolan, and I swear to God I always will," he held me close, and we fell asleep together until the sun rose.

23. And So

XXX OOO

I loved the little texts Reed would send whenever he could from football camp during the first two weeks of summer. It had only been 10 days and I was missing him like crazy. I hated how dependent I had grown on his company, and I worried a little about losing myself in him, but I couldn't ignore the fact that I thought about him every waking moment of my day.

Buck let me ride with him up north to Flagstaff to visit Reed on his last day of camp. When we pulled in to the practice field, I spotted Reed immediately. He was running through passing drills with a few different coaches. Watching him tuck and run from side to side, slipping tackles and staying on his feet—he was so gifted.

The gaggle of girls who were gathered on the bleachers, gawking at my boyfriend, didn't go unnoticed either. Despite how much I believed, truly believed, in us, I still felt pangs of jealousy over those girls with confidence that seemed to be lurking around every corner. I was satisfied when they giggled, flipping their hair, and called out to try to get Reed's attention as he ran off the field to get water. He just gave them a passing glance and smiled, turning right back to his destination. Better yet, he didn't know I was there witnessing it.

"So, I hear there's some fancy pants quarterback working out up here. Think he'll give me an interview?" I said in my best disguised voice behind Reed at the watering station. I must have tricked him a little because he turned around a little irritated, wiping the drips of water from his chin with his arm and looking down. When he realized it was me, he tossed his cup at the recycling bin and pulled me into his arms, kissing me, sweaty workout clothes and all.

"Oh my god, I've missed you," he kissed me and swung me around. "Did you come up with Dad?"

"Yeah, I hitch with the best," I winked, nodding at his dad, already working the crowd of coaches at the camp. The man was all business.

"Good, you can come to dinner with us then. We get to eat at the stadium club at the college. It's pretty good food," he smiled and ran back out to the field to finish up for the day. The bleacher of bimbos shot daggers at me, and I was satisfied.

———

Reed was right. Dinner was amazing. The kitchen staff cooked for football players, so the cornbread muffins, carvings of meat and gravy was flowing, constantly hot and ready. It was maybe some of the best food I'd ever had.

I sat with Reed and a few of the other quarterbacks working out at the camp. I loved listening to them 'talk shop.' It was also amazing to hear how much his peers respected him. It was one thing for our town to know Reed was among the best, but to hear it from the others who were just trying to sit at the table with him? That was telling.

Reed kept his arm around me at the table and held my hand when we walked through the food lines, except when he took my tray. He kept refilling my tea for me and even made me an ice cream sundae. I could tell he missed me, and that made my heart jump for joy.

Leaving that evening was hard, but Buck had to get back and there really wasn't anywhere for me to spend the night, not that my parents would allow it anyhow. I kept my hand to the cheek that Reed had kissed for nearly the entire first half of the drive home. When we were immersed in the desert finally, I heard my phone chirp and pulled it out to find a text from Reed.

It was sooooo good to see you. I've been surrounded by a bunch of sweaty dudes for waaaay too long ;-) I know I'm supposed to stay at my mom's for two weeks, but maybe I could leave early?

I snuck a text back, hoping Buck didn't think it was rude. I caught a grin on his face, though, and I knew he approved of Reed and me.

You can't do that to your mom. We'll manage. Besides, she hates me enough as it is. Don't make her hate me more :-p

I was only half joking. The more time had passed between my first meeting with Millie the more I realized the differences between how Buck treated me and how Reed's mother acted towards me. She was cold, and I couldn't deny it.

One, she doesn't hate you. But…you're right. She's been looking forward to this. I'll be able to come see you a few times I'm sure. Maybe you can skate me a MicNic ;-) Love you!

Love you, too!

I tucked my phone in my bag and shut my eyes for the rest of the drive, picturing Reed surprising me at work while I skate up to his window. For the first time ever, I felt like the lucky one.

MicNic's was turning out to be a far better summer gig than working at the pool. And I was able to volunteer with the Boys & Girls club once a week with their adaptive program for special needs kids. I loved the work, planning activities with the kids and celebrating their accomplishments. The more I learned about this path, the more I was sure it was the direction I wanted to take in college. I liked the idea of pushing limits and telling society to shove it just because something wasn't easy, and the kids in these programs proved that to me every single time I was with them.

Reed let me go on and on about my first volunteer day. I felt a little bad, dominating our conversation, but he was genuinely interested. One of the counselors at the club had given me some information about the special education program at ASU and offered to give me a letter of recommendation for my application.

Things seemed to be falling into place, only ASU was the one school that wasn't in the mix as far as Reed was concerned. I hadn't talked to him about it yet, but I had pulled the applications for Stanford and UofA from our guidance office and was going to fill them out just to see. I knew that those were his top choices and I couldn't deny I had fantasies of going away to college with him.

It had been a particularly busy day at MicNic's when my phone buzzed with a text as I ended my shift, unlaced my skates and pulled my uniform shirt off and stuffed the apron in my little locker in the back of the restaurant.

Knock Knock.

That was all Reed said. I scrunched my brows a little trying to figure out his puzzle, finally guessing with:

Who's there?

I waited for a few minutes for him to write something back, but he didn't immediately. I grabbed my purse, slung it over my shoulder and got my keys ready to head out the front to my car. I was walking backwards, waving to a few of the girls working the late shift when I backed into a hard body, a familiar body. My pulse raced instantly.

"Me," I heard Reed's voice whisper in my ear. I turned immediately and kissed him, keeping my eyes open to take him in and make sure he was really here.

"Always clever, aren't you, Reed Johnson," I smirked, poking him in the stomach a little.

He laughed a little and wrapped my fingers in his. "Yes, terribly clever," he said, leading me out to the parking lot. "Hey, I'll follow you home. Think you can get ready in a hurry? I'd like to take you to my mom's big benefit party tonight. I saved you a step and already got the OK from your mom."

He just looked at me smiling, anticipating. Truth is I would have been happy to walk through a sewer just to spend time with Reed, but my anxiety was doing a somersault at the thought of having to spend my evening at one of Millie's charity events. I would go, of course, but I would hyperventilate more than a few times before, during and after.

"Uh, spend the night dressed up with you? Count me in," I smiled, big and bright. *Sell it, Nolan. Sell it!*

"Good, just wear something simple and comfortable," Reed said, my mind immediately taking inventory of the few dresses in my closet that would work for this. I was pretty sure I was going to have to get creative.

When we got to my house, I plopped Reed on the couch next to my dad so they could catch up while I showered and sorted through every possible dress in the house. Desperate, I called my mom.

"Mom, it's me," I was panicky, and realized I needed to get a little perspective. "Nothing's wrong…I just, don't know what to wear."

I rolled my eyes at myself. My mom just chuckled on the other end at how girly her little tomboy had become. "Why don't you wear my black dress? I know it will fit you. You can borrow my strappy heels, too," she seemed so hopeful.

"Uh, you think I can walk in those?" I wasn't so sure. Again, she just laughed it off.

"You'll be fine. Be careful, and make sure you have your key. We'll be long in bed by the time you get home," she said.

"OK, thanks mom. Love you," I stilled as I heard my mom take in a deep breath. She would always worry.

"Love you, too, honey."

I hung up and went right to the simple black dress that was wrapped in plastic in her closet. It was a classic fit, small spaghetti straps and a tight curvy cut, ending right above my knees. I pulled it on with black tights and my mom's shoes and took a few practice strides around her bedroom. I felt a little ridiculous, but when I caught my profile while passing my mom's full-length mirror, I did a little bit of a double take.

I seemed older, and with the shoes, I was close to Reed's height. Picking my hair up, I decided I liked the way it looked with my shoulders bare, so I headed to my mom's bathroom sink and pinned my hair up in a twist, letting a few pieces fall like Sarah always does. With a small bit of makeup so I didn't have to worry about it all night, I packed a tiny purse with my key, phone and money and headed out to the living room where Reed was debating a replay on ESPN with my dad. They both stopped, mid argument, when I stood in front of them.

"Honey, you look beautiful," my dad said, swallowing a little and turning his head to Reed to give him a stare, or rather a threat. I loved it when my dad was fatherly.

Reed just stood and came up to me and took my hand, kissing it. "Your dad nailed it, you look beautiful," his dimples deep with his big grin and his green eyes crinkled on the sides in awe. It took my breath away.

"Thanks," I half whispered, blushing and turning my head sideways.

"Well, we better hit the road. I can't go dressed in basketball shorts with you looking like that," Reed joked.

I kissed my dad on the cheek and followed Reed out to his Jeep and we made our way to Millie's house.

Reed, of course, had a complete suit at his mother's house. In fact, he had a closetful. He put on a simple black one with skinny black pants that just made him look like one of those classic movie stars from the 50s like James Dean or Cary Grant. He had a white shirt with a thin black tie. I could eat him, he was so delicious.

The party was at a ballroom at a big hotel in downtown Phoenix, and it had been going on for about an hour when Reed and I arrived. I was worried about being late, but Reed assured me that most people were late to these events. He also warned me about all of the rich old men with cocktails that would probably leer at me in a creepy way. I wasn't sure I was leer-worthy, but I decided to keep my guard up nonetheless.

When we walked in, there was faint piano music playing and a woman standing on a stage singing jazz, exactly what I pictured it would look like in my mind. There were dozens of tables around the room where everyone had left their purses and jackets, most of the people congregating around the middle of the room. *This must be mingling, I thought.*

Reed squeezed my hand, sensing my unease, which shot up tenfold as soon as I realized Millie was approaching us. She was upon us quickly, and I wasn't ready.

"Reed, dear, I'm so glad you could come tonight," she planted fake kisses on both sides of his cheeks, careful not to smear her lipstick. She smiled tightly and turned to me, reaching out to touch my arm and giving it a squeeze.

"So glad you could come, too, Natalie," I am sure my eyebrows shot up in surprise. I was about to correct her, when Reed rescued me.

"Nolan, mom. We went over this," he gave her a closed-lip smile, grimacing and showing his disapproval.

"Right, right. I know we did, honey. Sorry, it's just such an… unusual name. It doesn't seem to stick in my mind," she turned her fake smile to me. "We're at the front table, there should be two seats reserved for you. Excuse me, though, I have to greet some more guests."

And in a blink she was gone, back to flitting about the room. This was where she and Buck were similar. They could turn it on and were both all business when they needed to be. It just seemed Millie was more business than pleasure, like 99 percent business.

Reed and I found our seats and sat down at the table, picking at the breads stacked on plates in the center. We were both starving. We giggled each time we scarfed down a roll, laughing about how uncouth we were amid this high-end dinner crowd. I teased like I was going to put one in my purse, and Reed actually stuffed one in his jacket pocket to one up me.

I was finally relaxing and having a good time when I caught something out of the corner of my eye that made my body jolt. I wasn't sure I had seen things right, so I talked myself out of over-acting and almost had myself convinced when I heard that familiar cackle behind me.

"Oh my gawd, Reeeeeeeeed," it was Tatum. "I thought you never came to these things?" She was moving right past me, walking over to touch him, reaching for his shoulder.

Reed's surprise was genuine as he stood and pushed his hands in his pockets, quickly closing himself off to her. "Tatum, what the hell are you doing here?" he accused.

"Oh, I'm on the Sigma charity board. We're one of the scholarship recipients tonight, silly," she was acting like nothing had ever happened. And I was invisible. "I wish I was at your table, I'm so far away, over there in the corner. Maybe I could switch with someone."

She was seriously getting on my nerves now. I coughed a little to get her attention, and she turned and looked down where I was still sitting. Her brow scrunched a little as realization spread over her. "No fucking way, are you serious with this shit, Reed," she was talking about me. Nice.

I decided long ago that I was done being bullied by Tatum Hernandez. I had rehearsed many comebacks during my showers every morning, and I was finally going to get to use one. "Uh, yes. Quite serious," I said, standing and pushing past her to link myself through Reed's arm and kiss his neck, laying my head on his shoulder. "I'm afraid all of these seats are taken."

I was beaming with pride as she lowered her brow and clenched her teeth. Never one to just let it go, she shot one more arrow as she turned and left. "Boy, you really rebound low, don't you Johnson?" she said, walking away.

Reed just grabbed me and held me close, afraid that I was wounded. "I'm so sorry about that, I had no idea, I swear," Reed whispered in my ear.

"It's ok, and I know. I'm stronger now," I just smiled at him, a little proud of my showing. Reed just kissed my head and pulled my seat back out for me, tucking my napkin back on my lap so we could resume our mockery of his mother's dinner party.

———

The rest of the evening was more of the same. Millie made a lovely speech and the evening ended up raising more than $1 million for youth scholarships in Arizona. Millie managed to ignore me for most of the rest of the night, despite being seated two people away from me. She spoke to and about Reed often, and I'm sure most of the other people at the table were wondering who the strange, awkward girl was sitting next to him. Reed tried to introduce me a few times, saying things like "I take that class with Nolan or I run track with Nolan," and gesturing to me. His efforts were always grazed over though.

She shook my hand again when we left, still treating me like the help. I noticed that she embraced Tatum earlier in the evening, like long lost sorority sisters. I am sure Tatum wasn't too kind about me to her, either. *Great, like I needed more working against me.*

Even with the painful shunning, I still had a wonderful night with Reed. And he was right, I did manage to catch the eyes of a few older gentlemen, though they were far less creepy than he had me believe them to be. Drunk, yes, but creepy? That was up for debate.

Reed put his jacket over my shoulders as he led me out to the Jeep, careful to tuck me in safely before shutting the door. He drove us partly back to Coolidge but pulled onto a side dirt road when we were in the midst of the mountains. I noticed the grin on his face and bit my bottom lip at the anticipation when he pulled off into a small camp area. He quickly shut off all the lights and cut the engine, unbuckling and reaching for my face, pulling me close to him, swift and with a hungry force.

It had been so long since we'd been alone and kissed with such passion. We clung to each other, grabbing and fighting for air between locked lips. After several minutes, Reed just hung onto my hair and face, pressing his forehead to mine with his eyes closed. I grabbed his wrists and closed my eyes with him, content.

"It's a really nice dress," he laughed, breathy. I just started laughing, too. He was adorable, and I loved him with all my heart.

We held each other close for a while longer, and my mind raced with how good it felt to be in his arms. But I also started to feel a sense of dread, and I was sure it was because I had seen Tatum tonight. Reed could feel my heavy sighs and nudged me a little.

"Something wrong?" he creased his forehead, biting his lower lip.

"It's nothing," I tried to hide with a smile. He wasn't buying it, though. "OK, it's just…Tatum's really close to your mom, huh? And she's going to be around. And…well, you're going to pick a school that's never going to be closer than 2 hours from mine, and…"

He stopped me with the touch of his fingers to my lips. "Shhh-hhh, don't get ahead of yourself with worry. For starters, fuck Tatum," he was bitter with his words there, and I knew why. "You never need to worry about her. And second, we still have our senior year, and we'll figure things out, so how about we just enjoy now, huh?"

He was so good at calming me. I just smiled and squeezed into his side more. So happy, this was where I wanted to be, now.

The night air was getting colder and it was close to 1 a.m. Knowing I had to get home, Reed finally took in a deep breath and started the engine again. I stared at the desert stars, so plentiful and bright against the black out here. My mind was still dwelling a little on college plans and I thought about telling Reed about my applications, but instead I decided to wait. I didn't even know if I'd get in, and he was right. We had a lot of *now* ahead of us, and I was wasting it.

We pulled back onto the main highway, which was dark and empty for stretches. Reed slid his hand over to grab my leg, squeezing it to reassure me. I put my hand on his and stroked his strong fingers, admiring his perfect arms. I loved the way his jaw looked as the light from the oncoming car cast a shadow over it, so strong and masculine. He was so much more a man, grown from the boy I noticed years ago. I was so lost in him and his features when I saw the flash of pain rush over his face in an instant as he jerked his hand from me and grabbed the steering wheel.

There was a screeching sound of tires and the smell of burnt rubber in my nose. I saw glass shattering in my lap and felt the strong pull of the seatbelt across my bones just as the swift punch of the airbag came slamming into my face, burning my skin upon contact. It felt like we were spinning, but I wasn't sure if we were even moving any more. There was a constant sound of a car horn and I heard screaming.

Disoriented, it took me a few seconds to recognize Reed's voice. "Nolan, Nolan! Are you ok, Nolan!" he wasn't himself, he sounded terrified, hurt. I pushed through the airbag material, pulling at the yellow bag in front of him until I could see his face. I gasped when I saw his steering wheel pushed up into him, pinning him to the seat, his arm bent awkwardly through the wheel and into the dashboard. Then I saw bone. Bone!

"Oh my god, Reed! Your arm! Don't move, don't move. You're hurt!" I fought to get to my buckle, pain shooting through my ribs a little as I moved. I could see Reed's face, it was ghost white and he looked like a frightened little boy. I reached for his face, holding it still in my hands and forcing his eyes to mine.

"Reed, you're hurt, do you understand me?" my heart beat deafening in my ears, shaking my entire chest and I was sure my hands were shaking from it. "Reed, just focus on me. Do not move; do not look at your arm."

It was broken. Badly. I wish I could take back what I had seen, but I made a mental note to myself not to look again. I was sure I would get sick if I did. I kept a hand on his face, my eyes locked with his, as I reached for my purse that was thankfully still tucked in my lap from the force of the airbag. I pulled out my phone and dialed 911.

"There's been an accident. I don't know where we are," I was operating on adrenaline now, my mind flashing back to Buck's heart attack. "Yes, I will stay on the line."

I kept my eyes on Reed. "They are pinging my phone, help is coming. Just stay right here with me, don't move."

I could suddenly register the sounds of the other vehicle. I heard a woman's voice and I yelled through the shattered front window, hoping she heard me. "Help is coming, stay where you are. Do not move in case you have injuries," my eyes still on Reed. His face was expressionless.

I wasn't sure how long we sat there, silent amid the chaos, before the flashes of lights and sounds of sirens were upon us. The firefighters pulled me from the Jeep and I fought to try to keep my eyes and hands on Reed. "Careful, he's hurt! Please, help him!" I screamed.

They laid me on a board and ran through a series of questions I couldn't even hear. Could I see something? Could I hear this, could I feel this, was there pressure here? I was fine, I wanted to tell them. I wanted to get to my feet, go help Reed. But they kept me in place and were soon lifting me on the board and into the back of an ambulance. I remember the doors shutting, the pinch of a needle in my vein, the sound of scissors up my mom's dress. A woman EMT was dialing my phone, and I could tell she was talking to my parents.

We were at a hospital soon, though I wasn't sure which one. There was a rush of florescent lights and dotted ceiling tiles and then silver doors that flung open and a new set of nurses and doctors in scrubs. They hovered over me, pushing, prodding, sticking for several minutes before wheeling me to a corner in the long hallway, pulling a curtain around me and then abandoning me.

I tried to stretch my muscles and sit up in the bed. I wanted to find my phone, wanted to know how long it had been. I needed to know if my parents were here, and I HAD to see Reed. I started crying finally, the release of it all coming out in full force.

A nurse swished the curtain open just then, holding a small tray with medicine and water. "Nolan?" she was using her calm voice, the one they train them to use. I remember this from Buck. I know this voice. "Hon, you were in an accident." *No shit!*

"Reed, is he here? Is he ok?" I was starting to fight her, trying to sit up. She put her hand on my shoulder, holding me down. I winced from a pain, a bruise I thought.

"He's here. He's fine. He's with the doctors now. It's ok," her words were better than medicine, the fight completely abandoning my body, leaving me exhausted.

"My mom and dad?" I was starting to cry again.

"They'll be here any minute," she reassured, pushing the water with the straw in it to me and giving me two pills to take. I swallowed and she was gone.

I stared without blinking at the curtain, wanting to just leave my little corner, but afraid to all the same. I was at Mercy. *Buck's hospital, I thought.* I focused on the sound of my heavy breathing and the regular beep on my machine, my only companion here behind the dark curtain. When I finally heard a familiar voice, I started crying again. "Mommy? Daddy?" I heard their feet speed up and the curtain was once again open.

My mom hugged me, again making me wince in pain. My dad just stood at the foot of my bed, holding his hand over his mouth, trying to hold it together.

"I'm ok, mom. I'm ok," I was reassuring her. *What the hell?*

"Oh my god, baby. We had no idea," she leaned back, wiping her own tears and then mine. Grasping my hand, she also reached for my father's. We sat there still for a while, just linked together.

We were finally interrupted when a doctor with a clipboard walked up to my bedside, flipping through paper and chewing gum. "Hi, Nolan," he was more chipper. I wasn't sure if I liked that either. "You are a lucky girl, you know that?"

He leaned over and listened to my heart and helped me forward to listen to my back while I breathed. "You wore your seatbelt, and that saved your life, you know that?" he continued. Lifting the blue gown I was somehow now wearing, he showed my mother the bruising on my chest and ribs from the impact of the seatbelt. I spaced as he started explaining the burn marks from the air bag and before he was done speaking I interrupted.

"Where's Reed," I stared at my father, knowing he would be the only normal person here with me now, the only one who would get me the information I needed to know.

"I'll go find him, honey. I'll be right back," he gave a half smile and tried to hide the pain in his face from seeing my injuries. He left my curtain world and I watched the spot he had been standing until he returned.

My dad didn't come back for almost 30 minutes. When he did, he had the answers I was desperate for. He had talked to Buck and said Reed had two broken ribs and they were working on setting his right arm. I gasped at the thought, air leaving my lungs. My dad smoothed my hair back and reached to give me more water. "He's going to be here overnight, honey, but he gets to come home tomorrow. He's going to stay at his mom's. But he's going to be just fine," he said, trying to keep me calm.

I let a single tear slide down my cheek, not even bothering to wipe it. *How could he be fine. He can't throw. How the hell did this happen?*

"The doctors said we could take you home tonight," my mom slid in to sit next to me, pushing a cold wash cloth on my head.

I just shook my head no. I didn't want to go. I couldn't bare the thought of going without Reed. "No, please. I have to stay. Please!" I was begging. "It's a hospital, I'll be fine here. Please!"

My voice was hoarse and my cheeks were sticky. I was sure I looked homeless, my hair ratted and my face dirty from crying. I watched as my parents exchanged glances, looking from me to one another. Finally, they relented, explaining they had to check me out so I would have to stay as a guest, sitting in Reed's room.

"I'll pick you up early tomorrow, OK?" my dad kissed my head while my mom helped gather my bag of belongings. I cringed as I saw her good dress, cut in two in a plastic bag. But she picked my chin up and smiled.

"It's just a dress," she smiled. "It gives me an excuse to buy a new one."

I just squeezed her hand again. Not really wanting to spend the night here in my loaner gown from the hospital, my mom worked her persuasive magic and talked one of the nurses into giving me a set of old scrubs. They were maroon, but at least they weren't open in the back, a step up from the gown I was wearing now.

———

My parents left and I stood in the hallway by Reed's room holding my phone wearing flip flops my mom bought at the gift shop. I couldn't seem to get my legs to move, so I just listened as Buck explained he would be back tomorrow and he would drive Reed to Millie's house. Millie had left just minutes before; I missed her, which was probably lucky as I'm sure somehow what happened has only made me a step lower in her eyes.

Buck stopped in the hall as he left, looking down at his phone and then pausing as he got closer to me, looking up and giving me a soft smile. "Nolan, sweetheart," he gave me a big hug and I started shaking. "Shhhhhhh, it's ok. He's going to be just fine. He's strong, my boy."

He gave me a wink and said he'd see me in the morning and I started to slide to his room. I barely made it around the corner, silent, and I saw his face, still blank. He was looking out the window at nothing. I slid closer, setting my phone on his small table and then pulling the wooden chair over to his head side of the bed. I curled my body up into the tiny chair and reached for his left hand, his right one buried under a slick, white cast. His entire right arm was held up with bars and chains, and he looked so uncomfortable.

He didn't turn to me right away, and his hand felt weak. When he finally looked at me, I could tell his eyes were puffy. I ran my fingers down his face, leaning forward to kiss his head. "Hey," I smiled, faintly.

"Hey," he said back, biting his lip a little, still pained. He was squeezing my hand more now. "You're ok," he let out his lungs, his mouth falling into a hard straight line.

"I'm ok," I swallowed, looking at his body, which was not OK. "Does it…hurt?" I motioned to his arm.

He turned slowly to look at it for several minutes before speaking. "Yeah, it hurts," he was chewing on the inside of his cheek, distracted.

He finally turned his head back to me, blinking a little, his eyes looking tired. "I'm staying," I said. I just wanted him to know so he could relax, and it seemed to help a little. "I refused to leave," I smiled.

He gave me a flat smile, his lips tight. The lines formed on his brow; he was thinking. I reached for his water cup and brought it to him, but he just turned and shrugged it off. Finally, he spoke.

"She was texting," he sighed. I wasn't sure what he meant, so I just shrugged, not understanding. "The driver of the other car. She was texting. She came in our lane, so fast. I swerved and we hit the highway marker. And a cactus, I guess."

He seemed to be far away, replaying the accident in his mind. I just brushed his head and tried to get him to rest.

"My dad's pressing charges," he said flatly, turning back to the window. A few minutes later, he was asleep. I watched him breathe until the sun was up, and finally I slept for an hour or two myself.

———

My dad picked me up just as Buck was arriving to get Reed settled and ready to go to Millie's. The two fathers shook hands, Buck putting his hand on my dad's back, almost a hug. I could tell they respected each other and were some comfort to one another, and it made me feel glad amid all of this bad stuff.

Reed had managed to eat a small breakfast, and was talking more this morning. But he still seemed off. I kissed him, but our parting felt empty. It felt like a routine, or an obligation on his part. And suddenly the deep bruising on my ribs wasn't the only internal injury I was nursing.

24. And After

TEN WEEKS. That meant five games. Reed wouldn't suit up for his senior homecoming match up, and there was a chance the Bears wouldn't make the playoffs unless Kyle, Reed's back-up, could pull off a miracle. He had only thrown the ball in a few games, and only when they were blow outs.

Reed had been back at his dad's house for almost two days, and I still hadn't seen him. He had called me the night he got home, but said he was going to bed early, tired and trying to get things settled. He promised to make it up to me yesterday, but then the entire day came and went without a single phone call.

His texts and phone calls to me grew less and less while he was at his mother's house. I tried to keep it in the rational box that told me he was dealing with this life-changing trauma, and fear that he wouldn't be the same. And I knew that mostly that's what it was. But I couldn't seem to equal out how he could be shutting me out now when I had so much to offer. I could be his rock, and wanted to be so desperately. I couldn't help but think that his mother's opinion of me wasn't at play just a little, either.

I drove to campus for volleyball workouts and stopped on my way into the gym to peer out at the football field. I saw Reed's profile standing next to his coach on the sidelines. He was talking to him and pointing at things while Kyle was working passing drills. Kyle wasn't Reed, and that was clear from even this far away. But he wasn't bad.

Heading into the women's locker room, I let my mind get carried away, wondering if Reed would be waiting for me after practice, or if he even realized I was here. I was navigating unknown territory, and I didn't know how to handle it. Reed was distant, but he still told me he loved me and spoke sweetly, when he spoke.

When I led the freshmen through running drills up and down the stairs, my mind flashed back to the first time I locked eyes with Reed as he flung open the heavy metal doors to the gym lobby. Those doors remained tightly closed each time we ran by today, but I still expected to see him standing there every time I passed through anyhow.

When practice was over, I packed up my gym bag slowly, letting everyone leave before me. I even thought about taking a quick shower before I left, something I had only done two or three times ever. But I knew I was just stalling. I was so afraid of walking out that door and seeing the dark lights over the football field and Reed long gone. He was driving Buck's raised Ram truck, waiting on the settlement from the accident to see what they could do about his Jeep. I willed that truck to appear in my mind and held on to the hope that it would.

When I finally walked through the gym lobby and let the warm desert evening air hit my face I shut my eyes for a moment, not wanting to know if he was there or gone. When I opened them and saw him sitting on the wall, I felt my lungs fill with air for the first time in days. His hat was backwards, his hair a little longer than normal and tucked behind his ears, curling out from the bill of his hat. He was wearing his long basketball shorts, Nike sandals and my favorite gray T-shirt; his cast, which now boasted a few signatures, was resting on his leg.

I bit my lip a little as I walked over to him slowly. I was nervous, like I was just now introducing myself to this guy who knew me so intimately. It was strange, and I missed the comfort we used to have.

"Hey, you," I said softly, trying to gauge his mood.

"Hey, yourself," he smiled faintly, reaching his hand up to take mine and sliding off the wall. He moved into me and kissed me softly. "I missed you."

I could still see the shimmer in his eye, but it was faded, worn. He seemed tired. Reed walked me silently over to my car, and I felt my hand sweating in his, something that had never happened before. The closer we got to my car, the more worried I was becoming, afraid that the next words from his lips were going to be to break up with me. I was so lost in these thoughts that when he finally did speak, I jumped a little.

"Thought maybe we could get some dinner?" he held my door open for me. "Maybe you could follow me home and then drive? It's kind of uncomfortable for me."

I could see that, there wasn't really a good place to rest his cast, and it looked so heavy. "Of course, I'm starving!" I smiled, trying to hide my worry.

He kissed me again, softly, and shut my door for me and I waited for him to back out to follow him home.

I struggled for something to say the entire trip to MicNic's. Reed seemed lost in his own thoughts, too. My mind was racing and fighting against the thoughts of our relationship ending, sick with anticipation that his next words would be telling me that we had to move on, apart.

Things were quiet over dinner as well. We sat across from one another in a booth, but at least now we had our food to keep our mouths busy. I let my eyes take in Reed's cast finally, slightly ashamed of staring at this glaring symbol of his weakness. Sean had written his name and football number on the cast and so had a couple of the other guys, but there was a signature closer to the inside that I was having a hard time making out.

"That's nice, some of the guys signed your cast?" I said, almost timidly.

"Oh, yeah," he just shrugged. I wondered if he'd want me to

sign it, or if that was even something you offered to do in a situation like this. I felt like a third grader.

He was picking up his drink and leaning back in his seat a little when his cast rotated and I was finally able to see the names hidden on the inside. Tatum. And Calley. I wanted to throw up right here all over the table. I could feel my heart speed up, and I was pretty sure rage was starting to brew in my toes and crawl up my legs. I had to be cool, because things were not good between us, and I didn't want to make them worse. But this? This wasn't ok.

"Uh…" I stalled, looking for the right words, crooking my mouth to the side and taking a deep breath. Reed just looked at me, shaking his head and wondering what I was going to say. "I'm sorry…but…did Calley and Tatum sign your cast?"

I was being so careful, and I hated that I was acting like this. Almost afraid of him, afraid of making him mad. But inside I was screaming.

Reed rolled the cast a little and looked at it and just shrugged a bit. "Oh, yeah. They were both at my mom's when I got back from the hospital, volunteering for one of her things. Whatever," he said as if it was no big deal.

No big deal. Perhaps it wasn't. Maybe I was making it a big deal in my own mind. Except, he had to know that of all names he could walk around wearing for two and a half months, these were possibly the only two that could break my heart, if only just a little. Instead of confronting him, though, I just swallowed my emotions and tucked them back deep down inside and plastered on my fake smile.

———

The first few weeks of school went about the same. Reed and I saw each other in the hall and in the two classes we had together. We held hands and he kissed my lips lightly when we parted. But there was no depth. It was as if we were characters in a play, carrying out our parts for a rehearsal, but saving the real emotion. I just didn't know exactly what we were saving it for.

Reed wasn't the only one to blame. I was just as much of a

zombie as he was, allowing him to ignore me until he had to come face-to-face with me, pretending that it wasn't bothering me. I just went on with my days and then sat awake until the late hours of the night watching my phone, each night thinking he would call. And then he didn't. I didn't either, though.

We texted the few times we had plans, but that was it. Even his texts were shorter. I still signed mine with XXOO, but his were just short one-word answers or times when we should meet. And we hadn't met, outside of school, for days.

Reed was spending most of his free time watching tapes with coach and working with Kyle. The team managed to win their first two games, though it was close. Our big test would be Friday when we played Southern Christian. I knew that this game was consuming Reed, and I also knew that he was counting down until the day he was able to take the cast off and work on his strength. The doctors had told him that he might be able to throw in the play-offs if we made them, but that he'd probably miss the entire regular season. His arm just wouldn't be ready in time.

I stayed late after volleyball practice just to watch Reed work with Kyle on Thursday night. Kyle was picking things up, and Reed was actually a pretty good coach. But I could see his frustration. When Kyle ran back to the field to work out with some of the other guys, Reed stayed at the sidelines and sat on the trainer's table, his feet kicking a little while he looked down at his phone. I watched him push his phone to his ear and then he jumped from the table and began pacing. He was rubbing his head and swearing a little. Then I heard him clearly.

"Fuck!" he screamed, pushing the giant water chest from the table and knocking down rows of cups, kicking at them as they fell. He shoved his phone back down into his pocket and just stood there, staring at the ground and the mess he'd made. Frozen, I wasn't sure if I should go help him, comfort him or pretend I hadn't seen him crack.

He was picking up the cups and kicking ice chips around when I finally got close enough for him to hear me.

"You ok?" I said, nervous.

His eyes shot up to me and then he just looked back down. "Yeah, I'm fine," he was short.

I couldn't play this game with him anymore. "You don't look fine," I stood, my hands on my hips. "How about you talk to me? Let me help."

I started to help him clean up the table and he continued in silence. When he reached for the chest, I took it from him and put it the rest of the way on the table. The act seemed to irritate him, though, and he shrugged me off.

"Just … just don't, Nolan," his brow was bunched together, like I had offended him.

"Sorry…" then I rethought my words, feeling braver. "I was just trying to help, Reed. You won't let me fucking help."

I turned to leave, starting to feel the anger brew in my tummy once again. I was sure I was going to make it all the way to my car without a protest from him, but he surprised me, stopping me before I was more than a few steps away.

"No, you're right. I'm sorry," he sighed. I turned and just looked at him.

"What's going on?" I pleaded.

He let out a heavy breath and looked back out to the field where his team was practicing without him. Finally, he spoke. "Most of the schools are pulling their offers," he finally admitted. I had feared this.

"Oh Reed," I went up to him and put my arms around him, but he still stood limp in my hold. "I'm sorry. I know this sucks."

I didn't want to patronize him. He didn't need that. He looked up at me finally and I saw a faint smile on his lips, but it quickly disappeared. He looked back down at his feet before talking again. "I still have Stanford and UofA," he said. "So I guess that's good."

I thought maybe now would be a good time to let him know I applied, too, just to make him feel less alone. "You know, I wasn't going to tell you until I knew for sure, but I applied to those, too," I bit my lip, anxious for his reaction. When he finally did look up, though, it wasn't the expression I had expected to see on his face. Instead, he looked concerned and baffled.

"Why would you do that?" he asked, sharply.

A little dumbfounded, I stood there looking at my hands as I wrung them together before I could answer him finally. "I uh... I don't know, I like their programs, too, and thought I would keep my options open? Thought maybe it would be cool if we went to the same school?" I couldn't believe I had to explain this. What did he mean, why would I do that?

"Oh, yeah. I guess that'd be pretty cool," he was flat. I fought against my tears and turned so he couldn't see me when I wiped my eyes a little and managed to get my emotions in check. I was about to ask him if he wanted a ride home when he interrupted my inner debate with myself.

"Well, I'm going to go talk things over with coach. We're going to go through some other tapes tonight, work on my game plan to keep the scouts interested. I'll probably be pretty late," he smiled, tight lips, just waiting for me to give him his out, which of course I would.

"Oh, ok. That's fine, I have a lot of homework," I lied. I didn't have a thing to do. Just like every other night, I would go home and sit on the porch, look out at the stars and let my mind get carried away with horrible, negative thoughts.

He leaned in and kissed me then whispered, "Thanks for talking." He turned and walked away and I headed back to my car wondering when we'd actually start talking for real. Or if he ever would.

Friday's game was a disaster. Kyle threw four interceptions and the Bears lost 41-7. I could tell Reed was pissed from my view in the stands. His dad was pissed, too, but still so much more approachable. When I was leaving the stands, I stopped to talk to Buck, hoping he might give me a glimmer of something to hold onto. Per usual, he pulled me into a giant hug and warmed my heart as only he could.

"Reed's having a tough time," I grimaced.

He just put his hand under my chin and tilted my head up to look in his eyes. "Hey, no getting down, you hear?" he insisted. "Reed will get through this. He's a fighter."

I wanted to believe him, I did. But it felt like Reed was losing the fight, and in the process, I was losing Reed.

I left Buck and met up with Sarah and she motioned to the fence by the field. I turned to see what she was looking at and saw that Calley and Tatum were standing there next to Reed's mother.

"What are they doing here," I am sure I sounded as offended as I was.

"No idea," she shrugged. "My sister didn't even mention that she was driving back into town tonight."

I hated that Calley and Tatum still lived together. It felt like a double betrayal. I hadn't told Sarah about Calley sleeping with Reed, but seeing them here and knowing that they spent time with Reed over the summer was making it harder for me to maintain my cool. Even worse, Reed's mother was talking with them. Accepting them, like she never would me.

I was only getting furious, and that wouldn't do me any good. I decided I needed to get myself away from the situation in order to think clearly. "You mind giving me a ride? I don't think Reed's going to come home for a while, and he's pretty pissed," I asked Sarah.

She stopped to stare at me for a while, I knew she understood more than she let on, but she finally just gave in and did what I asked. "Sure, I get it," she just shrugged.

———

During the entire ride home with Sarah I wondered if Reed even noticed I was gone. I also wondered if he stopped to talk to Tatum and Calley when they were with his mother, and if he was pleasant to them, unlike he had been with me lately. I wondered why his mother had shown up at all. She rarely came to his games, and Reed wasn't playing tonight.

By the time Sarah dropped me off, I had worked myself up into quite a frenzy. My parents seemed surprised when I came into the house so early. I think they expected me to be out with Reed. *Hadn't they noticed we hadn't been out on a date in weeks?*

"You ok, honey?" my mom asked as I walked in and stopped to sit on the end of the sofa for a few minutes.

"Yeah...just tired," I said. And I was tired, but I was also fueled with anger.

I headed back to my room where I sat on the edge of my bed for about half an hour, trying to talk myself into calling Reed. Finally, when I reached a boiling point, I dialed.

"Hey," he answered, short.

"Yeah, hey," I copied his tone.

We both sat silent for a few uncomfortable seconds and then he talked. "You just left? What the hell?" he seemed angry, which only set me off more.

"Yeah, I did. It looked like you had a lot of *fans* waiting for you and I didn't want to get in your way, you know, cramp your style," I was being a bitch now, but I didn't care. And I couldn't stop.

"Noles, you're being stupid, stop it," he threw back.

I didn't like that word – stupid. "Really? That's all you've got? I don't know Reed, you spend the summer with two girls you slept with, one who bullied me to near breaking point, and you're just going to chalk it up to me being stupid right now?" I was breathing heavy, fuming.

Reed just let out a long sigh.

"What's wrong, Reed, nothing to say to that?" I wasn't letting him off so easily.

"Nolan, you're overreacting. You need to let the Tatum thing go. We hardly talked all summer, and I was just being polite. Come on, give me some credit," I could hear his eyes rolling.

I sat there in stunned silence for a while, not sure what to say next. We were not in a good place, and Reed was just ignoring it because that was easy. But I couldn't ignore it any longer. I knew he was hurting from his arm and not being able to play, but he was taking it out on me, *on us!*

Taking a deep breath, I tried to calm down. "Reed, I know you're upset about your arm," he tried to interrupt but I kept going.

"But I'm still here. Here for you, to support you and listen to you. And when you show up with Tatum and Calley's signature on your cast but you can't even text me goodnight or give me the time of day, well I guess it sort of made me question things. Can't you see that, just a little?"

Silence. We both sat there soaking in my words and finally I could hear him moving a little, rustling on his phone. "You're right," he relented. "I'm sorry."

"Just don't shut me out," I said, hoping it would really sink in.

"I'm not good at this, failing? I just…I don't know how to not be whole. I feel stuck, and my options are all disappearing. It's just… scary, you know?"

He was talking. I couldn't believe I had him talking, and I was so thankful. "Yeah, I know. And it's ok to feel scared. And I know you don't believe me, but I know you'll be just as good when you get your cast off. I know you can come back from this, Reed."

He just sighed heavily. "Thanks," he finally let out, softly. "I gotta go. But I am sorry."

I could tell he was, but he was still not right. It was going to take some work to bring him back from the dead. But I was up for it.

"I love you," I said just before we hung up.

"Me, too," he responded, and my heart kicked a little not hearing the words, but I had done enough tonight. I wouldn't push any more.

———

Homecoming had arrived and Sienna, Sarah and I were prepping the gym and the classrooms for our senior lock-in. Reed and I were still strained, but I was forcing him to talk more, and he wasn't giving up. His cast was set to come off next week and he was determined to work hard and maybe get in one regular season game in. It looked like the Bears might just make the playoffs, but barely.

Tonight's game was an important one. We still had a shot without winning, but the door would close just a little more. Reed had been working with Kyle all week, studying game tape from the

Yuma games so he'd be ready for the pass rush. I impressed Reed a little knowing what that was.

He had come over for dinner last night and for a brief few hours we felt like we were back to where we were. He snuck holding my hand under the dinner table and even gave me a passionate kiss goodnight before he went home. He sent me a text to have sweet dreams, too, and I had looked at it about a dozen times today.

When things looked about set, I walked Sienna over to the band room before the game. I needed some alone time with her, and between her dating Micah and Sarah being with us most of the time, I hadn't had a chance to let her in my head much lately.

"So, you wanna tell me what's going on or do you just want me to guess?" Sienna was so intuitive.

I smiled at her and nudged her shoulder a little with mine while we walked slowly through the halls. "Things are…" I didn't know how to classify my relationship. We had a few good moments, but on the whole, my relationship was failing, fighting for air. Reed hadn't touched me intimately since the accident and even his kisses felt forced. "We're sort of stuck. Since the accident. Reed's so depressed, and I can see it. And he just won't let me in. What's worse is he's taking it out on me. Sienna, I feel like his arm is my fault somehow…"

This was the first time I'd said out loud what I'd been thinking all along. I was there when it happened, and if Reed hadn't been driving me through the desert at that time, he wouldn't have had that accident. He was taking me home from his mother's damn party, and she'd been hateful. But he was making me feel loved, and then everything changed.

"Nolan, you know that's crazy, right?" Sienna was staring at me. I just shrugged. "OK, this is going to take more than just a short talk on my way to band. Come in with me."

I followed her into the dressing room and helped her unpack her uniform and get changed. There were a lot of pieces to her uniform and it was weird being in the changing room while 30 other girls were all throwing jackets, jumpers, feathers and buckles around, trying to change before the game. Always the multi-tasker, Sienna laid her wisdom on me while she got ready.

"One, and most important, this isn't your fault. A bad thing happened, Noles. A really bad thing. That's all. It's shitty and it's terrible and it's been miserable for Reed, but it was a bad thing that happened, and there wasn't anything anyone could have done differently," she was lecturing me now, but I was prepared to listen. I just nodded.

"Good. OK, now that we have that down, I'm going to say something you're not going to like, but I'm saying it because I love you like a sister," she stood serious and moved to the side so we were a little away from everyone else, more private. I was nervous at what she had to say as I was pretty sure she was going to say everything I'd been thinking.

"Reed is being a bit of an ass and you need to call him out on it," she read my thoughts. "I get that he is going through something horrible, and I get his fear, but he's taking it out on you. That's not fair, Nolan, and it isn't healthy. I see you two. You walk around like you're in a trance. And he's not there for you, not really."

I just nodded, my eyes watering a little because I knew it all. "Nolan, he's got to fix this on his own, get his head on straight and get out of his funk. If he doesn't, he's always going to blame you, but only because you're there. You're an easy target, and you're just taking it."

I sucked in a sharp breath of air because I knew what she was going to say next. "Nolan, he's going to keep lashing out until you leave. And you might have to. I'm not saying that you can't find your way back, fix this freaking all-consuming relationship you and Reed have been in for what seems like forever," she was trying to be humorous to lighten the load she just threw on me. I adored her for it, but she was right. And I was glad she was here to give it to me straight.

"I know," I whimpered, reaching out to my friend who just gave me the hug she knew I needed.

"God, why can't Sarah be the one to give you the serious lectures," Sienna joked, rubbing my hair while we hugged.

I laughed a little and backed up to look at her, rolling my eyes. "Sarah doesn't do serious matters of the heart. Now, she'll kick his ass. But psychology? No, that's not her deal. That's yours."

Sienna laughed and nodded. She gave my arm a squeeze and I told her I'd see her at the lock-in after the game.

I walked out to the bleachers to find Sarah. I paid my entry and walked to the front of the bleachers to find where she was sitting and then I felt someone brush up behind me.

"Hey, I got snacks, want some," it was Calley. She was sipping on a soda and had a tray full of candy and popcorn. *Unfuckingbelievable.*

I nodded and just gave her a polite smile and led our way up to Sarah. We watched the game and I kept sneaking glances at Calley on the other side of Sarah. I wondered if she thought about what she'd done ever, if she knew I knew? She seemed oblivious, like nothing between her and I had ever changed or ever should, so I was pretty sure she didn't.

Not able to keep my curiosity at bay, I leaned forward to look at her. "Why'd you come to the game, Calley?" I tried to keep it light and pleasant, but I was really fishing to see if she was here for Reed.

She finished chewing on a licorice and then leaned forward to look back at me. "Tatum has a new boyfriend. Can't stand being in our apartment lately, he's over all the time. Thought I'd just come home for the weekend," she smiled a bit and then leaned back to keep watching the game. She seemed genuine about it, so I let it go for now.

The game was close, and we were losing by two with less than a minute to go. If Reed were in as quarterback, I know everyone would breathe a lot easier right now. But putting this in Kyle's hands left everything up in the air. We were at our last down and 10 yards out from the end zone. I stood and held my breath, watching Reed watch Kyle. Reed was motioning with him, I could hear him yelling and Kyle released and the ball sailed to the corner of the end zone, about five feet too far.

The entire crowd fell silent. Reed threw his hat and kicked over a table, pushing his hand through his hair and screaming while he turned around to look away from his team. He was pure anguish and helplessness. Everyone knew the numbers. Yuma needed to lose tonight for us to make the play-offs, for Reed to play in a game his senior year that mattered. Everyone in the stadium was heart sick. I looked down and found Buck just motionless, rubbing his chin in disbelief.

I locked my eyes on Reed and fell into despair for an entirely different reason. This was killing him. And he was gone. Those last 10 seconds that ticked off were exactly how long it took him to shut the door on everything. His face was pale and blank. And I was going to feel the brunt of it all. I knew this, and I had only a few minutes to prepare myself for it all. And for what was likely to come after.

I stood to find Sienna in the crowd and when my eyes met hers she gave me a sympathetic smile, just nodding to show she understood and was here for me.

"Come on, let's go get the gym ready. Not that anyone's going to come tonight," Sarah said, tugging at my shirt so I would follow her.

———

I sat at the entrance table with Sarah and Sienna finally joined us along with Micah. A few people started to stream in, which surprised us. They were mostly sophomores and freshman, students who didn't really have anywhere else to go on a Friday night. The upper classmen would be in the desert, I was sure. Drowning their sorrows.

After about 30 minutes, a few members of the football team started to make their way in. I was feeling anxious and every time the door flung open, my heart leapt and my breath stilled waiting for it to be Reed.

It was about an hour into the lock-in and time to close the doors for good when it hit me. He wasn't here. And he wasn't coming. Sarah and Sienna sat still next to me. They knew it, too.

"Maybe we can wait a few more minutes," Sarah said, trying to let me down easily.

I just shrugged and stood. "It doesn't matter how long we wait and you know it," I felt defeated. "He's not coming. He's fucking not coming!"

I stood up and stuffed my hands in the front of my sweatshirt pockets, looking down at my feet. I was so mad at myself for letting this happen. I was putting off the hurt and I was enabling him to take his frustration out on me. "I can't do this, guys. I can't do this," I was shaking my head, looking at both of them.

"I know," Sienna said, coming up to me to give me a hug. Sarah sat still behind her.

"You know he's at the desert party," I did know. Where else would he be. He wouldn't go home. He'd go somewhere to lose himself or sit in silence amid a crowd and throw himself a pity party.

"Come on," Sarah said, pulling on my sweatshirt and grabbing her purse.

"Where are we going?" I asked, a little worried at her idea.

"We're leaving. Sienna, can you tell Ms. H that I got sick and Nolan had to take me home?" Sienna nodded at her, knowingly.

"We can't just leave, we're in charge…" Sarah interrupted me.

"Yes we can, and yes we are. We're going to go tell Reed to stop treating you like shit. Are you in? Or do I need to do it by myself? Because I'm going to do it no matter what," she was unstoppable at this point.

I looked at Sienna for guidance and she just smiled. "Go, this is what Sarah is best at," she was referring to our conversation earlier. "You can't put this off; you're going to have to confront him eventually. You might as well go while you're packing a secret weapon," she motioned to Sarah.

She was right. They both were. I was terrified. It was all going to be over tonight, and in my heart I knew it. I guess I had been putting it off because I didn't want it to end, but the last few months had been so miserable, it wasn't really worth the heartache any more.

Sarah and I snuck out the door as Sienna locked up and we headed to her car. The drive through the desert was quiet and determined. As we got closer to the campgrounds, Sarah started to talk. "Nolan, you deserve better than this. I know I'm not a great model for relationships. I have a new boyfriend every week. But you're better than that. You and Reed aren't supposed to be like this… this is poisonous, and I won't let him destroy you," she reached over and grabbed my hand. She was right and I was so thankful to have her and Sienna at my side.

We pulled in and shut the lights off. I took a deep breath and gathered my inner strength before getting out of the car, glad I had worn my comfortable jeans and sweatshirt since it was freezing outside.

There were pods of people drinking on car hoods and in pickup beds everywhere. There was a new crowd added in, the new junior class and some underclassmen that wanted to get in with the 'cool crowd.' The thumping of the music was distracting, and there weren't many lights, so it was hard to see in the distance. Finally, Sarah recognized Calley's car and motioned for me to follow her.

Calley's car? My blood pressure was shooting up now and I was getting stronger with every step we took. We pushed past a small fire pit and found a few people sitting on a grouping of picnic tables. I recognized the silhouette of his back in the firelight and stopped in my tracks. Sarah was still looking around and hadn't noticed yet. He was sitting there with a beer in his hand and talking…to Calley. He could talk to her.

As if I was possessed by someone far stronger than myself, I stormed up to his table and flipped the hat he was wearing backwards off his head. That fucking hat, I always thought it was so adorable. I wanted to shove it down his throat right now.

"What the fuck," Reed said, turning to see who had done that to him. "Nolan? What are you doing here?"

Seriously? What was I doing here? I was about to unleash. I felt Sarah move behind me, catching up to me when she heard Reed's voice. She started, but I put my hand back, letting her know I was good. I had this. I wasn't going to be his whipping post any more. I loved this boy, the real one that I knew was still down there, but he needed to hear the raw truth. I was hurting, so I was prepared to serve it to him, unfiltered.

With a calm voice, almost scaring myself, I began laughing a little. "I know, right?" I giggled, mockingly. "Like, what would I be doing here...with my boyfriend."

I was serious now. "So, were you going to just let me know you weren't coming... maybe with a phone call tomorrow? You know, so I could just wait around and worry tonight. Or were you planning on not calling me at all? Maybe this is how you handle things, like the child you are. You just figured you'd ignore me until I got the hint and went away. Well, I got the hint, Reed. Ohhh, I get it."

My heartbeat was pumping through my ears now and my lips were quivering with anger. Reed just tossed his empty beer bottle into the bushes and slid down from the table. "Nolan, let's not do this now. Can we just talk tomorrow?" he was annoyed with my words, I was forcing him into a corner, and I wasn't going to stop.

"No, Reed. We can talk now. Funny, I see you don't have a problem talking to Calley," Reed's eyes shot to mine with a warning. It was too late, I was gone and there wasn't any way to stop the flow of venom I was about to let out. "You planning on making yourself feel better by sleeping with her again?"

Calley's eyes shot to mine and then to Sarah's, her mouth wide open with shock. She was getting up and shaking her head, trying to explain herself, but it was too late. "No, don't bother Calley. Reed told me about the little fling you two had. You know, while you knew I was in love with him. You and Tatum are perfect roommates, you know?"

I was so on fire I didn't notice Sarah behind me, shaking her head and growing angrier. But when she opened her mouth, I was suddenly reminded she was there. "How could you!" she shoved her sister to the ground, kicking dirt at her. "You bitch! You're my sister! How could you do that to my best friend?!"

Tears were pouring down Sarah's cheeks now and Reed and I were stuck in our bubble, just staring at each other. He was blank still, unfeeling. And that's when I knew I couldn't crack him. He was too far gone.

"You know what the kicker is?" I said, laughing a little to myself and shaking my head. "I got my acceptance letter to Stanford today. I was actually thinking about how we would maybe both go off to college together. God, I'm a fucking idiot!"

Reed was just shaking his head, indifferent to me. And then he locked his eyes right on mine. "Whatever. Like it matters, I mean... it's not like you could even afford it," he sounded superior. Smug. And his words cut through all of my bravado like a knife. Never had Reed made me feel less. He had never commented on where I lived, what my parents did or the fact that I came from something so very humble. He knew how sensitive that was for me, and yet here he was...exploiting it.

I froze and everything drained from me. Reed stood staring right back at me, locked together. He had put something out there that he couldn't take back. For a brief moment, he seemed like he wanted to, too, but then he just straightened his posture and tightened the line of his mouth. I had nothing left to say. That was it, and I knew we were done. Reed was too far gone in his own breakdown to realize he had just killed me, killed us with his words.

Turning to Sarah, I cleared my throat a little. "Please take me home."

She just nodded and put her hand on my back, leading me out of the wake of our damage. The thumping of the music was still going, but the crowd was quiet. I could hear Calley crying, but I didn't care. I was sad that Sarah had to find out this way, but I had to leave everything I had on the table.

———

Sarah drove me to her house and we locked her bedroom door and curled up together in her bed. I was too stunned to cry, and she was too angry about her sister to talk. We just stared off into space, her hand squeezing mine. She was my strong friend, and tonight had made her weak. I hated that she got hurt.

"I'm sorry I didn't tell you," I whispered.

"Shhhhh, it's ok. This isn't your fault, Nolan. None of it is," she was flat, but I knew she was with me. She had my back, and she always would.

———

Sarah and I finally fell asleep in the early morning hours. I woke up at 10 and nudged her after laying there for a little more than an hour, thinking. Thinking, it turned out, was not good for a broken heart.

"Hey, I'm sorry, but can you take me home?" I was quiet, a sharp contrast from the loudness of the night before.

"Sure, just let me hop in the shower real quick. I want to go out for a bit," she grimaced. "I don't want to be around while Calley's here today."

"I'm sorry," I started, but she stopped me with her hand up.

"Again, not your fault. Don't, ok?" she was genuine. I was grateful she didn't blame me, but I still felt badly.

Sarah drove me home and then headed out to Chandler to spend the afternoon at the big mall in town. My parents were out for the afternoon and had left me a note on the counter. "Hope you had a good time, honey. There's leftover pizza in the fridge if you're hungry. We'll be home later this afternoon. Love you, mom."

I couldn't eat now if someone held a gun to my head. I wasn't sure when my appetite would come back. I flopped onto my bed in my room and tossed my bag of things to the floor. Deep breath after deep breath was helping me to clear my head. I had come to terms with the fact that this needed to happen. I knew it was inevitable, and I knew that it was coming the second Kyle missed that pass.

Kicking my shoes off, I slid from my bed onto the floor, bringing my knees up and tucking them under my chin. I stared at it for a few minutes before finally sliding the box out from under my bed. I didn't have to open it; I knew everything that was in there. It was every letter, every card, every single thing that Reed had ever given me. There were pictures and stupid things that reminded me of him like the napkin from MicNic's that he drew a heart on and hid in my purse for me to find after our date once.

There was also a packet of information on UofA and Stanford in there with my notes from the research I'd done. Reed was probably right; affording Stanford was a bit of a pipe dream. But I was still going to try if that's where he had decided to go. Now, sitting here with my box of Reed in my lap, I felt ridiculous. I was redrawing my entire plan, just to be with him. And that wasn't healthy either. I had wanted to go to ASU my entire life, and here I was ready to throw that all away just to follow a boy to college. Who's to say he wouldn't have broken up with me as soon as we got there for some cheerleader?

Who's throwing the pity party now, I thought.

Suddenly, the box of mementos in my lap was the last thing I wanted in my house. It had to go. Standing, I pushed my shoes back on my feet and tucked the box under my arm and grabbed my keys and wallet from my duffle bag on the floor.

With purpose, I walked to my car and tossed the box in the passenger seat. Within minutes I was pulling up in Reed's driveway. Buck's big truck was nowhere to be found, but I saw what looked like Reed's old Jeep parked off in the garage. It looked like it had been fixed. I was glad for that. *At least something was able to be fixed from this awful accident.*

I grabbed the box and jogged up to Reed's front door and rang the door bell. It was one of those long-ringing bells, playing its song forever. Everything about his house suddenly seemed so pretentious. I was about to give up when the door clicked open and Reed was standing in the doorway, his body leaning against the wall a little. His face was still flat, which was going to make this easier.

"Here's your shit," I said, shoving the box in his hands and making sure his eyes saw right into mine. This was me, ending it. On my terms. Sure, it was childish to play the last word game, but nothing about the end of our relationship was mature. I might as well win at something.

I spun on my heels and headed back to my car, fighting every itch to turn over my shoulder to see his reaction. I didn't want to give him the satisfaction. In fact, I didn't even look in his direction when I climbed in my car and drove off, pulling a U-turn in front of his open doorway. I was pretty sure he was watching me leave, and I was glad.

Everything was going to hit me eventually, but for today I was going to be strong. I owed that to myself. And I was. Tomorrow, that's when I could cry.

25. My New Normal

THE ENTIRE TOWN seemed to be operating under an umbrella. Sure, there was still one more game to play. But it didn't matter. Not really. We were knocked out of the state tournament. And this was our last Johnson, so the odds of Coolidge making the spotlight again in the near future were slim.

I ran into Buck at the grocery store the morning after the big loss, and, positive as ever, he was hopeful. He told me Reed was set to get his cast off, and he was anxious to give the scouts one more look at his arm before signing season began. He still had a few tricks up his sleeve, and I felt a little better knowing Reed had his father in his corner.

I thought perhaps just getting to play once would lift Reed's spirits. But his unhappiness ran much deeper. When he was up, things still seemed possible; when he was down, though...well, I guess that wasn't really my problem anymore. Except I knew that wasn't true either. I'd never stop worrying about Reed. I was pretty sure I'd move on to college and spend my four years following him in newspaper clippings and daydreaming about how he was, hoping he was ok and hoping he was learning to be happy again.

I spent the entire Saturday holed up in my room, cleaning out my closet and listening to music. I pulled out a few of my favorite classic books, trying to get myself lost in the high-brow torture of the Bronte sisters, but I never made it further than a few pages. I wasn't going to homecoming. Not alone. And I knew Reed wasn't coming to get me. A small part of me was hoping he would ride in like a knight and shining armor and beg me to go with him, but when the clock ticked to 7, then 8 and finally 9, I quit that fantasy, too.

My mom was a little surprised that I wasn't getting ready for homecoming, and I eluded that Reed and I had a bit of a fight. She tried to pry a little, but I told her I wasn't ready to be upset about it yet, and she let it go. I knew she was worried, though, because she made excuses to check on me every hour or so throughout the night.

No matter how big of a jackass Reed was being, I still wanted my parents to love him. Such a dichotomy from how his mother felt about me. She didn't even acknowledge me when I was around. Again, though, not my problem anymore…except it ate away at me every moment I was awake.

Sarah texted me from the homecoming dance, wanting to check on me. She was also telling me what I really wanted to know, needed to know—that Reed wasn't at the dance either.

————

Weekends were easy, it was when I was at school, in the same room, building, campus as Reed, that things were hard. I was waiting for it to get easier, waiting for something to happen. Waiting to forget the last words Reed had spoken to me. I wanted confrontation, but I suppose that had come and gone. All I had now was, well, the now.

I couldn't help myself, but I stole glances at Reed when he walked through the halls, looking for hints at his mood, all the while waiting for him to snap out of this spell he was under and remember he loved me, to pursue me, to chase me and claim me again. That never happened, though.

Most of the time he was quiet, just floating from one class to the next, sitting and watching the lessons, not really participating. I had worried that his grades were slipping, but Sean told me he was still managing to ace everything and that he still had UofA and Stanford pursuing him. *At least something was going right.*

Reed's birthday had come and gone. There was no party this year, though Sean told me that Buck had tried to talk Reed into the annual barbecue. The UofA and Stanford hats I had bought him still lived on the top shelf in my closet, tucked away in a bag, waiting to be shaken out and delivered. But that wasn't going to happen.

I noticed that his Jeep was showing up in the parking lot at school again, and I was glad to see it fixed and in working order. It was a part of him, and it was the way I liked to remember him. His dad had put special plates on the back, UofA ones. I mused at his not-so-subtle act, also wondering if that was any indication of Reed's decision of where he would sign for next season.

The last Friday game was a week away. The school was set ablaze with the hype I'd grown accustomed to during the last four years. Streamers and banners were hung along the halls. Cheer-leaders were decorating the football player's lockers, many paying special attention to Reed's. I thought about how I probably would have been the one to do that a month ago. But instead, I hadn't spoken to Reed since the day I showed up at his door with his letters and my memories.

He hadn't texted. He hadn't asked Sienna or Sarah about me. And he and Sean talked about football and nothing else. It was like the last three and a half years had all been a figment of my imagi-nation, that we were nothing more than mere acquaintances. Less than, in fact, as even an acquaintance would make eye contact with me on accident once or twice.

I spent most of my nights working on my memoir project. It turned out I loved my creative writing class. And after a few phone interviews and inquiries with the special education program at ASU, I found out I could specialize in reading and writing disabilities. For the first time in weeks, my mind was excited about something, and I even found I could forget about the hole in my heart every now and then.

It was my turn to present in class today, and a strange part of me was eager to share something so personal. I had spent weeks working on my piece and had even shown it to our teacher, Mr. Bosch, in advance. He encouraged me to submit it for a scholarship award, so after perfecting it (with his brutal editing), I did. If I won, I would be able to pay for my room and board at ASU, which would be a blessing because, as it stood now, I was looking at driving two hours each day through the desert. I had earned a full scholarship for my tuition, but that was only half the battle.

I sat in the back of the class with my notebook bouncing nervously on my knee. Reed's desk was empty, and while I was worried because he never missed class I was also relieved. I wasn't sure I could stand in front of the class with his eyes on me.

We were nearing the end of our hour when I was finally called up front.

"Miss Lennox," Mr. Bosch called.

I walked up slowly, opening my notebook and taking a deep breath to clear my nerves. Public speaking was not my forte. I cleared my throat a little and slid to sit on the stool at the front of the room, thankful I could at least not worry about my knees locking. When the classroom door flew open, I jerked back a little and immediately flushed when I saw Reed walking to his desk, right at the front of the class, directly in front of me.

I swallowed, still looking down at my notebook, my hands fidgeting with the ringed binder. My nerves kicked into overdrive when I looked up again and saw Reed was smiling a little at the students next to him, his cast no longer on his arm.

"OK, class. Settle down. Mr. Johnson, glad you could join us," Mr. Bosch snarked.

"Sorry…had a doctor's appointment," Reed stood, pulling a pink slip from his pocket and handing it over.

"Yes, I figured as much. Nice to see your appendage is back to working order," even Mr. Bosch almost sounded excited, and I was pretty sure he hated football.

Reed sat back down and shuffled his feet a little, grabbing at the front of his desk and then settling his eyes right on mine. His bright-ness flattened a little and he bit his lip, embarrassed as he realized he had interrupted me. Heat rushed over my body and I forgot my entire purpose for standing up here. I was startled by Mr. Bosch's throat clearing and shook my head a little trying to find my way back.

"Uh, yeah…sorry, where was I?" my voice cracked a little. I snuck a look back at Reed and he was grinning at me, encouragingly. He hadn't smiled in weeks, and certainly not at me.

"Your reading, Miss Lennox?" Mr. Bosch said, leaning back against the wall near the classroom door.

"Oh, yes. OK," I cleared my throat again. It was only two pages, but I wasn't sure I could do this. I was sweating standing up in front of the classroom.

Deep breath…

My grandmother believed in angels. Not the traditional kind. Her angels didn't have wings, they weren't ghostlike and they didn't live in the sky. No. Her angels lived among us. She always said my mother was one. She said it was the way she looked after her family. Mom held us together when grandpa died, when grandma couldn't pay her mortgage and when my brother broke his arm and we didn't have insurance and had to drive hours away to find a doctor that would set his arm for what mom referred to as 'the generic price.'

Unflappable. Undeterred. Indestructible. Unwavering. All good words, but those are still human. An angel, though…well, an angel is something more. An angel knows your heart. And they know how to fix it when it's broken.

I paused ever-so-slightly, taking in a breath and willing my eyes to stay on my paper. I wouldn't look up at Reed, but I knew these words were hitting him. They had to. They were hitting everyone.

I have an angel of my own. She's 10, and her name is Nancy. I met Nancy two years ago, and she gave my life purpose by giving it direction. Nancy has Down syndrome, and she's fearful of many things. Mostly, she's afraid of being alone. Turns out, so am I.

Our first summer together, we conquered Nancy's fear of water. Amazingly, she's part of a swim team now and hopes to swim in the Special Olympics some day. As pen pals, we conquered her bullies. Young people can be cruel, and when they see someone with Down syndrome they also see an easy target. Bullies like to find where you're vulnerable, avoiding the challenge and instead going for the easy kill. For me, it's always been my family's small bank account or the fact that I don't like to wear a dress.

I looked up now, noticing Reed was listening intently, his eyes focused on the edge of his desk, his knuckles white as his hands gripped hard and his feet shuffled with discomfort. I continued.

Together, though, Nancy and I discovered that you can strip a bully of their power without even confronting them. All you need to find is your passion— something to love. For Nancy, it was swimming. For me, it was a boy.

And so this is where my angel comes into the story. What do you do when your passion breaks and your heart is broken along with it?

The boy I had been holding onto was suddenly gone. Not physically, but emotionally. I was lost. I'd been lost for a while. And I found myself on the road, driving to see Nancy. With her mom's OK, I picked her up from school, and together we went for ice cream. Without much preparation, my angel went to work.

"You look sad," she said.

"I am," I was always honest with Nancy.

Then Nancy put her small hand on the center of my chest and closed her eyes. Her act made me a laugh a little, prompting me finally to ask: "What exactly are you doing?"

"I'm taking your sad away and making it mine," she was serious, and I wouldn't dare laugh at this. "You can have my happy for a while until I get this figured out for you and give you your heart back."

Hugging Nancy, I cried and realized that, up until now, I hadn't done that yet. I had been holding my tears in, afraid to let them go. But now, as I did, I realized that maybe Nancy, my angel, had been my passion all along. And helping her, and kids like her, was what made me better than those who tore me down.

Nancy had suddenly made me strong when I felt weak. She took away my alone. My heart? That's healing, too. And loving someone isn't what makes me special, it's my ability to love…period…that sets me apart. At least, that's what my angel told me.

The bell started ringing just as I finished, but the entire class sat still. Uncomfortable, I just closed my notebook and slid from the stool and found my way back to my desk, my eyes looking down at my feet.

Saving me from the discomfort of this awkward attention, Mr. Bosch started to talk, explaining our next assignment and dismissing the class. I finally breathed with relief when people started shuffling their backpacks and leaving the room. Reed was the first to go.

Sienna leaned over as she was packing her bag and I noticed her eyes were glossy and red. "Holy crap, Nolan," she whispered. "That was good. Like…really good!"

I smiled humbly. I wasn't good at taking compliments. "Thanks," I said. "It felt good to write. I just sort of wish Reed wasn't here to hear it. I think…I think I made him really mad."

Sienna just shrugged it off. But he left the room quickly, and everyone knew who the boy was in my story. I was pretty sure that I'd just fired a warning shot, however unintentionally, yet I had no want for war. All I could hope for was that the truth in my writing would be enough to win over the scholarship judges now. At least my heartache could earn me that.

———

Reed ended up playing in the final game of the season, and as I predicted (and had promised him) he was just as good as he'd always been. Maybe even better. He threw for 350 yards with four touchdowns, and that was only in a half. It was certainly enough to keep several colleges interested, and Buck was back in business managing his favorite client.

I went to the game with Sarah, but she took me home before it was over. I didn't want to run into Reed after the game. Since I had read my piece in front of the class, I found myself avoiding him even more than before, something I was able to keep up for weeks.

The holidays passed quickly. Calley was home for the break and after not talking to her sister for the first two weeks, Sarah finally gave in. I had forgiven Calley and wanted Sarah to, too. But my loyal friend took a little wearing down to get there.

Sarah, Sienna and I were all going to ASU next year, and Calley and Sarah decided to move in together. It seemed that living with Tatum was too much, even for Calley. She had already moved out of their apartment and into a single dorm for the rest of the semester.

I didn't go out for track this season, deciding to spend my spring focused on my studies and scholarship applications. I knew I had a shot at the creative writing scholarship, but I didn't want to hang my hat on that alone. My parents were sure they could cover most of my schooling extras, but I knew every little bit would help, so I took on a few afternoon shifts at MicNic's, too.

Both Reed and Sean had decided to skip track for the season, too. I knew Reed's signing deadline was fast approaching, so I was sure he was spending every spare moment planning the best move with his dad.

I had seen Reed in class and in the halls, but I always managed to rush by without making eye contact. I thought I heard his Jeep pull down my street one night, but when I looked out my family's front window, no one was there. It had been months now since I'd heard his voice, and I could hardly remember the sound of it.

I spent most of my spring break toiling away at the school library. The computer lab had become my working office and I had a goal of sending out one new scholarship packet each day. I had managed to score a few with my efforts, though most were only $50 or $100 stipends, barely a dent in the parking fees. But I kept moving forward since every check meant one less day working at the burger joint.

My face was buried in my backpack, looking for my headphones, when I ran into Buck, literally. "Whoa, oh my gosh, you scared me!" I laughed a little, surprised to see a car other than mine at the school parking lot during the break. "Whatcha doing here?" I slung the headphones over my shoulder along with my backpack.

"Just picking up some of Reed's stuff. We have a workout down in Tucson," Buck smiled, winking. "They want to take a final look. I think he's got the starting gig locked up down there. I just hope I can convince him."

I smiled, my heart picking up a little knowing that Reed was just a few yards away in the locker room. I wanted to get inside before he came out. "Oh, I know if anyone can convince someone of something, it's you," I smiled, starting to walk past Buck, then suddenly halting when I heard his voice.

"So what exactly is pops convincing me of?" I flushed and suddenly felt panic stricken. I turned around nervously, looking at Buck for a life raft. But he just grinned and threw Reed's gear into the back and walked to the other side of his truck, leaving me to clean up my own mess, or leaving me with Reed at the very least. Yes, that man was tricky.

"Ha," I laughed cautiously, searching my brain for the right words. "Your dad just said he was driving you down to Tucson and making you walk back if you disobeyed." *Phew, that went ok.*

Reed leaned into the side of the truck, chewing on his gum and flipping the sunglasses from his eyes so I could see him. For the first time in months, they looked clear, the worry and anguish gone. He looked down at the bag now dangling from my wrist and then slowly up to my face, a smile shyly curling on one dimple. "Are you doing homework on spring break? You know, our grades don't really matter at this point," he was teasing me. God how I missed this.

"Oh, ha…" I shuffled a little in my stance. "No, just scholarship work. I've got a lot of dorm bills to settle for ASU."

His smile started to fade a bit, but then he closed his lips tight and forced a renewed one. "Ah, yes. That other school in Arizona," he joked.

"Yeah, you know, the one where all the smart kids go?" I was joking right along with him, winking as I talked.

"Reed, we gotta hit the road, kid," Buck hollered through the window he'd just rolled down.

"Ah right, hang on," Reed leaned in to say to him.

I stood there still, not sure of my next words, my next move, or if I'd be able to move at all.

"I gotta go, but hey…" he was looking down, his brow bunched and a bit of a frown on his face. "Maybe… maybe I'll stop by MicNic's later or something? Sean said you're working there right now?"

I just nodded. He smiled back a bit and then climbed into the truck with his dad. I stayed frozen, watching them drive away. Eventually I found my way back to my car. There would be no scholarship writing today. I'd be lucky if I could concentrate long enough to fill out my first name.

————

My shift at MicNic's seemed to drag. I'm sure it was because I spent the entire time watching the clock and calculating how long it took to drive from Tucson once the sun set. But Reed never showed. I think maybe part of me knew he never would. But it was exactly this part of me, the one that was hoping, that concerned me most. This part of me had been numb for so long, this renewed self seemed so foreign. And I wasn't sure if I could handle waking it up again.

I was able to get a few good scholarship days in after all, and by the time our break was done, I had sent out 24 new applications. Something had to come of this work. I was enjoying what was left of my break on the Sunday afternoon when my cell phone rang. I didn't recognize the number, since mostly Sarah, Sienna and Sean called me now. I thought about ignoring it, but instead I answered.

"Hello?" I was a little guarded.

"Hi, is this Nolan Lennox?" a woman asked on the other line. She sounded older.

"Uh…yes. Who is this?" I was suspicious now, and I think the woman on the other line could tell as she started to chuckle when she spoke again.

"I'm sorry for surprising you. My name's Kendra Sharpe. I'm a reporter with the Gazette. I'm doing a story on Reed Johnson, you know, talking about his amazing high school career and the accident. We hear he's signing with Arizona tonight and want to do a full feature for the sports section, local hero kinda thing," she was smart when she spoke. I was a little thrown. Why was she calling me?

"Ohhhhhh… kay?" I said, still not sure what I had to do with this.

She continued to explain. "Well, sometimes for these big profile pieces we like to interview friends and family, just to get a full picture of who someone is, if that makes sense?"

It did. "Yeah, I get that," I said, waiting to find out what I could possibly offer.

"Well, we know you were in the accident with Reed, and I was hoping I could just get your perspective on what happened…and how you think it affected Reed…" she was waiting, hoping I'd take the bait. But instead I was hyperventilating a little. I didn't know how to do this, or even if I should.

"I know it's an uncomfortable thing to talk about, and I'm sorry to call you out of the blue, but you're sort of my last piece to finish this article. I'd really appreciate just a few minutes," she said. She seemed genuine, so I relaxed a little. I didn't want to hold up the article, and Reed's story was an amazing one that people should know. I was excited to hear that he was leaning toward Arizona, too.

"OK, I guess…" I would be careful.

We spoke for maybe 10 minutes, mostly just clarifying facts about the accident and how much the students loved Reed and how the town really rallied behind him. I felt pretty good about the interview, until she asked me at the end how I was holding up after going through something so traumatic. That's when I got a little too comfortable with Kendra and let my mouth run unfiltered.

"It's been really hard. I mean, I didn't have the broken bones and injuries, but I've had the guilt. I guess a part of me feels like the entire thing was my fault, like I caused him to miss out on his entire senior year," this sparked her interest.

"Why would you think that?" she asked.

"He was driving me home. If he didn't have to deal with me then this never would have happened," as soon as I said the words I wanted to stuff them back inside. My eyes were wide in realization.

"Hmmmmm, I'm sure that's not the case," she was quiet for a

moment. No doubt quoting me perfectly, word-for-word. *Oh god!* "Well, I think I'm set on my story. Thank you so much for your time, Nolan. I really appreciate it. Hey, and good luck next year at ASU! That's where I went."

And then she was gone. I replayed the interview in my mind over and over. By the time evening rolled around, I had finally convinced myself that my words just didn't fit with the story and I would be safe. At least, that's what I hoped.

I searched for the story online and in the paper for days after the interview. Reed had made his announcement as she told me he would. They covered it briefly during sports on the evening news. My parents and I watched and cheered that he was staying in Arizona. I had finally brought my mom up to speed on what had happened between us, though I left out the part where Reed made a dig at our poverty. That still stung me a little, and it wasn't anything I ever wanted to share.

There were only a few weeks left before our senior year was over, and my homework was now pretty much non-existent. We were at the point where most of our classes were filled with busy work or movies. We'd been watching the BBC version of *Pride and Prejudice* in our writing and literature class, which was fine with me and most of the other girls in the class, but I was pretty sure Reed and the few guys taking our class wanted to nap.

I was looking forward to today's viewing because we were going to get to see the end. I liked that part, not just because it was swoon-worthy, but because the main character, Elizabeth, stood up for herself. We settled into our desks and Sienna and I were getting quite comfortable, prepared for Mr. Bosch to turn the lights off, when he instead slid to sit on his desk like he had an announcement.

"I know, I know. It's movie day. I promise, we'll get to the movie," he rolled his eyes a little. I wondered just how many senior semesters he'd endured. "But I had a quick announcement to make before we started, if that's ok with you guys?"

He pulled his glasses forward a little to look out at us over the tops, overdoing it for our benefit. Mr. Bosch was everyone's favorite.

"Well then, if I could get a drum roll, please..." A few of the students started patting their desks, and soon the room sounded like it was full of messy thunder.

"Nolan Lennox." My eyes shot wide. No, no...no attention, no thank you, no please? "If you could come up here, I have something special I want to present you with."

I looked at Sienna, my shoulders scrunched up to my ears and my body stiff. I had no idea what this was about, and I was not looking forward to standing in front of this classroom of students again. Hesitantly, I walked up to the front and turned, rigidly, to face my teacher.

At first he laughed a little and told me to relax. I leaned a little onto his desk and then just turned to look at him, bobbing between his eyes and my feet with my glare.

"Nolan, I am so honored to present this to you. I've never had a student deserve it more, and I wanted your fellow classmates to know what you've achieved," he was a little emotional as he spoke. "Your memoir essay was very well-received by the writer's college, Nolan."

I gulped a little, my heart pounding as I waited to hear what this meant.

"Class, Nolan entered her essay in a very competitive contest. Only three awards are given out, and students from throughout the country compete for this award. Nolan, you were given the Note of Distinction. That's the highest prize, and it means $5,000 a year for your education, provided you keep your GPA up."

I wanted to faint, but instead just held myself up on his desk, my eyes I'm sure as wide as they'd ever been. I vaguely could hear the others in my class clapping and whistling for me. I was so stunned, I think it took a few minutes for me to let it all sink in and to smile. I shook Mr. Bosch's hand as he handed me an envelope full of the information about my award as well as confirmation about my stipend.

When I turned to walk dazedly back to my desk, I caught Reed's view and the look on his face was so very much the old Reed, my Reed. He was...proud. Sienna gave me a huge hug and whispered how proud she was of me in my ear. I couldn't believe it.

I couldn't wait to get home to tell my parents, so I broke the school rule and snuck into the girl's bathroom to call my mom at work. I wasn't certain, but I think she cried a little as we spoke. And for the rest of the day, a weight was lifted and I felt invincible.

———

Ironing the purple silk gown was impossible, each time I flipped it I only seemed to add a new set of wrinkles to the mix. I still couldn't believe that I was graduating from high school and would be moving from my tiny room into a place of my own with Sienna. Sure, it would be a dorm room, one surrounded by hundreds of other 18-year-old pseudo grownups just like me. But it would be far from home, or at least the farthest I'd ever been.

My mother was excited for my new adventure in life, but I could tell my dad was having a hard time letting me go. We still had two months at home together over the summer, but my dad had already started prepping my car, checking oil, hoses, vents and parts I didn't know existed. He'd called Buck a few times, too, to get his opinion, and together the two of them had worried themselves into more than a dozen new parts for my old beater of a car.

I had practiced my speech for tonight's ceremony at least a hundred times. As much as I wanted to be valedictorian, I was also thankful that the responsibility had fallen into someone else's lap, and Sienna was worthy of the honor. I was content to be her number two. My speech was one that was pre-written by years of students before me—the traditional school pillars of pride. Sienna and I had fits of laughter the night before about the pillars and how silly the entire thing seemed. Preaching about character, adversity, discipline and respect to a couple hundred graduated teenagers who were thinking about the beer party that awaited them seemed nothing more than a tremendous waste of time. But my dad planned on filming the entire thing anyhow, so I would perform it well.

The sky outside was orange with the sunset and I was anxious to get to the football field for the ceremony. I heard a knock at our front door. Sarah was here to pick me up so I grabbed my gown, speech, purse and headed to the front room, yelling out to my parents that I'd meet them there. When I turned back to the door and opened it wide, Reed was standing there.

Always a vision. He was wearing a pair of khaki pants and a white dress shirt with a fitted black sweater vest over it that hugged his chest. Of course, his chest looked like it had already gone to college and took a pounding on the football field and come back a man. He had cut his hair some, but the curls were still there and the length swept to the sides and front just right. With the whoosh of the door, I also caught his scent, and between the sight of him and the smell that was now attacking my senses, it's a damned miracle I didn't just throw myself at him and forget the hurdles we had yet to overcome.

"Soooo...hi," he said coyly, in a tone that suggested he was wondering what was taking me so long to speak. I was pretty sure my ogling had been overt.

"Hi...uhm...happy graduation? Is that even a thing people say?" I was still nervous and clearly unable to think of clever things to say.

He just laughed a little. "It's what *you* say, so I guess that's all that matters," he smiled, flashing his perfect teeth and melt-worthy dimples. "I wasn't sure if I'd see you at the desert party after graduation, and I wanted to give you something...so, I hope it's ok?" He looked in the house a little to see if we were alone and then gave me a half-smile as if he was unsure of himself. We were both walking on glass around one another, but it was nice to see him struggle, too.

Reed pulled a box from around his back and held it out to me. I could tell it was a shoe box that he'd tried to wrap himself, which made it all the more adorable to me. "Thanks," I bit my lip a little, pulling the box into my chest. "I'm sorry...I didn't really get you anything. This whole graduation thing sort of snuck up on me, I've been so busy with scholarship apps."

That was a half truth. I had gotten a gift for both Sienna and

Sarah. I just didn't know what Reed was to me anymore, and after spending four hours at the mall trying to find something perfect for him with nothing to show for it, I just threw in the towel.

"Well, are you going to open it? I know you're dying to know, you can't handle surprises," he knew me so well. I was dying to rip the lid off the box. I smiled guiltily and then pulled the ribbon back that was holding the lid in place and flipped it open in my arms. When I saw the ratty old ASU hat sitting on top of a bed of crumpled tissue paper, my mouth went dry and I squeezed my lips together tightly to keep myself from going full estrogen with my emotions, my eyes already threatening to tear up.

"It always looked better on you," he smiled sweetly, reaching in to pull the hat out. He pulled the box from my hands set it on the ground and then looked me in the eyes as he reached for my hand and squeezed my fingers around the hat. "I'd put it on for you, but your hair looks really nice. I don't want to mess it up before graduation," he spoke quietly.

I just stared down at it, so touched at the thoughtfulness of his gift, but also mesmerized by his touch. I thought I would never hold his hand again, and this was the greatest gift I could imagine. "I'm real sorry, Noles," he surprised me with his words. He kept his eyes down, twisting his mouth a little as his spoke. "I fucked us up real good. And I never meant to be cruel. I lashed out at you, and it wasn't right."

I couldn't quite catch my breath. He had hurt me with his words. But I think it hurt even more because they came from him, someone I'd let in, let get close. "Thank you," was all I could say, just nodding a little but keeping my eyes on the hat in my hands and watching his fingers let go of their grasp on me. He leaned forward just a little and kissed my cheek, whispering in my ear just a little before he walked down my driveway and left.

"I never would have picked Stanford…too far away…" that was all he said.

The graduation ceremony seemed to breeze by, which was good since the temperatures outside had barely fallen below 100 degrees at night. Most of my classmates were fanning themselves with their hats by the time Sienna welcomed us all to stand and move our tassels over to signal our official end of high school.

Sienna and I went to Sarah's house after the ceremony to change into more summer-friendly clothing for the desert party. This night was for seniors only, and it was something every Coolidge student looked forward to, a rite of passage. I sat on the end of Sarah's bed, my mind off in the distance, while she and Sienna got ready.

"Nolan, you better hurry, or we're going to leave your ass here," Sarah teased.

"Sarah? Do you think I can borrow some of your clothes?" you would think I offered her $20 she was so excited by my request.

"Uh, yeah! What do you want? Tank tops? One-shoulder? Skirt, dress, shorts?" she was in her closet in an instant searching for me.

"I just…wanna look as hot as you can make me look," I was embarrassed by my own vanity and blushed as I asked.

"Oh, I can make you look hot," Sarah grinned devilishly. Sienna rolled her eyes as she went to work.

Sarah delivered on her promise, dressing me in her shortest denim cut-off shorts and a one-shoulder black shirt with a scoop neck. She pulled my hair up in upside-down braids, letting a few strands fall to the sides. I even relented and let her put mascara and smoky eye shadow on me. I felt bold, which I would need to if I was going to be bold tonight.

By the time we got to the desert party, most of our classmates had arrived already. The music was pumping, as it always was, but the sheer number of cars parked amidst the desert brush was far from inconspicuous. The local law enforcement was always on alert for graduation night, so there was a strict code among senior classes to follow the designated driver roll. Sienna was ours tonight, which was good because I was planning on downing a little liquid courage to get myself through the night.

We parked and started to walk to the center of the campsite

where most of the other girls were dancing, waiving red cups over their heads. Sarah grabbed one and filled it for me, putting it in my hand with a warning. "Go slow on this, ok missy?" I was new to this drinking thing and knew what I didn't want to look like when the night was over, so I just smiled and gave her an understanding nod.

Sipping slowly on my beer, I scanned the crowd until I found Reed and Sean standing over by the bed of Sean's truck, talking to a few other team members. Reed was laughing and smiling, such a refreshing sight. He was telling them a story about something, setting his beer down to show them something with his hands. He was animated and excited. I watched him for about 10 minutes before he noticed me. And when he did, I could tell my look surprised him—in a good way.

He didn't come over to talk to me for a while; instead he snuck glances in my direction from across the fire pits and in the shadows of the headlights that lit the brush around us. We were both flirting from a distance, doing a dance with our eyes. I would watch him walk to the keg and look for me in the crowd, biting his lip a little and looking away when he found me. And I did the same.

"OK, Noles, I'm cutting you off," Sienna reached for my cup. I had only had two beers during the hour and a half that we'd been here, but I was already feeling quite a buzz. Sienna had promised me she'd watch out for me, and I knew I wouldn't be able to disobey her, so I handed my cup to her and walked over to the cooler to grab a water instead.

I came back to sit on the hood of Sarah's car with Sienna, handing her a water as well. She was making a suspicious face, turning quickly to look in the other direction. "What was that all about," I called her on it.

She bit her lip a little and let out a deep breath, nodding in the direction behind me. I looked over to see Stephanie hanging all over Reed, her arm looped into his and her head resting on his shoulder. And this is what it feels like to get punched.

Unable to avert my stare, I tried to keep my courage up, the courage I had worked so hard to build with Sarah's make up and cheap beer. "It could be nothing," I didn't look away. "I mean, his hands are just in his pockets. He's probably just being polite."

Almost believing myself I was about to feel satisfied with my conclusion when Reed pulled his left hand from his pocket and put it on Stephanie's lower back and whispered something in her ear that had her laughing. Just then, Sarah walked by and I took her beer from her hand and drank it all in one tip of the cup.

That was probably a mistake. I was spinning a little more now, not fully sick but definitely not in the clearest of minds. I had given into dancing with Sarah in the middle of the party, mimicking some of her more provocative moves, though probably not looking as professional as she did. We got a few whistles when we danced together from the guys standing to the side, which only made me try harder.

My courage was fading quickly by the time midnight was upon us, and Sienna was working on Sarah and me to give up the dancing so we could head home. A lot of the partiers had called it a night, but it seemed sadder than it should to be leaving this party. It felt final. Over.

Making pouting faces at Sienna, Sarah and I finally gave in and gave hugs to several girls who, though we'd spent four years with them, we'd never really been close friends with. It just seemed like the thing to do tonight. Then, as if I'd just remembered why I'd come to the party in the first place, my eyes scanned the remaining crowd in a panic and I stopped in my tracks and grabbed hold of Sienna's hand before we got to Sarah's car. "Wait!" I shrilled. "I have to..."

My friends were so patient, understanding what this meant to me. Sarah was the one to finally see Reed and she pointed to him, hesitantly. She wasn't ready to trust him yet, and I appreciated her for it. "I have to," I took a deep breath, looking at them both before I turned and marched over to where Reed was standing next to Sean. I was relieved that Stephanie was nowhere in sight.

He saw me coming and pulled his beer from his lips, wiping his mouth on his sleeve and setting the bottle down on the edge of the truck before looking back up at me. He was about to say something when I didn't give him the chance. Wrapping my hands around his neck, I stood on my tiptoes and kissed him with every bit of passion I had left to give. He shifted backwards at first, stumbling a little from the force of my body into his. But soon I felt his arms reach around me, his hands sliding up behind my neck and holding me to him tightly as he started kissing me back.

I faintly heard Sean whistle and a few of the other guys pipe in with a "damn," but most of my brain was focused on making Reed remember. I hadn't gotten him anything for graduation because I didn't know what to give him; I wanted it to be something that would help him remember *us*. And I hoped that maybe, just maybe, kissing him one last time would do that.

Time slowly started to come back into focus as I felt Reed's hands slip forward from my hair to the sides of my face, holding me in place as our lips finally parted, our foreheads still pressed together as we clung to each other. No words. I had just hoped that this was enough.

Pulling away from him slowly, I looked up at him through my hooded lashes, my look as serious as I could force on my face. I walked away backwards at first and turned to join my friends. And once we were safely in the car, I let out a heavy sigh.

"If he doesn't know how you feel after that, Noles, he never will," Sienna said, turning the music up as we pulled out on the desert road and headed home.

26. Lost and Found

WHEN I DIDN'T HEAR from Reed the next morning, I convinced myself it was because he had hooked up with Stephanie and I was just an indiscretion he had snuck in without her noticing. When I didn't hear from him during the first week of summer break, I started to feel cheap and questioned how buzzed I really was.

I had seen Sean a few times at MicNic's during my shifts over the summer, but Reed didn't make a single appearance. I knew he would be leaving for school early, so when July rolled around, I gave up hope.

Becky was back in town for the summer and she and Sean spent most nights going out together. Sean was going to San Diego for college, putting the two of them a short commute away from one another. Sarah and Calley moved into their apartment early and Sienna and I spent a few nights at their place before the dorms opened so we could scope out the campus before the crowds of new students showed up.

When moving day came, my dad was in full parent-mode, questioning me about every safety feature of my car, wanting to know how many desk people worked at the dorm and how often the front was guarded. He lectured me on keeping our doors locked at all times and on not letting strangers follow me home. My mom rolled her eyes a few times when he talked and would try to undo his damage when he left the room, assuring me that she knows I'm a responsible girl. I knew he was just having a hard time letting go, so I took him out to MicNic's for one more daddy/daughter milkshake the night before I left for good.

Sienna and I spent the entire first day on campus loading our clothing, stereo, shoes, computers and other crap we were suddenly wishing we'd left at home from the parking lot to our dorm room five stories up. The elevator was slow to come, so we opted for more trips up and down the stairs.

I was hanging pictures on my cork board when two guys knocked on our door and called out from the hallway. "Ladies?" Sienna and I looked at each other in a panic, not used to attention from college boys yet. We started to giggle a little and both hopped down from the chairs we'd been standing on and walked over to the hallway leading to the door.

"Hey, we're your neighbors," the tall one with short blonde hair said, reaching out to shake our hands. He was at least a foot taller than I was and had a tattoo that covered one arm. I laughed a little inwardly, wondering how my dad was going to react to this when he came up to visit next week.

"Hi, I'm Nolan. This is Sienna," I said, shaking his hand and looking toward his friend, who was equally as tall but seemingly not covered in ink and with longer, dark hair.

"Hey, I'm Nick and this is Travis," the blonde said, smiling and making his way into our room a little.

Sienna and I just backed up and kept our guard up until he turned around in a circle and spoke. "Trav? Come check this shit out. They have, like, twice the space," he was comparing our room sizes like a kid would and it was funny and setting me at ease. "And their window is bigger!"

I started to laugh a little and then Travis spoke up. "Yeah, but we have a microwave. I see they didn't bring one of those," he smiled superiorly. "Maybe, just maybe, we can broker a deal." He was rubbing his hand on his chin scruff.

Sienna looked around and then jumped back up on her bed, grabbing the toolbox from the top shelf of her book case. "We have tools!" she bragged. We all started laughing at her attempt to one up them.

Nick and Travis had quickly become good friends. The next few mornings, Sienna and I knocked on their door to heat up our oatmeal. And, ironically, they had to borrow our hammer a few times as well. We made plans to attend a few of the orientation events together, and the boys introduced us to a few more of their friends. Of course, when I introduced them to Sarah, they started to show their peacock feathers a little, battling for her attention as most guys did when they first met her.

I could tell she liked Nick a lot, and I thought that maybe, just maybe, she might find herself in a relationship that lasted more than a week. I caught them making out in the stairwell once, but kept it to myself not wanting to jinx things for her.

School was starting soon; we had the rest of the weekend and the Monday after before classes officially began. I was sitting on my bed early Sunday morning, plotting out the location of my classes on the map and munching on an apple I'd cut up for breakfast. Sienna had gone out for coffee with Micah, the both of them had joined the marching band together and spent most of their afternoons at practice. Tonight, though, was all about me and my girls. There was a dance party for freshman in the atrium of the arts school and we had been counting down the days.

Sarah would no doubt spend the evening draping herself on Nick while Sienna and I pretended to dance in a corner, but it would be fun nevertheless. Seeing her with Nick was making me miss Reed more than I cared to admit. I had pinned a few pictures of him and I to the cork board above my bed and I often drifted off to sleep staring at them, pressing the depths of my memory to hold on to his voice.

I was packing up my map and getting things sorted in my backpack when Sienna burst through the door and came running in, throwing her body onto my bed next to me. Her eyes were wide with surprise, and I couldn't tell if it was in a good way or a bad way.

"Whhhhhaaaat...does that face mean?" I tilted my head questioning her even more.

"Oh my god, Nolan. Please promise me you're not going to freak out, ok? It's not that bad, I promise," she said. Of course, I was freaking out now.

"Yeah...I'm pretty sure I can't promise you that now," my heart was racing and a million scenarios were flying through my mind all the way from my tuition payment had been rejected, my scholarship falling through, to she hadn't really left for coffee but instead eloped to Vegas and came back married.

Sienna ground my imagination to a grinding halt the second she flopped the newspaper on my lap, folded to the sports section with a full-page color photo of Reed standing in front of the red and blue A on the mountain near his university campus. I looked up at her, my eyes wide now, too, knowing full well what I would find when I started reading the story. "Shit!" I grabbed the paper and started reading.

The first part was all about Reed, his projections for the year, how the UofA coaches had tracked him for years and expected great things from him. There was a great quote from Buck about how proud he was to see his son follow in his family's footsteps and a few quotes from Coach Baker about Reed's work at Coolidge and how he thought of him as a second son. I was starting to relax a little from the positive nature of the story when I finally came to the section labeled 'Accident.'

I gulped and looked up at Sienna, who was just staring at me, her mouth closed tightly, willing me to read on. As I read, I relived the entire night. The way they described his injury made the bile climb up my throat a little, and the quote from his mother about how scared she was for her son, describing the call she got from the hospital, almost made me feel sorry for her despite how terrible she'd been to me.

And then there it was, as if it had been covered in yellow highlighter, it jumped out to me in a flash.

Reed's then girlfriend had been in the Jeep with him at the time of the acci-
dent, and while she didn't walk away with the same injuries as the star athlete
who had been driving, she was left with a terrible sense of guilt.

"I guess a part of me feels like the entire thing was my fault, like I caused
him to miss out on his entire senior year," said Nolan Lennox, also a senior at
Coolidge at the time. "He was driving me home, and if he didn't have to deal
with me, then this never would have happened."

I know the story didn't end there. In fact there was an entire
column left. But that's where it ended in my eyes. I just dropped the
paper and flopped back on the bed, smacking my hands to my forehead, my mind racing with possibilities of how I could fix this. I
could ask for a retraction, I thought. Except she was accurate, and I
hadn't asked for any of this to be off the record. I just hoped it
wouldn't make sense with her story. But reading it now, I see the
emotion my words brought to everything, and the reason she
included them. I was screwed.

I heard Travis and Nick come barreling into our room while I
laid on my bed with my pillow over my face wondering if it was
possible to buy up every paper in southern Arizona before Reed,
Buck or my parents could read my gaffe in all its glory. I sat up
when I felt a second pillow hit me in the gut.

"Hey, what was that for," I smiled, rubbing my face a little to
snap myself out of my funk.

"Pillow fight with a girl, couldn't help it," Travis smirked, flirta-
tiously, but friendly all the same.

"I'm not much of a fighter right now, I'm afraid," I slumped a
bit, sliding the copy of the paper over to him and pointing to my
quote. I waited a few minutes while he read the entire story and
then I felt his stare when he turned to look at me.

"No fucking way! You dated Reed Johnson?" he was more
interested in my love connection to a quarterback then the fact
that I'd embarrassed myself in the biggest newspaper in the state. I
just shoved him a little to get him back on task and he leaned into
me whispering over my shoulder that it wasn't that bad, immedi-

ately turning back to ask me questions about how well I knew Reed.

Walking through campus that evening to the dance wasn't as exciting since I'd been hit with my news making quote that morning. I thought about texting Reed more than a few times, but we hadn't talked all summer, and the thought of trying to reconnect over the mess I'd made just made my stomach bunch. I hadn't heard from my parents, and I hadn't heard from Buck by phone or email, so I had an inkling of hope that the story slipped by others unnoticed. But I knew that was probably a delusion, since Buck was like a one-man clipping service for Reed.

The music pumped and lights cast shadows on the concrete walls and statues in the atrium of the art school. The picture was breathtaking, and for a while I was able to dance and lose myself with Sienna, Sarah, Travis and Nick. Just as I thought, Nick and Sarah paired off with one another quickly, leaving Sienna, Travis and I to dance uncomfortably with one another to the slow songs.

Micah ended up showing up an hour into the dance and stole Sienna away from our group easily, and since Travis really wasn't much of a dancer, he and I ended up sitting on one of the concrete walls, watching the crowd of bodies blend below us. Feeling my energy, Travis leaned into me a bit, causing me to look up at him a little. "Where you at?" he questioned. "Because I know it isn't here."

I just smiled faintly, he was right. Reading that story had done more than just thrust me into embarrassment from my quote. It made me miss Reed all over again, maybe even more than I did before. I wanted to go back and look at the picture more closely, knowing it had probably been taken just a few days ago. I smiled inwardly a little thinking about how Reed looked right now.

"I think maybe I'm going to go home, if that's ok with you?" I hated leaving him here alone, but I also knew Travis was a bit of a player and would probably be making out with a girl by the time the night was over.

"You want me to walk you? It's late," he was starting to slide down from the wall to stand with me, but I just put my hand on his knee to stop him.

"No, I'll be fine. There are security guards all over the walk, and it's not that far. I'll keep my phone out, though, and I promise I'll call you if I get jumped from the bushes," I joked, realizing he was already checking out a leggy blonde girl dancing near Sarah. He just nodded a little, smiled and walked away to work his charm.

The walk back was crowded with other freshman who were walking from the dorms to the dance and the recreation center all evening. It was only 9 p.m., so I didn't feel anxious about being alone.

I was at our dorm entrance in minutes and walked by the front desk where I flashed my card key that unlocked the main door. I noticed a few letters in my mailbox and pulled them out to flip through them as I took to the stairs. The first was a postcard from Sean from San Diego bragging that his weather was better than mine. The second was from my mom, sweetly telling me that she was proud of me and wanted the honor of being my first piece of mail. I wouldn't dare tell her that I'd read Sean's card first.

I was breathing a little harder by the time I made it up the five flights and opened the stairwell door to head down the hall to go to our room at the end. I saw the flip flops and bare feet first, stopping me in my tracks. Reed's legs were unmistakable, tanned and muscular, his college basketball shorts draped down to his knees. His long legs were jetting out from the wall, his body leaning against my door as he sat on the floor, his eyes closed as he listened to music through his headphones. His hat was pulled down a little over his eyes and his hands were stuffed in the pockets of his sweatshirt.

Not wanting to disturb him, he looked so perfect and peaceful, I stood still for a few seconds. He was everything I'd remembered, and somehow, over the few months I'd been away from him, he'd grown so much. My mouth went dry as I thought about my words in the paper, and my palms started to sweat when I realized he was probably here to yell at me for being so careless with the reporter and taking the focus off of his achievements.

For a moment, I considered turning around and going to find Sienna to ask her what I should do. But I kept forging forward instead. Finally at his feet, I kicked them a little with my own and he startled awake, pulling his hat from his head and running his fingers through his hair that was once again a little longer.

He stood awkwardly, stretching and trying to get to his feet. I held my breath as I waited for him to speak. When he didn't, I reached into my pocket for my keys and stared him in the eyes, sure I hadn't blinked for over a minute. "Wanna…come in?" I asked, sucking my lip in and holding my breath yet again.

He looked down a little, kicking his feet and stuffing his hands back in his pockets before looking back at me. "Yeah, that'd be great. The floor's a little stiff," he smiled, stretching his back a little as he walked through my tiny door frame. His body had definitely grown as he seemed to fill my room more than he ever had before. He had always towered over me, but now he seemed to double my width as well.

I followed him in and locked the door behind me out of habit. "You planning on kidnapping me?" he joked when he saw me do it.

"Oh, sorry, habit. My dad calls me to remind me," I rolled my eyes.

"I'm glad he does," he said, smiling and looking around our room. He looked over Sienna's desk and shelves with affection before turning to my side of the room. He picked up the small heart pillow I had brought from home and held it close before putting it back down and picking up the hat he had given me. He looked over the pictures on my cork board and straightened one of me and him. I swallowed hard as I watched him, my heart swelling that he was here in my personal space.

He walked over to the window and pulled the curtain back a little to check out our view. "You can see the stadium," he said, looking out at it for a while before closing the curtain again. I just nodded.

When he turned to face me, my body flushed and I thought briefly I might pass out. He leaned back and sat on the edge of my desk, his hands once again back in the pockets of his sweatshirt. He looked down for a long while, thinking, his forehead heavy with thought and his eyebrows drawn close together before he finally turned up to capture my gaze with his.

"Nolan, what happened…you know that it wasn't your fault, right?" I had feared this. I just gulped a little and nodded slightly, trying to make myself small. "Do you really?"

He was questioning me and moving closer to me now, standing straight. I was leaning against the wall opposite of him, against our closet door, and as he closed the distance between us I thought seriously about opening the door, crawling inside and locking it to wait him out.

He stopped when he was an arm's length from me, his eyes still pouring into mine. The green was mesmerizing, like a truth serum. "Nolan? Did you mean what you said in the paper? That you felt like this was all your fault?" he was even closer now. I closed my eyes a little at his question, afraid to look at him this closely.

"Sorta," I squeaked.

I heard the breath escape him and he stepped forward again, now inches from me, his arm leaning against the wall next to me. When I felt his forehead press to mine, I shook a little, trying to stifle my cry. I kept my eyes closed tight, not wanting to feel any of the guilt I'd tried so hard to escape.

"Nolan," Reed whispered. "*This*…the accident, our breakup, my season…none of that was your fault. None of it."

His hand was under my chin now and he was forcing me to open my eyes. Blurry-eyed, I looked at him, but quickly tried to look to the side, unable to against his force. He looked me in the eyes again, moving his hand to my cheek and bringing his other hand to the other side of my face, brushing the hairs out of the way. "Nolan, it wasn't your fault. The accident, it just happened. And our relationship, I'm the one who destroyed that. OK?"

I shook again, fighting against the full on cry that I'd buried deep down for months. Reed was wiping away my tears now and bringing me into his chest to hold me close. By instinct, I reached up and grabbed the fabric of his sweatshirt in my hands and squeezed tightly before reaching around his body to hold him back. "You never called. I waited…" I confessed. I kept my face flat to his chest, embarrassed and afraid of his response.

I felt his body stiffen a little and then I felt the air leave his lungs as he relaxed. "I wanted to…so badly," he kissed the top of my head with his words. "But I wanted you to live your life and make a decision just for you. I didn't want you to be disappointed, following me to some school and then watching me fail. I can't let you down again," he was holding me tighter now, almost as if he was afraid I would be the one to run away.

With his words, all fear left my body, and I felt strong enough to speak my heart. "Reed, the only thing that you ever did to let me down was give up on us. I love you, and I'd love you if you were a biology major without an inkling of athletic talent, I swear," I smiled stupidly as I tilted my head back and stared at him. I awed as I watched the caution in his eyes slide for just a bit, a small smile touching his lips.

His strong hands slid around me tighter now and he leaned back a little, lifting me off the ground with his embrace, holding me up a little to look me in the eyes as he spun me around and started to walk to my bed. He pushed me back against it and we fell down together, still holding on to one another. He leaned over me and tucked my hair behind my ears slowly, his eyes intent on his hands as he touched my face softly. Leaning forward, he pressed his lips to my forehead, then my cheek before coming to rest his head against mine again, his eyes staring deep into mine.

"I love you, too, Nolan," he said, letting out a deep breath. "And I swear, if you let me, if you give me another chance, I promise I won't let you down."

With his eyes closed against me, I just nodded my head, whispering yes against his lips before kissing him with all of the love I'd been holding onto, as if I'd been waiting to give it to him all at once. Wrapping my arms and legs around him, we quickly became tangled and hungry for one another, gripping each other tightly for fear of the night slipping away.

When I realized that almost an hour had passed, I stopped Reed from carrying our kissing any further and held his gaze as I smiled, a true smile, the first I'd had since that car had run us off the desert highway. He lay back and I nestled myself into his arm and tucked my hand inside the warmth of his shirt against his bare chest. "Hey, aren't you going to be missed?" I worried, hoping he wouldn't miss a curfew or anything.

He just chuckled a little. "Naw, I don't have practice until tomorrow afternoon. I have to get back by four. And I figure if I'm going to be making this drive a lot, I should figure out exactly how long it takes me," he smiled, looking down at me against him, and leaned in to kiss my head again before shutting his eyes.

I watched him fall asleep and felt soothed at the sound of his breathing. Somehow, we had found our way back to us. And we felt stronger this time. I knew that there would be bumps in our road, things to shake up the perfect I felt right now. But I also knew it was worth it, every second. The good and the bad.

Not wanting to leave his arms, I left the lights on and rested there until I heard Sienna's keys at our door. She shut it quietly, probably expecting to see me asleep, and stilled when she took in the sight of me staring at her, my finger to my mouth to tell her to be quiet. Her eyes shot up with surprise and I just smiled and nodded, biting my lip and letting her know that my wish had somehow come true, no matter that it had taken longer than I expected. She smiled back and blew a kiss at me and flipped out the lights, crawling into her bed.

I stared at Reed in the dark for another hour before finally succumbing to the sleepiness that took me over. And for the first night in weeks I didn't dream. Probably because I didn't need to.

~ THE END ~

The Story Continues...

REED AND NOLAN'S story continues in *Going Long* (out now) and *The Hail Mary* (releasing Jan. 18, 2019). The Waiting Series is complete at 3 books. Thank you for taking this journey with me!

Acknowledgments

---

updated in Dec. 2018

I don't want to rewrite any of the below acknowledgments. They are special. This book was my first, and it is the one I carried around for far too long afraid to finish. The words I wrote the day I published it are raw and from my heart, and they were read and rewritten to make them just right. I honor that, because without my past self, the one who was brave enough to share this little piece of me, I would never be the present me I am now, and I wouldn't dare dream of the future me I plan to become. So dream big. And I hope you continue on this journey. These characters…they are mighty special.

This book has been a lifetime in the making. I've wanted to write a coming-of-age love story since I was coming-of-age myself. I've spent more than a decade working as a reporter, freelance journalist, editor and digital media specialist, which has been a proven training ground for helping me tell honest stories that touch the heart. I hope I have been able to convey that same honesty in my fiction.

Waiting by the Sidelines is a special story to me. It is about those anxieties young girls feel over not being good enough, pretty enough, sexy enough, rich enough, daring enough to fit in. It is about wanting someone so badly but not feeling confident enough in yourself to put your heart on the line. It's about finding your center of confidence and then rebuilding it over and over again, each time your inner strength takes a hit. No one is impervious to heartbreak, and those of us who say we are, well, we're lying.

I would like to thank my parents, who have always believed in my writing and have known I could do this. I would like to thank my dear friends and family members who have urged me to put my story out there for the public (a special thanks to "Bulldog" Jennifer Stein, my own personal Vince Lombardi, who has made my success her number one mission). To my wonderful husband, Tim, who made me make time for this once and for all, and to my son, Carter, who wants to read mommy's book some day. He may be disappointed when he learns that it is not entirely about football.

Thank you Phil Scott for being the best big brother a girl could have and for teaching me all the right things about cars and "buying American." Thank you, mom, for the copy editing gene (and the copy editing). And lastly, special thanks to my girls, the members of 'Team Ginger,' who shared their creativity, inspired me and worked tirelessly to help get my story out there for others to enjoy. Thank you: Lesley, Mia, Debbie, Brigitte, Jayne and Kim.

Thank you for reading...

Thank you, from the bottom of my heart, for reading my book. If you enjoyed *Waiting on the Sidelines,* I would love it if you would share your thoughts with others. Please consider posting a review, lending this book or recommending it. If you do post a review, please let me know so I can thank you. You can find me at www.authorgingerscott.com or www.littlemisswrite.com. Please also consider liking my facebook page at www.facebook.com/GingerScottAuthor.

About the author...

Ginger Scott is a journalist and writer from Peoria, Arizona. An Arizona native, Scott infused a lot of her home state into *Waiting on the Sidelines*. A graduate and associate faculty member of Arizona State University's Cronkite School of Journalism, she had a hard time writing about her rival school in Tucson, but feels satisfied at the few jabs she was able to work into her story. Scott is an avid sports fan and loves the purity of high school football. In fact, she attends the local high school games regularly with her husband and 9-year-old son.

updated again

^^ *My son is older now. And my ABOUT ME is a little fuller. But again…I love the idea of seeing where I began. For those with similar dreams… know this—YES YOU CAN!*

XO

Ginger

Also by Ginger Scott

The Waiting Series

Waiting on the Sidelines

Going Long

coming in January 2019

The Hail Mary

Like Us Duet

A Boy Like You

A Girl Like Me

The Falling Series

This Is Falling

You And Everything After

The Girl I Was Before

In Your Dreams

The Harper Boys

Wild Reckless

Wicked Restless

Standalone Reads

Cry Baby

The Hard Count

Memphis

Hold My Breath

Blindness

How We Deal With Gravity

About the Author

Ginger Scott is an Amazon-bestselling and Goodreads Choice Award-nominated author from Peoria, Arizona. She is the author of several young and new adult romances, including bestsellers Cry Baby, The Hard Count, A Boy Like You, This Is Falling and Wild Reckless.

A sucker for a good romance, Ginger's other passion is sports, and she often blends the two in her stories. When she's not writing, the odds are high that she's somewhere near a baseball diamond, either watching her son field pop flies like Bryce Harper or cheering on her favorite baseball team, the Arizona Diamondbacks. Ginger lives in Arizona and is married to her college sweetheart whom she met at ASU (fork 'em, Devils).

FIND GINGER ONLINE: www.littlemisswrite.com